LEEDS

A Novel by Corey Phillips

American Backroad Publishing, LLC.

ISBN: 978-1-7373608-0-3 (paperback)

Book Cover/Title Page Illustrations copyright © 2021, by Corey Phillips

First print edition 2021.

Published under American Backroad Publishing, LLC., Saltville, VA.

Printed in the United States of America.

Table of Contents

Chapter 1: The Diagnosis

I never knew I would have a conversation with a ghost.

The room is cold and empty somehow, but he still sits within arm's reach of me. I want to reach out and touch him to know he's human, and not just a childhood fear. I remember thinking about these things as a kid, what it would be like to meet one. Then we grow up knowing it's an impossibility. But then I look at him and he's only an empty and emotionless physical vessel. A living individual that no longer feels inside. Ghosts must have emotion, though, because they are spirits of some form that were living at one point. But he isn't either and has neither spirit nor emotion. He is only alive but no longer amongst the living. I stare at broken war-torn shell and nothing else, hoping he will say anything that indicates a heartbeat.

He sits with one leg crossed over the other. His weathered hat is tilted low to cover his brow. His jeans are just as worn and tattered as the rest of him. A single strand of the material on his ripped pants near the bottom continuously gets tampered with between his fingers. He won't give me any clues about him. He is on constant guard and vigilance, even from a woman like me that is no physical threat to him. The room is always well lit for these sessions, but an icy darkness surrounds him. I feel almost frightened of his demeanor in such close proximity to him. Most male veterans wouldn't hurt a female. There is a slight country accent in the few words he has spoken, giving the hint of a southern upbringing. Though that doesn't calm my nerves around him either.

"How's your family doing with all this?" I ask.

He still sits there and raises his head to look at the clock. Rarely has he looked at me directly when speaking to me.

"They are fine, as far as I know. She gets her check every month on time. I guess that's all that matters to her now."

Nothing again, just silence.

"Do you miss them?" I ask.

"Every day. I miss a lot of things though, but there's nothing I can do about it now. She doesn't want me around anymore. I don't know if she ever did."

He takes a deep breath to look at the clock again. His hat is slanting in a manner so I can't get a good glimpse of his face. He's almost hiding from me. Men like him don't see it as hiding from others. It's just a continuous mistrust of everyone. They don't care to even bother engaging with others in public or even at home. They develop a distance from their own family, and they don't understand how or why it becomes an instinctual behavior for them.

"Does she try to talk to you now?" I ask sincerely.

"It happened months ago. It's just a matter of time before I get some divorce court paper in the mail or served to me at my doorstep."

Still, no reaction from him, just indifference. What can he be thinking?

"The courts brought you here. I understand that being forced in an environment like this doesn't support the idea of voluntarily saying anything to me. Is there anything you're willing to talk about, if not your family?"

He takes another breath, but it is more of a sigh on his part. He readjusts his legs to switch the crossed leg. A sour look of physical pain shows on his jaws and lips with each movement. An emotional pain and a physical pain he may feel he has to endure, no matter what I try telling him. Does he feel he deserves to be in pain, I wonder?

2

"What is it you think you want to know from me, Doctor?" he asks while readjusting.

"Do you care to tell me about your time overseas?"

I have only heard of scenarios like this, but never seen it in person. They never tell us how unnerving the atmosphere of a session like this could turn out. It's a total shot in the dark to ask these things. I have no way of relating to him. He notices his other pant leg is as frayed as the other one, but there are no loose strands to fidget with in his fingers. So, he just moves his hand up to his mouth to maintain a stance of deep thought. His breathing slows. He's well experienced at concealing what he is thinking, but he hasn't tried to divert the topic.

"Did something happen over there?" I ask.

"Sure. Lots of things happened over there. What do you really want to know? Have I ever killed anybody over there? That's all most people want to know. It's just a sad attempt for others to see if its anything like what they see in the movies."

"Well, has it happened before?" I ask.

"I can see you leaning in. I don't even have to look at you to know how eager you are, hoping I would talk about it. Your voice changed too." as he looks directly at me for the first time. "You're all the same."

"I understand if you had to defend yourself in…"

"You don't understand shit, lady. None of you do. At the end of your day here, you'll drive back home and type up some report about your day's work and a diagnosis. I bet you even got a home office with the walls filled with all your accomplishments and degrees, don't you? Your clueless about all of it. All of you are. Accept that as a reality and I might have a bit more respect for you."

That's the first time he's raised his hat to look at me and interrupt me at the same time. Sleepless nights ravage those deep, glaring eyes. They said it would not help by trying to relate to them. Though accidental on my part, he left a window to dig further.

"I didn't mean to imply that I understood what you may have gone through. You 're right. I'm not a veteran. I've never deployed. I don't even know what life is like as a soldier. I know nothing about it, other than what I hear second hand from others like you. My apologies for coming off that way."

He lowers his face to be covered by his hat again. Interrupting me may give him a sense of dominance in the conversation. His guard lowers, or at least he appears that way. I keep my shivering hands hidden out of his sight behind my clipboard.

"Can you help me understand? You can keep trying to hold all these things in, but eventually it becomes too much for anyone. I'm not trying to force you into anything you don't want to discuss with me. I know I'm a stranger to you, but you agreed to be here because you know something is off. All these things you hold on to may be overflowing somehow. I can't help you unless you try."

His jaws clinch as he stares at the clock again. He's not really looking at the clock, though. He knows what time it is and how much longer he is expected to be in here with me.

"I'll ask a better set of questions. Were you ever in danger over there?"

"Yes."

"Did you ever have to defend yourself?"

"Yes."

Trying to ask leading questions is a start. One wrong question here and that mental recollection period he is in may dissipate. He'll just shut down on me again, maybe indefinitely.

"Did you ever have to kill anyone when you defended yourself?"

"I don't know."

"What do you mean?"

He looks at me again and the hairs on my neck stand up. His voice grows threatening while he stares me down with no movement. The eyes typically cross back and forth to attempt looking at both eyes of the other person at the same time. But he stares right at me, right through me.

"Again, you wouldn't understand, now would you. I'll answer you again. I… Don't… Know."

"How could you not know?"

He lowers his head again to cover his face. Such a confusing answer, but somehow still genuine on his part.

"Doesn't really make a difference now, does it, Doctor? The moment we all come back we are nothing but empty shells. We are thanked and then tossed aside. The thanks we get become meaningless shortly after we receive them."

"Does it bother you not knowing?"

"It used to bother me. I just told myself it was necessary. Then later on, I didn't know how to feel about it. My wife asked me once. When I answered, I think it just scared her more than anything. It didn't really matter what I told her or if I had just said nothing. She would have gone away no matter how I answered that question. Maybe it was just all the excuse she needed."

"Are you guys still married? Didn't you have a son?"

"Yes, technically, we're only separated. Why?"

"Because there are counseling sessions offered for couples. It's more for those reintegrating after deployment. Can I ask how long ago your last deployment was?"

"Doesn't matter. I would save the effort for couples counseling for others that deployed more recently. They might still have a chance at that point in their family."

"Why is that?"

"She made it very clear to me she doesn't love me anymore. She hasn't in a long time now. What's the difference? She's gone, and it is what it is."

"Does it bother you she left?"

"She pushed me out of the house, really. But no, nothing bothers me like it should."

"What about your son?"

"I'm not talking about that here." as he snaps his head up to look at me and points his finger. He's just pointing a finger at me. But it is undeniably imposing. It's the fastest he has moved so far.

"Not here, do you understand?" he demands, while glaring at me again.

That attachment to his child is gone somehow. I wonder if he can even comprehend as to why.

"Ok, I'm sorry. That sounds like a rough topic for you. So, I'll just leave it alone. Have you ever felt the need to hurt yourself since you came back from overseas?"

"Sometimes, it crossed my mind." he says.

"Did you ever act on it?"

"They're just thoughts is all."

"Do you think about it now that your wife is gone?"

"Nearly every day now more than ever."

"Do you want to hurt yourself now?"

"I'm done answering these types of questions."

"Ok, we can change the topic again, but can I say one more thing on it before we move on?"

"What now?"

"Just based on what you have discussed so far, I think you're in a lot of pain that you can no longer digest. You may not even know how to cope with some of these things. Even though your family has separated, there are ways to move on before hurting yourself. We can show you how to manage these things."

"Oh, so we can all hold hands in some sort of group therapy session to hug and cry on each other's shoulders. Let me tell you something, Doctor. The sooner we all accept the idea that we're just tools, the sooner a lot of things become easier. Your *therapy*, as you call it, is nothing more than an effort to create this illusion that everything's going to be just fine. But it really isn't, is it? Things really don't get better, do they?"

He remains lost in some trance that a combat zone is everywhere he goes. Even in this very room. He makes points that he knows I can't argue with. We just had two of them last month commit suicide. None of them feel we are listening to them, because we aren't. We might hear them for a single hour session once a week, but then we send them back out the front doors where nobody hears them all over again. They know we all are scared of them. That's why most of them just want to go back to a never-ending war that has little meaning to anyone. They don't feel needed here.

"I had others come to me, ya know." he speaks up.

"What do you mean?" I ask. That's a random statement. He lowers his head again to hide under his hat. The loose thread on those tattered jeans is gone now.

"Other soldiers while we were there. They would ask me why we were there. They would ask me if we really are doing the right thing. Why do we care about some third world country in a foreign world that will go on living the way they have long after were gone? *Why are we here, Sarge?* I remember some of their faces. I think about them a lot and I can't get them out of my head some nights."

"They looked to you for reassurance. That's a good thing. What would you say to them?"

"I told them that we are the good cause. We are here to rid their nation of insurgent organizations and assist in rebuilding where we can. To aid in building their military and police forces until they can keep the peace on their own. Then we can finally go home and stay home. I lied to them. I lied straight to their faces and told them what we do is necessary and righteous in every sense. But some of them never came home. I lied to their faces over and over again. They were just kids. We were all just fucking kids. I lied to them and those same faces never came home."

He stares at the clock again. There's nothing else in the room to divert his attention. This may as well be an interrogation booth designed by the Veteran's Affairs. We even have our own special police force patrolling up and down the hallways to keep the staff safe. We build and send warriors to a foreign land and we don't know how to handle them here, because the monsters we make scare us. Even when that is all they know how to be at some point. He looks back at me with that same cold stare.

"Will you lie to me, Doctor? Will you tell me we did what was necessary and we'll all be home soon? Can *you* do it? Can you lie to me like that?" he asks. He knows I can't agree with that. It is only rhetorical on his part to prove a point.

"I would like to keep talking with you and understand you a little better. It helps me understand the best way to…"

"Our time is almost up here, Doctor."

"I know. I know, but can I ask you something else?"

"What?"

I have to try. Guys like him never come back here on their own accord unless it's for meeting some agenda for the courts or for the VA.

"I heard you say you mentioned some of your experiences from overseas to your wife at some point. Did you ever consider maybe she didn't judge you? She may have, more or less, misunderstood some of the things you were willing to tell her. I will tell you I am not here to judge you. No, I cannot relate to combat in the military, but I am *not* here to judge you. I am here to help you and to listen. Even if that's all I need to do to help you. Just to listen."

He looks up at me again, but not as stern as the last few times he made eye contact with me. Absolute silence. He looks at the clock and then slumps further into his chair.

"What do you really want to know, Doctor?"

"What are you willing to discuss with me?"

"That's not what I asked you. You're not listening again."

"Ok. Did something else happen over there?"

"You mean, like other combat situations?"

"Yes, that's what I meant. I just didn't want to sound so direct."

"It's fine. Yes, of course, there were more."

"Is there one you want to talk to me about?"

He sits there in silence again. How many incidents could there have been to think about which one to talk about? At least he is contemplating just talking to me about one. It's just frightening to think he has to choose which one to discuss. I sit back in my chair in a more relaxed stance like his. I don't know where he is about to take me.

"The locals had their own police forces in the districts we were in. They tried to set up outposts in various roadways. They started to go out with us on patrols. Having one or two of their own police forces there with us out on mission helped the interpreters and gave a level of comfort to the locals in the surrounding villages. We caught wind of a white flag with black inscriptions on it that had been recently raised over a mosque in the western parts of the area we patrolled. We knew what we had to do.

We went on foot most of the time. The dirt and gravel roads off the main highways were usually too dangerous to travel on while mounted in vehicles. We closed in on the mosque and then one of the local policemen got hit with an IED in the fields. The force of the blast knocked us all on our asses. When we started to get back up, we could barely register what had happened. His body went sky high, maybe even twenty or thirty feet in the air. It took a few seconds to come back down, actually. We just looked around at each other at first, wondering if we were all dead or alive. We all got splattered with blood and dirt from the blast and a random boot slammed me in the face.

They called in the medivac chopper, but we all knew he was dead the moment he landed on the ground like a sandbag. When the chopper left with him in it and the green smoke faded away, we all saw that white flag on that mosque was still waiving. We wanted to move forward, but we were ordered not to. At least, not to push forward until the EOD crews can clear the area. We all walked away. Some of the younger guys were relieved, but most of us knew it wasn't the right thing to do."

"Did it make you angry, the fact that you were ordered not to go any further?" I ask.

"Every day, I regret we didn't move forward. A life lost for no reason or justification. There were so many of our own lost like that, too. The local police had a funeral at their little outpost near our base for the man they lost the next day. A few soldiers from our base went, but I just couldn't go. I just couldn't."

He sits there looking down in shame now. I can't even respond to it. The floor is his, but I don't think he can take much more.

"I can only imagine the things you carried in your mind if there were more instances like that. There is life beyond war, though. I want you to know that and there are people that can help you find it. Even if it isn't me. It would be hard, going back there again into your memories, but it may be the only way to move forward."

No movement from him, just motionless, and that hat doesn't cover his quivering lips. He bares his teeth to hold back tears now. Such aggression forced into conformity. I wonder how many of them like him are out there, stuck somehow but still trying to move forward.

"You know the worst part about all that? It wasn't how I felt afterwards. It wasn't the fact we were basically ordered to move back like a bunch of pussies. It wasn't that someone else was killed."

He looks directly at me. I lower my clipboard on my lap, so he knows I am listening.

"When that guy's boot hit me in the face, I never did know if his fucking foot was in it or not. Was it that the boot was just blasted that hard in my direction? Or, maybe it just felt that hard because it was heavier with a foot inside of it still. I just don't know. Maybe I didn't go to the burial service because I didn't want to know if his dead body had a foot still on it or not. I couldn't remember that stupid little detail. I still can't remember, and now I'll never know."

The tears come rolling down as he stares right at me. He lowers his head down again to cover his face, but it's no use now.

"I guess it really doesn't matter now if his foot was in it or not. He's dead now anyway and nobody cares. Nobody even thinks to blink over one dead Afghan National, right? Anybody would view me in the same manner here in the states and move on with their lives without a second thought. What difference does it make for any of us now?"

He attempts to hide under his hat again with his teeth baring and jaw clinched. Going further may only make things worse, but I have all I need to know. There is one final question for him.

"I can only wish to understand the things you and many others have been though over there, and you say there are more incidents like this."

"Yeah. Dozens more. I lost count actually." he says.

"You have every reason to be angry. It is a truly natural human response after such an ordeal like this. You haven't made the effort to hurt yourself, which is good. Studies show that an untreated issue like this has a higher potential of ending in suicide. I know you don't want to hurt yourself, but the thoughts are there. There are things we can do to help if you want. Where will you go from here?"

"I think I'll head north to my old hunting grounds. Closer to home, but not at home. It's better that way. Safer..."

"What do you mean? Like, safer for you? How?" I ask.

"No. Safer for anybody else in my life at this point."

"You said you may go hunting? Do you own firearms?"

"I got a few. Enough to get the job done."

"I have to ask, is there someone else you want to hurt? Do you project this anger you have on any other people in your life, unintentionally?"

He looks up at the clock in more awkward silence. His front teeth should be broken with how hard he clinches his jaw. Is he thinking about how to answer the question or is he shutting down again? The clock must have rolled over a full minute of absolute quiet by now, an unnaturally disturbing quiet with no response from him.

"Are there others you want to hurt?" I ask again. Still no answer from him. He leans forward to adjust his pants back over his shoes and then leans back in his chair. He's not looking at me.

"Time's up, Doctor."

"Is there someone you feel like you want to hurt? Please say something." as I start to raise my voice from concern. If he does something terrible, they will look back and see I was his last encounter here. It could all fall on me. He stands up from the chair and moves toward the door. I don't have the spine to block his way out. One physical hit from him in this emotional state could put me in a coma. He opens the door but refuses to look at me as he steps out. I jump up in total fear as he starts to walk away. I raise my voice down the empty hallway.

"Please tell me, are you going to hurt someone?" I beg and then he turns his head to answer me while still keeping his torso forward.

"We're finished here, Doctor… *We're all finished.* All of us."

He turns his head forward again and keeps walking. Somehow, despite an emotional conversation for him, he still stands tall as he walks down the empty building hallway. Nobody around to greet him in the waiting room area. He makes no effort to check with a receptionist to make a follow-on appointment. There's just nothing left of the man I see walking away, completely alone. He's a true living, breathing, and completely conscious ghost, with no hope for a human life. I run down the hallway to get his attention. I see him opening the glass exit door as I turn the corner.

"The war didn't follow you home!" I yell to his backside. He stops walking to turn around and face me with the door between us. I move close enough to hear what he might say.

"Well… I guess I'll just have to go find a new one then, won't I? Tell me, Doctor, will you lie to me? Can *you* lie to me and tell me I'll make it home?"

Chapter 2: The Encounter

Only in the darkest of winter nights can someone holding on to their last glimpse of humanity ever find a sense of victory or peace, all at the same time. No place else seems to make much sense to me anymore. A desolate and gloomy world of woodlands that exists far away from all things is the only home I care to know now.

The scent of the pines that stains my clothes long after a hunt is over. The feel of the cold air coming in and out of my chest. That's what living feels like. Not fighting far away in some distant land for a cause that we no longer understand. That is not living. That's just a distraction to avoid accepting what comes for all of us. It's almost beautiful in a way, to be lost so deep in the forest and still find so much. To be alone with nothing to look back at. To be forgotten and to forget all things. To make a single kill worth hanging your hat on. That is being for me now. This is living. I love it out here and it smells like the rains are finally coming in.

All the smaller plant life sitting at the forest floor has their leaves tilted upwards, looking for that last ounce of moisture before the temperature drops. My breath becomes visible as the sun starts to lower. Varmint and squirrels scurry around, looking for their last meals beneath me before they bed down for the night to avoid the larger prey. They have no interest in the deer feeders though, as long as they are hung high above their reach. I can see other deer in the distance being drawn in by the scents that I scattered earlier. They carelessly scamper around the area, while completely oblivious to my tree stand and the rifle barrel that stays fixed on all of them. Clueless to their potential demise at any second.

A few degrees colder and the oncoming rains could turn to a solid snowfall, or at least a white dusting of the area. A deep frost is no surprise in the barrens this time of year either. No one cares to venture this far in. Not to just track one, anyway. There must be a million acres of pine in here, older than any man that has ever hunted in them. The last few days going deeper and deeper into these woods have shown multiple deer that has some promise to be a potential trophy rack. This one that I am after though stays difficult to take even a single shot at. His number of antler points is hard to count on the deer cameras that have spotted him in the area, but I know he is here. He must be at least a nine-point. The signs are all in my favor this time, from footprints to droppings within this location. The bark that he has scraped with his antlers during the rut spans a near four feet upwards on this massive pine I'm set up on. Climbing this tree with only spurs to set up the stand was no simple task but will be worthwhile in the end. This white stag will be mounted on my wall before this season ends.

The white stag is a reality that is just a rare encounter. A skin pigmentation that can be burdensome to some deer species, or that of a genetic albino type deer that can turn their coats dull white. These deer usually never make it to full maturity. This one's size puts his head raise at a near six feet tall. How I would love to stand toe-to-toe with him, dead or alive.

As for me and Marlin, we patiently wait alone in the coming darkness. She's old, but a few upgrades for the scope mounts, the new trigger job, a freshly forged chamber, and now she will stand the true test of time. She has already proven herself worthy of keeping from past takedowns. I move to use my night vision monocular. Several does, and a few younger bucks appear to still be closing in on the feeders. I slowly creep out of my ghillie blanket to catch a better view of them in the mono. Every movement has to be slow and methodical on my part to avoid all potential noise. One cross action could set a hunt back several hours. Even my breathing is controlled to exhale into my collar to keep it from being visible in the moonlight. I look to see over a dozen sets of glowing deer eyes reflecting out of my night vision, all well within shooting range of a 30-30, but I will wait for the worthy kill.

My monocular battery dies off hours into the night. Most of them are close enough to see moving while they approach the deer feeders, so long as the moonlight remains in my favor. How long it will be in my favor remains questionable with more passing overcast. It would be a shame to kill one of these smaller ones, but I will keep them in mind to prevent coming back empty-handed. One younger buck has some potential of a six-point rack, but not quite a trophy. A few have just found the salt bricks hanging from a neighboring tree. The others become more curious. Like timid children to a cookie jar, they cautiously approach the feeder. None of them are interested in approaching my pine tree. They know something larger has recently marked it as its own with the rut marks. Another ten-point buck from beyond shooting range watches over the closer approaching deer underneath the feeder. It's difficult to catch a full body glimpse, while he maneuvers in and out of sight through the surrounding pines. Now he might be worth taking the shot, but that may be my current lack of patience talking.

I see the ten-pointer sniffing frantically from the little moonlight that is available above the approaching rain clouds. Something has definitely got him spooked, and the rest of the herd looks in his direction. A single shot suddenly echoes through the tall pines followed by a male's voice yelling, a loud yell that is either hurtful or laughter. The herd freezes in place. The ten-pointer makes a few more agitated snorts. His breath lingers through the cold and then the group begins to raise tail and scurry away. They all move swiftly through the pine trees, with each of them panting heavily while their breath lingers behind in the cold. Completely quiet again. No tiny hoof steps or antlers breaking the shrubbery. Just nothing. That last shot from another hunter must have been within a mile or so. With the yelling immediately after the shot, it is undoubtedly one of local drunks celebrating a minor kill. The first person

I catch bragging about some young doe they took home will hear some cross words from me.

Knowing that my stay is now prolonged, time stops out here with each passing minute that feels like hours. Absolute silence, only the pines that lose needles into the marshy bottom underneath me with any light breeze. The cloud coverage allows another glimpse of solid moonlight to come into the area that I overlook from my stand. No guarantee of much more moonlight in the area, as that storm front is heading in closer with the wind that blows in my favor. My eyes take time to adjust to the darkness each time a cloud passes under the moon. Eternity passes and my adrenaline has just turned to outright shivering from the cold. Each time it goes full dark, I don't feel so alone anymore. Life is all around me in these dark woods, whereas I am the only one here to bring death. The moonlight appears again to brighten up the entire area and finally reveal him.

The white stag appears within range like a ghost from darkness.

He has a nine-point rack just as expected. I raise my Marlin and slowly release the safety and cock the hammer. He's lingering into my sights now, but his front torso is in my direction. I need him to turn for that clean shot in the shoulders, but he keeps staring in my direction. One wrong shot here and the round either bounces off the ground between his front legs or a head shot that ruins my trophy. As if the white deer hears my thoughts, he lightly prances closer. Chills run up my spine and the air somehow fell colder with each of his movements that close the distance between us. A little less than a hundred yards away now. My right cheek presses on the freezing stock of the rifle. I close my left eye as my index finger puts more pressure on the trigger with each of his passing steps. I just need him to turn. My timing needs to be perfect with the trigger pull at the bottom of my exhale.

I see you.

Keep your breath low.

Exhale into the collar.

Slow breathing.

Gimme that clean shot at those shoulders.

Easy does it now.

Just turn for me once.

Slight pressure on that trigger

You're mine now.

Just breathe.

A distracting branch cracks from a neighboring tree. No, just ignore it. I won't let this one get away. This white stag is coming home with me. I convince myself to keep my eyes on my target for the kill. He just won't turn his damn torso. He keeps staring right at me. Is he watching me? Can he see me somehow? I have just enough time to look away before the stag turns. What cracked that tree branch a few seconds ago? Nothing visible to my right. It's just too dark with the moonlight being covered again. I turn my eyes back to the stag through my scope again. He's gone. That's impossible. He was right there in my sights. My scope glass starts to fog up now. I need to lower my breathing to get him in my crosshairs again. I had him right there in my sights. I could see him nearly glowing in the dark with that white coat. I hear more breathing to my left, but it isn't mine. The hairs on my neck stand, but that's not the cold. The breathing is either getting closer or louder. The cloud coverage opens up for more moonlight again. I want to keep checking in my scope for the stag, but the breathing is too close to ignore.

I turn my eyes left to see a dark creature begin growling at me while perched on the cracking branch from the tree right next to mine. The dark silhouette raises a long and jagged horned head up between two enclosed wings. Each pant from its long face results in a short snarl as it stares right back at me.

"Jesus Christ… What the fuck are you?"

The tree branch lowers further with each crack under its enormous weight. I know that smell from its breath, the smell of fresh death from a recent kill. One cross move and it can jump onto my tree stand. The moonlight goes away with the moving clouds again as its branch snaps. A sudden demonic scream of tortured souls echoes into the barrens as its wings open up to break its fall. My body is motionless. I can't even find the will to turn my rifle on this thing. Its massive wings flap the freezing air hard enough to uncover my ghillie blanket. It's too dark to catch a full glimpse, beyond its massive silhouette and the moonlight that shines through the holes of its tattered and leathery wings. Each burst of wind from it hits my face with freezing air so fast, it brings a near instant numbness from the cold. It gives another blood-curdling yell as its frightful blood-red eyes focus back on me. Those crazed red eyes stare deep into whatever heart I may have left.

It hovers there, motionless, while flapping its massive wingspan. Its wings close in as it rushes me headfirst. All I see are teeth and clawed hands outstretched while coming at me with a speed faster than my first trigger pull in its direction. It bites and clamps down onto my left shoulder. Nothing has ever bitten me this hard on any prior hunt. It tries to throw me off balance as its jaws clamp down harder on my shoulder with each wing movement. Its upper claws sink into my torso and crack several ribs like twigs. My left arm is useless while its fangs are ripping deeper and deeper into my shoulder. It thrusts its head around like the winning pit-bull of a dog fight that ravages its weaker victim.

I pivot my rifle against the tree to shoot, but one of its lower claws pushes it out of my grip with little effort. My rifle drops and hits the ground below hard enough to blast the chambered round. The shot startles the creature and releases its jaws from my shoulder to look at the ground where the rifle landed. My left arm is suddenly limp now, and the blood feels as cold as metal while it drips down into my glove. It keeps its grip still, clamping down on my ribs so hard that I can't yell anymore. I can't even take a full breath. I swing with my right fist at its head as hard as my balance will allow on the tree stand that is buckling under our weight. I try a few more swings at its torso, but its left claw releases its grip to grab my only good arm now. I am helpless now as I stare at a demon, face to face.

A quick and struggled breath passes out of my chapped lips. It releases its claw from a protruding rib on my side. It still faces me, but it is lunging its neck back to take another mouthful aimed for my head this time. Its jaws open again to reveal a set of teeth that can make even the most aggressive grizzly whimper away. Got no choice now but to risk a fall from twenty feet up. It may be my only chance while it has less of a grip on me. Before it has a chance to clamp those jaws around my head, I rush toward it with all my weight. The creature loses slight balance but keeps a grip on both the tree stand and the pine. Startled and dizzy, I slam the side of the tree before I fall. I hang upside-down from one leg that is strapped to the deer stand with a safety cord. The tree stand is folding in on itself under my dead weight. The moment this creature puts all its weight on the stand again, we'll both go down. It reaches for my leg and clamps those massive claws on my ankle. Even with my ankles covered by my hunting boots, its grip is still violent enough to break the skin through the leather.

I use some gravity to bend my free leg inward to pull my spare boot knife and start waving it towards the last strap holding me up in my tree stand. I swing it viciously, at its outstretched claw, the safety cord, anything a blade can cut. I slit the safety cord with the third wave. The creature lets out another demonic scream as I begin to fall towards the ground. Its wings open up to guide it back to the tree. It struggles to find a grip on all four claws again before falling with me. Its head faces down at me and those glowing red eyes just stare at me in hatred while I tumble down through the weaker branches of the pine. The limbs bash me in the legs and face but don't slow down the fall. I hit the ground with my back hard enough to force out a gurgled cough full of my blood. My hunting stand lands just below my feet. I lost my knife somewhere in the fall. Even if it was near, I can't take a breath deep enough to make a reach for it.

All the hours in that tree stand have left the sandy ground I lay on frozen. My left shoulder burns like a heated iron each time I try to move. The frost on the forest floor seeps into my open wounds. I have to stay conscious, but I already know I'll keep fading in and out if I don't get a full breath in. Either my head or back hit the ground hard enough to hinder me now. I see the monster's breath lingering in the air as it maneuvers down the tree slowly. It's as if it is teasing me like a cat that knows its wounded mouse just lays here lifeless, helpless. It enjoys it, my vulnerability. Either the overcast is covering the moon again or I'm losing consciousness. If this thing is going to end me, I prefer to be unconscious. It crawls down the tree with little effort and a growl with each breath. Hard to keep my eyes open as it gets closer and closer to the ground. I made a mistake coming here. That scream. That yell. It's a howl that makes you fear the blackest of nights. These barrens don't belong to man nor hunter.

A sleet begins to fall that is cold enough to freeze my nostrils that are already clotted with blood. The salty copper taste fills the back of my throat. I've never felt colder while I feel my heart rate starting to lower. Everything gets dark as I fade in and out. I look up to see the night sky that lets moonlight come through the clouds. It stands over me during my last efforts of vision while still awake. So much trembling I can do nothing about now. I have to see it beyond this dark silhouette closing in. Face to face with the horns and red eyes, as it drools my own blood down on me. This demonic nightmare will make a mistake if it doesn't kill me now. Let me wake up from darkness just one more day, all broken and bloody, and I will hunt it down with all I have left. I'll search the depths of hell that it came from.

End me now and I'll wait for you there.

I know where you come from.

I know that place just the same as you.

I will gladly follow you to meet your maker or my own.

I will go down fighting again and again if I have to.

I won't have it any other way...

Chapter 3: The Nightmares

I look to my left to see her like a shining light in my own darkness. The world felt as if it completely closed down all around us. There were no concerns, and no more worries, and all became suddenly simple. Everything is warm again. We laid there, breathless and uncovered, but vulnerable to only each other. All we had was our love for the other and a happiness that we would forever have to fight for. But would never truly have it, ever again. I must be dreaming. I must be dead. I hope I am dead this time. I remember this moment, because I never wanted to leave this moment. I hope I can stay in it with her forever and not have to leave her this time. Her soft hands touch my face while I am lost in her long hair. Her bare chest presses against mine as we entangle our legs together as one. I feel safe in her beauty and her love for me. I stole her heart but could never give her mine.

"We're gonna make a baby.", she says to me as her eyes gaze through the darkness and right into my heart on a dance floor.

Every moment inside her, I feel alive. I feel wanted. Over and over again. My lips touch every part of her as she moans. The night was perfectly blurred from cheap wine on empty stomachs. We didn't care to eat at the hotel restaurant I took her to. She wanted me from the moment we sat down. Other couples, young and old, sit facing each other. Whereas we sit next to each other. Her hand slides under my belt beneath the table. My arm wraps around her small frame to harden her nipple underneath my coat that she borrowed.

When we get into the door of the hotel room, she drops down on her knees to take a mouthful of me in at the very entrance. She raises up to kiss me after as I take her top off. I leave her shirt stuck on her head over her eyes to keep her arms pinned in the air. I grab her as she still squirms to undress, but I lay her on the bed to tease her more with my lips. She's trapped but entertains the vulnerability with a smile from ear to ear under that shirt. I pull off the rest of her bottom skirt piece to taste her as her legs wrap around the back of my head. She tenses her hips up to my mouth so I can go deeper inside her. I lift to take her top all the way off. She tastes herself on my lips as we kiss, unforgettably hard and long.

It must have been all night like that. We would spread the sheets all over the room every time we wanted to get away from it all. Her hair a constant mess of being ravaged and me not knowing where she hid my clothes to keep me open to herself whenever she pleased. To have each other endlessly and tirelessly every night that we could have each other. She lay there again in my arms to pillow talk until the sun came up. Her lips right next to mine when she whispers, ever so gently. She rolls on top to slide me inside her again. I wish this would've never ended.

"Don't go. Just stay here a little longer with me, with us." she says.

"I don't want to go. I'm going to stay this time. I promise."

"Please don't go. Why do you have to leave?"

Her smile turns to a cry. Her hazel eyes turn black in front of me. Can she hear me? She's holding me so tight that it's hard to breathe. No, not this. It's not supposed to be this way. This moment wasn't like this.

"I'm not going anywhere I said. I'm staying here this time. I'll stay with you."

"You always leave us. Please just stay with us. Don't go." as she cries more and more with tears of blood now.

"Can you hear me? I'm not going anywhere?"

"Why are you leaving us again?" she says.

Her red tears fall uncontrollably. My arms and hands are locked around her body. I want to wipe her tears away, but I can't. Why can't I move?

"I don't want to go. I want to stay here. I'll do whatever it takes to stay this time. I swear I will stay this time. I don't want to go."

"All you ever do is leave. Just stay with us this time. Please stay."

"I am. I'm staying right here with you this time. I promise."

"You're already gone. You're always gone. We don't know you anymore. Even when you are here with us, you are still gone."

"Baby, I'm right here. I'm not gone. I'm right here?"

"You don't love us anymore, do you?"

"I never said that. I never meant to say that. I'm right here. I'm staying here this time. I promise."

She starts to fade away right in front of me while her grip on my chest grows tighter somehow.

"You don't love us. Even if you did, you were never here to show it." she says.

"No, that's not true. You don't understand. I want to stay now."

She fades away more. She gets up from the bed and walks away, but I can barely move. It's as if I can only move in slow motion and my chest sinks more and more. I can't breathe while my heart breaks into pieces behind her. I reach for her as she turns her back on me, but all I can feel are the sheets sliding off the bed as she covers herself. She walks towards the door with all the white linens dragging on the floor behind her. Her eyes aren't there, she can't hear me or see me.

"Can you hear me! I want to stay. Please God, just turn around and talk to me!" I yell.

She says nothing as she walks out the bedroom door and slams it shut. I jump from the bed naked to search the drawers for something to wear, but there is nothing in them. I run to the door, still nude. I step out of the bedroom, but the stairs that go down to the kitchen appear to be a mile long.

When did I come home?

I see her, still walking down the steps with just the white sheets of hotel linens wrapped around her. She makes it to the bottom of the stairs with the bedding dragging behind her.

"I'll stay this time. I promise!"

I run down the stairs and it takes everything I have to just jump down to the bottom steps. I go into the kitchen to see all the lights are on, but she is gone. Am I too late? Am I still at home or at the hotel? I don't want to leave. I have to find her. I move through the kitchen and into the living room. The television is on. My son sits there, alone, with toys surrounding him while watching cartoons. He wasn't born yet when I remembered those moments with her. He hears me coming in through the entrance way and turns around. I'm in uniform again. What is going on? It wasn't like this, was it?

"Hey there. Did you see where Mommy went, little man?" I ask him.

"Are you gonna yell at Mommy again, Daddy?" he asks with dried tears on his cheek. His eyes are hollow and blackened too, but he talks just like I remember.

"No, little man. Me and Mommy were just talking. Did you see where she went?"

"Are you gonna yell at me again, Daddy?"

"No. Why would I do that? You did nothing wrong, buddy. Where did Mommy go?"

"You never get to play with me and Mommy."

"I know, little man, but I'm staying home this time. I promise. Do you know where Mommy went? I have to find Mommy."

He stands up from his spot on the floor with and my assault rifle in his little hands.

"Oh my God! You put that down now, right fucking now!"

"You always yell at me and Mommy. You never play with us anymore, Daddy. Mommy says you don't love us anymore."

"Ok. It's Ok. I won't yell anymore. I'll stop yelling, ok? I promise. Just put the fucking gun down. For the love of God, just put the fucking gun down. Please, just put it down."

24

He walks towards me and uses the gun like a walking cane with the muzzle pointed upwards. Every step he takes closer, he hits the buttstock on the floor hard enough to set off the trigger. I reach out and motion for him to stop. I yell at him, but my voice isn't coming out anymore. He starts crying when I try to yell louder. He always cried when he heard me yelling at him or his mother. He keeps walking closer with the gun in front of him now. The muzzle is right in front of his face.

"You don't love me and Mommy anymore. You never want to play Daddy."

"I will… I mean, yes, I do love you, little man. Just put fucking gun down, please. How did you get Daddy's gun?"

"We miss you Daddy. Can you come home, Daddy? Mommy's crying Daddy!" over and over. He repeats himself more and more, louder and louder.

I grip the side of my head and ears to shut out his repetitive voice as he cries. He just keeps saying it over and over till it becomes a scream, as he walks closer. I try to yell at him to stop moving, but I can't hear my own voice yelling anymore. He steps forward again and slams the gun on the floor. I jump towards him to grab the gun while I land on the floor. He's too far away from me to reach and he moves further away while walking closer somehow. He stands there above me, still crying. His head is right above the muzzle. He slams the gun's stock on the floor and my ears ring as the bullet blast out of the chamber.

I can't hear myself screaming again. His blood splatters all over me. There's blood everywhere, and he lifelessly drops to the floor.

His grip is released from the gun and it drops to the floor right next to him. It sets off another round again when it lands on its side.

They won't stop!

The ringing in my ears. They don't ever fucking stop!!

What have I done?!

His blood drips down to his little fingers.

Gun shots fired!

Gun shots all around in my home.

The home I left behind…

Chapter 4: The Black Doctor

My body jolts from the additional shots fired. I'm still lying on the ground and still breathing. The pools of blood continue to fill my mouth so much that I have to turn my head to cough it out. More shots fired, and it's coming from my rifle. I know that sound and it is way too familiar to be any other rifle other than my Marlin. A man's voice is yelling, but I can't move my head enough from the dizziness and too weak to see what's going on. The air is still frigid and dark all around me. My whole body seems to have frozen to the ground from the moisture and frost. Vision is too blurry to see anything other than more muzzle flashes. He must have unloaded my magazine tube on that monster. Still fading in and out of consciousness. It's difficult to contemplate which nightmare is worse. The one I just had or still being out here.

The sounds of the creature's screams seem more ear piercing than the echoes of the rifle, but the gunfire suddenly stops. The yelling stops. I see a dark silhouette of a man standing over me. He's trying to talk to me but I either don't know what to say or I simply can't talk back to him.

"Hey, wake up fella! Can ya hear me! Can ya move?!" he yells frantically.

I blink my eyes and try to talk back, but nothing but a gargle of blood comes out and drips backward towards my upper lip. The drops of blood feel like it freezes on my upper lip before it reaches my nose.

"We gots to move ya fella!" he yells again.

He moves my arms to my chest and rolls me over to my right side. I try to think how long I had been laying here on the frozen ground. The back of my frozen head peels off the forest floor like an old piece of masking tape. Once he gets me on my side, then the coughing starts hard. Blood and vomit spew out and steam as it lands on the ground right in front of me. He props my leg up to keep me from rolling over onto my chest.

"Ya gots to say something to me, fella? Otherwise, ya too far gone to save out here."

I shake my head and try to speak, but nothing comes out again. I point to my shoulder that feels like the arm is out of socket. That's the only way I can talk back to him to let him know I'm still alive, but I'm fading in and out into darkness too often to speak back to him. He rips the shoulder of my jacket, either with little ease or he has a blade to cut it. Darkness again, but a quick gargle of blood to spit out wakes me back up. How could I still be alive after a fall like that? What the hell was it that tried to kill me out here? I can feel him looking at my shoulder. Pain shoots down to my chest and neck as he tries to move my arm. His breathing near my shoulder is the only thing that gives any hint of warmth as I lay here shaking in the cold.

"Gonna stitch that up for ya, but we gots to get ya to shelter if ya expect to live to see the light of tomorrow. Just sit tight right there now."

I close my eyes in relief as I try to say thank you. But he knows enough by now that it is too difficult for me to talk back to him. He remains in darkness too much to get a good glimpse of his face as I fade out again. He moves me to sit up on something and I look outward before my head falls back down. Not enough energy to even keep my head up at the moment. Consciousness comes and goes. I see her face again. She looks at me in worry. She always looked at me like that when I came home after being gone for so long. She's beautiful but I don't know how to tell her. My feet feel like they are floating in front of her of somehow.

"I wanna stay this time. I promise, no more hurt."

She says nothing back to me and slips back into the distance as I try to reach for her. My feet aren't floating, they are being dragged on top of the ground. He lays my head down on something. He is moving me somewhere. Several hours must have already passed as I see the light coming up on the horizon through the trees. The air is coldest just before the dawn. I can now smell the sea's saltwater and realize we are close to the shoreline.

Everything goes dark again, but I am still awake, I think. We are inside of a building. Everything wreaks of fuel. He lays the makeshift sled he dragged me on down on the ground. The light from the doorway closes as he slams it shut. I hear multiple pieces of wood dragged around on the ground to barricade the door. I don't hear a lock being turned or a doorknob.

"We gots to get you warm. Ain't no tellin' how long you were laying on the ground out there."

He rolls me over on to my side again. He has a propane camping heater he lights up on full blast. Just enough light to look around if I had the energy, but I still haven't caught a glimpse of his face yet. My whole body is just shaking as he strips my clothes off. The moisture left on them from the recent snow fall makes my pants and shirt feel as if they are peeling off layers of skin when they slide off. A thick wool blanket is thrown on top of me and tucked underneath my side. He lifts my head to lay another sheet underneath it.

"Drink this fella. I think you caught a fever lying around out there. Just drink this to fight it off before it gets you any worse than you are now."

He brings my head forward to an old coffee mug, and the smell is worse than the starting flames of the propane heater in front of me. I take a gulp, hoping it's a bit of water, but water does not go down as harsh as this. Its smell curls my nose hairs as I cough and spit up more blood.

"Come on, fella. You gotta drink a little more now, ya hear?"

As it goes down my throat again, an instant feeling of warmth comes over me more than the heater. My shivering goes away for just a moment before it all goes dark again.

"If you make it till the morning, well get that arm put back in place. Ya lucky it didn't bite that whole shoulder off of ya. Gotta have a few broken ribs from a fall like that, too. Ya must've put up a damn good fight with that one, didn't ya, stranger?" he says with a giggle. That voice, the accent, tells me he is much older than me, but I can't keep my eyes open.

He lifts the coffee mug to his own lips with a smile that shows a few teeth. I catch a glimpse of him for the first time as he walks over to the other side of the heater. All I can see is loose teeth. His skin is either covered in that much dirt or he is black. Not enough energy to keep my eyes open. Whatever he gave me to drink is setting in unbelievably fast. I keep my eyes closed to avoid a spinning view of the few flames inside the heater. My body warms for the first time in days now. I don't know how long I keep going in and out.

"This ain't gonna feel good here now, young fella. Bite down on this. When I get it back in place, you 're gonna wanna holler, but I can't let you do that out here. Alright now?" he says.

I'm not on the floor like I was. I'm on some sort of makeshift bed of sticks and needles covered with flannel blankets. He takes the pillow out from under my head, so I lay flat. He shoves a piece of pine bark covered in cloth up to my mouth. My teeth grind it as I bite down. He moves my arm around with one hand and digs around in the loose shoulder to catch a feel of the bone. I feel his fingers digging into the fresh bite wound. He braces himself against my torso.

SNAPP!!

I let out a growl while biting down so hard on the pine bark that I can feel a molar in the back of my jaw breaking off. That bone cracking and jarring sound was like no other. The sound of an instant pain that happens so fast you wish you had already been killed. Broken noses, mangled legs from car wrecks, and busted knuckles in fights never felt as jolting as that one. Hard to catch my breath as I try to spit out the bark.

"Slow your breathin down now, fella. I think it's back in place now. Ya breathing too hard, one of them broken ribs might dig into your lungs. Then we gots a real problem I can't fix there. Stay flat now, ya hear? Your ribs have gotta fix themselves for a bit."

He takes the now chopped-up cloth and bark out of my mouth. He digs his fingers around inside my lips as I try to catch my breath and takes something out.

"Looks like ya broke a damn tooth off in there, fella."

He chuckles under his breath and smiles at me again to show the few rotted teeth he has left behind his lips.

"Well, that's alright then, I reckon. You gots a full set in ya mouth before you broke just one little ol' tooth anyways. Can't remember the last time I had a nice set like yours, but maybe they can put it back in, so I'll just hold on to it for ya. Don't be swallowing any more blood now. You'll be pissing red as it is with all that you swallowed from that busted up rib. Lay still now while I finally get some of these gashes sewn up. Already got them cleaned while you were out."

He walks over to the propane heater and opens the match door. He carefully places a needle on the tip of some pliers and slides it all into the flame. He comes back a few seconds later with that sewing needle red hot as it sits on the tip of the pliers. He bends the needle against the side of the bed to give it a slight curve as it the glow fades off. There's that coffee mug again, and he dips the needle inside it before he takes a swig of his own. He hands me the mug to take another drink once I sit my head up straight. The rest of what was in the mug gets poured on my shoulder that gives a serious sting inside my arm that lets me know I'm still alive.

"Jesus! What the hell is in that shit?" I ask, while coughing.

"Just a little liquid lightning for ya, stranger. Just lay back down now to keep your ribs opened up and try not to move too much while I close this up. I already got the one on your face cleaned and stitched too while you were out."

"That stuff tastes like kerosene. Is that what you keep having me drink? Kerosene?" I ask.

30

He giggles as the needle goes in and my shoulder shrugs inward from the pain.

"Be still now, ya hear? Ain't no kerosene in that drink. If I put that stuff in my heater over there, it would blow us all to shit in a heartbeat. How would you know what kerosene tastes like anyhow?"

"Good point." as I lay my head back down.

"You just keep talkin or try to close your eyes while I do this. Once I close in the wound, you 're gonna feel it, for sure. So best you pass back out or just keep talking to take your mind off what I'm doing here."

"You a doctor or something?" I ask.

"Used to be back when I still lived around others, but that was a long time ago now."

I feel the needle moving in and out from one side of the flesh to the other. At least the drink is kicking in already. I stop watching him and lay my head back down when the dizziness starts.

"You called out a lady's name a few days ago when I first found ya." he says.

"A few days ago. How long have I been in and out?"

"Bout less than a week or so, *I think*. Ain't got no care for a calendar marker out here these days, so I can't really be too sure on that one either. Gonna close this one up now so it ain't gonna feel the best, but it'll keep it from infection. It's fishin line, so be ready. No yellin now, ya hear?"

He hands another piece of cloth covered bark for me to put in my mouth.

"This won't be as bad as when your arm was put back in the socket."

The line tightens up, but I can feel it ripping more skin as it closes with each tiny movement. Once he stops, he lowers his face in close to bite off the line that wasn't used.

"You took that one pretty well, stranger. Take it you had that done to you before?" he asks.

"Yeah. Once or twice."

"So, you gonna tell me who this lady friend of yours is. She your wife or somethin? I can go into the towns and call for her."

"Nobody in the nearby town knows me. Nobody even knows I'm even out here."

"Well damn fella, you really are a stranger in these parts, ain't ya?"

"Been a stranger everywhere I go for a long time now, ol' timer. But it doesn't matter."

"So, wanna tell me who she is?" he asks again.

"She's no one, and she's been gone a while now too."

"Lot of hurt in them last few words, young fella. Sounds like a bite that can't be stitched back up." as he focuses again on his stitching work.

The light coming in from holes in the side of the walls and the roof start to blur again. This house isn't very big, if it is really even a house at all. More like a small wooden shack that's been pieced together. I just want to close my eyes. He stays close to my side as I drift off again.

Chapter 5: The Recovery

I wake up to see my breath flowing up through the sunlight that shines through the broken holes of the shed. Sitting upright takes more painful energy than I can fathom, but I move anyway. My stomach growls in hunger. I take my first glimpse around, not to see the black man in sight of the small shed. Medical books are piled up everywhere and the heater had not been on for several hours. Though the place still smells of fuel everywhere. Cast-iron pots hang on the walls near baskets of fruit and vegetables that are drying out from the cold. There are jars of vegetables stacked on shelves near all the books by a few medical tools.

My clothes sit at the edge of the bed, neatly folded underneath my rifle. I remove the wool blanket to see my wounds for the first time. The side of my ribcage is badly bruised and spans across my backside. My shoulder is as stiff as a board and I can't stretch too much, or I'll rip the stitches right out. A small mirror and a bowl of water sit on top of a little table that has a candle lit underneath. I see the stitch job he did on my face in the mirror that gives me the look of being mauled by a tiger at the zoo like a dumb tourist that got too close to the fences. The candle has been lit for hours and down to the last few strands of wick.

It's a tiny candle, but it has kept the water warm enough to prevent freezing. I splash it on my face and take a cup of it in my hands to drink. I move back to my clothes and they smell clean. Not a clean smell from laundry detergent, but from that of being rubbed clean by pinecones and saltwater. Once I get dressed, I take a good look at my rifle. The scope has a busted sight glass and is now useless. One of the mounting rings has been broken off too. The magazine tube is emptied out and has been fired hard without cleaning. The iron sights still appear to be left at my last settings. A quick functions check ejects an empty casing, but all of it appears to be in working order, except for some new scratches in the wooden stock that could be sanded back out. I see my knife placed back in the holster as I slide my boots back on my feet. It takes another serious effort to put them on and tie them up, along with putting my jacket on too. The shoulder of my jacket is torn and lets in every bit of cold air right onto my stitched-up wounds. I look around some more while I catch my breath from the recent struggle, and I can't see any other of my belongings around me.

I step outside to see a quiet snowfall hitting the ground through the naked pine trees. It's like something seen in a painting that only uses colors variations of white and gray. My first catch of fresh air since it attacked me. Being so near death should make you feel more alive at a calm moment like this. But I feel nothing, even in a forest so alive with life in the cold winter months that never seemed so serene. I still feel nothing somehow. I'll just stand here and at least appreciate it, even if I don't feel it. I want to at least try.

"Pretty out there, ain't it, stranger?" he says from the other side of the structure.

I turn behind me to see the black man crouched down near a fire behind his shed.

"Yes, I was just thinking the same thing. Very peaceful."

I turn my body and try to walk towards him to warm up by his fire, but he jumps up from the ground as he sees me stumble in my broken walk.

"Hold on, there fella. Pretty sure you jammed up one knee and sprained the other ankle. Could be awhile till you can walk proper again. Just take it easy now, ya here?"

He moves to my good arm and moves it over the back of his shoulders to keep me from falling. We walk over to the fire and I see a fresh varmint of some form on a rotisserie made of sticks that have been used in the same manner before. The snow has melted all around the fire to reveal the moist sand at our feet.

"Ok now fella, just drop down here real slow like on your good knee and take a rest."

I do as he asks, not having a choice. As soon as I am settled upright again, a sharp pain presses through my ribs with each breath.

"Breath in your nose and out ya mouth. Or the other way around. Don't really matter, so long as you slow your breathin."

He steps away to stoke his fire and stir something in a pot that I didn't see while on the other side of the shed. He killed a large racoon that the bullet blast had torn apart. The skull is left broken in many pieces that have already fallen off into the fire.

"I take it you used my rifle to blast that racoon all to shit?" I ask.

"Sure did. Sorry I had to use your last rounds, fella, but I didn't think you would mind. It was a little too strong to expect much else left from that koon when the bullet went clean through. But I got enough meat salted up from it to go in a nice stew here. Never been much good with rifles anyhow but figured you could use a fine meal when you finally wake up."

"How long have I been out?" I ask.

"Pretty sure it has been the better part of a week by now, because it was two days ago when you last asked me that same question. At least your fever broke yesterday. Once you get some meat and vegies in your belly, we gots to take a look at those stitches and clean it up again to keep out any other infection."

"All right then. You sound like you know what you're doing. Do you live out here or just camp or what?"

He giggles as he stirs the pot. Whatever he is cooking smells like it will surpass old granola bars and frozen beef jerky left in my ruck. Wait? I lost my gear out there before he found me.

"Of all the things to ask me, stranger, that's it. That's the only question you gots for me are, *Do I live here or camp here he says?* Hmmmph." He chuckles a little more under his breath, but at least he appears in good spirits. And I have no choice but to smile back at him in the same humorous effort.

"Yeah, I guess so at the moment."

"No questions for now. Just have some of this here grub. Just take it slow. It ain't about how good or bad it tastes. It's about getting some food in your system."

He pulls out another coffee mug from beside him and dips it into the pot. He walks it over to me and places it in my hands. At first glimpse I see a few herb type leaves floating around inside the browned stew along with soggy green beans, maybe a diced-up potato or two, and some shredded dark meat more than likely from his recent kill.

"Ya need a spoon or somethin?" he asks.

"No thank you. This will do just fine. In fact, this is the first hot meal I've had in several days, even before you met me. It is much appreciated. I don't even know how to start to say thank you."

He motions with his shaky hands to signal me to stop talking, "Ain't gotta thank me, stranger. Helpin the hurtin and the sickly is what I used to do on a daily basis out here. A caretaker of the woods, so to speak. Until all the old pine rats strayed off into the towns. A few more days here, then you'll be on your way I'm sure."

He reaches for another coffee mug and pulls out that familiar flask. With his attire it would appear to be old hand-me-down clothes from the turn of the century, almost. But they have been stitched back together on many occasions with more sewn up places on his pants. A large jacket covers his upper part, but it's mainly made of rabbit, squirrel, and raccoon furs. His walk is funny and just as broken as my walk is at the moment. He is not a large man, but very homely looking with a straggly white beard that is combed in an effort to cover his missing teeth. The only piece that doesn't match that of a true mountain man that lives off the land is his hat.

The hat was a bowler cap that I've seen in western movies before. Usually, it's the Irishman in those western movies that wears one of those hats, but he has the added touch of crow feathers that make up most of the brim. Some turquoise beads line certain places of his front layers. A single ear is pierced with a bead of the same color.

"Once you're gone off, then it's just me left with chattin it up with the trees and squirrels again and they ain't much for conversation these days." he says.

"Wait, so you do live out here?"

"Sure do. Seems like I been out here for several lifetimes now. Even the natives are gone now too, but I decided to stay and help others when and where I could."

"Are you like a doctor or a medicine man or something like that?"

"Oh yes. I studied medicine back in them towns years ago now. My brother did too, and he went on with it longer than I did. Learned a lot from some natives that lived out here along the way about getting certain things to grow in the warmer months. I would help their sick and ill in return."

"Why live out here and treat so few people. I mean, don't you think they need people like that in the cities?"

"I'm sure they do, but it comes with a lot of headache too. Especially when they don't exactly care for men of color like me. Tried to string me up a few times for it, but I usually got away. I just felt I was needed more out here. Especially when the War Between the States ended, the soldiers started to make their way back home. Warriors like you too, that never really left the battlefields either."

"I'm not sure I know what you mean and believe me I'm no warrior."

He looks and talks like it is hundreds of years ago. He interrupts me, pondering his last response.

"Why sure, you are. You all look alike, and you can be spotted a mile away. I would always tell them the war would be over soon and we'll all be back home. Some of them had nothing to go back to. Almost felt like the ones that never got home were blessed in a certain way."

"So, you were like a medic in Vietnam or one of the other ones. I can't see you going as far back as Korea or World War Two? You're not *that* old."

"Nah, further back than that, but don't matter anyhow. It was their faces that stuck with me all these years. Faces like yours. A look of not understanding anything other than death. Or worse, just longing for it in some way or another."

I take a few more sips of stew in confusion and to avoid my curiosity.

"I'm sorry ol' timer, either you have spiked the stew with some of your famed lightning, or I hit my head a few times harder than I thought. Hard to keep a conversation with you at the moment."

A few giggles from him as he stokes the fire again and stands up to walk over to me. His boots are a high calve style boot like seen in old silver screen movies too.

"Alright now, let's have a look at that shoulder here while we got some good daylight."

He helps me take my arm out of my jacket and stretches out the rip already on my shirt. He examines it closely to see a few stitches have ripped out from what little movement I can commit to. He pulls out a small pocketknife and walks over to the fire to stick the blade right into the flame red coals.

"What are you doing now?" I ask.

"Gonna take them old stitches out your shoulder. That fishin line might do more harm than good if it stays in there too much longer. At least the cuts are closed up so they can heal on their own from this point. Gotta get those ones off your face too before they infect, but I'll get the mirror out so you can get those out on your own."

Each time the blade was close enough to the fishing line, it melted away, and he would use his dirty fingernails to dig the rest out. Once he is done with my shoulder, he walked back inside his shed to get the mirror I saw earlier. I took a few more sips of the stew and caught a few chunks of meat and vegetables in the mix. He sets the blade back in the fire to heat it up again and hands me the mirror. I take a good glimpse of my face in the foggy old mirror. Dried blood surrounds my stubble beard hair. I look dead already with all the cuts and stitches that are holding my face together.

"Let me get this shoulder bandaged up while you pick those stitches outta ya face. Gots a few more scars to impress the ladies now I bet."

I pick away the stitches in my face. The heated blade burns my hair of my eyebrows when it gets close enough. He didn't use as much line to close up these wounds around my checks. There's some scar tissue to keep it hardened in place as it is.

"You got yourself a woman out here?" I ask him.

"Nah, not for years now. Had me a wife once, but she fell ill with the tuberculosis and died off with a lot of them natives too. Town folks didn't care for the tribes still left out here. When the last few tribe folks left, they discovered they couldn't even the raise crops out here either, so a lot of them died for no good reason. Wasn't really worth stayin near folks in the towns after that."

He must be referring to the remains of a tribal nation that stayed away from reservations. Unless a place like this continued on that way they lived, even long after the Civil War. I can see how someone of his age would have dealt with Civil Rights issues in the 60s. That might make sense if he was afraid of working as a doctor in a populated area. Maybe he just helped returning soldiers from Vietnam as a field doctor of some form. That timeline would be easier to understand for his story. The last stitch comes out without issue and he uses my shirt to bandage up my shoulder and tie it off underneath my armpit. He manages to spread some sort of herb smelling cream on the shoulder wound while I was busy in the mirror.

"Well fella, you managed to sleep most of the daylight away, but that's good for you. Tomorrow, it's best we get you up and start walking around so that leg doesn't stiffen up too bad. Gotta keep it movin or it won't work the same ever again."

"I'd be alright with that." I reply after lowering the mirror.

I hand him his knife and mirror back and he walks it back into the shed. He comes out with a new coffee mug filled with frozen water and hands it to me.

"Just give it a few seconds and it will thaw out to be clean and cool water for ya."

"Thanks. Can I ask when we go for a walk tomorrow, can we go back to where you found me? I left a backpack covered up down on the ground level. There might be a few more rounds for my 30-30 in it and some other things there too."

"Sure thing. But for now, let's get you stood back up on your feet. Be dark here before soon."

He carries his pot of stew back to the shed behind me as I sit there in front of the fire and finish my cup. The snow fall comes down lighter when the cloud coverage breaks to let the sunset make itself known. When he comes back, he steps out his fire with his older style boots and covers it with the sand that surrounds it. Then he comes to me and drops to a knee to help me on my feet. With the sun coming out over the horizon as it sets, I catch a glimpse of the shoreline that I hadn't seen when I first came out of his shed.

"Take it slow now, fella. You'll get your bearing back soon enough, now."

"I didn't know you were that close to the shoreline."

I walk slowly with my good arm over the back of his neck again. His crow feathers rub against my face. For an older person, he has more than enough strength to keep me stable. He pauses so I can stand upright for the first time and take in the view. The cold air fills my lungs with moisture and my lips instantly taste of the salt in the air.

"I take it you two know each other?" he says.

"What do you mean?"

He points with his free hand out at a bluff that overlooks the shoreline less than a hundred yards down wind. The same white stag stands there overlooking the sea. The same one I saw before I was attacked. It still stands tall and proud. He knows we see him but doesn't have a fear in the world, just like the last time. We both stand still as the stag turns his attention in our direction. He just looks at us, with no other deer around. The old man's voice turns to more of a whisper.

"Oh yessum. You two know each other, don't ya?"

"Yeah. I've seen him before. I came out here to hunt that one down. Almost had him, too. Before, well… you already saw how well that hunt ended."

"Ahh, you ain't gonna get that one. He ain't supposed to be taken down, but folks come in try, anyway. Might even get a few shots off right in him, but he'll never go down."

"Enough buckshot will take him down next time."

"Didn't learn ya lesson the first time, did ya? That old white stag ain't supposed to go down. He's been around longer than both of us, and believe you me, I been around a long time."

The white stag turns its attention away from us and back to the sea for a moment before he slowly trots back into the tree line behind him. The old man and I stay paused in our tracks to see if the white stag would return. Then he looks back at me.

"You gots a lot to learn about these woods here, stranger. There're things at work here beyond what you thought you knew about the world. No matter how much ugliness you already saw in it."

I shake my head in agreement, as I have no point to argue with him on that one either. We continue our short walk back into the shed. He sits me down on the bed again and starts to lay my head down on more blankets, but I resist.

"No, no. I'd like to sit up a while if that's alright."

He gets back up to set the propane heater in the middle of the dirt floor. Taking a closer look inside the shed shows that the floor is uncovered. So, it's not a floor at all. It is just heavily compacted sand that has been stepped on and wet down enough continuously to make it feel as hard as concrete with each step. Even the heater sounds as if it is being set on a stone floor when he puts it in place. He steps out and comes back in with a tin can full of random candles. The cheap dollar store type. Only they appear to have already been melted or hand made.

"This here propane stuff sure beats oil or whale blubber like they used to use back in the old days. Gots a supply of this and boat fuel around back of the shed to last several lifetimes too. Used to be an old fuel station back in the day near the shoreline out there for gassin up boats and such. Got burned down some time ago and left a full supply for the taking. Nuttin much left of it now, even the old dock they used nearly washed away with a storm a few months later." He reaches over to me with another cup. "Here's some fresh water for ya."

The water is barely thawed out, but just enough to take several drinks for the second time. He lights up a flame for the heater and steps in and out a few more times to stash away some things outside the shed. Once he comes back in for the last time, he closes the door to barricade it with multiple pieces of secondhand plywood. I just sit on the bed, attempting to take a full deep breath in, but the pain in my ribs prevents it. My nostrils are filled with old dried blood and salty air. The old man reaches under his bed that I sit on to pull out another old military style cot to put together.

"I can set that up, if that's ok. I hate that I'm using your own bed already. Not that I don't appreciate it, I just don't want to burden you anymore than I already have."

He lifts his hand up again and motions me to stop talking as he smiles.

"Not a problem, stranger. A cot like this is already what you're actually sittin on. I keep a spare one case I gets me a woman to come around here and get a good poke at her. That way she gots something to sleep on too, if she decided to stick around afterwards, that is." laughing to himself.

He chuckles more under his breath, and I do the same. He reaches under the bed again for more flannel and cotton sheets to spread out on his cot once it is set up. For a loner, he seems to always be in good spirits. Despite the cold winters here, and that he has nothing more than a shed to live in with a few pots and pans, he couldn't be happier. He has nothing, but at the same time he has everything he needs in the world. He sits down and pulls down another coffee mug. But I know what that drink is that he pulled off the rigged-up shelving he had strung up to the wall next to the hanging vegetables. I can smell from here and that it his own moonshine.

We both share the remnants of the stew as the light coming through the cracks of the shed turns to darkness. He drinks his lightning and I take in more water as it thaws out near the heater. He babbles on about his life out here in the woods alone and how simple things are out here for him. You would think he hadn't talked to another person in years. Not much to say on my part for long periods of time while he talks and gets tipsier by each sip of his mug. Sometimes, all people want is just for another to listen to them. It is a simple thing really, but beyond these woods in the standard society that we are both aware of, nobody cares to listen to anybody, no matter how loud they might scream. He hands me over a coffee mug filled with lightning as he continues on his rant.

"Here ya go. It'll either lighten you up or put ya down for the night, one. Good for ya though. Keeps the blood a flowing nice and real loose like." he says.

The more aware I become in my current situation, the more this drink burns as it goes down. Burns so much, it warms me more than the flame of the old man's heater in the middle of the sand filled floor. He laughs a little as he sees my cringed facial expressions with each sip out of the mug. Before I have time to set the mug down beside me, he tops it off again from another larger jug he seems to have pulled out of nowhere from behind him.

"Propane, boat fuel, and moonshine. You seem to have enough to go around for years but what else do you need out here, I guess." I tell him.

"Ain't that the truth. Be nice to have some fried up taters on a plate now and then, but hard to grow out here with the soil being so salty and sandy this close to the shore."

"I'd be glad to buy you a decent meal when I get back to the towns. Hell, I'd even get you as much groceries as you need to bring back out here, unless you got a place to stay in the towns. We could take some there too?"

"Nah, don't even worry about it, young man. Ain't exactly keen on going back into those places. Supermarkets and telephones? No thank you, but I do appreciate the return kindness." he says.

"Well, you have to let me repay you somehow. It's…"

"It's not necessary. You're doing more than you think by just being here."

"Alright then. Well, now that I think about it, my wallet was left in my ruck covered up out there in the woods where you found me. Hopefully it's still there, or I just made a false promise."

"Sure, it's still there. Ain't nobody crazy enough to travel this deep into the barrens. Except you, that is. Drunk or crazy enough, one. Which is it?" he asks.

"I would like to think just *determined*, maybe?"

"Ok, so that makes you crazy then… That's alright though. Being alone long enough will do the same thing to any man." he says with a smile.

"Nothing wrong with being alone. Been doing that a while now too."

"Yeah, but you weren't always alone. Where ya, young fella?"

"Not much gets by you, does it? But, neither of us are drunk enough for that conversation."

"I think I know enough by what little you have already said, but say no more, young man. I'm sure you got things you wanna know from me though, don't ya?"

"Absolutely, well… um. First off, how did you get me here and how far off are we from where you found me?"

"Sure thing. After I shot off your rifle for you a few times to scare it off, I took your rifle and a good strong walkin stick that I had and made a sled with it using some more flannel. Dragged you back here on it and near broke my stick, well cracked it to make it useless, anyways."

"How far did you drag me?"

"Took bout uh half a day's journey north to get to my little home here, I'd say. So, you're actually deeper into the barrens than you were when I found you. Just closer to the shore is all, really."

"That's quite a distance?"

"Ain't no thang to worry about. Especially when you gots enough lightning in you to make your legs like young again. I'll get another walking stick though."

"How'd did you find me?"

"Just follow the screams, really. I heard one earlier that night. A man's scream, then total silence. That's the part that kept me worryin. Wasn't really the man screaming that kept me up, it was the quiet that came after."

"I think I know who you're talking about. I heard the same thing before I got jumped too."

"Well, I couldn't find him. Then I heard it again. That God awful yellin' that will stop you dead in your tracks. You weren't too far away from me when your rifle started soundin' off, too. I found you just in time, but I stepped on your rifle by mistake. It just sat there watching you. Not looking to kill ya yet I guess."

"Are you kidding me ol' timer? That thing, or whatever it was, attacked me and I damn near jumped out of the tree stand to get away from it, or at least take a shot at it myself. But what makes you think it wouldn't have killed me?" I ask.

"Last I recall, I found you lying on your back, swallowing your own blood. Cause you already looked dead on the inside before you even fell out that tree. Not much of a hunt there now for anything lookin to kill then is it?"

"Well then, before we both get too deep into that bottle of lightning you keep stashed near your cot there, why don't you tell me what hell this thing is." I ask.

"It is a long story, stranger. One you ain't gonna wanna believe."

"It takes a lot to surprise me these days. Tell me what it is I don't know. I've honestly been trying to just convince myself that some sort of mangled bear is what nearly jerked my arm out."

"You just sit back and take a few more swigs for this one, then. It's about the only thing that'll help you sleep tonight after I tell you this story. The proper story of how it came to be. That one, oh yessum, it goes way back to the early 1700s, I do believe…"

Chapter 6: The Legend

The thunder rolls throughout the night like a stampede. It troubled even the fire in our tiny log home to keep up with the winds that blow down into the chimney. Leaves and brush slam against the already cracked windows that overlook the town square. The moans of the harsh breeze and the cracks of the thunderstorm are not enough to cover her piercing screams. Screams so loud, nothing stops the growing fears of neighboring homes from what they knew would happen nine months later.

"Get it out!! Get it out!! Get this damned bastard child out of me now!!" my mother screams.

"Call for the midwives, son." says my father.

The look in my father's eyes fills with terror and tears. He holds his head down in his hands in a state of absolute shame. He reaches out to try to comfort her, but she slaps him away. If she weren't holding on to the bedposts, she may have tried to lash on him more with her fists, but the screams took all of her strength and breath away. Her entire body lay naked on the bed as she stretched her legs open and bent upward to her bare breasts. Not a single effort to cover herself or her filth in an attempt at decency. The flame light gives sight to the blood that pours out her wound onto the bed covered in the forced-out wastes of her bowls. Her screams become mere gargles with her own blood that spatters out of her lungs and nostrils.

"Call for the midwives, now! She won't wait any longer!" he yells again.

"Yes, Father."

I rush out the door into near darkness. The only way to see my given path to the front of the house is the lightning that strikes with every other second now. I open the door to see three midwives already standing near the property entrance while trying to keep their lanterns from fading out from the pouring rainfall.

"We heard the screams. Is it time, young man?" says one woman.

"Yes, ma'am. My father says she cannot wait any longer. Please come in. Hurry." and I lead them through the entrance.

"I wish I could say you are blessed this night, young man, with another brother or sister, but I cannot say that for it be a lie against God's good Graces. I ask that you tend to the younger children." she says to me after seeing other children in the top loft looking down.

"Yes ma'am. I will do so."

I take their coats and their head wraps to dry on the rack near the door. My mother continues to scream and curse at my father sitting on the other side of the home. The three midwives stop in an icy shiver as they listen to her harsh words that are viler than the blood and smell coming from her womb.

"You're here! You're here! Now get this thing out of me. Just get it out! Cut it out if you have to!! Just get it out! Let it be a bastard devil and get the damned child out of me, now!"

One midwife approaches the bed and stroke my mother's forehead, hoping to calm her. My father just sits down next to the bed in total silence and sadness. His hands shake as he uncovers his face to see the horror.

"Can you help her?" he asks the midwife. She appeared the oldest of the three.

The midwife moved her attention down to my mother's swollen stomach that raises up the few blankets my father tried to cover her with while I answered the door. Her torso raises higher than I ever remember with any of my other brothers and sisters, but this is different. Something

48

is trying to push outward. Her screams pierce through my ears. My younger brothers and sisters cover their ears in fright as they look down from the loft above. The midwife tries to push on her stomach to turn the child, but whenever she touches my mother, a hand pushes back harder from inside. She tries her best to turn the baby as the other midwives join in to hold my mother down. They push my father aside and turn to my mother, still trying to thrash her way out of their grip. They turn to my father, who is frozen in dread. They can't gather his attention, though.

"Either help hold your woman down sir or take these children elsewhere.", yelling at my father to gather his spine. He doesn't move, and the thrashing from my mother grow more violent. All of my brothers and sisters just sit in the dark loft of the house, watching in shock as their mother cries in agony and a foul cursing that would have had her beaten by my father on a normal day. My father just stands there watching mother's belly raise sharply. As if the child inside can rip out of her stomach with little effort.

I take my siblings out of the room and to the bunk houses where the slaves used to sleep. All the younger children keep their ears covered and they refuse to move their hands away from their ears to wipe their tears. I point them out to walk through the rain and the storm to get to the bunk house. I have my eldest sister hold the lantern for them, but the lightning stays bright and constant enough to brighten the entire property and beyond.

"Please come with us," my youngest sister asks. "Don't stay."

"I'll come to you when this is all over. Stay there with the others and keep warm."

My sister tries to hold my hand tighter, but I wipe her tears away before I motion her to follow the others. I turn to hear my mother screaming and my father's prayers at the top of his lungs. I quickly close the door as they walk away to the bunk house and turn around to see my father sitting at the head of the bed while winding up a cloth. She doesn't stop screaming and thrashing as one midwife moves her hand inside the wound. The smell is a familiar smell that brings a sense of vomit to the inside of my mouth. The midwives struggle to keep her still.

"This child ain't turnin around. He's gonna come out feet first or he'll break her ribs trying to push out. We have to open her wound longer to help it come out or she won't be able to breathe no more." says the head midwife.

"No!! No!! Just kill it! Just end it now! For the love of Christ just end it all!!" screams my mother again. Her sweat mixes with her tears and matted hair of her forehead. She looks up to my father, who stands over her head now and pleads to him. The first time I have seen her lower her voice since the storm and her labor began hours ago now.

"Please, kill me. Just kill me. Kill me, please. Forgive me and end me, please. Don't let it come out. Kill me, I beg you. Please don't just… Wait… Wait… No…"

He lowers the tightly wound sheet on her mouth to muffle her pleads that turn to more of a gargled scream, and then the thrashing begins again. One midwife steps away to fetch a knife out of the fireplace. The blade shines a bright orange that lights the surrounding area as she gives it to the lead midwife that sits between my mother's legs. My mother's muffled screaming forces more blood from her nostrils and out of her wound on the midwife. Somehow, she keeps a steady hand with that scalding hot knife as old and feeble as she looks.

"We gonna make the cut now, Momma Leeds. Try to breathe and stay awake with us. Tis almost over now." she says, while readying the blade.

One midwife turns to notice me in the doorway still. She is younger than the others and has a sternness that I have no issue leaving unquestioned.

"You there, young man, help hold your mother down. Your father's near too drunk or full of dread to keep her steady."

My father continues to hold her head down and gag her like cattle that knows it is about to be branded as that glowing knife comes closer. Me and the other midwives hold her hands and legs upwards, me on one side and the two on the other side. When the knife goes down into her skin near her groin, my mother doesn't even stop screaming to catch her breath. The smell of burnt hair and fleshy foulness makes one midwife vomit on the floor next to us. My father looks away as he continues to pray in more of a mumble now.

"God forgive me." is all I hear him mumble under my mother's screams.

"Her sacks broken all over now. She is losing too much blood with the child trying to push out feet first. I cut the wound open, but we have to hurry. The knife didn't cauterize the cuts." says the midwife.

She scrambles as she tries to soak up blood from all over her face and hands. She cleans up what she can on my mother in a hurry and slings the soaked linen onto the floor.

"One of you women, you come over on my side with the clean cloths ready and take this knife away." She looks to my father "You take that linen out of her mouth! Least let her breathe before we start pullin."

My father doesn't respond and backhands me as I attempt to gather his attention to do as the midwife asked him. Only after he gets the chance to slap me does he take the gag off of her. My mother's screams subside to gasping for breath and coughing. The other midwives scramble around to do as the head midwife asks. The room feels hotter by the second, with the fire that just received a gust of wind down from the chimney. The midwife turns her attention to me for a moment.

"Tis almost over, young man. It's best that you hold your bearing like you been."

She notions to my father to place the linen back over my mother's mouth. He had already cut the sides of her lips open from the last time he held her down like that. My mother grips my hand tight as I hold one of her legs upward towards her bare chest. Her thrashing turns to moaning from lack of strength now and the midwife forces the wound open wider to slide one hand inside. Once one hand is in, the other is forced in next. The moment of calm from mother ends as the midwife moves around inside her. Her moans turn to muffled screams again. The wind and thunder follow relentlessly while pounding on the roof that leaks in various corners of the house.

"I have the baby's feet! We need to get her to calm down or she'll kill herself and the baby. The cord is wrapped around the legs?!"

The midwife struggles to get the baby out to his torso. One of the other two midwives screams in fright. She lets go of my mother's leg to drop it down on the bed.

"That's no umbilical! It is a tail!! That child has a tail!!"

Everyone is screaming. My mother's thrashing pauses, but her moaning turns to groveling and growling of an unimaginable pain. This is not like the last time I remember from my youngest sibling. The smell is worse. Her pain is worse. Her bleeding is flowing more than I could remember as the lead midwife continues in her efforts.

"Devil child or not, it still needs to be taken out."

The baby's feet dangle outside of her wound to see what looks like a rope wrapped around one of them. The feet already have pointed nails. My father stops his prayers to look over and see the deformity for himself.

"Blasphemy! You see what you have done, woman! Do you see for yourself the evil that you have spawned on us all?! A child of witchery and damn all of you other women to hell for aiding it into this world!"

The midwife that already let go of my mother's other leg runs in panic and beats down the front door of the house to go outside screaming into the storm. My father thrusts his arm out at the other midwife still holding my mother at her side to strike her unconscious. He removes the linen still on my mother's lips as the lead midwife is still struggling. He leans in close to my mother's face while she whispers to my father in her exhaustion.

"Kill me… End me… I beg …"

He moves the linen, now spun tighter in his wrists, to clamp it down around her throat.

"Hold her down!" says the midwife, still struggling, but she cannot see what I see. My father is trying to kill my mother, but she won't let my grip go while chocking under my father's grip.

"The child is almost at the neck! Hold her down, damn you!!" the midwife tells me.

I try to reach for my father to push him away from my mother, but my mother's grip is too strong. He places all his weight on the linen as he lowers down under the side of the bed to strangle her.

"No, don't Father!!"

I reach for the dish of water on the other side of me with my free hand and slam him on the back of the head with it. He stumbles down to the floor as she gasps and gargles for air again. Her eyes bloodshot, and her lips still bleeding from the sides. I try to lift her leg back up for the midwife, but it is no use. My mother has gone limp and too weak.

"There's something stopping the rest of the chest from coming out. Push Momma. Push for the life of your child! Push!!" she yells.

My mother wakes up from a death that we thought my father had already given her. The rope on the child's feet squirms as the tail of a lizard would, just like what the other midwife screamed before she fled in terror. Its hands appear gnarled and mangled, with blood soiled fur all around his arms. Its hands are claws that flex in and out like the rabid hands of a wild animal. My mother struggles and tenses her entire body for a final push that splatters more blood on the midwife.

"Get it out!!!!!" she screams.

Her screaming voice is painful to hear from an already ravaged throat and sliced lips, but she shakes and stops her struggle.

"The child is out. It is out! Oh Jesus! Oh, my heaven's name in Christ!!." The midwife stares at it in horror. It thrashes around while screaming an unholy scream as she holds it into the light. Red eyes and a long face covered in blood and bile. My mother lets go of her grip on my hand and, with tears and sorrowful weeping.

The midwife still screams with the child in her hands. "The child *is* a demon Momma! Oh, my God!"

"The wings of a demon! Oh, God please no! Please let my eyes befool me!" cries out the midwife.

I back away from the both of them. The midwife just stares in fright as its blood-soaked wings slowly twitch. They are the naked wings of a bat that flutters around the streetlamps outside at night. My mother tries to sit up. The midwife is motionless, except for her trembling hands that still hold the child.

My father gets up from the floor to see the horror that is before him in the midwife's hands.

"Send that Devil back into the flame!! Now woman! Or else you will doom us all!!" he says.

The midwife looks at my mother and then looks at the fireplace. Before making a commitment to either direction for the child, the baby wakes in her arms with a blood-curdling scream. Not the scream of a new child born unto this world and looking for the comfort of its mother, but the gargled scream of a tortured being that had just made an escape from the depths of an eternal fire in Satan's grasp. It grows and stretches in the midwifes hands while she is too mortified to move from her frozen stance. It fiercely lunges out of her hands and at the midwife's throat. It grips her neck as she struggles to rip it off during each furious bite. It clamps and chomps on the mid-section of her gullet too hard for the midwife to even scream. The child jumps off her from her shoulders after it makes the last bite, the bite that leaves her blood spraying from her neck faster than the rain fall. Her blood splashes my face as I run to her aid, but she drops to the floor holding her neck before I can get to her.

"Father, the rifle!!" I yell at him. "Get the rifle!!"

The demon child cowers and stumbles into a darker corner of the house as its wings try to flutter. Those flaming red eyes pierce through the low light right at me, straight through into my soul that is filled with a dread and terror that I cannot hide. It stays low into the darkness, but those eyes gaze back to my mother. She tries to move to the edge of the bed but is too weak. My father lifts from the floor to reach out towards the mantle over the fireplace. The flames burn bright with the wind that blast through the front door the other midwife left open when she fled out to the street screaming. The demon child is twice the size it was when it was first in the midwife's hands. I try to cover the midwife's throat with some linens that were already thrown on the floor. Everything is soaked in blood. Blood spewing from the midwife's throat, blood from my mother's wound and cuts in birthing. The umbilical still hangs from her wound on the edge of the bed. The old midwife struggles in my arms to stop the bleeding from her throat, but her eyes go full white in front of me. Her body goes limp and I hear the death bells ringing in my ears.

The demon child walks out of darkness while still growing somehow. Its clawed feet struggle to keep balance on the uneven flooring of the house. Its horns reach the low ceiling of the loft with each step towards my mother. It grows with a freakish speed that I cannot believe. My father holds the rifle in hand, ready to take the shot. The eyes burn brighter than the flames it stands in front of. The face is not round but long. The teeth protrude from its horse like snout. Its wings seize to flutter and wrap around its body. My mother, on the edge of the bed now, continues her whimpering as it comes closer.

"Shoot it! Father shoot it!!"

"Come child. Come kill momma, now." says my mother in her own gaze of horror.

"Shoot it now Father!!"

He cocks the hammer of the black powder rifle and startles the demon child. My mother turns to my father and gives a sinister look of hate.

"Let it take us. Let it claw your soul down to the Hell you belong in too." she says.

My father just stands there frozen in tears and terror. He lowers the rifle down. And then it screams. I drop the midwife's cold and now dead body to cover my ears. The demon child screams at the top of its lungs so loud, the windows shatter. My ears ring with its shrieks.

"Father shoot it!!" at the top of my lungs over the demon's screams.

"God forgive me." he says in tears.

He lifts the rifle but does not point it at the demon child. He turns it around and points it at himself. He struggles in reaching for the trigger that is too far away from the long barrel, but close enough to end his own life. I lung towards him to stop him from the unforgiveable.

"No, Father!!"

The demon child's screams grow louder as the gun fires and sends my father's head to shattered bits all over the side of the wall. In a swift motion, the black powder smoke fills the room to mask the demon child's movements, but I can still hear it screaming.

The wind from the front door clears the room. Blood is everywhere and all the broken windows have smoke filtering out of them. I rush to my naked mother, that remains in a state of sadness and shock to see what her newborn child has become in front of her as it approaches again. It now stands taller than beyond my height. Those bat-like wings keep most of its boney body covered. The horns are that of Satan's horns only seen in a biblical painting. I stay in between the demon child and my mother, toe-to-toe with him as it glares down at me with those fiery red eyes. Little motion from it as the smoke clears, just staring at me while my mother keeps crying her sorrows. A few short steps towards me as claws clap and stomp on the rickety wooden floor of the house.

"Come child, come."

"No mother. Leave it be. This is not your child. This is the Devil's own. It is not your child, mother! Stop calling for it."

It stands only a few feet in front of me and lowers Its head inside its wings that keep its midsection covered. All becomes quiet. He just stares at me standing in front of my mother's birthing bed for moments that seem like an eternity. He opens up his wings to outstretch a dark and fury arm that ends with claws. Its claws are large and sharp enough to collapse my face in. Its skin is loosely covered with fur as dark as the night skies. As the wings are open, his bare teeth show, still covered in blood from the midwife's throat, but slowly being drained off from its excessive saliva. It reaches for me and I stumble backwards on my mother's bed. Its claws are only a few inches from my face, but it is not attempting to be as ferocious as it was. I turn my face as it reaches closer. It is too frightening to look at with those eyes to assume it may reach out at me or my mother out of a saddened sense of curiosity. The chaos, the turmoil, and the death that surrounds this home, and somehow, it remains curious.

"It's there. The demon child is in there! It's going to kill them!!" someone yells from outside.

The midwife that ran away just moments ago has returned with a mob of armed men outside of the home. The demon child screams at the top of its lungs and slashes my face as it backs away. My mother screams in her weakened voice.

"No!! Don't hurt my child!!"

Multiple muskets fire off to the inside of our home at the demon child. I duck below the bed again and drag my mother down with me to take cover from the gun fire. Dozens of lead shots fly into the room at the creature. We lay down flat on the floor to see the dead midwife staring at me in a lifeless trance. The demon child does not fall from the lead blasted into his body in multiple places. It only stumbles with its footing on the flooring. More blood fills the room in all directions. My mother lay next to me as she screams and covers her ears.

"Hold your fire men!!"

"It already killed two of the women in there!"

"Where did it go?!" one man asks.

"It is climbing up the chimney!! Look at the tail! The tail of Lucifer as it climbs the chimney!"

"Back up to the front of the house, men! Send more lead at it as it raises its head from the smokestacks! Hurry, now!!" one yells.

It is the preacher man that came to the home to pray earlier in the night before my mother's labors began. The mob outside carries torches and pistols outstretched at the roof as they back away to view a clear shot at the chimney top. The third and cowardly midwife tries to run inside to help the other two women, but the preacher stops her from coming inside to aid the others.

"No, miss, it is too late for all of them now. They are in God's hand of judgement now." he says.

"It hasn't come up yet!" one yells from outside.

"Shoot at the smokestacks until it does. Don't let that demon raise its face without swallowing our lead!"

"The monster is too massive! It's not coming out!" one says they all scramble in confusion to get a clear shot.

"The creature is stuck! The damned creature is stuck in the chimney! Shoot it down to Hell before it can get out!"

The gunfire that goes off to show at least a dozen more men and hunters outside. The black powder flames match the lightning and booms louder than the thunder with each musket that is fired. I can hear the bricks from the breaking chimney fall and bounce on the roof top while I cower on the floor with my mother by the bed still.

"Mother, we have to go! They'll kill us both! Mother!"

The musket fire muffles my mother's screams. She thrashes out of my grip to run to the front door at the men outside, still indecent and into the rainfall. Her umbilical still trails behind her and wipes a trail of blood to follow.

"Stop it!! It's my child! It's my burden!" she yells to the men still shooting.

"Hold your fire men!!" the preacher man yells.

The chimney smoke remains in the room from lack of moving out the top. I crawl below the eyesight of the bed to a window on the side of the house. The men are still yelling, and some shots are still being fired at the roof top. I cut my hands from the leftover broken glass of the window that was shattered earlier from the creatures screams. After I maneuver my way out the window seal, I stumble down to the cold and wet ground. The smell of fresh gunpowder and smoke lingers all around the house. The rainfall has only worsened to develop streams through the yard. I can hear my mother still begging outside the front door.

"Burn it all, men! For the eternal flames it shall return to on this day!!" says the preacher.

"Throw the torches in! Keep shooting the chimneys!"

"Don't let it out!! Send it back to hell!!" another shooter says.

"No!! Not my child!!" screams my mother.

"Burn it all!!", all of them agree with throwing torches into the open door.

More shots fire off as others take a knee to reload their muskets. My mother stumbles down the doorsteps, watching torches being thrown over her and through front windows and door of her home. She is too weak to move any closer towards the mob, only to beg at the top of her already ravaged lungs. I move quickly and low to stay out of sight to the bunk house. One of the older children peering through the window slide open the door to let me inside. They are all still inside and remain unharmed, but most of them huddle up into a corner away from the door and windows. I tend to all of them before I look back to the same window. My youngest sister stays close to my side.

"No. Be quiet and stay close to the others. Do as I say, now." I tell her.

"You're bleeding?" she says.

"Go back with your brothers now. Just stay away from the windows and cover up."

I push her away towards the back of the shed with the others. My blood-soaked hands leave an imprint on her sleeping gown. I look back out the window to see the inside of the home engulfed in black smoke. The flames begin to rise above the same window seal I just crawled out of. The midwife that fell unconscious by my father's hand is awakened from the smoke and flame. Her screams slowly disappear as she attempts to escape. Her body is already engulfed in flames and loses the ability to struggle or scream as she goes limp to the floor while still inside the home. The burning smell of flesh and hair travels through the air as the rain begins to subside, but the thunder and lightning still rages on. Some of the men have their muskets raised at the roof top, ready to fire. My mother, still collapsed at the front of the house, pleading, begging, and crying into her hands. They won't even cover her nakedness. They have no remorse, as they force her to watch her home burn. The preacher man approaches her and reveals him standing over her like that of a wounded animal that needs its suffering to be ended.

"Do you see the evil you have brought into this world, woman! The death that surrounds your life for your wicked deeds and blasphemy!"

"She's a witch!" another man yells. The crowd begins to chant the same things.

"Devil worshiper!"

Several of the men lose interest in keeping their rifles pointed upwards at the roof. They assume it is still stuck in the chimney and is now taking its last breaths in the flame to burn with the rest of the bodies still in the building. He's still there. They just don't see that the demon child already crawled out and is now crouched down behind the remains of the chimney. Those eyes firmly planted on them as they glow hotter than the flames that surround the sides of the building. It watches its mother suffer in shame and humility, just as I do. If only he would gather their attention. I could get my brothers and sisters away from this madness.

"String her up!"

"That is fitting for a damned witch!"

"Fetch the ropes from the carriages."

My mother screams with her gargled voice as they drag her to the tree outside the front of the burning home. She does not have the remaining physical strength to struggle as they drag her to the tree. Only screams, moans, and continuing to scorn them.

"Cover her head with the cloth. No decent and God-fearing folk should have to see the panic in her eyes as she faces her judgement, before her last breath!"

The men feverishly gather the ropes at the preacher man's request as he pulls out a Bible and begins to read several passages. A cross held in his pocket is pulled out and pointed at my mother. The last vision my mother sees before they drape a cloth around her face is him looking down on her with that cross in hand, as he chants some unknown scripture at her. She only looks back down as they cover her face and drape the rope over her neck. My hands shake in dismay to see what I am watching. The rope is slung over a strong branch and tied off to a horse that shuffles its head.

"Confess your sins now! Accept the blood of Jesus as your lord and savior now, woman, before it is too late. I beg you! Rid us of this evil you have brought down on all of us, and I pray that the Lord in Heaven may forgive you!" the preacher man says.

She looks up with her face covered in the black cloth. She tries to cover her nakedness with her own hands now. *Please mother, say something to stop this insanity, anything.* She stands up, while covering her breasts with one hand and her wound with the other. Her throat clears to yell her last grim words of nothing but hatred and contempt in its darkest form.

"Damn all you arrogant bastards! You will rot in the stinking flesh with me in the lake of forever burning fire and brimstone. Before that day in forever darkness, you will suffer tenfold as I have on this night. He will come for you and all your children and remind you of your own sins for the generations of your children's children to come. I have only brought you the Hell demon you all rightfully deserve in your own worship of a false prophet! In that hell my demon child brings, he will feast on your animals, your cattle, your farms be burdened, and then your children will die by his hand. Their mothers will continue the suffering until the day of reckoning comes for you all!"

The preacher stares at my mother's covered face in absolute fear and shock from the words he just heard. He drops to a knee and begins to bow in prayer. All eyes focus on my mother and the preacher's chants. Not a single thought to look back at the roof. Those glowing eyes that were watching the sorrows of my mother are now vanished into the storm. The beast is upon us all in the world now as it screams into the night while flying away. Only the wings that flap into the stormy night can be seen with the remaining streaks of lightning flashes.

The man that tied the rope to the horse slings a leg over the saddle to move forward as the preacher continues to pray for my mother at the top of his lungs. The slack of the rope tightens on the ground first, then the tree branch begins to bear her weight. Her loose hands uncover her shame and begin to grip the ropes around her neck as her legs raise off the ground. Her feet thrash around like the slaughtering of a live animal at the butchers to release her afterbirth and umbilical down to the ground. It splashes the preacher with her blood and urine as it thuds into the ashes and leaves in front of him.

"Blood... Her blood is on me... *Her blood is all over my hands!*" yells the preacher.

The crowd watches in horridness as my mother speaks her struggling and choked last words.

"My child... comes for your soul..."

Chapter 7: The Wolves

Most of the night is spent further understanding such a story. With or without his famed lightning drink, I still refuse to believe what I am hearing. Demons and devils are nothing more than a weak man's fears. The next morning, we woke up hung over, or at least I did anyway, to set out early. My legs are limp from the many days of lying around, attempting to heal my chest and shoulder. Everything remains stiff as I move around the shed and make my way outside. I grab my lever action that has been left by the door for the last several nights. It's only natural for me to remain in constant concern where it is at all times, even in my drunken stupor. A few dry biscuits and frozen water for each of us before we head out to where he found me. Where I was almost killed by this thing that he claims to be a demon born forever ago from a human mother that damned it as a devil child while still inside her belly. The cold air fills my lungs and reminds me I am still alive as I step outside. The snows falling is constant now and keeps the horizon in a state of gray for miles into the ocean.

"You seem at peace every time you step outside in the mornin." he says from behind me.

"Seeing sunset or sunrise is about the only sense of peace that comes to mind these days."

"Your buddy sits up yonder on the bluff again. Looks like he gots a fondness to you. I usually only catch him up there once or twice a week. But he's been up there every mornin since I brought you back."

Sure enough, the white stag looks over the beach just as I turn around to do the same. My rifle sits in my hand, but he looks back at me without a concern, despite trying to take a shot at him a week or more ago. I am reminded of how I first saw him. That fearless look gazing towards me in my rifle sights on that dark and fateful night.

"He walked right towards me the night you found me. I was covered to where nothing could even see me, but he looked right at me somehow."

"Ah, that ol' buck. Like I said, he's been around a long time. He's here for you now. He looks after all of us, including ol' farts like me. Best you feel safe or feel warned when he's around."

"What is he?" I ask.

"What you mean?"

"Well, you keep saying he's been around forever. Is he some sort of good omen or something? I hate to tell you, but I lost my lucky rabbit's foot years ago, now. I don't know if I believe in that sort of stuff anymore."

"Say what you want, stranger, but he watches over us and waits. Been waiting a long time now too, I reckon."

"Waiting for what?"

"Not sure to tell the truth. The natives claimed that when two of them were finally spotted together, all the wisdom of all the chiefs would come down onto these lands."

"Right. More mystics..."

"Not much of a believer in things beyond yourself, are ya?"

"After some of the things I have encountered, you wouldn't be much of a believer in anything, either. You don't know me at all though?"

"I know enough, young man... All the sufferin' you've seen. All the hurt you made it through and still breathin the air you take in as we speak, and you think there's nothing out there beyond yourself that tries

64

to do some good for this ol' world? Humph... Now that's some arrogant horseshit."

"Ready to head out. I could use a pleasant walk in the woods to get my mind straight again."

He nods his head in agreement, knowing that I just avoided the conversation. I have nothing to add to it at the moment. I look back to see the white stag disappearing into the coming snowfalls as we head out. A near perfect camouflage for him if a blizzard comes, but he just stands there tall and proud, waiting. We walk into the pines until he is out of sight while overlooking the bluff.

We walk for miles on top of the snow and frozen sand that crunches under our feet with every step. Difficult to keep up with him at first, but he looks back to check on me as I struggle less and less with each step. Still painful to the touch if I move my chest the right way, but at least my shoulder is only stiff and not throbbing like it was. The marshlands thaw under the snow and it filled several holes with muddy water under each footprint behind him. Each tree appears dead and lifeless with mountains of pine combs at the base. My rifle turns to a walking stick for me that puts the dirty stock into the ground to help keep my balance. The noon hours push the snowfalls away and the old man comes to a dead stop in his tracks several yards ahead of me. I catch up to see why he stopped from what feels like a sprint for my busted knees and ankles.

"Everything looks different in the daylight hours. I take it we are close to where you found me?"

"Nah, we close, though. We just come up on somethin' else. This must be the fella I heard yellin before I came to you."

A man's body lays there with his lifeless face frozen in terror. Three out of four of his limbs are missing. Not only missing but torn from the torso with bones dangling from broken meat. His guts are swollen from the inside as open claw marks have allowed intestine to spew out like a dried and frozen sponge that has just received water. One eye is missing, with bone being uncovered from his scalp. Several smaller animal bites are obvious the closer I move to what is left of him. More than likely other scavenger type animals or coyotes getting their share of a free meal. But there are other bite and claw marks that match my own. As I walk around him, I recognize the smell from upwind is rancid from his own rot. The other side of his face is caved in with the jaw bones drooping to the side. Every opening of his bitter face, natural or not, drips with brown and soiled blood that has been smeared with curious licks of animals. I gaze around to see if any limbs are apparent in the area, but I see nothing. Not a trail of the body attempting to struggle, no other limbs, no rifle, not torn pieces of clothing, just nothing. As if he was dropped here, out through the trees from the skyline.

"I've seen this fella out here before. He usually sets up a camp closer to the towns." he says.

"Do you know his family? Friends maybe?" I ask.

"Sorry to say I don't. Nobody deserves such a death like this though. Looks like ol' Leeds done a number on him."

"This Leeds Devil? This thing can't be real."

"I told ya, it's just a pure evil beyond all of us. He's out here and breathin' just like you and me."

"Oh, boy. Here we go *again*."

"Bear or wolves don't kill just to kill. They kill to protect or because they are scared, one. Ol' Leeds though, he kills just to kill. He kills to put fear in you. I take it he likes a good hunt. Just like you."

"Right. More about this creature."

"Still don't believe me?! Take a look at this fella. Ain't no bear gonna do a number like that."

I reach down to roll the stiff body over. It tore most of his pants to shreds, but the back pockets are still in place. A faded ring from a can of dip on one side and a square indention on the other. His wallet is still on him.

"Well, isn't much left of him to even carry back to the towns, but at least his wallet is here. Once we get to where you found me, I'll be able to make my way back and tell the local authorities where to find him. His name is… or was, Rick Clauson?" as I look into his wallet and see his ID.

"Won't be much left of him by the time you get them back out here." he says.

"Still gotta try. Can't blame his family. They deserve to know he isn't coming back home for dinner in one piece tonight."

"Well then, I'll give it a few more days and then I'll come back out here and give the man a proper burial myself. I'll put a marker down so as you can find it again if the family wants him buried closer. Far as I can see, he belongs to the barrens now." he says.

The old man hands me a set of small and tattered clothes that he carried under his coat and motions me to cover the body. Seen plenty of bodies before, but never on any open grounds where I have been on the hunt while stateside. The cloths unfold only a little and cover most of him, as there isn't much left to cover. I place rocks around the edges that have to be unburied from the melting snow to keep the cloth from moving. Any smaller coon or coyote desperate enough for a piece of frozen dead flesh will move it off his corpse, though. I rip a piece of the cloth off to tie it to a hanging branch on the nearest tree in case the local cops can get back here before the animals take the rest of him. The nearest branch would be about ten yards away from him, and of course it would be just beyond my reach without being able to jump. I grab my rifle and try to maneuver a branch closer to me to tie off the cloth.

Snow and needles fall on top of my shoulders, along with a limp dead leg that was stuck a few tree branches above and out of sight. It lands on my face, knocking me to the ground and almost breaking my nose. I feel like a thick needle is trying to push between my eyes when it strikes my face from the force of the fall. I push the limp leg off of me frantically.

"Son of a bitch!!"

"What's a matter?!" he asks.

"Dammit, just got knocked on my ass." as I struggle to get up.

"That fella's leg came down from them damn trees?" he asks me in a worried tone.

"Shit. What the fuck is his leg doing up there?" as I brush off the filth. "Yeah. It was a few branches out of my view."

"He gots two others sitting up there somewhere I bet."

"*What?*"

"Yeah, his other leg and one arm." he says as he looks up in a level of concern I haven't seen from him before.

I stand back up to gather my bearings and grab my rifle. The old man just pauses again as he looks upwards into the pines. The air grows cold as the old man shivers. Multiple owls all around us, just staring in silence. Great horned owls with yellow eyes staring at us from all directions above. Perfectly still. No wind nor other sounds of nature to hear, just dead silence from both of us as dozens of owls glare down on us. There must be at least twenty or thirty of them, just watching.

A whisper from within the winds. *"Come feast with us."* Over and over in my head.

Tiny little feathery horns grow on the sides of their heads, but those black and yellow eyes are the most awful feature as they appear dead. No movement from them at all.

"What are…"

"Shhh. Stay quiet and stay still for a bit. Just stare right back at them." he interrupts me.

"How long have they been there?"

"Ain't no tellin'. But he watches too. They tellin' him we're here."

"What are you talking about?"

"Ol' Leeds wanted us to find the body."

The winds pick up and turn to whispers through the trees again. I don't know if he hears the same thing I hear. *"Come feast with us."*

"You got that man's wallet for the family?" he asks.

"Yeah?"

"We best be headed out then. Ain't much time before dark falls on us. Just back out of the area, real slow like, ya hear?"

"Come feast with us."

"Did you hear that? What are they saying? What do they want?"

"Just start walking. Trust me. I'll tell you more on the way. Let's just go on and get now."

Their heads slowly spin backwards and all the way around to watch both of us leave the clearing. They seem like lifeless dolls that turn and look the further away we walk.

"Come feast with us."

I have never seen owls that big, nor that many in one spot. Did my eyes play tricks on me, or were they closer to the ground than I thought? Am I hearing things? If all of them go down to nibble at the body, it would be hard to find what was left of him with so many of them.

I walk backwards with my rifle in hand at the ready, but I would like to hope two dozen massive owls don't know it is actually empty. The only sound is our feet moving over and through broken twigs under the thawing snow, as they turn their heads and stare. I turn back around to walk forwards when they are out of sight, but then they all flutter away into the skyline and fly away together. So many of them could be mistaken for a flock of some other type of bird. Most owls are solitary creatures that may be seen near their roosts or nest. Not a sound from them, even as I see their wings flapping above the trees. The perfect and silent predator, even while in motion by the masses.

"Wanna tell me what the hell that was all about?" I ask as I catch up to him again.

"Don't really know what to say about it. Death surrounds you."

"They're just owls, ol' timer."

"Still trying to convince yourself more than me, I see. Owls watching over us by the dozens. A body torn and thrashed apart by the limbs to be hung up in a tree like an ornament? When you gonna get it? When you gonna understand that this place doesn't belong to us. No matter how *big* you think your *empty gun* is, it ain't gonna matter out here."

I tire of hearing this old coot tell me what it is he thinks I need to know, and I stop in my tracks. I give a loud sigh, so he knows my frustration. Not worth yelling back at him or getting frustrated with him. He saved my life, but I won't be badgered by this drunk anymore. He stops to turn around and sees me glaring at his back side.

"Struck a nerve finally. I do pray tell. You got somethin' you wanna say?" he asks.

"Why don't you just answer the question straight for me ol' timer. Level with me on this."

He walks closer to me to avoid yelling, "Been out here a long time, young fella. Seen a lot of happenings in these woods that go way back to when the tribesmen were still here, to other hunters that turn up in pieces. Some listen, some don't. Maybe I just got used to the idea that ain't nobody gonna listen to me."

"I'm listening now. So, quit the bull shit and give it to me straight. What's going on out here?"

"Alright then."

He walks closer to me as we stand face-to face in the woods. It would be a comfort to see him act serious for only a few minutes to get it all out in the open.

"Ol' Leeds never really left. Them there owls you saw, they watch out for him. A thing that was never wanted by his own. He's taken hundreds of lives. When cows or sheep weren't enough, it would go for the drunks and the hunters. None of them were enough, though, so it went after the children. Dozens of them. It won't stop, not ever. The only thing that might stop it is the very flames of hell that he came from. But...",

"But, what?" I ask.

"He didn't kill you."

"I just got lucky that you found me."

"Nobody gets lucky with ol' Leeds."

"I don't understand?"

"A murderous creature spawned from the devil and a mother that damned it back to hell. Has he met his match with you? That why you still breathin'? How much killing and suffering do you know about? How much hurt have you put on your fellow man?"

"Well, that's different... I had my fair share. More than I bargained for, actually."

Interrupting me to lean in and lower his voice further, "And so has he…"

"Devils and demons… It's just hard to believe sometimes. There has to be a valid reasoning or an actual creature that explains what happened to me and that other guy. A freak of nature or something."

"You best get to believin', stranger. It seeks to massacre the innocence of all. The innocence it never had. T'was born of the flame and will die of the flame. And it will take anyone it can back to the same fire with it. But for now, we best be movin' on too if you expect to make it out of these barrens before nightfall."

We continue our walk deeper into the woods until the scent of the ocean fades away. As long as I keep moving, my limbs and shoulder loosen up more and more from the blood flow. It doesn't take long to make it to my hunting sight. My deer stand lay on the ground in a few different pieces. Empty shell casings are scattered in a few different areas, but most of them only shine through the light snow dusting on the ground that has thawed. My boot knife lays nearby, shining with the lowering sunlight. My ruck sack sits buried under more foliage and an extra ghillie blanket about ten yards away from the tree I threw myself out of. The old man picks up the broken deer stand and examines it while I dig into the ruck sack.

"Expect you and got much use for this here anymore?" he asks.

"It's too banged up. I'll have to get a new one now."

"Can I keep it?"

"That's not a problem. What are you gonna do with it?"

"Maybe I can fix it and bend it back into shape or something. I'll find use for it."

"It's all yours then. Be my guest."

Frost and snow have nearly glued my ruck in place from being frozen and thawed out again on multiple days. At least it is still here and nobody else found it to rat it out for their own benefit. Water from my canteen is still frozen, but a half-empty box of 30-30 for my marlin is ready to go. More ghillie blankets and map layouts of the areas I have hunted while looking for the white stag, GPS unit, basic gun cleaner kit, and a few MRE type rations are all still in place.

I load up the rifle and chamber a round as the old man looks back at me as I struggle to sling the ruck sack on my shoulders. It's painful on the shoulder at first, but at least it wasn't heavy enough to cause more damage. I make sure the dead man's wallet didn't fall out of my side pocket. The old man looks upwards again to see the broken branch and clawed bark area where I was attacked.

"Holy cow. How high up were you before you dropped?" he asks.

"I was pretty high up. At least twenty feet, or so."

"What took your arm out of place, the fall or ol' Leeds?"

"I guess I'll have to give that credit to *ol' Leeds* as you call it."

"Startin' to believe me now, I see."

"Have little choice, really. I can't argue that something attacked me, and you've been out here longer than me. Long enough to know what tried to kill me, anyway."

"Was your big hiking bag still in place?" he asks.

"Yes, it is. It's a tough one. I've had it a long time."

"Expect your heading on your way back now?"

"That's right ol' timer. I need to make my way back about six or seven miles inwards into the towns. I parked my truck off the side of the road, so I should be there before dark."

"You gonna make it with that bum leg?"

"I should be fine. The locals are probably searching for that dead hunter we saw. I'll hand in his wallet and tell them where to find him. They'll send back out a search party to recover it."

"Won't be much left of him I expect."

"Well, still gotta try. At least for the man's family. It's the decent thing to do at this point."

"You gonna tell them what happened to you?"

"If they ask, I will, but they won't believe me. Some stories are best left untold, I guess. Whether I got the bite mark to prove it or not."

He pauses, knowing that we are about to part ways.

"I can't thank you enough for helping me like you have. I don't have the means to repay you, but if you come with me into the towns, I would gladly do so…"

"You have done more than you think by just being here."

"You mean get busted up and land on my ass?"

"Well, besides that. But I ain't going into the towns. Ain't no place for folk like me there. They got a real problem with dark skinned folk like me. Nicer out here anyways. Peaceful and quiet. Just like I like it."

"Right, didn't see too many blacks there the short time I visited but those days that you keep mentioning have been over for a while now."

"You gots a home to go back to?" he asks.

"Not really. Just an apartment that stays empty."

"What about your lady friend you were talkin' to in your sleep when I first found you?"

"Like I said, she's been gone for a while now too."

"No peace here and no peace there for you, is there?"

"Pretty much."

"There's an old Native American tale from the tribal folks that span up and down the entire eastern parts of the sates. They told it for men like you a lot." as he props up next to a tree.

"Alright, then. Let's hear it." as I prop my weight on the rifle.

"They tell it like this. They say there be a pair of wolves inside all of us. These two wolves are ferocious and cunning, like warriors. Like you. But one of these wolves is bad, and the other wolf is good. They are always fighting with each other. Constantly attacking and hunting down the other one our entire lives here on Earth, but on the inside of all of us. They both talk to you and guide you on your chosen path more than you think. They are both hungry, all the time. The good wolf knows faith, love, peace, empathy, and kindness. The bad wolf only knows hurt, anger, sorrow, and resentment. I'm sure there are more words to describe the both of them, but it was so long ago when an old tribal leader out of the Appalachias told me about it. No matter though, the wolves always keep on fighting each other."

"So, which one of them wins in the end?" I ask him.

"The one you *feed*, young fella… The one you *feed*."

He looks at me with such sudden honesty while standing there. Intriguing story. A lot of truth to be told behind the morale of that one, but no words can express them. I approach him closer to take off my glove and shake his hand for the first time since he found me. I hope I see him again when the authorities catch up to the remains.

"Are you sure I can't convince you to come into the towns with me?"

"I'm fine. It's best now you head on your way. I'm sure you'll be back before you know it."

"Right, they might ask me to help them recover the body."

"Well, not what I meant, but somethin' like that. You watch yourself if you make your way back in here. You know where I be near the shores in my lil ol' campground."

"The police or sheriffs might come asking questions. I never caught your name?"

"You white folks gots a name for everything, don't ya?"

"Yeah. I'll admit that, but if you got one, I'd like to know who it was that helped me out here?"

"They used to call me James."

"Well, *James*. Again, I can't thank you enough for helping me."

"You go with God now, young fella. You gots a journey ahead of ya now."

"Will do, James. Will do."

He shakes my hand for a while in silence, as if to study me with that same toothless grin he has. Cryptic old man, nothing more. We go our separate ways without a second thought. If I get to the towns before too deep into the night, a deputy's office or police department is my first stop. I may have to lead them back here. Or, better yet, if they have a general map of the area then I can use my GPS deer tracker tool. I pounder ways on how to explain all this to whoever I find. There's no better way to deal with this other than to take it head on when I get back.

Darkness brings more snowfall again as I make it to the road. Half a mile down and I see my white dodge sitting right where I left it, camouflaged under a sheet of snow already. When I get close enough to my truck, I notice another car behind it. It's a sheriff's deputy car. I stop in the ditch line to stuff my rifle onto the side of my ruck sack, but the barrel sticks out, pointing to the ground. Not a good idea to approach these people armed, especially if they are already out looking for a missing person. Surely there's been a missing person's report by now. It's been over a week. I get closer to my truck and see there's nobody in the white deputy patrol car. They may be out in the wood line searching. If they saw me, they would have shined a search light on me by now. I see the engine is still running the closer I get.

"Freeze!!" a voice yells from nearby.

I stop dead in my tracks. "Hello? Who's out here? Is that a deputy? I won't move, ok?"

I hear snow crunching from the other side of my truck as the light gets shined in my face. I see a service type Glock pistol silhouetting in front of the flashlight. Only cops carry a light with their gun in that manner. Not the first time I had a gun pointed at me, though.

"Get your damn hands up!" he says.

"Ok, just don't shoot. I'll do as you say."

He walks closer, but the light is just too bright to get a clear image. He is a large man. Not an imposing man, he just has an enormous belly. The flashlight is too blinding to see anything. They won't risk getting within arm's reach of someone, but he keeps getting closer.

"Drop down to your knees and get them hands behind your head, now boy!" he demands.

"Ok. I will. There's no problem. But listen, I'm wearing a large bag on my back and…"

Lights out as I get knocked to the ground from the side of my forehead near my eye with something without warning. Floaties everywhere all over again. Overzealous fuck heads. This is worse than

OC spray. May as well shoot me now and ask questions later. I could respect that more than getting blindsided by some fat deputy. Haven't been arrested in a long time, not since I was still in uniform. My transition back into the civilian sector is not going so well for me these last few weeks.

Chapter 8: The Sheriff

It seems I have been patrolling around the town for hours into the night. Drake sits in the back, ready and able as soon as I turn the strobes and the siren on. Ears are up and eyes are alert. He knows we are about to go to work. I don't always need him to hop out and do his thing for me. But he is always ready. He had his tail blown off when an IED hit us on our patrol years back when I was still in the service. Most civilian contractors that tagged along with us on patrol with their bomb dogs are only in it for the money, a nice six figures for a few months out. Whereas those of us in uniform and full gear risk it all to stay above the poverty line. They view their bomb dogs as an expendable tool and nothing more. Soldiers out in the operating basis look to the comfort of a dog. Stray and farrow cats that meow all night outside the tents. Mangy underfed dogs from the locals that are just there outside the forward bases knowing some soldier will give them a free meal in exchange for a temporary friend.

Drake is a black Strafford mix with who knows what else. Maybe even husky with those two different colored eyes of his. It scares most people at first glance and that works in my favor. Lean and muscular is all they see behind those two eyes, one brown and one blue. He may have had his tail blown off years ago as a newly trained bomb sniffer in the field, but he definitely saved my ass that day. All of us on patrol that day, actually. When I got back stateside after my national guard unit went back to inactive status, I made sure he came home with me. Got him recruited into a special program to retrain him to be the drug dog for the Sheriff's station. He is tough and loyal as a best friend can be. I see him in the rearview mirror with his mouth closed and tense. Even the nub from what is left of his tail is perfectly still in the back of my speeding department issued SUV. I always wonder how he stayed on all fours in the back of a moving vehicle.

Not exactly a hot pursuit for this one. Changing lanes without using a signal. There's been word of a dark blue BMW that came through the area once last week out of AC trying to sell off weed, speed, or heroin to younger folks before the weekend. Younger skinny white male, longer hair, scruffy beard, and a nose piercing. What he does to afford a BMW beats the hell outta me. Been looking out for the vehicle description for a few days since we got wind of it. I have the strobes on but turn the siren back off. I can see him doing something in his passenger seat. There it is. He just threw something out the side window, hoping I didn't see it in the dark. These morons just never learn. I turn the siren back on, shine the spotlight on his back glass and get on the loudspeaker.

"LOWER YOUR SPEED AND PULL THE VEHICLE OVER, NOW!!"

He turns his four ways on and slows his down speed to show he isn't trying to get away. He pulls over near an alley way that he may not know is a dead end. I run the plates and call the stop in to the station. The strobes stay on and the plates come back expired and registered out of Atlantic County. It doesn't get any easier than that.

"Stay for now, Drake. Just wait for my signal." He turns his head sideways to give me a frown, as he is always eager to jump out and scare somebody.

"Don't look at me like that. You almost got me in trouble last week going after that wife beater like you did on that domestic call. Remember that one? Did his finger at least taste good?" I ask sarcastically. He sits back down below the dog cage out of site. Animals are like children when they get embarrassed. I step out and shine my service light right into his side-view mirror so he can't see my hand already on my revolver. It's a brisk winter night that keeps my breath lingering behind me in a fog. Not a lot of movement from him, and I can see his hands already on the steering wheel. The window is cracked open. That's strike three for this guy. I knock on the glass.

"Roll the window down, sir."

He fumbles to turn the ignition back on enough to roll down the window, but he forgot his passenger window is still down. What an idiot. The window goes down, but I can smell it already outside the vehicle. He refuses to look at me, but he is nervous.

"Um... What can I do for you, officer?"

"It's the Sheriff's Department. Do you know why I pulled you over?"

"Umm... speeding? But, umm... No, not really?"

"Were you speeding?" I ask intensely.

"Umm... Maybe, I'm not sure."

"You don't know if you were speeding or not?"

"I don't, umm... I don't think so. I mean, I didn't even see where you came from."

"You're mumbling and slurring your words. Have you been drinking tonight?"

"No... No... officer. I'm not old enough to drink."

"How old are ya, kid?"

"I'm 20 sir... officer. I was... Um."

"Again, it's the Sheriff Department."

I give him a long awkward silence with the light shined down on him that makes turds like him feel like an eternity, wondering if their life just went to shit in a one-horse town they don't even live in. I've seen this a lot the last few months. State troopers can't catch these guys because they stay off the interstates when they leave the Atlantic City area.

"I pulled you over because you were changing lanes without proper signal, young man."

"Oh, shit… I'm… I'm sorry, sir. I thought I did something worse by accident or…"

"Gonna need to see your license, registration, and proof of insurance. Ok?"

"Oh… Yes… I umm."

He reaches into the center console and I unclip my holster for safety to have my revolver ready. That's another strike for this guy. Most times, men hold a license in their wallet and the reach for it in their back pocket first. The first thing he did was go for the center console as he stammers his own words still. Then he goes for the glove box and shuffles random paperwork around. I never know what's in these ridiculous amounts of vehicle compartments nowadays. Some cars have too many to count.

"Is this your vehicle?" I ask as he still shuffles around random paperwork and empty packs of black and mild cigars. It doesn't smell like cigar smoke in the car. It smells like marijuana, but I haven't said anything to him about that yet. I'll bring it up while he is still nervous and frantic.

"Did you throw something out the window a few streets back, young man?"

"Umm… No… Yes… It was… uh."

"Yes or no? Which is it?"

"Um… No officer… or… Sir."

"Are you sure you didn't throw something out the window right back there?"

"I don't think so, but here is my license sir."

"You don't *think* so?"

He reaches out to hand me the license. I see the needle marks on his arm, but he tries to keep them covered with a long sleeve of his hoodie on top of them. His veins are prominent, and his hands shake a lot. Could be the nervousness, but it looks more like tweaking to me.

"I… I… umm… I don't know where she keeps her registration, Sir. This is my mother's car, but I… I know she keeps it insured. I just don't know where all that stuff is at the moment. I... I can call her and see if she knows..."

"Nope, this is fine for now. I want you to sit tight and try to reach her, but I'll be right back with this for you. Just sit tight for a bit for now, alright."

As I walk away, I hear a sigh of relief from him. He thinks he's about to get off on this one. Usually, it is an indicator when the officer appears to be mild mannered about the situation by not checking all documents on a traffic stop that we are gonna do a license check and then we let them go. He knows this because he has been stopped before. Before I get back into the SUV, I re-clip the safety on my holster. I turn the spotlight off but keep the strobes on. Drake looks up from behind the back seat through the cage. I look at the license. Twenty years old out of Atlantic City. He may not even know the registration is out of date by a month. The ID photo makes him look healthier than he does now, so his bad habit is a new development within the last six months. *Justin Rowlands*, what a typical rich kid name. I check the record and sure enough, I see prior traffic stops and a prior arrest for paraphernalia, but no active warrants. I keep the kid waiting in suspense for a few minutes, but I don't call it in to the station as to what I am about to do.

"Ready to go to work, Drake?"

He jumps up on all fours in the back of the SUV and pants with his tongue out.

"Alright boy. You just wait for my signal. Gimme few minutes."

That's the second time I had to tell him that. He yawns and grumbles as he lays back down again behind the back seat.

"I know. I know I already said that, but I mean it this time. Soon as I open the back hatch, you know the drill. Ok? No fingers this time."

I step back out of the SUV with his license in hand and unclip the holster safety again. The last time I had to pull out this model 69 revolver was for a black bear that came into a park near the school grounds, but it was just to spook it off with shot shell I keep in the back of the SUV. This Justin kid would be stupid to make things worse for himself. Rich kids from the city are too scared of guns anyway, but I won't let my guard down, just in case he is tweaking that much. I approach the back side of the BMW and rub my finger across the rear quarter panel on the driver's side. He still has his window open, despite the bitter cold. Is he too high to tell how cold it is?

"Ok, Justin. Your mom's registration is expired by a month, but I won't hold it against you."

"Oh… umm… I… Thank you, sir. I'll have to get this fixed for her."

"Right, but I see you've been arrested for drug paraphernalia in the past. How'd that turn out for you? Did you make it to your court date for that one?"

"Umm… Yes, that was handled months ago."

"So, here's the problem, Justin. I can smell it from here before I even approach your window. And I know you *don't remember if you threw something out the window* or not, as you stated earlier. Do you mind if the vehicle is searched?"

He goes quiet and still doesn't look me in the eye as he lowers his head down in instant regret.

"Do you mind if the vehicle is searched, young man?" I ask again, but he is still silent.

"It's my mothers' car. I don't think you will find anything."

"You don't *think*?"

I reach into my pocket for the key fob and open the back hatch so Drake can come out. The rule for him is to make his presence known before he can do anything. He hops out and trots over to sit in view of the side-view mirror for the driver.

"Justin, do me a favor and look in your side-view mirror there and tell me what you see."

"Ah shit," he says.

"That's right. Oh shit. Now, you wanna tell me what you threw out the window before he comes over here and starts barking the moment he approaches the window and smells the same thing I do?"

"It's… It's my Mom's car."

"Ok, Justin. Have your way. I'm done playing this game with you. Drake SEARCH!"

He moves fast and sniffs out the passenger side first. Justin just lowers his head and slumps down in his seat further. Before Drake even gets to the passenger side, he barks and jumps his front paws up onto the trunk. That's the first place to check.

"Drake SEARCH!"

He moves down the passenger side as I point and lifts his front paws into the passenger window to bark at Justin. This is when Drake likes to have a bit of fun. He gives the cue that he smells something inside the car while barking and growling at the driver. Justin freaks out enough with one glance at Drake then he screams. He is already trying to crawl out the driver's window right in front of me.

"Holy fuck!! What kinda fucking dog is that?!?!"

Justin drops to the ground within arm's reach of my foot, trying to get away from Drake, who already made it into the passenger seat. He jumps back out of the window to come around to the front of the car. Justin is still trying to get on his feet, but crawls backwards on all fours as he sees Drake coming around the front of the car right at him quickly, teeth bared and all.

"Drake, HEEL!"

Drake stops inches away from him to just stare and growl with his teeth still baring. Justin is mortified and in near shock. If his hands weren't shaking before, they are now. I look up at the automatic key fob for the SUV.

"I sure do like these fancy door openers in our new patrol SUV," I say sarcastically, before putting it back in my pocket. I lean down to talk to him face to face while Drake keeps his same frightening posture directed right at him.

"I think Drake likes you... Now, what's in the damn car, boy?"

He keeps looking at Drake, wondering if his face is about to be torn off as he still growls and drips slobber on the freezing pavement next to him.

"Look at me Justin!"

He still glances at Drake, but I get his full attention when I yell.

"I got probable cause from your prior arrest record and the smell of you alone to tear this vehicle apart, for what we both know is already in there. Add in the fact I witnessed you throwing something out the window, *and* all this started over not using proper signal to change lanes, shithead. It does not help your situation to lie to me anymore. Make things easier on yourself kid, and tell me what's in the damn car?"

"It's drugs."

"No shit, sherlock. What kind of drugs?"

"A few ounces of pot and some H."

"Where?"

He keeps glancing at Drake in concern still until I slap him in the face.

"Where dammit?!"

"Uh… There's some under the passenger seat and some in the trunk, but it isn't mine."

"Have you *ever* seen an episode of cops, kid?"

"Huh?"

"Do you realize they all say *it isn't mine, I swear.*"

"But… But it's true. I… I swear."

"Get up and place your hands on the vehicle. Drake, HOLD!"

Drake changes his demeanor from fierce to best friend again. He trots away and sits in front of the SUV near the front bumper, but still in eyesight of me and the kid while I search him.

"Anything in your pockets I need to know about?"

"No… No sir. Just a lighter and a half burnt black and mild."

I find it and smell more weed. The worst part is, it's not even good weed. It's just the cheap shit that is left over from roaches that were already used. I call Drake back over and let him sniff it up for the scent while I hold Justin in place. Justin turns to look at him as he runs back over to his backside. Drake takes a big whiff, and he has the signal.

"Drake, FIND!"

Drake takes off down the road to find whatever was thrown out the passenger window. I keep patting him down, but I never cuff him. I haven't pulled the cuffs out in months either. I lead him over to the SUV as he lowers his head and starts sobbing. He slides into the back seat without issue or question. Could be too stoned or tweaked to realize he isn't cuffed. The cage between the front and back seat doesn't give taller perps a lot of leg room. The sense of claustrophobia in the back of a sheriff's SUV keeps most of them talking when reality sets in. The cruisers are even smaller, but we only have a few of each at the department in this county.

Drake comes back a few seconds later with miniature bong in his mouth and wagging his nub of a tail. Once I close the door on Justin to see him cry like a girl, I look in the front area of the SUV for a spare evidence bag and gloves. Drake hands the bong off to me into my palm and he gets a good job nod from me. I walk around to the back-passenger door and let Drake jump in to sit in the seat right next to Justin, to keep him from doing anything else stupid.

"Drake, HOLD!"

He sits within inches of Justin to stare and growl at him again for giggles. All I hear is Justin squirming around and probably pissing himself as I close the door behind Drake. The child safety lock, and that a vicious drug-sniffing dog is sitting next to them, keeps them at bay. The evidence bag is small but fills up quick. Wallet, cell phone, the few baggies of pot, car keys, and roach clip under the seat. The trunk has piles of unwashed clothes, bottled water, and a mildewed loaf of bread. Not the typical trunk cargo of a drug dealer. I move it all aside and lift the spare tire hatch. Sure enough, two baggies of white heroine sit underneath jack stand. Jackpot, but this is not even a creative effort to hide this shit compared to what I have seen before. Nothing else worth throwing into evidence. I walk back over to the SUV to see Drake still having his fun with him. Just the presence of a dog like him freaks most of them out and he loves every minute of it.

Justin is just sitting in the back with his head down, and still concerned about what Drake may do. I search through his wallet in the front seat. Expired credit cards, a mechanics card for a body shop, a flattened condom, and a few doctors' office cards. This guy has no life according to his wallet. I take the drugs out of the baggie. He sees I am searching through his things, but I have called nothing in yet.

"Am I under arrest?" he asks.

"Did I say you were under arrest?"

"Well… Um, no."

It seems light and laced with either baby formula or sucrose. Only two tiny little bags of it, but no other items that typically go with it. No spoons or needles. The marijuana is also cheap and maybe mixed with parsley or something along those lines. I lift the baggie of heroin up into the dome light.

"Do you know you got ripped off for some of this shit, kid?" I ask.

"What's the difference. These school kids around here will smoke the crap that gets swept off the floor in this area. Nobody can afford the good stuff these days, anyway."

"Oh wow, Justin. You just bumped yourself up from possession to distribution. What about the H? Do you sell that stuff around here too?"

"I told you. That stuff is my mom's. It's her car, remember? I forgot she still had it."

"Right, all of this stuff is your moms."

"It's true. She's in rehab. Just look in my wallet and you'll see the card for where she is at."

I shuffle through the various business cards in his wallet. Behind the automotive repair shop car is one for a rehab center based in Camp May, just south of Atlantic City.

"I take it you plan on committing yourself in too, right? Hey, maybe you and your mommy can be roommates there. How long have you been on this shit?"

"The pot's mine, sort of. The H isn't. I don't do that stuff."

"What about the marks on your arm, then? You take a piss test down at the station, what are you gonna pop hot for? How's that gonna look in front of the judge when you go in for the last arrest you had for paraphernalia?"

"Just do what you 're gonna do. You won't listen to me, anyway. Nobody ever does."

"Aww. *Poor little Justin.* Enough with the woe is me shit, kid. I've heard it all before."

"Then what are you gonna do to me?"

"I'm gonna let you go back to the station with me, Justin?"

"What?"

"Yeah. Today is your lucky day, kiddo. But I gotta do something first."

I take cell phone photos of everything in his wallet, mainly his license and address. I keep the card for the rehab center. The keys and the weed go back in the bag with all the other crap he had. The H stays on the seat and I start looking through his cell phone contacts.

"I tell you what, Justin, I'm gonna start calling every contact you have in this phone until I know who you are selling to and who you are buying from. Sound good to you?"

"Wait?... What?"

"Yeah. I'm gonna start calling random numbers from your phone. No matter who picks up, I'm gonna tell them that you and I are having a nice and long conversation in the back of a sheriff's patrol vehicle."

"Please don't do that... Please... Sir, I am telling you the truth. I'm not a dealer and I don't have a dealer. This is my mom's stuff and I take a few hits here and there on the weed. That's it, I swear!"

"Then what's with the marks on the arm?" I ask.

"That was a weed eater accident. I told you I don't do that stuff."

"A weed eater? *Really...*"

"Yeah, I mow lawns and I tried to fix the head spool while it was still running, and the throttle dug into the ground and wrapped the wire around my hand."

"Were you high then, too?"

"No. Everything you see there is my mom's stuff. I tried to mix some of the heroin she had left with sugar to make it look like more than it was. I tried to sell it off, but some people knew it was fake already. It only gives a normal user a weak buzz. I just needed the money is all."

"Money for what?"

"My mom's room at the rehab center. Detox in a private room isn't cheap, ya know."

"You're telling the truth, aren't you?"

"Yes. I told you that I was. I had to walk away from school. She lost her job at a casino resort…"

"Shut up!... Am I gonna find the number to this rehab center on your recent calls list?"

"Yeah. I talked to one of the nurses there just yesterday. I was trying to get an update on her."

I search through the phone contacts and compare it to the number on the rehab center business card. Sure enough, the phone number called out to around 1:30PM yesterday matches the same one on the card. He wasn't tweaking. He's just scared shitless, and Drake isn't even interested in him anymore either. This kid has enough problems.

"How long has your mom been on this crap?"

"This is her second relapse with it this year. My Dad was thrown in jail for it last year, then she had to go start finding her own dealer."

"And you don't use this shit?"

"No. Never. I hate needles."

"You can smoke it too, you know."

"I wouldn't know how to do that. Even if I did know, I wouldn't try it."

"Why is that?"

"I drove her to the hospital after she ripped one of her ears off when she was freaking out on that stuff. I see what it does to her and other people like my dad. Cheap weed is nothing compared to it."

"Jesus Christ, kid. Her own fucking ear?"

The radio speaker comes in from the station.

"Hey there Sheriff, another unit said you were on a traffic stop, over?"

"You're the fuckin *Sheriff*??" he says while sitting there shocked in the back seat.

I sit there in silence thinking about how to handle this one, but I was already committed to getting what I need before I heard this sob story. I step out of the SUV, but the H stays on the passenger seat. I open the door on his side to let him out. He steps out and I can see Drake is already stretching out in the now opened and warmed up passenger seat. I hand him his wallet, keys, and cell phone out of the baggy as I push him to lean against the patrol SUV. I dump the marijuana out on the street. A true junkie would have wigged out and started to try to sweep the shit up with their hands, but he just stands there and looks at the ground as the freezing rain starts to soak it up at our feet. I look right at him as I respond to the station on my shoulder mic.

"Hey Sherral, Sheriff here. Just a turn signal was out on a kid's car passing through. Let him go with a warning. Pretty quiet night out here. Gonna call it a day soon. Over."

"OK then Sheriff. Anything else for me for the night?. Over."

"You know the drill. Pack it in and lock it up for the next shift. Have yourself a good one. Over."

"Will do Sheriff. Station over and out."

Radio silence again as Justin looks directly at me, man to man, for the first time.

"What are you going to do?" he asks.

"I'm gonna let you go home. But know this, if I see you here in this area again I pick you up and throw you under the jail with my four-legged friend that you already met. Understood?"

"Yes sir... I... I won't come round here no more. I'm sorry..."

"Shut up, shithead! I'm calling the rehab center tomorrow you claim your mother is at. If they say she doesn't exist there, then I call you in to the city PD and they do me a favor of adding another turd to one of their jail cells and not mine. Don't make me regret this because I'll come for you. Don't say shit to me. Don't even thank me. Just get the hell out of my sight. And remember, I got your address. I got your name. I got your number. And now, I know your damn face. Think about it, kid. Now go on, get the fuck outta here."

Chapter 9: The Broken Home

Me and Drake make it home without stopping off at the station. I drive the patrol SUV anywhere I go, on and off duty. The day has worn me ragged with no energy left. Drake hops out and trots to the door to walk around in circles until I can let him in. The lights are still on, so I know she's awake, still waiting for me. Not waiting for me to come home and ensure a safe day at work or to cook a decent meal for me. She's just up and waiting for me to come home. My heart rate is up, and simply coming in the driveway has heightened my blood sugar again. Stress is a mess that throws so much of your health off. Yet I am about to walk into another stressful situation. I open the door and Drake goes right to his chew toy, near his bed. He goes through at least one of those a month just gnawing on it until he falls asleep. I've even caught him with it in his mouth when he sleeps.

"Jay?! I'm home."

No response, but I see the house is still a disaster, as always. I can smell that she's been smoking in the house, too. I look in the kitchen trash can to see multiple shot bottles of vodka have been emptied.

"Jaynese?! Are you home?"

"Yeah. I'm in here." She says from behind our bedroom door. I walk over and open it to find her wrapped in a bathrobe, with a towel on her head. The cigarette in her mouth has an ash on it a mile long. She takes another swig of something and ashes on the bed. Even though she appears to have just showered, she is dry. She has been in her robe for a while.

"Did you go to Atlantic City? Do you bring some home? I need it really bad. Did you bring it?" she asks anxiously. Her hands shake as she attempts to relight her cigarette again. She's antsy and in need, like a child that doesn't know any better. Like a child that comes out its alcoholic mother and relapses before it is even a day old. A child that never stops crying.

"Yeah, I got some. I didn't have to go all the way to the city though."

"Give it here then. C'mon, I need it now, jerk off!" she says as she jumps off the bed and approaches me. Not to come to me and greet me home after a day on the job, but like a beggar on a city street corner that prefers money to support their bad habits over a decent meal.

"Jay, you don't need to keep doing this crap. Have you eaten at all today?"

"The fuck you care. Just give it to me. I need it now!"

"I do care, don't say that. Just calm down."

"I'll calm down as soon as you give it to me right now, jerk off. Where is it? I need it."

"Can I convince you not to do this again, Jay? Please."

"If you don't give it to me, you worthless fuck, I'll go straight to the city and suck off a shitload of cocks behind a casino again to get my damn fix if I have to. Those old white gamblers love shootin a load down my throat and you won't stop me this time. Where is it now! You don't fuckin understand?!"

She cries and flails around in front of me and drops to her knees. That's what happened the last time I pushed her into rehab. I won't argue with her about that and she knows it. The city PD found her strung out and nude by a dumpster by a resort hotel in AC. I reach into my uniform chest pocket and hand over the two baggies of H. She grabs it and runs to her nightstand like a teen that just tried to get away with shop lifting candy at a gas station. Her "goody bag", as she calls it, was stashed away somewhere she knew I would never find it when I sent her to rehab over in the city the first time. Now she has no shame in leaving it next to the bed on her nightstand.

"Where'd you get it? Is it any good?" she asks as she pulls out the spoon, needle, and the rubber tubing that drops on the floor. "Shit!"

"It was from some kid that was trying to sell it off in town. He already said it was mixed with…"

"Ah, who gives a fuck. There's more than enough in there to get it done." she says.

I sit and watch her as she mixes from the chair in the room's corner. Drake's already snoozing out in the living room on his doggy bead. Not a care in the world. She squeezes the needle syringe outward to get every ounce of it from the burning hot spoon. She started a fire in the kitchen a few weeks ago trying to use the stovetop iron to heat up the spoon. She wraps the rubber tubing around her off hand and holds the end in her mouth to keep it tight. She tries to talk with the tubing in her mouth.

"This is the last time. I swear it. Then I'll stop, ok."

"You say that every time, Jay. I'm through doing this for you. I got a line on a rehab clinic from the kid I got it from today and I'm calling this in tomorrow morning."

"Shut up Jason! I gotta find the fuckin vein again. Come here and hold the tube in place."

"You know I won't do that for you."

"Worthless Sheriff of a worthless town and has a tailless dog. You're a few verses short of a sad country music song, jerk off."

She finds her vein as the needle goes in. She's used that same needle spot before. I watch her every time to make sure she doesn't keep pumping her body full of this shit. She used to be beautiful and energetic. We used to be in love. We used to be a family. But I don't recognize my Jay anymore.

"I did something good today." I tell her as she drops the tubing out of her mouth to let the blood flow through her arm again. Only about five minutes before she is lifeless on the bed. Maybe ten knowing how cheap the H really is. We always used to talk about my day. Only the good things worth hearing about, though. Now she just passes out on the bed drooling into the pillow.

"Yeah, you did good. You scored a few good bags." she says as she sets the stuff back into the goody bag. But it drops off the nightstand. She doesn't care to reach for it either.

"No, not that. I think I helped that younger kid out today. The kid I took this stuff from."

"Is that so?" as she props her feet up on the bed. She doesn't realize her head towel is falling off.

"Yeah. I think he got scared of being caught again. Drake sure did a number on him too."

"Yeah?" as she slurs her words with eyes blinking slower by the second.

"I think maybe he'll stay away from all of it now. He said he was trying to get money for his mom. It was a sob story, but I called the place he said she was at…"

"This shit is so good to me. It's better to me than you ever were. It's better than fuckin."

"I called the same place up and sure enough, his mother was detoxing there. For the second time. The kid was just trying to make sure he could afford the bill, so she stays there."

"I'm a mother." she says as she stares off into the ceiling.

"Yeah. I know."

"You let her die. Now I'm not a mother."

"That's not true. You know that."

"You let them all die, Jason."

"Don't say that."

"You don't even fuck me anymore. I haven't seen your dick in months now. Do you even still have one anymore, jerkoff?"

"I won't do that while you're using. You know that."

"Right… No fuckin, then no more babies for you to let die again…"

I watch as she drifts away. She looks at me and lifts her robe up to see her naked underneath.

"You can come fuck this. Nut up inside this. I know you want to."

"No, I don't. Not like this. You need help, Jay."

"Come and nut up inside me like you like to, Jason. I'll give you another baby girl to lose for us again. Come fuck..." as she plays with herself in front of me. She's just in pain. That is what I try to convince myself of when I watch this. This is her escape. This is her release. This isn't the Jay I remember. She's lost inside this sorry thing laying on my bed, either pissing herself or getting herself off one. She does both often when she gets her fix. My Jay bird is gone for now.

"Did you hear what I said, Jaynese? I said I think I helped someone today. Are you there?"

Nothing but mumbles from her now. Lost inside her own trance.

"I'll change the sheets in the morning for you again. Can you hear me, Jaynese?"

I stand up to walk over and put out the cigarette she left on the ground lit. She looks at me and grabs my arm, but I just pull away.

"You're shipping out tomorrow to get help. Enjoy your last fix on me."

I can't stand the person laying on my bed, but I watch this every time, hoping by some undeserving miracle my Jay bird will just come back to me. Her arms open up the top of her robe to show her tits to me. Her eyes are just drifting everywhere on the ceiling. I put the needle and the other baggie back in the bag and slide the nightstand drawer closed before I walk out of the room while I turn the light off.

"Goodnight, Jaynese."

I close the door behind me and head to the kitchen. Drake jumps up and follows me there but roams off down the hallway. I look into our empty fridge, wondering if anything miraculously appeared for groceries. Nothing. Just more of Jay's booze and a few of my own Millers. Too lightheaded to drink right now without checking my blood sugar first. Drake comes back from the bathroom with my own "goody bag" gripped in his mouth. Animals just seem to know certain things about their owners, I guess. He knows where I keep it, too.

"Thanks buddy. You did good today, yeah. You did good."

He stands there on all fours and then sits in front of me, wagging the stub of his tail on the floor.

"Yeah, don't worry buddy. I know what you want."

I move over to his stash in the cupboard. Beef Jerky, that's his thing, and it always has been since we met years ago in the desert. I give him a few slices and then he walks away to his bed and enjoys with his chew toy. Not the best meal for my situation, but it's good enough for a man and his dog. I pick up the "goody bag" he left me at my feet and open it up to check my blood sugar and heart rate. The strips fall all over the floor in my shuffling through the bag but didn't spread far. I prick my finger and slide it into the tester. All seems normal for now, but maybe I'm just tired at the moment. I don't even know what time it is. Drake hangs out on his bed near the kitchen most nights. I shut down all the lights and lock the only door that never gets used. I have enough uniforms to last a solid week if she doesn't do the laundry. After a decent shower to wash the day off of me, I'm up all-night playing housekeeper mostly when she is passed out on our bed. I refuse to be next to her in the same bed when this happens.

I make my way to a different room, a special room where I am reminded of better days. I'm in here more often than not over the last few weeks. Jay hasn't stepped in here since we lost her. The walls are fitted with pink and purple girls' drawings next to a bin full of stuffed animals. She was old enough to get her first twin size bed before she went missing. Barbie posters and dolls everywhere. Even a pink 19-inch flatscreen television that I put a Dora sticker on for her birthday last year. The clothing drawers haven't been opened since she was gone, only to put in her last set of clothes that were going through the wash before she went to school that day. It's a cute room that any kindergarten girl would love.

Now, it's just me with the dialysis machine under the purple nightlight. I still smell her on her pillows. Jay still doesn't know about my kidney failing out on me within the next couple of years, if not sooner than that. She never comes in here, even when she's clean. It was only a few times a week at first with the dialysis happening at the clinic. Now I go through this process multiple times a week when I sleep. If I sleep. When I close my eyes, it happens easiest in here. In my little girl's empty room full of memories. Maggie's picture is covered with dust. Everything is lined with dust, but I don't have the energy to keep cleaning things. Just clean the catheter, plug myself in, turn the machine on, and rest as best as I can on a twin bed with pink sheets. I miss her so much. I miss both of them, but they are both missing from my life, along with so many other things now.

I shut my eyes for a mere half hour before my cell phone goes off. Drake comes in the room to ease his own curiosity, too. I hope it's just the dialysis machine peeping, but I know otherwise. I pick it up and it's the station calling.

"Hello,"

"Sheriff?"

"Yeah, and I hope this is life altering? It's after midnight."

"I know, it's Rachel down at the station."

"What's going on?"

"Remember how Ricky Clauson was called in missing from his wife about a week ago?"

"Yeah, did he turn up in a drunken stupor again, like last time?"

"No, but we got a guy here that found him when he was out hunting. Looks pretty busted up."

"Is he another one of the local drunks too?"

"He had Ricky's wallet on him, Sheriff."

"What?..."

"Yeah. One of the deputies picked him when his truck was spotted outside the reserve areas."

"Has he said anything?"

"He says he knows where Ricky's body is at."

"Dammit. Keep this quiet until I get there. Keep him in the interview room. I'll be there within the hour. Who brought him in?"

"Davis did, and he's in there right now with him."

"Son of a bitch! Get him out of that damn room and wait till I get there!"

"*Understood. Do you want us to book him? Davis said he tried to assault him when he was looking over his truck.*"

"We both know that's bullshit. Do nothing else till I get there. Got it?"

"*Ok, Sheriff.*"

"And get Davis out of that damn room with him! I'll be there soon."

I hang up the phone and see Drake silently standing in the doorway.

"Ready to go to work again, boy?"

He quietly barks his typical response. Those two different colored eyes light up under the nightlight that has the black light bulb in it. I unplug the catheter and the machine beeps, showing the four-hour cycle didn't even make it halfway through. The insert bag is wasted, but the toxin bag is full already. I keep a spare machine at the station in case I have to pull an all-nighter. The yellow has left my eyes for the time being and my skin color has gone back to normal. It doesn't take me long to get ready, and I feel slightly refreshed. When I'm done playing homemaker after I get home, I always set everything out for the next day before I turn in for the night. I would rather live at the station if I knew beforehand how time consuming it was being in this position. The office would be big enough for a cot or maybe one of those college dorm futons. Then I would never have to come home to this mess and a junkie wife that has nothing good to say. If Maggie were still here, things would be different. I would have a reason to come home. My Jay bird would come back to me with a reason to stay clean.

The ride to the station doesn't take long. Drake hops out and follows me in. Me and Drake have our system down pat now. Some of the female deputies and Sherell, the admin clerk on the day shift, are fond of him. But Drake is very selective of some of the male deputies. Rachel is the first person I see standing outside the door.

We had a great thing before I took up the position after Maggie was born. Me and Rachel were just deputies back then when we first hooked up. She moved to a different county for a while after that long term fling but came back after I asked her to take on the second shift here at my station when I got the Sheriff's position handed to me. No strings attached for the two of us now, but we both still feel a lot for each other. She's way more educated in the judicial system than me. She doesn't belong here, more like in a metropolitan department with a detective's shield. Not in a small-town county Sheriff's Department. She even has the look of an educated professional woman and any guy would be thrilled to have her in their life anyway they can. If only it were a few years ago, along with a set of healthy kidneys that don't drain poison out of a tube two or three times a week, we might have been more. But we both know otherwise now.

"What's going on, Rachel? What do we know?"

She follows me and Drake through the front door of the station. I take out the keys to unlock the other entrance beyond the main entrance, behind the visitor's booth. The door is propped open with a random firebrick already.

"You morons will think twice about leaving this door propped open when an idiot leaves the drunk tank and wanders out into the street!?"

They do shit like this on the second shift when there're no calls that come in so they can step out for a quick smoke. Even though I yell so the entire station can hear me, none of the four deputies look in my direction, as if they didn't hear me. I kick the brick out of the way as we keep making our way into the station.

"Talk to me, Rachel. What's going on?" again, as I keep walking through the entrance.

"Ok, we picked him up just outside the wildlife preserve area where the white truck was spotted. Davis said the guy went at him, so he had to rough him up to get him cuffed and into the patrol car."

"Who called in the white truck?"

"One resident that lives at the trailer park near there. He said they were just coming off the shift at the plant when they drove by it. Been parked there for a few days. They thought nothing of it thinking it was just a broke down vehicle or out of gas one."

"Ok, who called it in?"

"I didn't catch a name yet."

"Get me a name and their statement first thing in the morning. Find them."

"Will do, Sheriff."

"Who was with Davis when he checked out the truck?"

"Nobody."

"Are you serious?" I ask.

"I said the same thing, Sheriff. Davis clocked him pretty good on the side of the head."

"Where the fuck's Davis?"

"He's still in there with him."

"I said to get him out of there till I showed up!"

"I know, but he insisted on grilling him still."

"Get in there and let him know I need to see him right fuckin now!"

"Ok.

"Where's the guy's stuff at?"

"It's over on the table near your office?"

She walks away to the interview room and I make my way to the evidence table. Another deputy is already gloved up inventorying the guys belongings. It all lays spread out over the table for viewing. A boot knife, a bowie knife, a 30-30 Marlin with a busted scope, a military styled ruck sack, a small hygiene kit, a few bottles of water, a box of ammo that is almost empty, his wallet, Ricky's wallet, a large section of a ghillie blanket, cell phone, gps unit, a mono night vision device.

"What have you found so far?" I ask the deputy, looking over everything.

"Not much, Sheriff. Just typical gear for a hunter. But, he says he's been out there for well over a week. I have found no food beyond old power bars and MRE rations."

"Where's the truck? What kind was it?"

"A late 90s model white Dodge pickup. It's back behind the station, locked up in the impound gates. Looks like he'd been living in it, but I haven't gotten to it yet."

I walk into my office and glove up. Drake stands post in front of the door, looking at the same table we all are now. He knows I expect nobody to be in that office without me. He raises hell if anybody tries to come in without me walking with them. I go for the wallet and pull out the driver's license and anything else I can find. Rachel walks up behind me and I hand it to her. Davis wobbles his fat ass right behind her.

"Look him up. See if he's got a record, anything. I wanna know everything about him ASAP. Davis, wait by my office."

I pull out every card and I see an expired military type ID, only expired a few months ago.

"Wait, Rachel, look him up within the local VA, too. See if he has registered with them and discharge papers may be public record at a home of address by now. Burlington County is the closest VA I can think of."

She takes the cards and heads to the admin computers of the front desk. Davis lifts the lever action rifle and starts examining it. I take it out of his hands in a snap.

"This could be evidence, so keep your hands off until I talk to him." I tell him. He gives back a snarled look in contempt.

"He killed him, I already got him to…"

"I thought he only mentioned knowing where a body was at?"

"Well… yeah. Isn't that enough?"

"No, it isn't *enough,* Davis. Hands off and wait for me in my office."

I tell the other deputy to search the truck after logging everything in. Drake stands outside the office and I motion for him to hold in place.

"Don't matter what you hear, boy. Just sit tight right here."

Drake just pouts again and lays down on the floor. I open the door to see Davis parked on the small couch in my office already.

"Ok, Davis. I'm gonna give you the benefit of a doubt for now. Tell me what happened out there and why you went without backup?"

"It was just a call on a broke down white pickup on the outskirts of the wildlife preserve area. Figured it was just a bunch of hunters that wondered into state park territory and the game wardens weren't taking the call. I show up and started running the plates, but nothing came back on the registration other than his name. I stepped out again to shine a light in to see if anyone was inside, and that's when he jumped me from the wood line. He had the rifle on him. Didn't have much choice, Sheriff. I just had to clock him on the side of the face to get him to calm down."

"He just jumps you out of the blue. If he had a visible weapon, why didn't you just shoot him and claim self-defense if you were that scared?"

"He went at me anyway, even after I bashed him in the head. When I got him on the ground and got a good look at him, I realized I never saw him before."

"Did you make yourself known before you approached the vehicle? Why wasn't this called in?"

"Once I searched him and found Ricky's wallet, I radioed it in and called for a tow to bring in the truck. I kept him cuffed in the back of the car until...."

"Wait, what do you mean you didn't recognize him?"

"Well, it's just more paperwork, but we got him for assaulting a deputy and now a potential murder too, right? I swear, Sheriff, if my cousin is out there dead and frozen then I'll..."

"Then you'll what, dumbass?! Murderers don't carry off with the wallet of the person they just killed for no good reason. Think, stupid! Nobody knows who he is, and he doesn't know anybody here. They gonna say he just came here looking for trouble for no good reason too?"

"That's bullshit, Sheriff! He's just some bum lookin..."

"Shut up! With a record like yours with multiple complaints of excessive force, you're fucking lucky you still got a badge in this station.

Now let's add in falsifying statements under color of authority. Think about it while you take the rest of the shift off, dumb ass. If he did kill someone out there, then your history is gonna come up later in the damn courts as a bias testimony. This is why you always call in for back up to confirm your statement. Why can't you think about these things? Now, take the night off and get outta here."

He puffs up as he gets off the couch and walks out in a hurry. Rachel stands outside the door next to Drake, still pouting on the floor.

"Jason... or... Sheriff. We found him from his registration out of Georgia. He's got a domestic violence, drunk and disorderly, but no convictions on either. Beyond that, his home of record shows both parents deceased and a spouse up in Maine somewhere. I didn't think to write the spouse's name, yet. Honorably Discharged less than a year ago."

"Did you find anything on his service? Discharge papers, DD-214, anything on public record?"

"No, but still searching."

The other deputy that was inventorying everything comes back inside from checking out the truck in the impound lot.

"Anything in the truck that can help?" I ask.

"Nothing, Sheriff. But he's definitely been living in it for a while. I photographed a lot of open and empty booze bottles floating around the back next to an air mattress set up in the camper bed."

Everybody in the station looks at me to wait on my next move and I head to the looking glass outside the interview room. He sits there leaned up against the corner. His clothes haven't been cleaned in days and the shoulder of his coat is ripped up. He is thin, and fast built but without a decent shave in a while. Though the military fade style haircut is still visible. He's changed his seating position from where we sit perps to have a direct view of the door. That's not how the chairs are placed when questioning happens. His eye is still bleeding from a recent hit from Davis, but he is wide awake and very alert.

"Rachel?"

"Yeah, right here." speaking from behind me.

"Where did you say he was from?"

102

"Georgia. Why?"

"Benning…"

"What?" she asks.

"Nothing, but he is probably combat arms. I need you to keep searching for his military service unless you hear him talk to me about it. Get me an MOS on him and somebody get me a phone book or a notebook or something heavy."

"Are you gonna do what I think?" asks the other deputy.

"What's an MOS?" asks Rachel.

"You idiots have seen too many movies. Just get me a damn phone book or anything heavy."

Rachel comes back with a stack of folders banded together. I move closer to the door but still able to see him through the one-way mirror. I slam the folders against the floor to make a loud snap on the floor that goes off throughout the station like a shotgun blast. He shoots right up out of his chair in shock and runs over to the door and tries to open it. He pounds against the door with all his weight then diverts attention to the glass to try to look through the one-way mirror by cupping his hands over his forehead to darken it. No luck on his part in knowing what is on the other side, but his heart is racing.

"Ok, He's combat experienced too. I know his type. Were gonna give him a few minutes to calm down in there, then I'm going in to have a chat with him."

"How do you know he is combat experienced, Sheriff?" asks Rachel.

"Cause we all look alike… Just keep the camera rolling and have someone stay close to the outside of the door in case this gets fuckin ugly, ok?"

Chapter 10: The Mirror

This room is claustrophobic and hot. I would never cuff a detainee with their hands in the front. I never got a good look at the building with one eye being swollen shut now. There is at least one exit in the front, but it guarded by a check-in desk or some administrative puke manning the front door. At least one other female deputy came and got Davis's attention while he was trying to grill me for answers. He isn't very good at it, though. Poorly lit and everybody that I have seen seems tired. It must be into the morning hours by now. If they assumed I had done anything, they wouldn't even be talking to me. If they had proof beyond me carrying the guy's wallet on my person, I would have been arrested by now. This is just a test from the fat deputy to see if I admit or confess to something.

The door is knocked on from the outside, and another deputy walks in with what appears to be a small package and two coffees held in one massive hand. I haven't seen this one and the room feels hotter with him in it. He walks in and looks me up and down and shakes his head when he too notices that they cuffed my hands on the front side. He is a large man, an imposing man of good posture, but older. Somewhat muscular, but more of a meaty brawn that could overpower a smaller guy like me. But I am younger and faster than he is. I can tell by his painful walk that he has had a few rough years behind him. He sets the two coffees and package down on the table next to me and pulls out a set of keys from his pocket. He carries a revolver, but not a big one. The other deputies I saw carry a semi-automatic pistol of some form, a typical Glock or MP police issue. This is a small town, but it isn't in the wild west. Why a revolver?

"Good morning." he says.

I say nothing back as he approaches me and reaches for my hands to take the cuffs off. They were put on so tight that I almost lost circulation, but it's not the first time I've been cuffed. He tosses the cuffs on the table, looks at my face, and holds up one finger.

"Ok, look at my finger and follow it back and forth. Tell me, do you feel dizzy like you're going to faint or vomit?" he asks.

I shake my head no to both.

"Turn your head so I can get a good look at that eye. I need you to relax a bit, nobody's gonna touch you here. Yeah… You got clocked pretty good on that one side. Can you still see out of that eye?" he asks.

I shake my head yes.

"Ok, you get dizzy or start to feel nauseous, like you need a doctor or something, you just tell me. I'm gonna leave you uncuffed for this. Take some of these old patrol wipes I had stashed and clean yourself up in front of the mirror there. No funny business, got it?"

I shake my head yes again as I stand up to get a better look at myself in the one-way mirror. I look like a total shit bag right now. How many could be standing behind this mirror if I have to get out? He hasn't given me a reason to push back. He is already sitting in front of the chair where I was sitting. Leaned back with a leg crossed over the other. But his eyes are as stern and serious as he watches my every move. That face and the seriousness of his eyes do not match his relaxed posture. Not like any other law man I have met before. They lean in and try to back you into a corner to make you feel more isolated from the outside world. I turn and sit back down in front of him after I wipe the dried blood off my check and eye. I haven't seen a package of patrol wipes since my last visit to the commissary on base back in Georgia. He moves the table to the side so there is no barrier between us.

"Coffee?" he asks, as he slides the extra cup over to me. "It might be a few hours old by now, but they make a decent cup after it gets warmed up for fourth or fifth time."

I take the cup and cautiously sip, but I refuse to lose eye contact with him. He does the same to me as well and reaches into his shirt pocket opposite of the badge and pulls out a pack of cigarettes with a lighter. He takes one out of the pack.

"Do you mind?" he asks.

I think I know what's going on. He wants to "play" buddy with me to get to me. He lights up and motions to see if I would prefer a cigarette, too. Why not as I take one out of the pack. He uncrosses his leg to lean in and light mine up for me. Still looking me in the eye, even when he lights mine up. We both lean back, and he crosses his legs again. I slide the ashtray near the edge of the table closer to us as he takes a sip of his own cup of steaming hot coffee. He sits and stares while saying nothing for several minutes.

"Well, I met the *bad cop* already today. So, this must make you the *good cop*?" I ask.

He gives a slight grin. "Neither. I'm just the Sheriff."

"Well now. An actual Sheriff. I'm flattered."

"Don't be sarcastic with me. This could be a lot worse." he says as his grin fades. "I'm not here to have a dick measuring contest with you. Let's get right to it. My deputy says you went at him out there when he was looking over your truck?" he asks.

"Nice try there. You all talk the same just looking to hem up anyone over anything. *Just let the courts deal with them*, that type of thing?" I ask.

"You're not under arrest here. You haven't been read your rights as if you were being investigated for a crime. Anything you say to me here can be thrown out, and I can't hold it against you. You can walk out anytime you please."

"But you're not gonna let me do that, are you?"

"Nah. I need details, not a confession. Save all that shit for the movies." he says, while taking a drag of his Marlboro.

"But you just said I could walk out anytime I want."

"Yeah. I said that. But, as soon as you walk out, I'll turn around and arrest you for interfering with an investigation, operating a vehicle with an open alcoholic container, public nuisance, hunting without proper license, assault with a deadly weapon, assaulting an officer, resisting arrest, and… Well… Whatever else I can think of that applies to your being here. You'll be booked, your picture taken, appear before a judge when they get to you. The whole nine yards. But, you already know how this works. Don't you?"

They've looked up my record already. This guy means business. But with all the potential charges he just spatted off, he didn't say murder.

"Listen to me." he says as he put out his cigarette. "I have a pretty good idea what happened out there. Did you know who this guy was that you say you found?" he asks.

"No, but we found him dead out there. I'd never seen him before. I don't know anybody in the area here."

"*We*… So, there's more than one of you? A hunting group or…?"

"No, it was just me and another guy that lives out there near the shores. We both came across the body after he helped me out when I got attacked by the same thing that killed this Ricky guy. He found me almost dead, too. Whatever killed Ricky, almost did the same thing to me. Knocked me outta my tree-stand from twenty feet up."

"Who is this other guy that helped you?"

"His name was James. He's an older black guy that has a living shack, or something like that out there near some abandoned fueling docks on the coastline."

"*Right*, I think I know who and where you're talking about." he says as he rolls his eyes at me.

"Well, James heard the gun shots from Ricky and went looking for him, but he found me first. I told him the cops might want to talk to him, to help track down the remains. He'll tell you the same thing I just did. We found him like that."

"We'll see if we can track him down. Did you hear Ricky's gunshots too?"

"Yeah, but I didn't think nothing of it. Just a bunch of drunks taken down a doe or…"

"Was Ricky, maybe, shooting at you?" he asks.

"No, I never said that. I don't know for sure what it was he was shooting at. It's like a mangled rabid bear or something that almost killed me before James found me almost unconscious."

"Does this *James* have a last name?"

"He may have mentioned it, but I can't remember." I really can't remember if I even asked for his last name before we went our separate ways. I start to scratch my head to think until the Sheriff speaks up again.

"*Right…* An older black man, homeless, came to your aid, and he lives in the woods is your alibi. Listen, if this was a *hunting accident*, understand how this may play out in a courtroom. You got a deputy in there that claims you jumped him and found a missing persons wallet on your person."

"I didn't kill him. Something else did. More than killed him. It tore him apart at the limbs."

"Ok, then…" as he sits back and collects his thoughts. Hard to tell where his mind is at if he thinks I did something to this other hunter or not. The room is warm enough to start sweating now.

"Many people don't look at us the same as other folks." he says.

"What do you mean?" I ask as he lights up another cigarette and offers me one, too.

"Us… Veterans… they don't look at us the same. There's been so many studies about this type of shit. Most of them come from doctors that have never even picked up a damn weapon." he says.

"They know they train us to be lethal. We are trained to be dangerous and do dangerous things that most people only see in video games. We do just that when we leave this place to go to some distant desert fighting in a third world country were even toilet paper is a hot commodity. We are rewarded for doing what we are trained to do there, to be lethal. But that gratitude only comes while still in the ranks. We do those same things out here though, in the *real world* as they call it, then we get punished for doing things we're expected to do. Now just how fucked up is that? To be put down like that?"

"You're not telling me anything I don't already know, Sheriff," as I shake my head. Where in the hell is he trying to go with this crap?

"Right… When they need us, they'll always call? But when they don't want us, they are terrified of us. They feel threatened by us somehow. Isn't that crazy? Here's where it gets even more fucked up. The studies from professors and shit like that, ya know they say that in today's current society, *America* I mean, an estimated four percent of the population show traits of being sociopathic enough to take a life. As in to actually intend to kill someone and end a life. For whatever reason, doesn't matter. The fact is that they are willing to end someone's life if given the *opportunity*.

Now, here's the caveat to that, as there is a difference between a sociopath and a psychopath. The sociopath, that's the four percent now, only has the ability or willingness to kill someone if given the opportunity. However,… the psychopath feels compelled to manipulate the situation they are in and create a moment so that they *can* commit to their desire to end a life. It's simple really… the psychopath creates an environment to where they can kill, but the sociopath kills only when it is opportunistic. Either way, they are both *willing* to make the kill and fall in the four percentile. Here's the creepy part of it. I question how many of each type fall within that specific four percent of society, whether it be the sociopath or the psychopath. Even worse, how many of that four percent, of either type, make their way into the military ranks being totally unnoticed of these traits I just mentioned?"

"I'm sure I could say the same thing about law enforcement personnel."

"What do you mean?" he asks.

"How many of this four percent carry a gun and a badge on a daily basis?"

"Good question. That being said and knowing that four percent can make their way into any branch of the military, or to entertain your thought process and apply it to law enforcement, can we blame them?"

"What do you mean?" I ask.

"Well, ya know. If they resort to the extreme violence they are meant to do. The type of violence that they are expected to do. Can we blame them?"

"Well... No, I guess not. But... It depends I guess."

"It depends?"

"Yeah... I mean, I guess... I don't know."

"Let's put you in the judge and jury seat for a second here. You got somebody like you or even me on trial. You've heard the case and you know the details, through and through. But let's complicate this a little and say that the individual on trial has been legitimately diagnosed as the four percent of the population that has an anti-social disorder like I just explained. It could have been a mere hunting accident but knowing that there is a diagnosis in place for that person who falls in the four percent, it brings into question as to that individual's true intent. Maybe they have been diagnosed with a type of anti-social disorder, but it was never properly treated. Maybe they haven't been properly diagnosed and that issue of falling into the realms of the four percent was used as a benefit in a different environment where it was needed. But now, that individual is back here, in the real world. The real world where the four percent is deemed the "*scary* people". Can you blame that person on trial for committing such an act of violence? Can you really be that shocked to discover that they have killed *again*?"

"I... I don't think so. Where are you going with this?"

"So, what would you, as judge and jury, do? Would you give this guy a break and help him seek the clinical help he or she needs? There are all kinds of counseling, therapy, medication, you name it, that could help someone like that reintegrate back into the norm of things, without being deemed a continued threat to those that may not understand them. Of course, they would have to accept some ramifications and responsibility for committing an act such as killing when it wasn't necessary, but only when that person is mentally coherent enough to understand that what they used to do was right in one environment, but wrong in another type of environment."

"I… um…"

"Or would you see that he or she was aware of what they were doing, all along. That people are not born with the desire to commit violence, thus discrediting the four percent notion. This leaves no choice but to accept the concept that falling into that four percent category is a choice, and not necessarily a genetic trait or mental illness. Therefore, you as judge and jury have to punish them accordingly. What would you do?"

"What?"

"What would you do, if you were judge or jury dealing with an individual like that? After you knew they committed such acts of violence, but you also knew they fell into that four percent?"

"I… uh…" This is really confusing, but hard to argue with. I've openly admitted to being dangerous to so many in my life, but I didn't want to believe it either. What if I did something to someone? They said this would happen. They said it would be hard to remember things sometimes.

"Listen to me." as the Sheriff interrupts my concerns. "If there was an incident out there, hunting accident or otherwise, it can be dealt with beyond just watching the hammer drop on you. That's all the courts care about these days, anyway. Just get the damn conviction, throw the person in an overcrowded jail, and nothing more. There are means to get the help people deserve. Especially, guys like us."

"Guys like us?"

"Yeah, guys like us. I was in the service same as you, man. You've just gotten out a lot more recently than I did a few years back now. They all look at us the same. A problem. A person who threatens their safety with just our mere presence in a room with them. Because they know what we are all capable of. So, tell me, what would you do if you were the judge there in that scenario?"

"Neither."

"What do you mean?" he asks.

I know where he is going with this now and he almost had me. "A" for effort there, Sheriff, but we're nothing alike. I didn't even notice his entire stance had changed in front of me at some point. He's now leaned toward me in his chair within arm's reach. Those eyes still stare directly at me, though.

"I would do neither."

"That's not the option in the matter. You…"

"You said *if* I was judge or jury in this matter," interrupting him for the first time. "I would do neither. I would stop listening to what others said about him. I would stop making the worst assumption and let the person actually talk. You said it yourself, *Sheriff*. People that make up these statistics, those turds probably never even picked up a damn gun in their lives. They would never know what that person needs after the things they had to do… And you 're *nothing* like me."

"How so?" he asks.

"You hide the idea of being part of the four percent behind a gun and a badge. Do you tell yourself that speech in your head on your way to work every morning? Tell yourself that what you do is the right thing because your type is necessary? How many times have you said that speech to yourself or told others that same thing after some petty crime and you lock them up, anyway? That's a great show, Sheriff. You had me going there for a sec, I won't lie. But I didn't kill anybody."

"How's your wife doing?"

"We're not going there…"

"Oh yeah we are. You already know we searched your record. Have we upgraded from a pathetic drunk to killer now? Let's make a road map for the jury on this one. Domestic violence, to divorce, to discharge from the military, to *pathetic and whiny* drunk living in his truck, to assault with a deadly weapon, to murder one. Seems like a believable scenario to me. Especially if I was a judge or jury."

"Well, it's a good thing you 're neither."

"No, you're right. I'm neither. I'm just the Sheriff." he says again. How many times is he going to remind me of that? Insecure prick.

112

"And you're just as fucking miserable as I am. That's the only thing we got in common here. How's *your* wife, sheriff? You ever given her that same speech?"

"This isn't about me, asshole. You're the one that came in with cuffs on after resisting arrest and interfering with an investigation."

"If you would close your damn mouth and let me talk. Your investigation would go a lot quicker. And that resisting arrest charge would never fuckin stick. Not after that whole comment on how I haven't been given my rights yet and I can leave anytime I want. I already told you people; I don't know what I saw out there. Must have been like a rabid bear or something like that."

He goes quiet for a moment. Maybe I have him stumped, but light has just turned on in his head.

"You said earlier that Ricky had been *torn apart*. What do you mean? Torn apart like how?"

His demeanor is totally changed now. He isn't even looking at me. He's staring down at the floor. Almost worried about something somehow. Paranoid and lost in some deep thought.

"Yeah. It ripped his arms and legs off."

"But were they hanging from the trees?" he asks sternly.

"What?"

"His arms and legs, dammit! Were they left hanging in trees near the body?" as he stands up in front of me. He's on edge without warning. This entire conversation he was calm until now.

"His limbs were hanging from the trees, weren't they?" he asks with an uneasy voice.

"I… I don't know what I the hell I saw out there, anymore."

"You go from saying a damn bear attacked you both, to now you don't know what attacked you?! Tell me what the fuck did you see out there?! Tell me right fucking now!"

The Sheriff jumps me and lifts me by my jacket off the chair. Holy shit, he is strong, but not very nimble. My jacket rips the rest of the way. He kicks the chair I was sitting on aside and tries to pin me against the back wall. His eyes have a crazed yellow tint to them. As my legs dangle inches off the floor, I jerk my leg up to knee him in the torso as hard as I can to throw him off balance and he growls in pain. He raises back up again to throw a hard right jab that has enough power to go straight through me, but I duck just in time to see him punch his massive fist into the wall right above my head. He jerks his arm out of the destroyed sheetrock as I jump onto his back to choke him out. I have a good grip on his shoulders, but he is too large to wrap my arms around his top half.

There are multiple frantic bangs on the door. Once the other deputies come in, I am done for, but not before I take this miserable jerk to the ground first. He lifts us both upright while I am still clamped to his back and he thrashes about to break my grip. In a sudden burst of raw strength, he rushes to the mirrored glass backwards to slam me into it as hard as he can. Once, and then twice, to shatter the glass on my backside and knock me out of breath to drop to the floor. I try to get my bearing back while on all fours and gasping for air. He is down on one knee trying to do the same, but an aggressive bark comes from outside the room. A dog comes rushing at me through the broken glass of the one-way mirror. I stumble backwards to get away, but this thing is ready for the kill.

"Holy fucking shit!" as I scurry backwards on the floor to get away from the clamping teeth of a pit bull. I glance to see two different colored eyes as it gets ready to lunge as I back into the corner.

"DRAKE, HOLD!!" yells the sheriff.

The dog stops in its tracks but keeps inching its head closer to my face. It's the second time this week I stare down a set of jaws that can break bones. It keeps growling as I try to find more corner to back into. The banging on the door from the other deputies outside stops and they rush to the broken mirror too and look in, but he holds up a hand to signal them to back off. The Sheriff stands upright while holding his side. His torso is bleeding through his uniform right where I kicked him with my knee.

"That's a good boy, Drake." says the Sheriff. As he walks closer, he looks at my ripped-up shirt to see my cuts and bite mark that are still healing. He kneels down to me in the corner and pushes the dog out of his way, but still allows it to stay close to keep me at bay. He reaches over and moves the rest of the sleeve off my shoulder to get a better look at my shoulder that will never heal without scars.

"I'm gonna ask you one last time, before I let my friend here ask you." he says as he still tries to catch his breath. "What the hell did you see out there? Just tell me dammit."

"I told you, I don't know what I fucking saw out there… *But you do. Don't you, Sheriff?*"

He steps back in disbelief. He knows what is out there. He knows all of it. He knows everything.

"Your gonna leave my damn town, but not after I lock you up till all this shit is over with."

"What's a matter, Sheriff? Worried I'll find this thing before you do?"

Chapter 11: The Search Begins

That bastard busted the cap on the catheter when he kneed me. I rush out of the interview room and Drake follows behind, knowing I am hurt. A few deputies and even Rachel are outside the door, still trying to get in. They rush in at him as soon as I am out of the way. I hear them scuffling around inside the room to get him back in cuffs as I make my way back to my office. This has happened before on the job, but only when I am wearing a vest and didn't cover up the catheter properly. I open the office door and Drake rushes in to wait by the locker where my medical supplies are stashed.

"Sheriff? Sheriff? Are you ok? What the hell happened in there?" asks Rachel as she stands by the doorway.

"Asshole got me just right with his knee." as I open the locker. "Close the door, will ya?!"

"Ok, ok" she says.

"Catheter cap, fucking tubes, where is all this shit?!" as I scramble through all the gear and medical supplies. They stay nestled in a bag near the spare dialysis machine. Only two left, but I can always get more down at the hospital. I take my bloodied uniform off and toss it on the desk. My undershirt soaked in most of the bile and blood from the tube.

"Jason?" she asks.

"What?!"

"Just calm down for me, please. Tell me what happened in there?"

I pinch off the tube to get it to stop dripping bile now, but blood surrounds the entire incision site. It slightly ripped the surgery area open. I try to manage all the crap that keeps falling down out of the locker, but there is just so much piled up inside on top of all the rounds and riot gear that never gets used. I feel her hand grab my shoulder to turn me around.

"Don't, I'm fine! I just need to get a cap back on it so it…"

She holds my shoulders from behind. I remember that touch. "It's me, Jason. Calm down and take a seat. Go on, just sit down… Please."

Drake walks over with my spare goody bag in his jaws. He knows when my heart rate is too high. Sweat is pouring off my forehead, too. She leads me over to the couch that sits in my office.

"I need the machine and the pouches right beside it there…"

"I know… I know… Just sit down catch your breath. I will get it."

I take the goody bag from Drake to check my heart rate and sugar levels. They are both way higher than normal. I have to lean back to keep the catheter from pinching my torso. Rachel walks over and takes the cap from my hand that wasn't busy pinching it off.

"Here, just let me take the…"

"No, just hush," as she puts a single finger over my mouth. "We've been here before… Just sit back and let me help you. Ok?"

I shake my head yes. The catheter tube cap is replaced, and she cleans up the surgery incision site where the tube goes into the stomach area.

"When's the last time you had a treatment?" she asks calmly.

"I… I was in the middle of one last night when you called, but I'm fine for now.. Now listen, we need to keep running his name on the computer and see what…"

"*We* are not doing anything right now. Just look at me for a sec. Christ, Jason. Your eyes are tinting yellow. Sit back. How many hours do you need on the machine?"

"Uh… That's the older machine. It doesn't work as fast. So, I…"

"Look at me." she says to me.

I look right at her like she asks. The years have not been helpful to either of us, but those dark brown eyes can calm any man down to look right at them. She puts her hand on the side of my face.

"I'm right here. Look at me… I'm right here, ok Jason. Let's get you plugged in and relaxed. Then you need to tell me what to do here, ok?"

"Ok, Rachel."

Half a dozen tubes and bags all over the floor. Drake lies on the floor, staring at both of us as she sets up the machine. His ears twitch back and forth as it makes its random beeps and buzzes from priming up. It takes a few minutes to start to feel anything. As soon as it starts, though, the exit tube fills with blood and bile. As long as the blood goes away down the exit tube, then no major damage was done. It clears up fast and I can start to feel it do its job as my heart rate lowers.

"Is there any word on where you are on the donor list?"

"Not for months now, Rachel. Kidneys are scarce these days, I guess."

"Wanna tell me what happened in there with him." she asks.

"Was anybody watching the tape."

"You know that camera only does video. We were all watching from the glass until you went at him. Then we realized nobody knew where the spare key was. The key was in your pocket."

"Right. Ok." as I slow down my breathing. "I need a map to point out where the body is at. I think I know the area he is talking about, where he found Ricky's body. Tell all those guys out there not to talk to him and just keep him locked down in the holding cell for now. We're gonna have to go recover the body and… Uh, we need to contact the radio station to put out a message."

"You gotta calm down. Did he kill Ricky?"

"I don't think so, but he tried to tell me he met James Still out there. So, he's still full of shit one way or another. He said he and James found the body and he had been dead for several days."

118

"James Still has been dead for over a hundred years. He tried to get you with that old tale?" she asks as she closes her notepad and kneels in closer to me. The machine beeps a few more times just below her. She readjusts the tubes that scattered all over my lap.

"What *did* he tell you?" she asks.

"Ricky's body was torn apart. Something left the limbs hanging from trees."

"That's sick. Who the hell would do that to Ricky? He was just another nine-to-five guy that drinks too much like anybody else around here. Are you sure that's what he said to you?"

"It's not a matter of who did it, it's what?"

"What do you mean?"

"It doesn't matter for now. I'll explain it all later. I need a map and we gotta send a message to the radio station to put out some information. We gotta put this town on lockdown."

"We can't keep doing this. Nobody's gonna go for it again this time. The last curfew like that was..."

"Was what, Rachel? What was it to you? Unnecessary? Pointless? A waste of effort? You and this town can feel free to stop me when I am finally fucking dead!"

"You don't have to be such a jerk about it to me, you asshole. I'm sorry I left here to find something better, but I came back, dammit. Came back to see you shacked up with some twat outta the city with a kid in the mix. Is that why you're a dick to me? Because I came back after you asked me to, and now you gotta see me every day. Well, guess what, asshole, I gotta see you every day, too! And it kills me knowing that you don't give a shit as to how much I still care. That you're driving yourself insane looking for someone that just isn't there anymore. She's gone, Jason! Maggie is gone!"

"You don't know that! You don't know anything! Now, get the hell outta my office."

"Please, Jason, just please listen to me!"

"No, you listen, God dammit! I want some fucking discipline around here. I come in this place every day and feel like I manage a bunch of damn cub scouts right outta high school. Maggie's out there! She's out there and I WILL FIND HER! I WILL! YOU FUCKIN' WATCH ME!"

She backs away and tries to hold back tears. Her jaw clinches in anger towards me. She resents me now in knowing we can never be what we were that seems like another life ago.

"Now get me a fucking map! This town is on curfew no matter what you or the mayor fucking says, tonight! When I bring back Ricky in a few different body bags because his damn limbs are scattered all over the fuckin barrens, then you will all shut up and do as you're told. I want a message written out for the radio station to make a public broadcast ASAP! I want the prisoner transport van fueled up, loaded with our crime scene gear, and ready to go, cause we're all going out there! We are all going out there so you can see for yourselves that I'm not crazy and I know what needs to be done! Now do your fucking job and quit giving me shit about it!"

"*Who are you?*" she asks.

She turns her back and starts to walk out of the office. She won't let me see her cry. She never would, but I know she is wiping her face. She comes to a stop at the door but refuses to turn around and look at me. She refuses to look at a lost and soulless monster that lives by medical machines going beep into the night, so she stays facing the door. A deputy comes rushing in before she turns the doorknob.

"Sheriff! Sheriff! We just got a call. Someone found one."

"What? Someone else found Ricky's body too?" I ask.

"No, not him. Uh... Well, they think it's a body."

"They *think*? What the hell does that mean?"

"Well... Uh... Cause there ain't much left of it. Whoever it is... Or was, Sheriff."

"Jesus Christ... It's happening again." as I lower my head.

"And there... And there's some reporter outside, Sheriff. What do you want me to tell them? Do you want me to send them away?"

"Tell them the mayor is on his way and he'll be glad to get his face on camera." I look right at Rachel as she stares back at me in shock. "Rachel, will call up the mayor's office now to make sure."

"What do you want us to do with the suspect, Sheriff?" Rachel asks as she glares back at me.

"Let him stew in the holding cell for a while. He'll have no choice but to leave the area after this is all said and done or be arrested and brought up on all the charges I can think of. If he's lied to me or somebody lied to him about this James character, then we'll find out soon enough. Until then, he's nobody and a waste of our time. Let him cry his way to the VA with his own damn problems later on. We have bigger things to worry about now beyond him. I need everybody out of here for a bit, but you have your marching orders. Now go. All of you."

I pull the kids business card for the rehab center out of my wallet out to make the call. I tell them I need my wife picked up with full discretion. They ask me what she is using and the last time she used. They claim that if she had been using within the last few days, it wouldn't be advised to take her in right away. But I lie through my teeth to get them to agree to come and get her. Get this damn junkie out of my house and don't bring her back until it's my wife again that I see. Not this sad excuse of skin and bone that is laid up at my house now. I give them all the information they need and set a time for the padded wagon to show up at my front doorstep to take her back to get clean. She'll be safer in detox while all this shit is going down, no matter how much it costs.

I've only been on the machine, locked away in my office alone with Drake for an hour when Sherral makes her way in and hands me a slip of paper to read. I didn't realize that the day shift had already made their way into the station for the morning.

"What do you think, Sheriff? This is kinda like the last one that we did. Just made it look a bit more official like."

She stands over me as I read over it. "Looks great. I want several hundred copies of these, and I want whoever doesn't come with me to start posting them all over the place in town and as far as our jurisdiction allows. Have them talk to the business owners to tell them the same thing. Tell them I'll be working with the radio station later today to relay the same message."

"I don't think we got enough paper and ink to print that many out, Sherriff."

"Then find it Sherral. You're the administration here and nobody else. That's stuff you're supposed to do. Go on now and make it happen. Go buy it if you have to. I do not care at the moment. Just steal the paper from the damn school if need be." Hard to yell at her as she hobbles out, but she might stroke out if I did that to her. But the county won't let me replace her until she croaks over. She might outlive me at this point.

I step out of the office to rally the morning shift and bring them up to speed. Rachel is still here but gives me a look that tells me that shift work during a time like this doesn't apply. Can't blame her and I won't tell her to go home either. She's the best deputy I got right now. A few deputies stay behind to keep our only suspect in custody inside the holding cell area. The others will make the efforts to post up the flyers in town. Rachel is nearing the end of her shift, so I send her to reach out to the school principals in person to get their thoughts on what they want to do as far as keeping the schools closed with the information we have. We load up and head out in a convoy with me riding shotgun in the inmate transport van. Drake sits in the back behind me but keeps in view out the front wind shield as we drive froward. A deputy patrol car ahead and behind us. The Mayor is still outside the station being a typical politician and creating a diversion. We leave the area unnoticed, traveling on the county route where the last body was spotted. Another deputy patrol unit is already standing by on location.

There has only been solid daylight for a few hours now, but not enough to break through the overcast that is drizzling freezing rain on top of all of us. We block off the entire side of the road, and I step out first to see my youngest deputy. Greeves is a good guy. Younger and inexperienced, with barely any facial hair, but a good guy that knows the area. He grew up here with the people and knows most of the faces. He approaches me right away, and I notice another pickup truck parked in front of him.

"Hey there Greeves. I take it that is the person who spotted it?"

"Yes, Sheriff. This is his property's edge, and he was gathering up some firewood when he saw it."

"Name?" I ask.

"Randal Davis, but no major relation to our Davis down at the station."

"Right. Everybody's related here. I always forget. How far off the roadway is it?"

"It's into the wood line about fifty yards."

"Does he know who it is?"

"No, Sheriff."

"Did you go in?"

"Only far enough to get a visual. Wasn't going any further in without somebody else here."

"That's good. I'm glad you waited till back-up arrived. But you got a visual, right?"

"Yeah. That's right."

"Do you know who it is?" I ask.

He looks down for a bit, and I step closer to him. When I get close enough, I see his face from under the hat. I see his eyes are moving from side to side and his face is pale white. I would blame that on the cold. But he's just terrified and in near shock from whatever it is he saw in there.

"Greeves, look at me... Do you know who it is?"

"I don't think anybody is gonna know who it was, Sheriff. There's nothing left."

I turn around, motion for everybody to step out.

"Ok, I want to see this side of the road to stay blocked off and one deputy out here controlling traffic. Any reporters approach and let me know via radio ASAP. Let's pull out the crime scene tape and start blocking off the area. No civilians are to approach the wood line in either direction from this point to at least fifty yards, going both ways along the road. Let's pull out the cameras and the crime scene gear. I want evidence baggies and everybody that comes in with me needs to be gloved up… Greeves, look at me…", as I walk him over to his patrol car. "I want you to take this Davis guy back to the station and get his statement. Talk to no one, unless they have a gun and a badge. Do you understand?"

"Ok, Sheriff." he says.

"One last question then you're gonna tell the witness what's going on and head out with him. If it was that far into the wood line how did he spot it in the first place?"

"Oh… Yeah… He said he saw a bunch of birds hovering real low into the tree line and some were flying their way across the road, too. He thought there may have been a dead deer carcass or something that had been run over and thrown into the wood line somewhere nearby and…"

"Birds? What kind of birds?" I ask.

"He said owls."

"Was he sure? Maybe like vultures or crows or somethin like that?"

"No, Sheriff. He said it was definitely owls. I asked him that same question too."

"Ok, let the witness know what's going on and head out. And remember… Talk to no one."

"What are you gonna do, Sheriff?" he asks.

"Well… We're gonna go in and see how much a dead person can tell us."

Chapter 12: The Great Escape

This Sheriff doesn't go by the books in this tiny little town. The cage only has a latch locking system with a single padlock on it. There are no guards, and I have spotted no cameras anywhere in the building beyond the front entrance and inside the interrogation room. Where are all the deputies at? Nobody is watching me. The Sheriff has made his presence known with that other female deputy I saw earlier. The dog is a serious problem though. There is no escaping that four-legged monster that creeps the fuck outta me. I hear some scrambling and foot traffic moving around in the next room, but as soon as things go quiet is when I make my move. Daylight comes into the windows that have a half-rigged bar system bolted around it.

The holding cell is nothing more than a large chain link cage you can pick up for cows at a farmer's market. A bed to lay on and a small toilet in the corner that is covered by a shower curtain that wraps around it. What do ya know, the cage doesn't even go all the way to the ceiling. I have climbed tougher things in basic training with pounds of gear on my backside and I wasn't in shape then. I keep the noise low as I lower down on the other side of the fencing. I make my way to the door before I turn the lights off to look beneath it to see if there is any more foot traffic outside, but all is quiet. If anyone were to look through the slender glass window on the door, they would only see the lights are off and think nothing of it. Law enforcement usually wears certain types of shoes that are recognizable from under a door, but there is nothing but old desk chair wheels and the dust that has settled.

The biggest concern would be seeing a set of dog paws walking in front of me, but I don't smell a dog from the other side of the door. Only the slight smell of the same old stale coffee the Sheriff offered me during our conversation. I slowly open the door but keep my head low to the ground. The first place a concerned person would look at for an individual is at eye level. No one ever thinks to look down to see a person's face or weapon at the floor level. No foot traffic and no feet visible at the few desks I see all the way to the front of the entrance, except for one. Those are not typical shoes for a deputy or cop. It looks like an older woman's shoes. It's not every day that you would low crawl through a Sheriff's station. I keep low and open the door as far as needed to get a full view of the room. The interrogation booth is in sight and the glass shattered from earlier has already been swept up.

I raise my head at waist level to get a better look at the room, but there is only one person with her back turned to me at the moment. She gets up in a struggled movement and I duck down to avoid her view. She is not a deputy but old enough to have retired at least a decade ago. I haven't seen her before, and she hasn't seen me since they brought me in. She doesn't notice me as she goes away from her desk to heat a new pot of coffee at a small table in the corner. I keep low crawling beside the desks to make my way to the entrance door. That door was locked when I was brought in and may pose a problem. There is a sliding glass window for the front desk clerk, but I can't remember how wide it opens. I see a tiny fire brick holding the entrance door open. What kind of Sheriff's Department is this?

You never leave an entrance unsecure like this. No time to question a good thing. The older lady is still messing with the microwave and doesn't realize its unplugged. I slowly open the door and move the brick out of my way to inspect the camera that faces the receptionist's front desk. As long as it doesn't rotate to the front entrance we are home free, but without my gear and truck, I'll never get very far as soon as they realize I'm gone. Some of these fat ass deputies may not be on top of their game, but the Sherriff will come for me with a fury. Time to take a risk as I slide out the door on my belly and put the brick out of the way to close the door behind me.

It wasn't a sliding glass window. It only has a small opening on the bottom to slide papers under neath it and a slot opening to talk through. I stand upright to see the older lady still committing to making a new pot of coffee and I knock on the glass window. She looks back at me, startled and confused, as she walks over to sit back at her desk. She is just a receptionist but doesn't recognize me. She has never seen me before. She smiles, which lowers my concerns for not making a clean exit.

"Hello Sir. How can I help you?... Oh, my goodness. Are you ok? You look like you got hurt in a car wreck or something?" she asks.

"Oh... Um... Yes I did. I got banged up pretty bad. They just let me out of the doctor's office, but they cleared me good to go." This couldn't be easier for me.

"My goodness, young man. You look like you got lucky in that one then. Boy, I tell ya. Come winter storm season, these guys are always on call with people sliding off into a ditch or hitting each other on the main roads going too fast." she says.

"Nope. I'm good. Just slapped my head on the steering wheel a bit. But it didn't mess up the truck last I checked. Just a ditch I slid off into is all. So... Uh, I wasn't sure who to ask about my truck. I was told they brought it in and to head to the Sheriff's Station and it should be there."

"Oh... Right." she says as she looks around for paperwork. "A white dodge pickup truck, right? I think I saw that one when I came in earlier."

"Right, that's mine."

She shuffles through some paperwork but does not know what she is looking for. "Well, I can't find the release paperwork on it, but the Sheriff is out at the moment. I'm not sure how long he will be out. So, I'll just have you sign off on this one and I'll fill in the rest later when he gets back. Or better yet how long are you in town for?" she asks.

"Well, not very long. I was just passing through when I slid off the road last night."

"My goodness. Well, I'm glad you're ok at least. I remember when I slid off the road a few years back. I thought they would never get it out then. Messed up my ankle pretty bad then."

"Well, looks like it didn't mess you up too bad, miss. You 're still upright and walking, right?" I say with a smile. I could play along with this for a while. She'll tell him what I nice young man I was. She'll tell them that she handed off the paperwork for me to sign. She'll say she was clueless about me being locked up in there in the holding cell. Then they will realize their department is an absolute shit show. Maybe I don't have to worry about orchestrating a clean getaway.

"Right, still up and walking at seventy-two." she proclaims.

"What... I would have never guessed a day over mid-fifties?".

She giggles and smiles back while still searching her desk for paperwork and pen. Always good to indulge people in a compliment. It keeps their guard down, but the more time I spend here, the less luck I have. Two deputies walk in the front door from behind me, reeking of cheap cigarettes. They are lost in their own conversation about a steak house down in Atlantic City. They don't pay me any attention with the receptionist not appearing concerned or worried either. I turn my head away from them, so they don't see my recent bruising.

"Yeah man... It was like a forty-dollar plate at that casino me and the wife go to all the time when we dump the kids off at her mom's, but it is well worth it." one deputy says to the other.

"Dude... I haven't had a juicy prime like that in a while... Ah crap. We must have not put the brick in the door. Hey there Sherral! Can you open the door back up? We locked ourselves out again."

She gets up from the chair to let them in. "You boys smoke too much. Isn't it too cold to be out there, anyway?" she asks them like a mother that scolds her children. She comes back to her seat. It's just a matter of time before they realize the light in the holding cell area is off and I am not here. They just go right to the coffee area, though. She slides the paperwork under the window with a pen to sign the highlighted area, but the rest of the document is blank.

"Oh, don't worry about it." she tells me. "This sort of thing happens all the time when vehicles have to get towed back into town. If we know them, we rarely even go through this process."

"No, I understand. Somebody's got keep up with what's going on here." as I sign the form with a random name. "So, tell me, miss. Is there any way of knowing where all my gear was taken to? I had a hunting rifle in the truck, so they may have taken it out for safe keeping somewhere?"

"Here? Na, they wouldn't have anywhere to lock it up, anyway. I would check in your truck to see if they locked it up in there with a trigger lock for safe keeping over at the bus garage area behind the building. That kinda works as our impound lot for the station too." she says.

"Ok, then. That works." I tell her as I hand the paperwork back to her after not filling out any information. "Well, just be sure to tell the Sheriff I said thanks for his help when he gets back. Speaking of which, where are all the deputies at today. I thought I saw a lot more patrol cars earlier?"

"Oh, you may not have heard. There has been another bear attack that hurt some people. They're putting the town on curfew tonight to keep the kiddos safe."

"A bear?" I ask.

"Oh yeah. Must be a big one too because it already hurt one person. That's where the Sheriff is at now." she replies.

"Well, hopefully all is well in your quiet lil town here, but I'm out the door. You take care miss and thanks for your help."

"No problem, young man. You be careful out there. They're calling for another cold front coming in tonight and it'll bring in some more snow too. Probably a good thing he's putting in a curfew tonight. I hate driving in the snow this time of year. My lil car and my nerves can't handle it anymore. I'll call the bus garage and let them know you're coming by for your truck."

"Will do miss. Thanks again for the info." as I turn around to see the front door of the building. I stop to look up at the camera and notice it was looking at my backside while I was playing with the receptionist. Hopefully she doesn't get in too much trouble from watching me leave out the front door. I give the camera a salute anyway, just for the asshole Sheriff to see whenever he realizes I am gone.

It's pushing past midday outside now. Just enough time to get out of the area before this curfew and the band of dumbass deputies see I am missing from the sad excuse of a holding cell. I turn the corner of the building to see the cluster of school buses, ambulances, sheriff's vehicles, and sure enough, my white dodge sitting next to a few cars that have seen better days. It is all fenced in, but it served little purpose, as they left the gates wide open for anyone to just walk in. The garage had a few workers or mechanics in it, and what appears to be a foreman sitting in an office. The mechanics just sit around, smoking and joking, without a second glance in my direction.

"Can I help you?" the foreman asks.

"Yes, the sheriff's station sent me over to pick up my truck. I went off into a ditch the other…"

Interrupting me with a scold, "Oh yeah, right, they just called over about that one. White dodge pickup truck, right?"

He turns around in his chair to look at the wall of keys and searches through them with a clip board of paperwork in his hand.

"I'll just need your ID and a signature right here saying it was picked up." as he pulls my keys off the wall. I sign a random name without hesitation, and I pull out a random business card that I grabbed off the receptionist's desk when she was looking for paperwork. He doesn't know that it isn't an actual ID while I hold it in my hand, even though he just asked for one. Wow… If I was a lesser individual, I could take this town for all they got.

"We'll be shutting down the garage for the curfew soon. So, if you gotta go through your stuff, you gotta do it outside the gate and then head on out. They just kind of threw all your stuff in the back-camper area. You trying to sell that old Marlin off anytime soon? That sure was a nice one you had in there? I bet old Jeppiess would love to add that to his shop down the road there."

"Oh, you saw that. Yeah, people have been trying to buy that one off of my dad when he was still alive too. I'm sorry but I'm not from around here, but what is *Jeppiess*?" I ask.

"Yeah, they don't make 'em like that one anymore. Hard to find them like that since the Marlin company went to crap in a basket. Anyway, Jeppiess Pawn and Outfitters are on the other side of town there. He's got all kinds of hunting gear, but a lot of the older firearms like yours just sit in there for years. Not too many collectors round here. Can't afford 'em unless you use them."

"Jeppiess Pawn? I'll have to check that place out. Sorry, but did I hear you say curfew?" I ask him in a dumbfounded voice.

"Yeah, another curfew in effect. Looking for that damned ol' bear again. Least that's what they blame it on. Anyone out past a certain time is subject to arrest."

"I'm lost. I thought they were worried about some hunters that had gone missing. Are they worried about a bear strolling through downtown now too?" I ask. It's always best to play dumb with, well... dumb people.

"Damn, boy, you really ain't from around these parts, are ya? You got a few hours to be out of the area or locked down inside somewhere, plain and simple." he says as he snarls back at me. If I only had a dime for every time I heard, *you ain't from around here* since I showed up over a week ago, I would have a lot more cash in my pocket by now. I take my keys off the counter and walk over to my truck. I see multiple sheriff patrol vehicles and a school bus behind another gated area on the other side of my truck. My curiosity gets the better of me, but I have made it this far already without incident.

I move past my truck to take a closer look at the school bus all bashed in and busted up. One of the front wheels is turned sideways under the engine housing from a major impact. Maybe running off into a ditch? It shattered the entire windshield on the driver side and stained a dull brown. This thing is weathered and covered in dust. It has been sitting here for a while. They locked the folding doors shut from the inside. I look down the side of the bus and see more brown stains and splatter marks. It's old dried blood that has been weathered and also surrounding claw marks. Deep claw marks that penetrated the sheet metal on the side right through the name of the public school district.

"Hey! You ain't supposed to be in here, fella!" yelling at me from across the parking area. It's one of the garage mechanics I saw earlier joking around when I was at the foreman's desk.

"Oh, I'm sorry. I was just here to pick up my truck, and I saw this mess back here." playing dumb tourist now. At least he is younger and seems more approachable.

"Oh, that one. Yeah that's a pretty sad sight to see there." he says while shaking his head. I walk out of his way and make my way back to my truck and he pulls out a pair of keys to close the gate to this area and locks it up once I'm out of his way. I notice the gate has a specific sign on it when he closes it that says *authorized personnel only*.

"What happened?" I ask.

"Welp. That was before I moved back here a while ago. Bus Driver got himself killed by a bear after he slide off into a ditch."

"Did he slam through the front windshield or something?"

"*Or something* is my best guess. With all those claw marks on the side, they ain't no tellin', because I don't believe that whole "bear" story either."

"Were there kids on board going to school?" I ask.

"Yeah, but nobody knows what happened to them. Almost a dozen of them, but I don't know the entire story. The mayor has tried to get the Sheriff's department to take it out of here to the scrap yard for a while now. But the Sheriff just comes in and says the same thing every time. *It's still evidence of an ongoing investigation* or something like that. They never could find all those kids. Pretty sad cause one of the kids was the Sheriff's lil girl, I hear. A lot of them parents already moved away to start over somewhere else. Especially after the state PD came in and called off the search. The Sheriff, he just won't let this one go."

"What about the driver? Did they find him?"

"Oh yeah. They found him. But he was more than dead, and his innards were torn out. Bear don't do that kinda damage to a person. Like I said, it happened before I moved back here. They found most of him in pieces, but they said the one thing missing was his heart. But I'd like to think that part is just a rumor though."

"You moved back to this little town?"

"Yeah, after a few semesters of college. That didn't pan out. I came back, and it was the biggest mistake I made thus far."

"Really...?"

"Yeah. I was raised here, but every time we go through one of the Sheriff's lockdowns, more businesses just close their doors for good and more people just move away."

"Should've stayed in school, right?" I ask jokingly. As I take one last look at the bus behind the now locked gates.

"Right. Well, mister. Gotta have you pull on out. We gotta close up the main gates now. Sorry to rush ya after an accident and all. But it looks like the truck came out cleaner than you did."

"Not a problem. I'm be outta your way in just a sec."

As I move to my truck, it makes sense why the Sheriff went at me like he did in the booth. This is just as personal to him as it is to me now. I can see my rifle through the back glass as I unlock it. It's the most critical item that needs to be there, along with my wallet still in an evidence baggie. I start her up and head out the gate unnoticed. I drive down the road to a small gas station to fill my tank. A deputy vehicle enters the gas station as I pull in to fill up. It wasn't one of the same guys from the station. It was a younger one that still had spots on his face under that hat of his. He jumps out and places a sign on the door regarding the curfew. Why the sudden rush to lock the area down? Something else has to have happened, like the receptionist said. Nobody is out and about. Once the truck tank is filled up, I walk over to inspect the flyer.

By order of the Mayor and Sherriff's Department
All residents are mandated to abide by township curfew no later than 7PM tonight and may resume normal activities at 7AM the following day until further

notice. This is in effect due to dangerous wildlife concerns that have been made known within the last week. The Sheriff is requesting that you call their office immediately in the event of spotting any and all threatening wildlife within the area, before, during, and after curfew hours. Sheriff's Department contact information is written below. We highly advise residents to remain indoors during curfew hours and that children remain attended by adult supervision at all times. Please tune in to our local broadcast station for any changes in the situation. Any and all persons not abiding by the information relayed in this curfew order is subject to arrest and fines.

Seven o'clock? That's plenty of time to restock on goods. I step back over to the truck and look up and down the empty road to see a single red light that flashes yellow. I decide to take a drive through the main street. The town looks like it came out of a rerun of the Andy Griffith Show. Except there are no happy town folks walking up and down outta the local grocers. Once I pull into a grocery store, I see they are still open and head inside the entrance to find the ATM.

I look around inside the grocery area to see a few shoppers remaining, but most of the workers are sweeping and closing up the store. Nobody sees me by the entrance. The ATM shoots out so many twenties I can't even fit them in my wallet. I add it all together with the few fifties I already had in hand and head back to the truck. I can always find food in any type of wooded environment and stay warm with most of the dirty clothes I still got in my ruck. What I don't have are enough bullets to go back into the woods to kill anything worth killing. I'm gonna need a lot. The magazine tube will have to be filled to the very end and more 30-30 rounds to spare on my person too.

The town appears dark beyond the single traffic light. If this pawn shop is already closed, I'll have to wait and hide out behind an empty business until morning before heading out again. Hopefully it is easy to find, like the guy at the bus garage said. I don't want to do this, but I've got no other choice now. There is nowhere else to go and I know what I have to do. This is what I am supposed to do. I start the truck up to see the outside temperature on the gauge cluster begin dropping in front of me. This journey will only get colder from here.

Chapter 13: The Body

"Ok, once we're in far enough and we see the remains, I'm gonna need a twenty-to-thirty-foot radius around the body. If you see footprints, clothing, weapons, claw marks on a damn tree, or anything beyond the actual remains, do not touch it! Do not move it! We need photographs of everything before attempting to move the remains and have them identified along with cause of death. What we are looking for is evidence, evidence, and more evidence as to what caused…"

One deputy is lighting a cigarette while we are prepping to go into the wood line, oblivious to anything I am saying right now. I walk up to him and startle him as I approach and flick the cigarette out of his mouth onto the road beside him.

"Oh… Uh, my bad Sheriff."

"Yes, deputy. It will be bad if you get ashes in my crime scene and footprints all over the damn place, because you're not listening. Any clue what I just said? What if I told you the bear was spotted in the area less than a few minutes ago?"

"I think we would've seen a bear by now. It's just a body."

"Well, I guess it is a good thing you got a strong stomach, then. I tell you what. Why don't you grab the shotgun out of the van and take point then, shithead?"

He walks away from me to the van until I stop him. "Pick up your fucking cigarette while you're at it, too. We fine for littering in this county last I checked." He bends over to pick it up. The two other deputies are nervous and under dressed for a walk in the woods this time of the year. The other comes back with the shotgun.

"Is the county coroner on the way?" I ask the deputy, looking out for traffic.

"He is, Sheriff. Should be bout a couple of hours."

"A couple of hours?!"

"He's coming all the way out of the city again."

"Let's get this going. We'll start losing daylight by the time he shows up."

The deputy with the shotgun moves out first. I keep the crime scene duffle bag on the side of my off-firing hand and unclip the safety on my holster. The air is frosty, but the smell is just lingering in the trees. It's the fresh smell that tells me the bowels haven't even begun expanding their gasses yet. We walk in until the road is just out of sight and we see it. I hold the crew and they spread out as soon as I toss them the police caution tape to spread around the area. Two of them make the circle around the body. Shotgun lead boy stays with me. I snap two long-range photos for distance reference from the road to the remains and close in.

"I need you to walk behind me. Try not to blast me in the back with that scatter gun and walk in my same footsteps. The other two guys are maintaining the perimeter. So, I just need you to keep your eyes peeled to the ground to see anything out of place, but a set of animal prints. Ok?"

"Ok, Sheriff."

"You'll be fine. Just do as you 're told. It's a bear. Nothing more. Just keep moving behind me."

We move in closer and I can see the other two deputies have already made it to the back side of the remains. There it is. That beautiful scent of fresh blood splashed from one tree to the next. That's Leeds alright. That's his call sign. The body is left strung upside down on a pine tree. As I move closer, I see it isn't hanging. It has been nailed upside down and stripped naked from head to toe. Both feet were nailed

136

through with a large square peg. I drop down to a knee and open up the evidence bag and glove up. These stupid things are never big enough as I rip a glove trying to slide it on. The deputy behind me vomits from the horrid sight of the body hanging lifelessly upside down, frozen in a panic with arms torn out from both sides.

"Get back to the fucking patrol cars and direct traffic before you puke all over the crime scene, fuck head. Go on. Now you can have yourself a smoke when you get there."

"I'm... I'm sorry Sheriff. I... What the hell did that?"

"Just get back to the road... Now... and leave the shotgun here next to the bag."

The deputy makes his way back and I hand signal the other deputies to hold in place for a 180-degree vantage point surrounding me. I grab the camera again and turn the flash on. The sun tries to come and go under overcast and my breath fogs the viewing screen if I hold it to my face for too long. The throat has been slashed open by a massive set of claws, but I have seen no footprints from claws yet. He's done this before. Ol' Leeds likes to sling them around like a toy when they are bleeding out and screaming for their last desire to live. It ripped the arms out first. A person can live after having their arms torn off. Neither of his arms are in sight on the perimeter. But it slit the throat last to finish the job. Give me a sign. Tell me something, anything. The nubs of one shoulder bone are bloody, but it broke the other arm off at the bicep area.

The camera goes off with multiple flashes at a time as I get closer. Why is it upside down? Where are the arms? Not a lot of cover in the immediate area to keep the body hidden. Other than the wood line near the road, this section is cleared out. Almost as if an entire audience was watching this sick monster work. The footprints everywhere are hard to see in the near frozen marshiness of the ground, but they are tiny. Not a normal man's footprint. Kids may have been here before this poor bastard was torn apart. If a child saw this mess, I would like to think it would have been called in by a parent. Several of the footprints from tiny feet have already filled with blood. Some of them are darker blood than others. The kidneys give out that darker blood like that from not being filtered in the blood stream yet. Those prints were there before this bastard got himself killed for whatever reason, so I snag a few more photos of them too. I look closer at the square peg that is slammed into the feet. Not something that could be bought at a typical hardware store. Something that would have to be made from a metal worker. It has forced the nail into the large pine through the achilleas tendons to hold the entire body up. I scroll down the body with the camera, taking flashes every few seconds.

A single knee has been scrapped down to bone, but the other leg has over half the calf muscle torn out. He must have been trying to run before it caught his leg. Those claws have to be massive to do that type of damage to a calf muscle, or maybe it was bitten off. What was this guy doing out here? There's too much frozen brown blood everywhere for the kill not to have happened here. What are you doing Leeds? What do you want from us? I keep scanning down to see his shriveled cock dangling over open and bloodied intestines. The small slit in the gut just above the groin differs from the last one, though. Only a small piece of intestine hangs loose, but it is doing its typical gaseous bulge. This poor fuck has been hanging here for at least 24 hours. The body starts to blimp up around the gut after about 18 hours in. The face has had over half the beard ripped off. Everywhere has claw slash marks from head to toe. There are no smaller claws or bite marks from other scavenger type animals looking for a free meal. There is no sign of other animal life anywhere, actually. This much blood slung around, and I should at least see some koon or coyote prints somewhere. But there is nothing like that anywhere around me that I can see.

"You ok in there, Sheriff?" one deputy asks on the hand walkie.

"I'm good. Just keep your head on a swivel out there for me, yeah." as I wave to him near the perimeter with a thumbs up.

The camera snaps more photos of the joint sticking out where one shoulder used to be. The throat muscles are enlarged. I have only seen that when someone is left screaming for too long and crying for help for hours upon end. Lots of veins protrude from the neck and shoulder area from excessive blood flow while being left to hang upside down. But he was still alive when nailed to the tree. Blood wouldn't flow that fast to his head and neck if it wasn't beating. The other shoulder still has some bone visible from the upper arm area under the torn muscles and veins.

I used to think I would never get used to the smell when I would do these things. But you can't look at this corpse as a person anymore. That person is gone. It is a means to understand what did this to him and why. These trends are hard to understand beyond placing blame on absolute madness and horror from something that just wants to kill without reasoning. There has to be something to answer why it keeps doing this and why it becomes more frequent each time it happens.

The head is stretched downward to look at the forest floor with the mouth wide open as if he was screaming till the very end of it all. Frozen in his last breath, ending with a tortured and demonic demise. I lean down on my stomach to get the camera at the ground level to take the picture from multiple angles. I stand back up to look at the camera and see that one eye is missing, but there is something stuck inside the eye socket. I lean back down again to get a glimpse of whatever it is shoved inside there. I adjust the head and take a better photo of it while it is still inside the socket. His other eye is wide open and bulging from his skull. He looks right at me without movement from that eye.

"Sorry fella. I know this must have been scary. But you gotta tell me what happened here somehow." as if he would come back to life and try to answer back. But nobody answers, and he doesn't even blink back at me. Just a lifeless and frightened stare from that single eye only a few inches from the ground.

I move back to the evidence bag and pull out a pair of needle-nose pliers from the small tool kit. I walk back over and lean back down on the ground. I have to be careful moving this head around or this whole body will rip off the giant nail holding it up by the feet. I slowly pull out a small piece of rolled tissue or paper that is too bloody from the outside to see what it is. More photos as I pull it out of his socket. I stand back up to place it on an evidence bag, but I need to unroll this before it goes into the bag. I remember the last ones had something like this in their eye socket. They all had one eye yanked out of the socket with the brain chord still left in place, but most wouldn't look close enough to see what is inside other than a hollow place where their eye used to be. It unfolds to about the size of an index card, but there is no blood on the inside of the folds.

"Still good, Sheriff? You were over here a while." asks the deputy I left to control traffic.

"I thought I said to make sure vehicles that pass by don't get too curious."

"Yeah, but I figure the one guy puking his guts out on the side of the road would divert their attention more than a deputy waving them by could. Not a lot of traffic right now, anyway."

"Can't argue with that. Gimme a hand here and pull out the tweezers from the evidence bag. This piece of paper might rip on me if I'm not careful here."

"Ok.", as he walks over to the bag. When he comes back with the tweezers in hand, he stops to stare at the body hanging from a tree head down.

"Try not to look at it, kid. That's somethin you can never unsee. Hold on to this camera here and start taking pictures when I get this thing unfolded." as I hand him the camera.

"I thought evidence like this always had to be processed?"

"True, but if it is evidence that is immediately actionable in the investigation, then it is worth the risk of outside contamination."

"Where was it? Laying near him or something, Sheriff?" he asks.

"Nope... Inside his eye socket."

"Are you fuckin serious? What the..."

"Don't get your nerves up, just stay calm, keep looking at me, and focus with that camera. Just try to ignore the dead guy hangin around behind me while I open this up to read it."

"Jesus, Uh... Ok."

He keeps snapping photos when it is fully opened. A few bloody spots seeped into the inside of the note. That cursive is old looking and reddish brown. I hope it's not blood, but I wouldn't be surprised at this point either.

"What does it say, Sheriff?" he asks.

Follow me and I will make you eaters of men.
Come to thy table and we shall devour thy own heart of darkness, together.

"The hell does that mean?" he asks.

"Didn't go to Sunday School did ya, kid."

"Well... I..."

"It's a Biblical reference, dumbass. *Fishers of Men.*"

"I knew that. But it is written *eaters of men* not *fishers of men?*" he says.

"I'll have to do some research on this one when we get back. Could be a direct stab at the teachings of Christ, or even a reversal of it. I can't remember much about what it says about fishers of men. This is just implying the exact opposite. Was there any word on the coroner?" I ask.

"Oh... Uh, still no word. Sheriff, what's the opposite of *Fishers of men?*"

"It was part of Jesus' teachings to aid in retrieving souls to salvation. The opposite of retrieving souls for salvation would be to retrieve souls for damnation, I'm guessing. Like I said, I'll have to research it more, but it is borderline sacrilegious type deviation of the actual text."

"I didn't know you knew so much about that stuff." he says.

"Well, it's one thing to know some of it by memory, it's another to follow it. Did you get some pictures of it before I put it in the evidence bag?"

"Yeah, I already did?"

"We got no immediate follow-on action here with what we got. We're losing daylight soon. There's one more thing I wanna try before we pack it in and have the coroner do his thing with the photos we got."

"What are you gonna do?"

"Well, I gotta friend that might help us find some missing arms. Radio in and have that barfing idiot open the back doors of the transport van to let Drake out if he isn't too busy still yakking his brains out on the side of the damn road."

He radios in with the hand mike on his chest to have Drake come down. He trots out in a hurry to zig zag around trees and the few bushes that are near the wood line by the road. He comes right to me and sits a few feet away, as always eager to please.

"Drake... FIND?!"

I point to the body, hoping he can catch a scent on where the guy's arms are at and he goes right up to it to sniff around. Dogs are better than deputies, especially when they don't puke at the sight of the first stiff body they see. He seems to have trouble to pick up a scent trail with all the blood scattered everywhere. He's got a good nose on him, but he may not sniff through that much dried and frozen blood on the ground. He moves around the tree in circles, waiting for the next command. He goes back to the body and keeps trying to pick up a scent, but he's giving the indicators that it is no use for him. There's just too much throwing him off at this location, and he keeps looking back at me in disappointment.

"Come on, boy. Give it one more good go... FIND?!"

He whimpers. He only does that when he thinks I'm disappointed in him or he sees something he can't get to. He moves around to the back side of the tree and attempts to raise his front paws up on the pine. He keeps pawing the pine and then barks towards air. Not an aggressive bark, but the bark of concern for something he sees.

"Did you photograph the back side of the tree already?" I ask the deputy.

"No, Sheriff. I thought you already did before I came."

"Well, get the camera ready, then. Let's have a look at what Drake has found for us."

We both walk around, seeing what Drake is looking at. I didn't notice on my first walk around the body that the square peg was driven through his feet protruding out the other side of the tree another three or four inches.

"There were no signs of hammer marks on the top of that peg driven through his feet."

"Holy shit. That ain't no damn bear. What could do something like that?" he asks.

This pine is at least a foot in diameter. The deputy takes another photo from a different angle.

"Put your hand or your pen next to a nail in a photo so we can have a size reference." I tell him.

He does as I ask. The amount of force that it took to drive that square peg through that deep in one attempt must have been incredible. All while the victim is still alive. There is no hiding it anymore, but I refuse to openly say what I already know it is. Just in case I am driving myself insane. The last time Leeds done this, it was just strung up and dismembered. It's almost like he crucified this one and hung it face downward. I see Drake is still attempting to paw his way up the tree to get a sniff at the nail.

"I don't think you're gonna get that nail outta that tree there, boy... Drake. HEEL!"

He keeps pawing the tree with his front legs, then back down to give the same concerning bark.

"Drake... HEEL!",

But he doesn't listen. He keeps trotting around in circles, giving that same bark, and starts moving to the road. He won't make his way back to the vehicle unless I tell him to. He comes back frantically as me and the deputy still stare at this giant nail coming through the back side of the tree. He goes back to sit on his hind legs near the crime scene gear, but he isn't panting. His mouth is closed.

"Are you spooked, Drake? Believe me, that guy is very dead already."

"Sheriff, he wasn't lookin at no nail."

I turn to see the deputy looking straight up into the massive pine canopy. Yellow glowing eyes stare down on us. Every branch of the pine above us is filled with them, several dozen if not more. Those are owl eyes with the silhouette of the horns beside those lifeless yellow beads that glare down at us both. They don't even appear to be breathing or moving, just watching us. The winds howl, but they still don't make a sound or even move. Their feathers even appear lifeless from that high above us. They would usually flap their wings to adjust against the wind, but these aren't normal owls. The winds speak a dark and familiar whisper into the area. *"Her blood is on your hands."*

"Did you hear that?" I ask the deputy.

"Hear what? What do you mean, Sheriff?" he asks.

"Her blood… Your hands."

I remember you.

"Sheriff, what are we gonna do?" asks the deputy.

"Come feast with us."

I will find you and you can count on it.

"She's in here with us."

"Sheriff?" asks the deputy again.

"She'll always stay with us."

"Sheriff?!!", yelling at me now and grabbing my shoulder.

"What?!"

"What are we doing here?" he asks.

"Just keep the fucking noise down and call those other two deputies in on the radio."

He calls them in on the walkie and tells them what we are looking at and I move to the body to see what it is gonna take to get it off the tree. I move the torso around and see that the backside is frozen to the tree in multiple places and bare muscle with meat sticking to the bark. The back side has been skinned with multiple ribs broken inward, so that it gets stuck to the tree when it got cold enough. It was skinned alive like a slaughtered animal at a butcher house. The wind is picking up as the surrounding trees creak and moan.

"Come feast with us."

"Take a picture of this backside while I still have it lifted and get the camera along with the evidence in the bag. Get all that shit packed up ready to go."

The other two deputies make their way to us.

"Oh my God, Sheriff, that whole back side is skinned up down to his lungs and ribs!?"

"She'll always stay with us." says that same whisper in my ears as the wind picks up.

"I know, just take the damn picture and put the camera away." I point and tell the other deputies what needs to happen. "You grab that shotgun and keep it aimed at those fucking birds. You, I need you toss me that body bag outta the crime scene gear then get back up to the vehicles and tell them to get ready to roll out. We're outta here within the next ten minutes. Let's go. Move your asses now dammit."

"Jesus Christ, Sheriff… Are those owls?!" he asks before getting into the gear bag.

"Stop yelling and do as you're fucking told. Move it and let's get this body loaded up."

He tosses me the spare body bag as the last photo is taken. One moves over to help me pry the frozen and lifeless corpse from the tree. The nail rips more of the ankle off when we break it loose. The foot just dangles on the calve, only held on by a few ligaments now. Drake is running around us in circles as we all rush to get the body in the bag and gather up the gear. I haven't ever seen the wind pick up this fast in the winter like this. The darkness came way too fast from the overcast. I hear the van and cars starting up near the road when they honk the horns. Some of the other deputies are yelling orders at each other. I scramble to help get the gear on top of the body bag and see that the owls are still watching us from above. Not a movement from them, and those yellow eyes get brighter while their shadows get larger and darker.

"Get me that crowbar out of the crime scene bag and set all the gear on top of the body. Get it all carried up at the same time. Move with a purpose dammit. Go now and leave me the shot gun."

"Sheriff, what are you doing. We need to go. We can't do anything out here like this."

"I need that nail outta the tree. Get that shit to the van now and be ready to move as soon as I get up there."

The two deputies fight off the wind and the cold and start moving the body and gear back to the road. They slip and slide on snow and sand as they move to the van. Drake stays close to me, but he has already tugged on my pant leg once to convince me to get to the road, too. I jam the crowbar underneath the massive square peg. It's gonna take all of my weight to yank this thing out, but I need to know where this nail came from. I hang there on the crowbar, trying to get it to loosen up from the tree, and it doesn't budge an inch. I look up above the nail to see the owls are fluttering their wings now. Those black horns look as sharp as razors beside their yellow eyes. I hang around and bounce my weight on the crowbar with my legs and it starts to wiggle.

The wind stops and a scream is heard loud enough to pierce the ear drums. Not a scream of pain, but a scream of absolute terror to my very core. It's here. I prop my feet up against the tree to push against the crowbar with my legs and my weight again. It frees up with the last powerful jerk of my heaviness and I drop to the ground on my backside hard enough to knock my breath out. The deputies are by the wood line near the road yelling at me and motioning me to move to them faster, but I can't hear them over the screams coming behind me. It's a scream I remember well. A scream that turns into a demonic roar the closer it gets to me. A scream that will always wake me in the night for as long as I still breathe.

I get up to see Drake is still by my side. I grab the shotgun and square peg in the other hand with the crowbar. I turn around to walk backwards with the shotgun pointed further into the forest. I look up and the owls start to flutter away in unison with another demonic scream. They lift off the branches and stay close to each other as they fly low under the canopy. They fly towards the screams and I keep the shotgun sighted on as many as I can. When I get close enough to the road, I run the rest of the way. Everybody is already in a vehicle ready to go and I jump into the back of the van that they left the back doors open for me to hop in quickly. Drake jumps in right before me and I throw the nail and crowbar near the body bag in the back. I leave the van's double doors open to keep the shotgun ready if something follows us out of the wood line.

I call on the radio to do a head count of all personnel by name.

"Are we up?! Did everybody get into a vehicle?! Give me a count, dammit! Time now!"

They all sound off one by one that they are there and what vehicle they are in.

"Sheriff here in vehicle three. We are all up and accounted for. Along with the pup and one cold one coming along for the ride with us back to the station, over..."

One deputy turns around in the front passenger seat.

"What the hell was that out there, Sheriff!?! What is that damn thing?!" he asks.

"I don't know, kid. Let's just get the hell outta here for now. Drive it like you stole it."

"You gonna keep that door open and that shotgun pointed out the whole way back, Sheriff? You're gonna freeze your nuts off back there."

"I'll keep it open until I don't see any more fuckin pine trees."

"Sheriff, you're bleeding." says the other deputy and points at my torso.

"What?"

"Yeah, right there on your stomach."

I look down to see blood draining down from underneath my jacked and vest down to my pant pockets and leg. "Dammit, not this shit again. Must have clipped the cap just right when I got that nail out and dropped to the ground."

He keeps looking at me from the passenger seat in concern. "Don't worry about it, kid. I'll be alright." as I close the back two doors.

The deputy driving the vehicle answers the hand mike. Somebody calling in from the station, but it is too muffled for me to hear it in the back of the van. I reach under my vest and jacket to tie off the catheter tube while he is responding on the radio. Drake hops over the body bag and plops down next to me to put his head on my lap. I try to keep my breathing slowed down, but I haven't had to run like that in a while. The driver puts the mike back down in the radio holder.

"Well?" I ask the deputy.

"Uh… we got some good news and bad news back at the station, Sheriff."

"Just tell me something good please."

"We reached out to the broadcast station and they'll be posting the announcement on the local station tonight on the curfew. They're gonna do it the same time they call off school for the blizzard storm warning coming in tonight. All the flyers were posted out throughout the town already and most of the businesses closed early for the night."

"Well, that's good news that somebody did their job. What's the bad news?"

"The coroner made it to the hospital already."

"How in the hell did that happen? He would have had to drive right by us. We could have used him out there for this shit."

"Sherral said he wasn't comfortable stopping this far out into the barrens with the blizzard coming in and all. Probably the same reason the game warden or animal control guys never showed up with us, too. They didn't think we would mind."

"No, of course not. No, no, no, I don't fuckin mind at all. Fuckin assholes. I'll deal with them."

"Well… that's not all, Sheriff."

"You have more good news, right?" I ask.

"Well…"

"Spit it out."

"The guy we left in the holding cell from this morning…"

"Yeah. What about him?"

"Well… He's gone."

"You mean like let go by the city PD. Did they come pick him up for something else since we've been out? We didn't find any warrants on him when we had him in questioning this morning."

"No, Sheriff… He's… Like *gone,* gone." he says.

"You gotta be shitting me, *right?* Please tell me this is some stupid joke or something, *right?*

Chapter 14: The Trade

We only had the shop open for maybe an hour when we caught news of the curfew. Not a customer for a few days, until he walks in with a rifle sheath slung around on his backside. My wife stood up from behind the counter with a concerned look on her face. Not a lot of strangers roll into our small town during the snowy hunting seasons, much less in our tiny pawn shop. Maybe it is the large door letting the air in, but the shop gets colder as he walks in.

"Sorry, young man. We are closing down soon for the Sheriff's curfew coming on tonight."

He just looks around and stares at everything behind me on the gun rack. He looks to his left and right to see all the gear he is surrounded by. No word from him yet, though.

He wore tattered jungle style boots with his dark pants tucked in above the laces. His black Carhartt was ripped up on one shoulder, but maybe still served its purpose against the cold with the collar up. Those jackets have enough pockets to carry a pistol in them without being noticed. His green gloves had hardened knuckles on them. I catch his right hand that holds the strap of the sheath has the index finger cut away from the glove material. He had a broken and feeble walk that contradicted the young age of his bruised face. A military style fade of a haircut with a full dark beard that was trimmed around the cheeks and neck at one point. He walks past my wife at the counter but gives her a head nod that calms her nerves, but only slightly. He approaches my side of the shop and lays his sheath on the glass display. Not a word from him as he opens up the sheath when I motion the ok with a simple hand gesture. Most experienced firearms users know the drill when walking into an establishment with a firearm, especially if they are not a familiar face.

"I think you'll want to keep your doors open for this one." he says.

He reveals an original JM stamped and vintage 30-30 lever action Marlin with the bluing worn from heavy use and weather. A slight scuff on the stock and signs of a scope mounted previously. I try to keep my excitement hidden, as we never get such a rarity in the shop.

"Are you looking to sell, pawn, or trade, young man?" I ask.

"Trade." he says as he points up behind me.

I turn around and see he is pointing at another lever action rifle on the shelf. A dusty stainless all-weather Henry 45-70 lever action that has never sold since it came in on pawn months ago. I pull it down and hand it to him for viewing and he lifts the barrel to look down the iron sights, simultaneously opening the lever to inspect the empty chamber.

"Your Marlin 30-30 is a near collector's item, but the 45-70 is newer and retails for more in the bigger cities. What do you say to a straight up even trade, young man?" I ask.

"That's a deal, so long as all boxes of your most potent cartridges go with it." he says with and intimidating sternness not common to folks in these parts. I motion to my wife to get up and turn the shop sign around to say CLOSED. He turns his head to look at what she does then focuses back on me.

My mouth opens with a stutter before I think to register what is being said, "Ain't nothing in these parts that needs a shot that big to take down. Bear ain't even in season yet. What are you huntin out there in those barrens with rounds that cost damn near a dollar apiece?"

He looks at me with a dark glare as he lowers the rifle and sets it on the glass case next to his. "No, not a bear… Something worse."

"You sure are a serious fella, aren't ya?"

He reaches into his pocket and I place hands on both firearms that sit on the glass display case in front of me. He keeps his hands in for a few seconds, but long enough to show how nervous he is making us.

"Um... Is there something else I can help you find in here before we do up the paperwork on this one? Maybe some gear or something for your next hunt or?"

He pulls out his hands from his pocket and lays out a wad of cash to lay it in between the rifles. There must be several hundred worth of twenty-dollar bills sitting in front of me.

"Well... We, uh... We agreed to a straight up trade on these rifles, young man. I'm not sure what to do with all this."

"Now for the next deal. You 're gonna take half of this and we're gonna forget about paperwork on this rifle for now. And for the other half of that pile of cash, I'll be grabbing enough gear until you say I have reached that amounts worth in merchandise."

My wife looks at me as she comes around the back side of the counter on my side. She can't stop glancing at the pile in cash in front of us, and then she opens her mouth.

"Sir, we gotta do the paperwork on the rifle trade. Sorry. But as far as the merchandise, you can buy whatever you need. You could by half the store with all this." she says eagerly.

"Not worried about the receipts or whatever. By all means, keep whatever documents you need to maintain your inventory records. It's the background check that is gonna be a hold up for me. That and other *locals* that may come in asking about me."

"Who are you worried about asking about you?" I ask.

"Maybe the local Sheriff's department and Lautenberg."

"The Sheriff hasn't walked in here in weeks and I don't know anyone named Lautenberg."

"Well then. Just take the cash and you got nothing to worry about, do you?" he says.

The last time I took a risk like this, I almost lost my FFL certification to sell and buy guns, but this is a lot of cash in front of me.

Me and the wife damn near live in the pawn shop now to avoid utilities in two different places, so our home doesn't have to be heated in the winter along with the shop, too. No customers in days and we may have to close our doors for good if we can't make it through the winter this year. If it comes to it, I'll just close the doors for good and nobody will ever know we skipped the background check on him. He walked in with a rifle already, so surely he is cleared to possess a firearm, anyway. I look at the wife, but she gives me the head nod for thinking the same thing I am. He doesn't look too patient or friendly, just a serious lookin fella.

"Ok. I'm good with that. So long as you can show me a hunting license or something like that. I don't wanna find out you took this grizzly killer off my hands to go knock off some liquor store or somethin like that." I ask.

"Sure thing." he says as he reaches into his back pocket with hesitation. Every time one of his hands or out of sight for even a second, I wanna piss myself. He pulls out his wallet and shows a military ID, hunting license and conceal carry from another state. Georgia, it looks like.

"Some of these are older maybe even out of date at the moment, but I haven't made it to go get the newer ones yet." he says.

"Good enough for me. Damned court houses are always so packed anyhow. I'll get this Henry cleaned up for ya, and we'll count the cash while you have a look around the store. Ok?"

"I know how much cash is there. So, don't get greedy with me. You're already walking out way ahead in this deal." he says.

"No. No. No. We don't do that. We're good Christians around here. We ain't never tried to swindle someone like that. That ain't no good to do people that way."

"Right… Excuse me, miss?", as he turns to talk to my wife. "Does this area have a post office nearby?" he asks her.

"Um… No, they closed that location and moved to the next county over. Were you trying to pick something up from there or something?" she asks.

"No, miss I needed to mail out a letter along with all the paperwork he is about to write up on this trade." he says.

"Oh, I can do that for you, young man. I can send it out with the outgoing mail tomorrow or Monday. Here, I can even get you an envelope for that if ya need one." as she reached eagerly under the display case.

"I appreciate that." he says.

He moves to walk throughout the store in a hurry and kept bringing things back to the counter. He knew exactly the things he was after. Like a list was already developed in his head. Deer scent, ghillie blankets both white and woodland camo, ammo pouches, a rifle sling, a small bullet holder to go on the stock of the rifle, a small pup tent, matches, mag light with spare batteries, more batteries, 500lb rated nylon rope, flint and steel, a fillet knife, camel pack, hand warmers, field wipes, construction style knee pads. The pile just kept getting bigger and bigger in front of me as I wiped off the Henry 45-70. It is like he is taking everything except for food and the clothes on his back.

"Are ya heading out on the hunt soon, son?" I ask.

"Why do you ask?"

"Oh… It's just they're calling for a major storm front coming in soon and it's supposed to get down to the single digits before morning. Then we're gonna get covered in snowfall for the next few days after that. Maybe some rain or sleet first, but mostly snow. You got what you need to stay warm out there? Maybe a bundle of firewood, too? You haven't reached your spending amount yet, but I haven't rung anything up either."

"Is the paperwork ready?"

"Oh yes… Uh… I'll just show on here you had a valid conceal carry license and military ID, so it should void any issues. I just need you to sign here and the back copy is yours."

"No problem."

He signs his name and takes the back copy, then he turns to my wife. "Miss, did you say you had an envelope?" he asks.

"Oh, yes, right here is one for ya. Did you need it stamped or anything?"

"That would be helpful if you can spare?" he says.

"Of course. If you need to write out the address of where it is going there's a table over there near the front door where people sit and fill out their paperwork for a firearms purchase."

"Thank you." as he moves over to the table and sits down.

"I'll just get all this rung up and bagged for ya, but I don't think you're quiet at the halfway mark of all this cash, son."

"Do I smell a fresh pot of coffee brewing somewhere back there?" he asks.

My wife answers for me before I can think about what he asked me. "Yes, we always keep a fresh pot going on chilly days like this." she says.

"I tell you what, if you pour me a cup of that nice smelling brew, get all that gear loaded in the camper of my Dodge parked outside while I write on the back of this purchase receipt for the Henry, you can keep the change of what's sitting there. Yeah?"

"That's awful generous of you sir, but that's a lot of money."

"Are you saying you don't have a need for it?" he asks as he moves the chair and sits facing us and the front entrance.

"Well, we've been struggling here for a bit. Not a lot of paying customers can afford much these days." says my wife. She gives me the look that may put me on the couch downstairs in the shop's cellar tonight if I don't stop asking questions and do as the fella asks.

"Sounds like many people in this town are in the same boat. You need it more than I do." he says. "I won't need it where I'm going. Don't worry and just keep the change."

I get all the items bagged up and me and the wife take them all out to his truck as he asks. He sat there for a while, looking out the large front windows of the shop. Even after she brings him a fresh cup of coffee, he still sat there for what seemed like forever. "Thank you, miss." is all that comes out of his mouth. Then he writes on the back of the carbon copy receipt for the trade-in paperwork. He writes fast, but I can tell it is good handwriting. I don't spell things too good myself. I just have the wife print things out from a computer or register. I have no clue what he is writing, and I don't want to disturb him as long as he has been sitting there already. I move to box up the rifle that he traded for, and he looks up again.

"Leave the rifles where they are for now." he says abruptly enough to startle me.

"Oh… I uh… Sorry I was just gonna box the one up for ya."

"Just leave it there for a bit… Both of them, if you don't mind? I'm almost done here."

"Oh, that's ok. We'll wait."

"Count your cash. I'll be outta your hair in a sec."

"Right." I was so nervous I forgot to count all the twenties. I hand it over to the wife to take it to the back room, out of sight. She knows to put stashes like this in the safe as quickly as possible. He stands up from his chair as she walks out of sight and licks the envelope to seal it shut as he walks up to the counter.

"Now the ammo?" he asks as he sets the envelope down near the two rifles.

"Oh… Yes…" and I reach under the display case to pull out the three boxes I have for the 45-70 and one bag of hand loads. I set them on the counter in front of him. He looks at the baggie full of hand loads and pulls one out to inspect in the lighting. He looks at it with a keen eye and attempts to dig his fingernail into where the casing meets the round.

"Those are hand loads from a local we buy from now and then. He used to pack 'em full of over 400 grains. That's more than the few boxes of the Hornady factory rounds we got here too."

He stays quiet and keeps looking at the round in the light, almost as if he is admiring it. "They sure are lady killers, aren't they?" he asks.

"That they are. Too much recoil for me, though. I wouldn't even try to take down a mule deer with something that big without breaking my shoulder." I try to laugh under my breath to ease the tension, but he pays me no attention. My wife comes back out from the back room and gives the head nod that the cash is locked up in the safe.

156

"Now listen very carefully." he says. "Two things. Number one, all that extra cash is for your discretion during this trade in deal. Ok?"

"Ok."

He lowers the bullet and starts loading rounds one by one in the side gate of the Henry.

"I'm sorry, sir. But you can't be loading up a firearm like that in here."

"Are you going to stop me?" he asks.

"Well… I…"

"Don't worry. I'm not going to do anything to you fine folks. If I was, I would have done it by now. Right?"

"Well… Right." as I turn to look at my wife, who is as concerned as I am.

"Number two, I will be coming back for this old Marlin you just took possession of. I don't expect you to not try to sell it. But we both know nobody around here can afford to pay what it is really worth. Right?"

"Right."

"Now, if I don't come back for it within the next few days, then somebody else will. No matter who comes for it, he'll pay whatever your asking price is. Understood?" as he keeps slowly loading rounds into the side gate of the Henry.

"Yeah, that makes sense. So, we're more or less like holding it for ya. Uh… The Marlin?"

"That's right." as he keeps loading. He hits the tube limit in the fifth round and looks up at me.

"Only five rounds can fit in this rifle tube at a time?" he asks.

"Well… Um… One in the chamber would make it six total. How many of those grizzly killers do you really need?"

He lifts the gun and points it to the ceiling to chamber one round out of the round tube. He lowers the hammer at the same time. He lowers it back on the table and loads the sixth round into the tube from the side loading gate.

"Right. Six will do for now."

"How will I know if it's you or this other person who is coming back for it?" I ask.

"Like I said, if it isn't me within a week it will be somebody else a while from now."

"Who?"

"You'll know that it is somebody that is here to pick it up on my behalf, but they'll have the means to pay for it the same way I did. They will have this receipt in their possession too. So long as this place is still here, right?"

"Right, but it'll probably be you that come back for it?"

"Hopefully." he says. "This ol' Marlin is an important rifle for me."

"I can tell. It'll be good here for a while."

He looks at my wife and slides the letter on the glass display top towards her. "I trust this will make it where it needs to go."

"Yes, sir. I will stamp it tonight and then I'll mail it out first thing Monday morning for ya."

He slides the other boxes of ammo into the pockets of his jacket and it droops down from the weight. He picks up the Henry rifle with his off hand and reaches out to shake my hand with the other.

"Pleasure doing business with you fine, folks. I can't thank you enough." He turns around to walk out with the loaded rifle in hand pointed at the floor.

"Wait… What do I tell the other guy that comes to buy it back if you don't come back for it?" He turns his head to talk from the side of his neck as he keeps walking towards the front door.

"You just tell them I went hunting and there is nothing more to tell."

And he kept walking out the door to turn the corner to his truck. I hear the truck start up and he pulls a U-turn in the road to travel back the way he came. I turn to look at my wife as she gives the same sigh of relief that I just gave.

"Who was that guy." she asks.

"I don't know. Military is all I saw from his ID cards he pulled out, but that was a lot of money he just threw out at us, just to come back and buy the same gun off us again later."

"Maybe he was working with the police or the Game Warden or something to find that bear that's been offing people in the woods, ya figure?"

"I don't think so. Haven't seen him before and I know all the Game Wardens and deputies around here. He looked like he just came out a damned war zone. Did you see his face, how it was all bashed up?"

"I know. He looked pretty rough. What do you think is in this letter he wrote on the gun trade paperwork?"

"I don't know. He was sitting there writing on it for a while."

"It's going all the way up north even further than here. Maine? What if it was like a death threat or somethin to somebody? He looked like a…"

"No! Don't even think that. Just don't open it and send it out like he asked. I wouldn't want to know what he would do if he found out otherwise. I damn near shit myself when he started loading up the Henry right in front of me for Christ's sake."

"I know. I walked right out and saw he was loading it up. What do you think he's going after in these parts with a gun like that?" she asks.

"I don't know. Ain't much in this area that needs something that big to take it down."

"Are you sure about that?"

Chapter 15: The Neighborhood

We show up back at the station just in time before the snow makes itself known. I have already put the APB out for the escapee as we were traveling back to the town. State troopers and surrounding counties know what to look for. Even though I know where he is going, it's best to follow protocol for these things. Sherral stands outside the office knowing she can't go home yet. The coroner meets up with us at the station instead of the hospital. I chewed out the county office all the way back into town for letting him come into town first without meeting us there at the scene. We transfer all the evidence and the remains to his van before he heads out. There is no need to have a conversation with him or give an update on what's going on. He knows his job well enough to wait until a full autopsy is down on paper before a debriefing. I hand the camera off to Sherral.

"Get all these photos from today printed out. I want two copies of everything. One for me and one for the coroner. The photo printer should have enough ink to make it happen now, right?"

"Right. Ok, Sheriff." as she walks back inside.

Some of the other deputies help move things over to the coroner's van and I grab the crime scene gear to take it back into the office. The station seems quiet and the second shift hasn't made their way in yet. It's pushing five o'clock now. So, I still have enough time to get things done before I head home. I step into my office and Drake follows me in to see two deputy badges sitting on my table with resignation letters. It happens every time we go through this here. Bodies pile up and deputies start to walk away. Businesses close their doors and locals move abroad closer to the cities. It doesn't take long for Sherral to come in with the photos already printed out.

"Hand this set to the coroner before he takes off with the remains then come see me in my office with today's video footage of how the hell this guy got out of my station unnoticed."

"Ok, Sheriff." while keeping her head down and leaving the office. I stare at all the photos to look for anything I may have missed, but I'll check them out, side by side, at home with the photos from the few bodies photographed from last winter. She walks back in with the video disk from today's footage and I slide it into the computer.

"Any idea when he approached the front desk?"

She replies frantically, like a child that knows their daddy just came home to whip their ass and send them back to bed. "Um… It was a few hours after you guys left. I did not know he was even here. None of the other deputies even told me he was here."

"Just stop talking, for Christ's sake, and let me find the damn footage. Stay right there. You get to watch this too."

As I scroll through the footage, another deputy walks in and takes his badge off in front of me and sets it with the others.

"I'm sorry, Sheriff. I didn't…"

"Get the fuck outta my office and go take on more shift work at the local factory, like the others. You should have never taken up the badge if you didn't have the grit to do the things that had to be done in this type of work. You'll have my recommendation and nothing more. Now go."

"You're not surprised?" he asks.

"Nothing surprises me anymore. Just leave."

He walks out, and I keep scrolling through the footage. I see the interrogation from earlier today and the camera that focuses on the front desk to look at Sherral. Just after midday, I see him crawling on his belly out to the door beside the front desk. It was not even a few seconds after the two deputies that just turned in their badges stepped out for a smoke. They leave the door propped open with the same damn brick I am always moving out of the way to make sure the door closed. He stands up to face her and they have a full-length conversation on camera. He signs paperwork and appears approachable to her. She is even smiling and chatting back with him. Son of a bitch. Those two deputies walked back in the building and move right past him. He turns around to walk out the front door to give the camera a smile with a salute. That mother fucker saluted the damn camera.

"How long you were here by yourself, Sherral?" I ask.

"Once the deputies saw that the light in the holding cell area was off and he was gone, they turned in their badges. They didn't want to stick around till you guys got back. I have been the only one in the office ever since. Sheriff... I'm really sorry. I just didn't know..."

"Save it. Where is the truck at along with all his gear?"

"The bus garage foreman said he already got it. They thought you had given the order to let it get picked up by the owner. Was he under arrest? Did he do something to those people out there?"

"No. He was just another hunter who found one of them. He isn't a threat to anybody. There's already an APB out for him and the State Police have the interstates covered as much as they can with the snows coming in tonight. But I already know where he's going."

"Where? Who is that guy?" she asks.

"It doesn't matter. Listen to me, Sherral. You've been with this station a long time. I know you've seen at least three different sheriffs come and go here..."

She sobs in front of me, knowing what I am about to say. "Sheriff, please. I didn't mean to be a burden. I just try to help as much as I can. I just didn't know. Some of these newer deputies that come in, they just don't know how to handle things like the old days when my husband was here as the Sheriff. But that was over 30 years ago. He's gone now, and this place is all I got now. Please don't. I'll try harder with all these newer computers and stuff. I just don't..."

162

I hold up my hand from behind the desk to get her to calm down. "I know… And you're still needed here. These new deputies that come in are nothing but a bunch of damn kids that wanna play cops and robbers. This isn't like the old days you and I both remember when it comes to some of these newbies. That's why my desk is piling up with resignation letters so fast. That's why you need to stay until you tell me you can't anymore."

"You're not gonna fire me?"

"Wouldn't be my place. You've technically got seniority over me in this station. Here's what's gonna happen. You're gonna take this disk and delete all the video footage. All of it. Me questioning him and the footage that shows him waltzing out the front door."

"Do you think they'll find him?" as she wipes her nose.

"I think he's gonna go out there into the barrens and get himself killed. But it doesn't matter right now. I got somewhere I gotta be. I will hand in all the paperwork from today on another day. You're going to hang out here and delete this footage and get all these resignation letters ready to be submitted to the county. I need Drake to hang out here with you for a bit, while I take care of something."

Drake looks up from chewing his toy on the couch and moves his ears to listen in.

"What about the blizzard coming? I can't drive so good in the snow." she says.

"Have a deputy from the second shift take you home and… Rachel. Yeah, have Rachel drive you home and let her know to bring Drake by my house later tonight. But tell her to wait for my message before she comes by with him."

"Oh. I forgot but one of the second shift deputies just called in earlier today. Said he wasn't coming in tonight because he was sick or something."

"Was he sick yesterday?"

"Well… No. I don't think he was."

"That's another resignation letter to get ready, then. He just doesn't have the spine to show face."

"I am sorry about all this. This happens every year around here like this as soon as things get ugly. I wish my husband was still here to help you guys out. He wouldn't stand for the stuff some of these younger deputies try to pull."

"It's not your fault. I didn't exactly leave this place in excellent hands when I took off. Guys like your husband were a whole different breed back in them days. Wish we had more like him around."

"You act like him a lot. All you veterans look the same, though."

"Well… I'm flattered, but don't go tooting my horn yet. Shit's about to get a lot uglier around here for a bit. So… Three badges on my desk and one resignation via call in. How many does that leave us to work with."

"We got Davis that you sent home earlier this morning. Rachel. Greeves. And you."

"What about some of those guys that were with me out there today?"

"They already took off. One of them left something on my desk before he left."

"That's another resignation letter for me then. Just four deputies and me? That's it?"

"That's it, Sheriff."

"Fucking Christ… Is the town on curfew now at least."

"Right. The mayor had it broadcasted for us too after Greeves put up the flyers. The mayor made it sound like it was his idea. The schools already shut down for the weekend."

"Of course, that weasel would say that. Ok, on top of what I already told you needed to be done, I need you to call in to the state PD and let them know we need some assistance with a body recovery tomorrow after the storm lets up for around mid-day. Let the game warden know the same thing to see if he will come out too. We could use a wildlife expert out there if there is anything left of this guy to bring back to the coroner. Have Ricky Clauson's wife bring in a shirt of his or anything that can help Drake sniff it out. We've got a general location of his last sighting, but do not tell his wife anything if she comes in and asks. We can't disclose anything until we know for sure it's him."

"Ok, is there anything else?"

"Just go through the list I just gave you before I take off." I grab the keys to the SUV along with the photos and have Drake hold in place as soon as he jumps off the couch. I make my way to the front exit as she follows behind me, talking my ear off.

"I gotta delete all the security cam footage from today. I gotta submit all the resignation papers for all those other guys. Gotta call the game and wildlife station and the State PD to see if they have help that can come in tomorrow around mid-day for a search party...."

"And what else?" as I walk out the security door to see her on the other side of the front desk through the glass.

"Have Ricky's wife come by with a shirt of his or anything that has his scent on him. And Have Rachel take me home and Drake to your home next."

"You got it. Don't stay here too late into the second shift. They'll be in within the hour. I'm gonna need you here in the morning. If it's that bad out, then one of us will pick you up again. I gotta go. If anybody needs me, just let them know to call me ASAP. I won't be far."

Drake comes over behind the front desk to sit next to her as she pets his forehead. He knows she always keeps some jerky hidden in her desk somewhere for when I'm not around to do the same after he has worked hard all day. I turn around to walk out the front door into darkness. The only thing visible is the quiet snowfall through the one streetlight that doesn't work on the main road through town. I head home, but the ground isn't covered enough for the four-wheel drive to kick in. I get the phone call voice messaging notification while driving down the road in the SUV.

"Good evening, sir. We understand that a loved one is in need of medical rehab services. We are the transportation services, and we are currently in route to the address provided. If you could call us back at your earliest convenience or we can converse more with you and the individual when we get there. Thank you and we'll be there within the hour."

Dammit. That call was about 30 minutes ago. These guys don't waste no time. With as much as I am paying these people they shouldn't be. The last time this happened I had to drop her off there, and she went quietly. This time isn't gonna be so peaceful. I pull into the snow-covered driveway to see her outside on the front porch, smoking a cigarette in the same robe I saw her in last night with a winter jacket on top. Children are already out playing in the snow at the neighbor's houses and trying to make a snowman on the street corner. I step out, and she doesn't even notice Drake isn't with me.

"Why did you leave last night? I could have been there strung out on that bed you left me on near butt ass fuckin naked." she says.

"Get in the damn house. Don't be talking like that with kids out here running around."

"Don't tell me what to fucking do, jerk off. I heard the radio announcement. It's happening again, isn't it? It's fucking happening again, isn't it?!" but she leans down to put out her cigarette and toss it into the yard anyway just to walk into the house in front of me. I walk in and see the spoon all blacked out and burnt up on the coffee table. Both baggies are empty on the table along with her goody bag. The needle is dried but covered in blood.

"Jesus Jaynese. Did you use up the other bag already too?" I ask.

"Yeah, but that cheap shit didn't last long. Good thing I ain't a diabetic cause all it was fucking sugar you got your hands on. Feels like you had your fun though after I passed out. Did ya get your jollies off before or after I pissed myself?"

"What the hell. I don't do that when you're on your damn fix. We gotta get this shit cleaned up."

"Have your way with me, did ya? Fuckin answer me, jerk off."

"I answered you! And no, I got called into work. You gotta go clean up. I'm tired of seeing you like this! I'm tired of coming home to this, day after day!"

Yelling at her always backs her off. Most days I can sit there and take it and try to talk to her enough to get her to calm down. Most of the time, like now, she is too strung out and twitchy to even know what comes outta her mouth.

"Now get outta that nasty ass bath robe and go clean up. I clean this fucking house! I gotta take care of you and feed you if you even eat that day! And I gotta go to work to pay the bills every fucking day! Now, if you want me to keep giving you anything, you'll do as you're fucking told. Now go shower dammit, before I flush what I got down the toilet."

"You got more. I need it…"

"Not right now. You've already had your fix twice today."

"Just give it here, then! What the hell? Why do you make this worse for me! That's all you do is make everything worse for everybody! Just give it…" as she rushes me and starts hitting my chest. She slaps the badge off my pocket and hits my face a few times before I get my arms around her.

"Stop it. Just stop it, dammit."

"You never give me what I need! You never help anything!" as she thrust outta my grip. She turns back around to face me. Her eye shadow was the same she has had on for days now, but tears have come through it. Her hair is all matted up in what used to be a ponytail. She wipes her face off with shaky hands that have needle sores up to her arms.

"If you want what I got for you, then you gotta go get cleaned up in the shower, right fuckin now!" and I point to the shower as she stares in shock.

"Or else, what? You gonna slap me around like some of them old dicks do near the resorts down in Atlantic City. Least they pay me for it."

"Shower now! I'll bring you some fresh clothes in the bathroom. Get cleaned off in the bathroom, then I'll give you what you need. Now go!" as I look down and just keep pointing to the bathroom.

"You're a fuckin asshole, Jason. I already know why you left last night, anyway. Give it to your old bitchy girlfriend in uniform again, did ya?"

"Just go, Jay!"

"Fine. Fuckin prick."

She walks off and slams the bathroom door shut. I've got less than twenty minutes before they show up to clean this crap up. I go to the bedroom and grab her a fresh change of clothes and underwear. The room reeks of burnt carpet. I strip the bed. If I had a fireplace, I would have thrown all the sheets and dirty clothes in it from the smell of her piss and cigarette stains. More old needles and twisted up spoons from too much heating and cooling from lighters. I pack a bag of a week's worth of fresh clothes for her. She wears the same few clothes over and over and doesn't realize how many clean clothes she has in the dressers still. I throw all the dirty clothes and sheets into the laundry room that rarely gets opened by her. I grab the bag of clothes and open the bathroom door to set her clean clothes on the counter for her when she gets out.

I head back to the living room to clean off the coffee table and the random rubber bands that get flung everywhere from her arm. More needles between and under the couch cushions. I rush back to the kitchen and grab the entire trash can to throw everything I can see drug related in it. Magazines with cigarette holes. More towels filled with puke from when she is having withdrawals. Empty coke and beer bottles on top of the floor with half-smoked cigarettes. It all goes into the trash can when I get a knock on the door. I clean most of the nastiness and drugs up, but the smell will take a deeper cleaning and airing out to get rid of over the next few days.

I move to open the door and two people stand there in shock that a law enforcement guy answers and is the first person they see. They both wear all white, one male of stronger build and a female with a soft face. Hopefully, she is the one doing the talking about this. I already know what the other guy is for. It's a good thing Drake is back at the station. He might take a chunk outta one of these people's ass, no matter how nice and calm they try to be.

"Oh... Uh... hello officer. I'm not sure if we have the right address, or?"

"No ma'am. You've come to right location."

"Is the patient in some sort of legal trouble?"

"She will be if she doesn't try to go with you. Do you guys have a means to get her to your vehicle?" I look behind them and see a van that appears more like an ambulance, but it has no lights and the name of the rehab center right on the side of it. So much for a discretionary effort on their part.

"Why in the Hell is that van right in front of my home?" I ask.

"We're sorry, sir. We didn't know if some of our more discreet vehicles are tough enough to make it through the snow." he says. "We have a stretcher, sir. But we only use that if the patient is withdrawing or violent. We can't use those unless it's a court mandated detox."

"I'm the Sheriff here. So, believe me when I say that it is more than court mandated."

"Is there a crime that has happened? I don't want to get into any legal issues. I'm not sure if we can do that without her permission." she says.

"You have my permission. That's all you need. She may get violent during this, but it needs to happen. If your facility has any problem with this, they will have the court mandate first thing in the morning. She's in the shower now, cleaning up. This is her bag of clothes and some hygiene stuff for her stay. I already told the admin person there everything they needed to know on this."

"Ok then. When was the last time she used?"

"Recent enough that she may not be withdrawing, but not recent enough to *not* be violent."

The male wastes no time and moves back to the van for the stretcher and sets it outside the door out of site. Me and the woman sign the needed documents and she goes over the steps she will take to keep Jaynese calm.

"Jason? What's going on?" as Jay comes out of the bathroom and I still have the clipboard in hand. Her hair is still wet, but at least appears more relaxed from getting cleaned up. The female nurse steps in while me and the big guy stand by the door.

"Hello Jaynese. My name is Sandra. We're hear from the Camp May Rehab Clinic. Your husband contacted us to help." She speaks softly and low enough to divert focus away from herself and Jay looks back at me, scolding.

"You son of a bitch..." she says to me with her eyes tearing up.

"Jaynese. Please understand. Everyone here cares about you and wants to help you get through this." The female nurse continues. "I know it is a hard process for anyone, but we can get through this together. Why don't you come sit down and we can talk about this for a bit to help you understand what's going on. Ok?" as she reaches out for her.

Watching this person give birth to my child and then watch her get strung out on heroine again later. Stabbing herself with needles day after day. Doing whatever she can to get her fix. Doing whatever she can to ease the pain of losing our daughter. Watching her stop smiling for months at a time. Watching her become a frail skin and bones with sores on her hands and feet that get infected. I don't know who she is any more.

I can't remember how beautiful she used to be holding our baby Maggie up to her chest in the morning. How happy we were together in the beginning. It's all gone now, and I helped her slip away into this mess day after day. I made this monster come back to life every time. I can't stand the sight of this thing in my home. I want *us* back, but I know she is gone forever if she can't break free from this mess she has become. All I can do is stare at the floor in silence, waiting for her to react like she did last time they came to our home for this. Waiting for her to beg and plead not to make her go to one of these places again, but it's the safest place for her now.

The female nurse attempts to coax her to sit down, but I know this will not be a pleasant intervention type of moment she is used to. As soon as she touches Jaynese, she goes into a fit of anger and slaps her violently to run back into the kitchen. Me and the big guy go after her as the nurse sits on the couch, shocked. I grab her from behind after she trips over to a dining room chair. I turn my head to the side, so she doesn't head butt me in the nose while screaming and thrashing around in my arms.

170

"No! No! I'm not going back to one of those places! You can't make me go!" she says while clawing at my forearms wrapped around her tiny frame. The male nurse runs back to open the front door after checking on his partner. They both get up in a hurry to bring the stretcher inside the front door with the snow flurrying inside the threshold. They both grab her legs and notice the needle marks and infections all over her feet. She isn't strong enough to overcome me, much less three sober adults pinning her down on the stretcher.

"Jaynese, please just stay calm! Get a hold of yourself! They want to help you!"

"Fuck you, Jason! You worthless bastard! You fucking did this! You did this to me! You fucking did this and you're gonna get more people killed! You're going out there again and you're gonna get more people killed. I HATE YOU! I FUCKING HATE YOU! I hope you die out there this time. You're gonna let more children die out there in the freezing cold!!"

"Miss, please calm down. We are only trying to help. Everyone here wants you to get better." says the female nurse while somehow maintaining her calm demeanor that she initially had. The male nurse makes the effort to strap her down. First her feet held by the female nurse while I keep my body weight on top of her torso. She moves the straps over her thigh and midsection, and I turn my face to see her crying and moaning as she thrashes her head around, screaming in my ear.

"We gotta get an IV on her. She's dehydrated." says the male nurse.

I move so they can keep strapping her in place and then I put both hands on each side of her head to get her to stop thrashing around and screaming. She cries with tears running down to my fingers. I try to wipe them away, but she won't even look at me.

"Jaynese! Please don't be like this. They're gonna make this all better this time. They're gonna help you this time. Please look at me. Please just look at me." I ask.

She turns to me and the screaming turns to a painful moan. The same moan she gave when she was giving birth to our Maggie in the hospital. The same day she moaned and screamed our beautiful girl to life, and I held both her and Maggie in my arms together for the first time. She whispers through her cries and moans. "Please, kill me. Just kill me. Kill me, please. Don't let me go back there again. I don't wanna go. Kill me, please, I'm begging you. Please don't just... Wait... No!!! Oh my God, no!!!" as they strap in her arms and her forehead to the stretcher.

I keep my hands on her face, wondering if she knows I am still here. But she only closes her eyes and returns to screaming and moaning at the top of her lungs again and again. She fidgets and tries to keep thrashing around while strapped in and being rolled out the front door. I grab some throw blankets and get them to stop before they wheel her out into the cold. I try to cover her up as much as I can, but they keep wheeling her down the walkway. The female nurse comes back for Jay's bag I packed for her as the male nurse wheels her out to the back of the van.

I stand on the front step only long enough to see that all the houses in the neighborhood have their lights on. If they aren't peeking out their windows wondering what the screams are, then they are out on their front porches watching from there. The children that were outside playing in the snow have been called back into their homes by the mothers that have witnessed the same thing the entire neighborhood saw. A junkie that was sent into detox by her enabler. They all knew it all along. I drop to the ground and sit on the step with my head down. I wanna rip my heart out to stop feeling this. I want to cry, but I don't remember how. The nurses come back and say something to me as I sit in the cold and then they move back to the van full of screams and moans to drive away as quickly as they arrived. I watch it drive off and stay sitting on the freezing steps, still in uniform.

The neighbors all around my home look at me from their windows and open front doors, but they don't let their kids come back out to play in the snow. They all slowly turn their front lights out one by one to leave me in darkness, alone in front of my house. To see me alone with just the silent snow that falls weightlessly to the ground to keep me company.

Chapter 16: The Mosque

They drive right by me, heading back to town in their little sheriff's convoy. I don't know if they even realized their back door of that van was open still. How could I be surprised at that one after walking out the front door of their station with no one even noticing? I move out of the snow-covered ditch and back to the truck to keep covering it up in the white ghillie suit and brush piles. When enough snow comes down on top of all this brush, you would have to walk right into it almost thirty feet off the road before you notice it. Snow, brush, white ghillie suit that has been torn up to cover anything reflective on the truck, and now the nightfall has it camouflaged.

The snow never bothers me. It's the rain that makes a journey on foot this far that much more miserable. I stay hopeful of a few hours of sleep in my completely hidden truck, off the roadside this time, but I head out to into the woods the same route I used to get back. I have to make my way back to James. He knows more about what this thing is than I do. The way that Sheriff went at me, I'm not the only person that has encountered this thing and walked away to talk about it. As long as he claimed he had lived in these woods, he has to know how to kill this thing. I stare at the wood line from the road that has had no passing traffic for hours. Even the Sheriff's little convoy had tracks that are now covered in several inches of snow, but at least it's quiet.

The pines stay perfectly still, lifeless and breathing under the snowfall at the same time. No crickets… No owls… only the endless ringing in my ears. This place was my haven. My home away from a home that I lost months ago. Now I have no place to feel at peace in. Not while I know it's still out here. I hope it knows it made a mistake crossing me and not ending me. I hope it knows ending it is all I have now. I hope it's scared. I have no other purpose. Killing it is my purpose. I told you I would go down again and again. I told you I follow you to the Hell you came from. I hope you're ready.

I bypass my hunting spot where it first attacked me and come across the other hunter's area where he was attacked. The sticks where limbs were hanging and the one that fell on top of me have been cut. James has been here and buried him properly, just like he said he would. He must have climbed a few limbs to get some of the higher ones cut down. I kneel and switch batteries for my single night vison monocular. All the shit I purchased at that pawn shop and I didn't think to grab more batteries for this damn thing. Seven to eight hours should be plenty, as long as I shut it down and not leave it on standby mode. My GPS unit uses the same batteries if it comes to it.

A small cross makes itself known with the hunter's hi-vis vest wrapped around it. It shines like a new penny through my monocular, but the unearthed ground does not have as much snow covering it. Piles of recently dug dirt and snow are set aside all around the gravesite that he left visible for someone to find the remains. But why so little dirt on top of it? I move in closer to realize it is not a controlled effort at leaving so little dirt on top of it, but that of something that has dug it back up after he buried it. I hope it didn't come at him when he was trying to bury this poor bastard. I inspect the body that is still frozen in horror. The temperatures have kept it from rotting too quickly and filling the air with a putrid scent. There's a fresh injury to this guy.

A chest injury that has ripped open his rib cage to see all his innards. The chest cavity shows all his intestines, liver, and stomach that has already dispersed its fluids. The chest is pried open a foot wide from the middle and I can't see the heart, even with my mag light. These new claw and bit marks are well over a day old and some freeze has already covered part of his torso. Why just the heart and nothing else? Why hasn't any other animal come for a piece of the free meal? The amount of force it must have taken to open up the ribs like that, straight from the middle without a blade, tells me what did this without a doubt.

So, it eats. It eats the living but prefers the dead, maybe? Is it a scavenger or a predator? And it leaves everything behind for the woods to devour. Except for the heart. Not so mystical after all. Only a natural living breathing creature needs nutrition to survive from one day to the next. A creature that comes from somewhere unearthly would not need to eat to survive. It's a thinking creature. A creature that looks for vulnerability and is highly opportunistic. A creature that has specific tastes. This answers some questions, but not enough to know how to find it before it finds me first.

I take the better part of the rest of the night to make my way back to the coastline, using the GPS that helps in following my old route that took me outta the woods. I stop every hundred feet just to listen and look upward and all around me. I look upwards into the night sky through the trees to see what I feel is watching my every move, but nothing makes itself visible. Snow piles up on weaker branches and falls down in piles. Gravity and smaller varmints are to blame, but nothing out of the ordinary this early into the morning when things are waking up. Moon light tries to push through the snowfall, but the overcast won't let it in yet. A burst of single digit air freezes my nostrils and looms until the moon makes itself known through the black and grey skies after a few miles.

I come across his encampment when the salt is in the air.

"James!" as I call out to see if he emerges from his little hut. "James... Are you there?!"

I look around the snow-covered ground and the fire pit we sat by outside is covered in snow. There isn't even a hole in the ground where it was supposed to be. His hut is covered in shrubbery, and the forest weeds have taken over it. I was sober and alert when we both left here, but nobody appears to have been here in ages, if ever. This can't be. I spent days here with him, though some of those days were unconscious on my part. Before approaching the hut any closer, I walk around the area to look at the beach front and see the old remnants of the washed away docks within the sand that he told me about. Fuel cans, driftwood, and trash remain covering the area as smaller waves attempt to wash more away into the sea. More fuel cans sit around his hut but are covered in rust from not being moved in several seasons of snow and weather.

"James, where are you?!" I ask, but nobody calls back out. Nobody has been here in months. This is not like I remember it. This can't be happening. The only other place to look is inside the hut, but I look on the bluff to see nothing again. Now that I remember very well. Every time we stepped out the few days I spent recovering here with him, that white deer would overlook the area, but out to the sea. He isn't there at the moment. I walk back around to see more shrubbery and lumber piled up on the outside of the door. So, somebody has been here. I remember he would pile up some of the stronger pieces of lumber on the inside at night. I drop my ruck where the fire pit used to be and ready my Henry as I approach the front of the hut.

"James?!" I call out again, but no answer.

I place the rifle to my firing hand with a finger outside the trigger housing and start moving wood to the side of the hut with my left hand. I grab the right piece of wood and the pile goes falling over to the side. I ready the rifle up to my shoulder and kick the door inwards, but it rips off the rusted hinges and falls to the packed sandy floor inside. Dust settles as a few squirrels jump through the holes of the roofing. I walk inside with the rifle buttstock against my cheek, but there isn't enough room in here to maneuver around.

There's nothing inside beyond more rusted fuel cans. No medical books or sleeping cots anywhere. His heater is still in place but covered in cobwebs and sandy dust. The indoor plant hanger has nothing but dead roots hanging from the side of the pot where critters enjoyed a free meal. The large wash bowl and smaller kitchenware is gone. There's nothing here as I look around. Then I see my old busted deer stand from the first attack. I pick it up to examine it, to be sure my eyes aren't playing tricks on me. The same safety cord I cut dangles off the bottom. It appears covered in dust and sand from age, too. The fabric is tattered and stained with blood from the bites of my shoulder. This can't be real. Where did he go? He had no means to carry away everything he kept in this little building. I step back outside and look in it again. A dim morning sun tries to fade in and out through the few openings and doorway of the hut. Or maybe it is still the moonlight. I don't know anymore.

I drop my Henry next to me on the ground and fall to my knees. What's wrong with me. There's nothing here. No one is here. Nobody has been here. Was I even here? Was anybody ever here? They said this might happen. They said I might see things. They said I could have nightmares. But this can't be real. Somebody stitched me up. Somebody put my arm in place. I stick a finger in my mouth to look for missing teeth, but all of them are still in place. I strip my shirt off outside the hut in the cold to look for the stitching scars on my shoulder and the bruising all over my rib cage, but those are all still there. I don't understand. It's just not fucking possible. Am I really as far gone as they I'll said I would be?

"Allahu Akbar! Allahu Akbar! Allahu Akbar! Allahu Akbar!
Ashhadu an la ilaha illa Allah. Ashhadu an la ilaha illa Allah.
Ashadu anna Muhammadan Rasool Allah. Ashadu anna Muhammadan Rasool Allah."

Where am I? That call to prayer only happens in certain places. I remember it well. I remember it every morning and all throughout the day. Five times a day. I remember the scratched speakers tones they would have set up on their mosques. I remember their faces. It never rains like this there. It was never this cold there to make the rain seem so freezing. The rain just seems to be hardened and near frozen already, but it never rained there when I was there. I turn to look through the clearing of the woods behind me and a mosque sits there as all the males walk to it with heads down. They slip their shoes off to make a pile before they enter with their kneeling rugs in hand.

"Hayya 'ala-s-Salah. Hayya 'ala-s-Salah.
Hayya 'ala-l-Falah. Hayya 'ala-l-Falah.
Allahu Akbar! Allahu Akbar!
La ilaha illa Allah."

It's always so loud in my ears. Every morning and every night. We stay respectable to their religion. We all kneel during the call to prayer as they enter to the mosque, so as not to discredit them, but this time is different. Their heads are down because they are crying. The women on the balcony of the mosque are also crying and screaming as they pray to the skies, bowing and raising multiple times. They pray and cry to the heavens, despite the rain or sleet that can return to snow at any moment. I wish it would snow for them here. The snow is more peaceful than the rain. How are they here? How am I here again? How has this hell followed me home again?

The call to prayer is over, so I raise up off my knee to readjust my gear and helmet. I lean over to grab my M4 back off the ground. That prayer never stops, even after the loudspeakers are gone. It used to be beautiful when I first heard it over there. Now it is a dreaded sound. I look over to see the interpreter, and he looks back at me with his lifeless eyes. Black eyes from the hemorrhaging of the back of his skull. They filled his chest with shrapnel and bullet holes as he stands up alongside me. He has trouble walking while his torn up and skinned knees collapse under the weight of his rotting body.

"Tarjimon, are we clear to go in now?" I ask while repositioning my M4 in front of my magazine pouches without trying to point it at him.

"Yes. They mourn their loved ones like this and they must bury the dead after a single day of prayer for those they lost." He turns and points with a single hand to the mosque, but they shredded his clothes with the back side of his arm burned up. His fingers are missing, and his nose doesn't stop bleeding as he splatters me with blood and rot as he tries to talk while spitting through his decaying lips. He falls down to the ground lifelessly at my feet as I ignore him and walk to the mosque in full gear.

"Wait, I will come with you inside. I will tell them you came to see the bodies and they will understand why you are there." he says from the ground with his face planted in the mud.

I walk closer and the frozen rain falls harder the more I close the distance between us and the mosque. The entire team stands behind me. All of us in full uniform and gear covered in sweat and rainfall as we struggle with several pounds of gear on us. We move to a smaller building on the back side of the mosque to see them all laying there in a row. We won't enter while they are in prayer. At least five men, dead with family standing all around. Most with bullet wounds to their chest and torso. They stay laid out on display for their families to grieve and mourn before they are put into the Afghan ground.

"You can go inside now." says the tarjimon. "They are waiting to speak with you inside the mosque." He points his nubs of his remaining arm into the mosque. He decomposes and falls apart in front of me more and more each time I turn to look at him. His jawbone hangs from his cheek and his belly bloats in front of me from bile oozing out his bullet holes. I step inside to see more bodies laid next to each other and elders gather around to chant more prayers in their native language.

"These men were victim of someone coming in for a pray and spray with an AK. Do they know what he was wearing?" I ask the interpreter. He limps closer to speak with the elders. They point and explain what happened, and he tells me in return. They cannot recall other than he was wearing all black when it happened the night prior, but one had the first shot fired to the back of his head. They point to the bullet holes in the wall that confirm my assumption on the "pray and spray" method and I move closer to examine it.

"Who was he? The one that they say was shot execution style?" I ask the terp.

"He was the Mullah. He has spoken with *you* before." he says.

"Where's the body?"

He points his arm, of near skeletal remains now, to the corner of the room with his dead body on top of a special shrine. A younger boy, maybe 12 or 13 years old, sits next to him on his knees as I examine more bullet holes all over the interior of the mosque on the other side of the body. My gear makes me clumsy and I knock over a bowl that was sitting next to the dead mullah.

"Shit... Tarjimon, tell them I'm sorry. I meant no disrespect to the remains."

He tells the other elders as I ask and they reply back to him, motioning their hands. "It is ok, they say. You meant no disrespect. They know you are here to help them find who did this."

I bend down and drop to a knee to pick up the bowl I knocked over. They filled it with his teeth from being shot in the back of the head. I take my gloves off to scrap them up back into the bowl and the younger boy comes over to help. He looks at me in tears as he picks up the teeth with me. His Afghan attire is covered in moisture under his neck from wiping his face with it. He pauses after we finish picking up the teeth and I hand the bowl back to him. He just holds it with both hands as he looks at them.

"Koja tu waqteke zesht me'aayam?" he says in his language. He keeps holding the bowl to look at the teeth and then look back at me. *"Koja tu?"* again and again with those tearing eyes and quivering lips as we both kneel down beside this dead mullah.

"Tarjimon?" I ask, while the boy is still kneeling in front of me. "Who is this boy? Did he see who did this? Ask him... He's trying to tell me something."

The boy stands back up and places the bowl of teeth next to the body where it was. The interpreter tries to speak to him, but he keeps shaking his head no and bows again in prayer.

"We gotta roll." I tell the team outside. "We'll come back after they bury their dead. We can't do anything right now like this out in the open in broad daylight. Tarjimon, who is the boy? What did he say to me?" I ask.

"That's the Mullah's eldest son. He says he wasn't here when it happened. We must go now as they pray again." he says.

We all move out as fast as we came into the area. Out into the rains and the team of soldiers disappear behind me, one by one. I turn back to look at the mosque crumbling down to the ground with the screams of everyone inside. Gun shots fired all around. I raise my M4, but there is nothing to shoot at. It was over for all of them in that village before it even began. No bullets zooming by anywhere. Just the hard Afghan soil that claims the mosque into the ground as dust, with the rest of the corpses inside it still. They died for nothing beyond talking to us just once. Talking to me just once is all it took. I turn to the interpreter to see him face down in the mud again, showing his backside with multiple exit wounds from AK rounds. I roll him over to see his face still trying to breathe.

"Tarjimon? Tarjimon! Can you hear me?! Get the fuck up, you damn coward. Get up. What did he say? What did that boy say to me?" I ask, while slapping him to keep him conscious from the blast.

"He didn't talk in my dialect. I cannot say for sure, sir."

"Then try dammit. What the fuck did he say?! *Koja tu?* What does that mean?"

"He asked you... He asked you, *where were you? Where are you when the wicked come?* He asked *where you were when they needed you* in some sort of Dari language or dialect." The interpreter turns to dust in my hands. The only thing left on my gloves is his blood that remained stained on them. This isn't real. This can't be real again. I should have taken the damn pills they offered. This can't be happening again. This was over ten years ago. These woods are fucking with me again. This creature is in my head somehow. None of this is real. Get outta my head.

"This isn't fucking happening again!" I scream out loud into the trees.

James' hut falls apart in front of me under the weight of the frozen rain. It turns to rubble hidden by the overgrown shrubbery around it. The Afghan boy still stands there on top of the crumbled hut in the rain holding the bowl of teeth.

"Koja tu?" he says.

"Shut up! Get the hell away from me!!!"

The rains get heavier as the freezing air turns it to ice and hail. I'm not there again. I'm in the woods. I'm in the Jersey Pine Barrens. None of this is real. I pick up my Henry Lever Action and hold the cold steel to my forehead, hoping to wake up or come back to the woods. I turn and see him still standing there crying out when the call to prayer rings through my ears again.

"Allahu Akbar! Allahu Akbar! Allahu Akbar! Allahu Akbar! Ashhadu an la ilaha illa Allah. Ashhadu an la ilaha illa Allah."

This is America. I'm on American soil. This is my home. Not yours. This is my haven. The rains get heavier, and I look to my feet to see teeth falling all around me into the frozen snow. Teeth are falling on my shoulders and forehead, bouncing off my Henry. I lean down to the ground and scoop them up in my hand, hoping it is snow. But its human teeth falling all around me. Teeth of the dead. Human teeth that fall harder and harder on my back side as I'm leaned over. They cut my neck and forehead as I move to the tree line for cover. They bounce off the back of my hands as I try to cover my face while moving. The boy just stands there crying out the same thing. The teeth bouncing off the frozen ground, the call to prayer, the noise, and all I can do is yell back at it as I grab my ruck while running into the tree line.

I jump under the downed limb of a massive pine and keep the ruck on top of my head. Everything is quiet again. Only the wind and falling freezing rain shaped as teeth that are slowly turning to snow flurries again. The winds pick up to make the pine I sit under creek and moan. I have to stay under cover. I have to keep my head down. Never go out into the open like that. They'll always get you in the open like that. Never let them see you vulnerable in the open. Always remain near cover or with camouflage at the minimal. I need both cover and camouflage out here or they'll come for me again. They'll shoot more of us down one by one. They all need to die. They all need to burn for what they did.

182

I hold my Henry close after I prop up the ruck on the branch to give me some cover. This is a lever gun, and it shoots a 45-70 caliber showstopper. This is not my old M4 semi-automatic assault rifle. I'm here. Not there. I'm here. Not there. I close my eyes and try to hold my breath in to lower my heart rate. In your nose and out of your mouth. In your nose and out of your mouth. Slowly. This is home. This is not a faraway land. This... Is... My... Home. The wind keeps picking up with the snow flurries and tosses the snowflakes around hard and fast enough to cause a white out all around me. A dust storm would be the same thing. Leaving all of us blind and helpless amid a combat zone. Hard to breathe. I uncover the gator neck from my mouth and look to the sky for fresh air and tell myself it is only snow and wind that is howling through the trees. I crunch the teeth all over the ground with each step.

My eyes adjust to the dark overcast of the early morning to see through the branches how they have all been watching the entire time. Those countless yellow eyes looking down at me as I move further into the tree line for more cover if it rains teeth down on me again. They sit there high above, motionless. Their eyes don't even blink as they look down on me, moving around on the ground like a wounded animal. They are just waiting to come down on me once I give in and accept a horrible fate of being flogged and ravaged to death by countless owls. I lay on my back against the tree and point the rifle up at them. I take aim, knowing that this caliber is strong enough to blast through at least three or four of them if they are sitting in a row.

The wind bounces the tree limb that the one or two sit on that I have in my sights. They stare right down at my barrel from a near thirty feet in the air. Not a single movement from them to maintain their footing in the wind and snow. The shot will have to be timed perfect to get more than one at a time with that limb bouncing.

Gimme that clean shot with two of you fuckers in line...

Slight pressure on the trigger...

Squeeze, don't pull...

Just breathe...

"Come feast with us…" the same chilling whisper in the wind calls out to me.

The round exits out of the barrel like a thunderous bowling ball blasting out of a cannon from the side of a warship. I take the shot and the rifle kicks my injured shoulder down into the ground, but I take the pain with a low growl beneath my breath. The sounds echo into the open sea, but none of the owls move. Not a single flinch or flutter from them after the smoke from the muzzle clears.

"Come feast with us…"

The Afghan boy is up there with them, sitting on a branch. *"Koja tu?"* he says.

"What are you doing up there?!" I jump up off my back and try to find a branch to climb to get him. I can't let these owls take him. I won't let these woods have him.

"Koja tu?"

"Just stay still up there! Can you hear me?! I'm gonna try to come up and get you! Just stay there ok?! Don't look at them birds! Just don't look at them! I'm coming up!"

I scramble around at the forest floor to look for another tree that might have higher branches. Nothing appears within reach, so I run to my ruck in a hurry to pull out my spurs to climb. They are in here somewhere to stay handy. I look back up as I keep looking through my gear.

"Come feast with us…"

The boy moves around on the branch of the tree next to the owls that are perfectly still. A rope dangles at his feet. Oh God, no… Not like this. Don't do this to me. Please God no…

"Kid!! Can you hear me?! Don't do it! Just be still and I'm gonna come up to get you! Stop moving! You're gonna be ok!!"

"Koja tu?" as he pushes himself off the branch.

"Dammit… No!!!" and I try to run under him to catch him. He stops with the crack of a neck, and his feet dangle just above my reach. His toes and legs tense up as he grabs the noose around his neck. I watch him choke to death in horror while being too low to help him. All goes quiet again. All wind ceases as he hangs there just above me, and I can't hold back my screams of hatred. A forever feeling of twenty or thirty seconds and he stops twitching and gurgling above me.

"Come feast with us..."

They still sit above him, looking down at me. None of this is real. I'm not listening to this anymore. I stand up and pull the lever to chamber another round and fire off at them. I keep shooting and scream at them at the top of my lungs until the magazine tube is empty and they continue to sit there unharmed. The Afghan boy looks down at me too now as he hangs there. His eyes blink back at me as he sways left and right.

"Your boy burns with us." he says while hanging with a twisted neck.

"You're not real!!!" I scream through my scratching throat.

"None of you are real. I'm here to stay. I'm not running this time."

"They all feast with us. All the ones you left to burn."

Out of breath as I frantically reach into my cargo pocket of my jacket to reload the Henry through its side gate.

"This is my home. This is my land. I'm not going anywhere until you are all dead and gone back to the Hell you came from. You tell this monster! You fucking tell it to come out of its fucking hole!"

"You will join us soon..." it says. The voices echo through the winds and into my mind over and over. They don't fucking stop.

The body drops to the ground after the rope snaps and worms around on the forest floor as the boy continuously gasps for air as if he is still dying, repeatedly. He becomes covered in teeth and snow before my very eyes until he disappears into the white out. The owls above flutter and jump into the air simultaneously as I keep my rifle sighted on all of them. They fly up above the tree line in unison to develop a pattern of circles like vultures that await the opportunity to come down and ravage on a dead animal on the side of the road. They fly in circles above until fading away into the white out of the gray skies above. The wind ceases, but I keep the rifle up at the ready on an empty horizon.

"You go tell that bastard child I'm right here waiting..."

Chapter 17: The One that Got Away

I don't know how long I sat on the porch steps after that van drove away, but I muster the strength to get back up and go inside to an empty home. I strip my uniform and fix up my catheter before I shower to clean the day off me. I grab my things out of the patrol SUV and set up shop with the portable dialysis machine in the garage. A double effort tonight for the dialysis machine for missing the last few scheduled attempts. An hour in and I feel the rocks in my torso loosening up and my skin goes back to a normal color.

I send Rachel the text to bring Drake by after dropping off Sherral at home.

I have used the garage as my office at home for a while now. Jaynese didn't care to go much further than our bedroom and the living room to watch TV. When I'm not trying to get some sleep in Maggie's Dora themed room, I am in here looking at case files all over the wall. She didn't even have a vehicle to park in here. She sold off her car at some point earlier this year to get her fix. She got a stash so big that time; it was like it doped her out of her mind for two months straight. I couldn't find where she hid it in the house during the little time I choose to be home now. Broken-in denim jeans and a white undershirt feel good for a change after a hot shower. I carry the machine around with me at my side like a small briefcase as I walk through the house. As long as it is charged, it can last for the rest of the night, but I plug it into the wall outlet of the garage anyway, after I grab the last few beers out of the fridge to take with me. I guzzle them down to take the load off my shoulders.

I hung the pictures all over the place in the garage. I had Sherral back at the station print me an oversized map of the area to pinpoint where all the attacks have happened. I slip into my bag and pull out the pictures from today. I plop down on the old couch I dragged in here after getting new furniture. She almost burned this one up in the living room with her lighter, but I cover it up with an older bed sheet. I sit and stare at all of them. Every photo of everybody this thing has left us to find. The bus driver, the guy from today, all the clothes the children had on but not leaving any signs of where they were. I resized the note from today larger to fill out an entire paper. The notes of all the locations we searched on the oversized map and when we searched them. A photo of the stake that was rammed into the tree somehow. It's all here, right in front of me, to drive myself insane over all night, every night until I find them. Until I find her and she's in my arms again.

I hear a car door slam outside in the driveway. I can hear a familiar bark. I step up to look through the smaller windows of the closed garage door to see Drake and Rachel making their way to the front door. Nobody knocks as she just walks in. She and Drake always got along well. He would let her know if something was wrong inside the house.

"Jason... It's me. I'm here with Drake!" yelling from the front door.

Drake hurries into the garage, already knowing where I am. He hops on the couch next to me and nudges under my arm for a bit of attention.

"Hey there ol' boy. Did you miss me? You were only gone for a few hours." but he moves in to lick my nose, anyway. Rachel walks in through the house in uniform, looking for me.

"Right here, Rachel." As I raise the last of my beer to grab her attention from the kitchen.

She comes right in with a concerned look. "I thought you weren't supposed to be drinking while you plugged into that machine?"

I ignore the concern. "Thanks for bringing Drake by, Rachel. I take it you already took Sherral home too."

"Yeah. She brought me up to speed about everything. You guys had a rough day out there." She moves over to look at all my handy work to see all the photos and the map with pinpoints all over it.

"Yeah. Rough may be an understatement for today. A lot of those guys turned in their badges after what happened. We barely got enough deputies to keep the station going now."

"What are we gonna do?" she asks.

"Well, for starters. You're gonna call up Greeves and Davis and let them know to call it a night out there wherever they are patrolling. At least one of them should be held up back at the station if any calls come in."

"Yeah, it's Greeves that's still there now. Davis is out and about making sure nobody went out after we put the curfew in place. Had a driver slide off the road into a ditch after leaving the school late for the day, so he went helped them out with a tow. Beyond that, the town's pretty quiet. I don't know what's keeping people in more. The weather, rumors of a bear, or…"

"Or what?"

"You. Everybody knows, or at least everybody thinks, this is all your fault this town is falling apart. I don't know what to tell people anymore." She leans in to pick up the photos of the school bus pinned on the board next to the map. "Everybody's scared, Jason."

"I know, but we still have a job to do. When you call Greeves, let him know to have any 911 forwarded to the next county over. We're short manned. I need you guys to turn in for the night and get some sleep." She nods her head in agreement as she looks at the photos of the bus and the photo of what it left of the bus driver when we found him.

"We never dealt with anything like this in the city when I was at the department over in AC." as she studies the photo.

"I know. I'm sure you spent most of your days rounding up druggies and drunks out of the casinos there."

"Pretty much. A few of the pimps and dealers would get themselves brought in with a gunshot wound, but those idiot perps would never go very far with their weapons that they did it with. Most of them would keep it in their cars. The job was just too easy for us sometimes. Stupid and mundane shit, day after day out there in the city." she says.

"Is that why you came back?"

"Yeah. I missed this old town. The simplicity. The people I grew up with. Working with you."

"Well... I'm glad you came back."

She holds up the photo and points it at me. "I've never seen a person be able to dissect a crime scene like you can. To look at all these things and just seem to know so much. I wish you could have come with me. We would've been great there."

"I would have never lasted there. You know I enjoy being the big fish in a little pond."

"Yeah, I know." she turns to look at me. "You look a little better than the last time I saw you yesterday. Did you take your medicine?"

"I'm drinking it up right now." as I point at the beer on the old coffee table. She just turns and shakes her head like a disappointed mother. "You know that crap just makes me tired and loopy. I just gotta keep the machine going most nights and I'm good to go the next day."

"Right... Where's Jaynese, tonight?" she asks.

"If you didn't know, it would have been the first thing you mentioned and you would have never set foot in the house in the first place if you knew she was home. Everybody knows. Everybody even stepped outside to watch the show a while ago. I'm sure you heard already."

"Yeah, they came and got her for detox again. Had a compliant about the yelling from one of your newer neighbors."

"It's the safest place for her right now. They suggest no contact for the first few days."

She keeps looking at the different photos of the bus. "What's out there, Jason? We went searching for all those kids for days before the state PD came in a called it off. I was right there with you guys the whole time, but you're the only one that saw anything. You found the driver's body and the clothes from all those kids. Even Maggie's clothes were left there with them."

"Yeah, I know." as I look down at the photos of the body from today. The screams from today were the same as that day I found the bus driver. The freezing cold we were up against in the middle of winter. Even poor Drake could hardly keep up with us during the search. Everyone was too tired to keep going, but I did, and I saw it clear as day. I'll never forget the thing I saw for as long as I live. I look over to see Drake passed out beside me on the couch.

"He's had a long day too, being out there with us." as I point to him, and she grins.

"You didn't answer me... What did you see out there?" she asks as she puts the photo back on the board in front of her and turns to me. All I can do is keep ignoring her, but that never worked before. She walks over to me and sits on the coffee table in front of me.

She raises my head up to her. "It's me, Jason... You can tell me. You've always been honest with me. Just tell me what is out there, what took Maggie?"

"You wouldn't believe me if I told you... took."

"What?" she asks.

"You said *took*, but you didn't say killed her."

"I know. Nobody's dead until there's a body to prove it. Right?" she says.

"I'm glad I'm not alone in knowing that."

"Does this thing have her? This thing you saw. This thing that keeps leaving dead ones for us to find?"

"I think so. I think I'm losing it too. I think I scare myself sometimes more than it scares me."

"You never scared me."

"*Yeah*, I know."

190

"What do I need to do. Just tell me, Jason. I'm right here with you all the way on this one."

"You need to leave and let the others off for the night. We are heading out first thing in the morning to go after the previous body mentioned to us. Ricky Clauson has been missing over a week, but he isn't dead until we know he is dead." I get up with the dialysis machine still beeping in hand to start pointing at the map. "We got a tentative location of an individual that helped the man that waltzed out of our damn custody earlier today near here. I know you said he may have tried the old "Black Doctor of the Woods" story on me, but he may have mistaken him for someone else that is out there." I point to the location on the map near the shoreline. "That's the old fueling point, but the docks are washed away. We find whoever helped him, and we find Ricky. We go from there."

"Makes sense, but what about the guy you questioned earlier this morning?" she asks.

"He's nobody. Just a whine-bag veteran with a death wish. Have the state police remove the APB bulletin and get him off the radar. Chances are, he's already out there in the barrens."

"How do you know?"

"I know his type. He's headed out there to go after this thing and he don't plan on coming back."

"Why is that?"

"Because we all think the same."

"What do you mean?" she asks.

"Nothing… It doesn't matter. I wouldn't be surprised to see him strung up somewhere too. This thing is gonna keep going after whatever it can, anything that crosses its path. The bodies are piling up though, and they are coming in more frequently. I don't think it got to finish the job with the one we found today. The guy's heart may have still been in place, but the coroner hasn't confirmed that, yet."

"The hearts were always missing. I remember that."

"More than missing. It ripped them out with a serious amount of force. I won't be shocked to see our escapee in the same manner."

"So, you're using this veteran guy as bait?"

"Exactly."

"I didn't think of that."

"Well, if you were this creature, would you rather take on a group of deputies packing weapons? Or one nutty veteran with a death wish? It will go after him first. It will probably kill him. But it's a chance we gotta take. One dead loner versus twelve missing kids. I think I can live with that."

"How will we know if he came across it?"

"Just follow the screams or the gunfire when we get out there."

"What if he is dead already?" she asks.

"Well, if he's smart, he's hunkered down somewhere in the storm. He'd be crazy, or a lil too dedicated for his own good to be out there in weather like this."

"That was my next thing. What about this storm we're going through? There talkin single digits, freezing rain, more snow, the works on this one, Jason. What's going on now, it's just the start."

"Dress warm is all I can say. We'll try to make our way back into town before night fall or if it gets too bad out there during the daytime hours. We go in with some serious firepower and take no chances on this one. We're going deep into the area but not far enough in to where we wouldn't make it back in time before it gets too late. Before we push out tomorrow morning, Sherral should already have a line on some state troopers that may come out to help us and the game wardens in the next county over. We got Drake with us that can sniff almost anything out, too. Are you on board with all this, Rachel?" I ask as she keeps staring at all the points of the map and photos.

"Yeah, let's get out there and finish this." she says.

"That's my girl. Ok, as soon as you head out call in Greeves and Davis and let them know what's going on. There are no more shifts patrolling tonight. I need you all on your best with a decent night's sleep. You'll have to pick up Sherral on your way in. I'm gonna need her on the phones with a dispatcher to be ready to redirect any calls if anything comes in on the 911 horn."

"Are you gonna get some sleep too?"

"You already know what I'm gonna say to that."

"Yeah, yeah, yeah…" she says sarcastically.

"I'll sleep when I'm dead. Go on, you know what to do. You gotta head out now. I know that Crown Vic isn't the best in the snow like this."

"Ok, is there anything else that needs to get done?"

"Everything else can wait for a briefing first thing in the morning and we'll lay it all out when we have a count on who's coming."

She gets up from the coffee table she was sitting on for a bit and walks over to pet Drake, who migrated to a different end of the couch to snooze as soon as I moved to point out things on the map.

"I can stay here if you need me to. I can help you with…" she says as she walks to the door and stops in her tracks.

"Can't let you do that, Rachel. You know that."

"Ok then."

"Thanks for bringing Drake home. Thanks for everything."

"Of course. I gotta take care of my two boys." she says, while turning back to look at me with a smile. I unplug from the dialysis machine to follow her out the door of the garage into the kitchen area.

"You're the best deputy I got. I wish I had a few more like you instead of some of these local boy scouts that are more worried about getting their drink on."

She moves to the front door and opens it so that we both stand outside and see the snowfall that doesn't feel as lonely now.

"Well, you still got me. You always did. I just wish…" she stutters.

"Don't say it."

"But…" She walks back from the front door to hug me. Her soft hands slip up and down the back of my neck. I remember those fingers. I miss her in more ways than not, but things are different now. We had our moment and we both let it slip away. She holds me tight just like I remember and raises up to try to kiss my lips, but I raise my hands to lower her head to kiss her on the hair line instead. I look back at her in those wanting brown eyes. We are right next to each other but still so far apart somehow. How could I have ever let this one go? I lean in to talk low to her. "Just don't say it. Not tonight. Not now. You don't have to say it because I already know."

She lowers back into my chest and I kiss the top of her head again as she still holds on to me.

"I'm just glad you came back." I tell her.

"I came back because you asked me to."

"I know. Go home now. Get some sleep. Careful driving out there in this." She lets me go but holds my hand while trying to walk away.

"Goodnight, Jason."

As she drives away into the night, I give her a wave. I'm two for two in one damn night. Watching a woman that I love to leave me on the steps of my home alone with the snowfall to keep me company in the cold of night.

I move back inside to see how late it is, and Drake hasn't moved an inch on the couch in the garage. I can hear him snoring from the kitchen. I lock the house down and set the thermostat to go up against the freezing temps outside. The lights shut off and Drake is sound asleep. The dialysis machine beeps its ending cycle but I hit the restart after replacing the drain bag to run it all night tonight to make up for missed dosages over the last few days. I go to Maggie's room and leave the door slightly open, so the light doesn't wake Drake. He'll need his energy tomorrow too.

I drop to a knee to pull the box out from under Maggie's bed. The long slender weapons box is covered in dust. I only keep it this close to me to remind me what it is for. If Maggie were still here, she would never know this black box existed. I filled the box with military gear from back in the day. Photos, records, uniform pieces, unit patches, and it all stays here this close to me every night to remind me that sometimes I have to do what's necessary. I move the old, moth-eaten uniforms and gear aside to pull it out.

My M4 assault rifle is as clean as the day I left it in this box, hoping I would never have to see it again. Lots of memories with this old AR. Took a lot to purchase it from the last unit they assigned me to once they discharged me. I don't know why I kept it, just to put it in a box never to be seen or used again. But I need you now more than ever. This is a better use for this weapon. A good use for a good cause. Not for some deployment to earn another officer a set of stripes to get closer to his General rank. We gotta end something that needs to end. We gotta kill something, but not to satisfy a political cause. We gotta kill to keep the ones we love safe and brought home. That's why I kept you and why I still keep you close.

Drake wakes up to come strolling in Maggie's room to ease his curiosity. He knows the things that happen when he sees this assault rifle out getting wiped off.

"Don't worry, boy. We're gonna go get shit done this time. You remember? Just like the old days, right buddy? You and me against the world out there in the desert… Well, a blizzard anyway."

He sits down on his hind legs but looks outside the room to see an empty and dark house.

"Oh, Rachel left buddy. You'll get to hang out with her again more tomorrow."

He drops to lie down in front of the doorway to let me know he is pouting again.

"Oh, come on dude. Just be glad you ain't got no gonads to have to deal with women in your life. I've got too many of them to deal with as it is."

He sighs through his nose. If dogs could only talk, but he would still be man's best friend until the end of it all.

"Maybe we can find you a nice dame to bring home when this is all over? You're fixed so you can't knock anybody up anytime soon. So, are you like a nice French poodle kinda guy or do you like to get some strange from them nasty ass strays? Bitches love a dog in uniform ya know."

He gets up to stretch and yawns before he walks out to drop on his bed and gnaw at his chew toy outside the room.

"I meant that in a good way!... I'm just saying."

I look down to see the tough box has dozens of magazine and a near lifetime supply of 5.56 NATO style tracer ammo. Just holding it and doing quick functions check makes me hesitant. I look down the red dot sighting optic and replace the battery to make sure it turns on. It never worked as a scope like some idiots thought, it's just a reflex sight for fast response. The attached surefire light still works the same once replaced. The screams and terror that came with this assault rifle and it's stayed by my side all along under my missing daughter's toddler bed.

No more screams after this, though.

Time to do right by this.

Chapter 18: The Bait

Any knowledgeable hunter knows a prey needs to be drawn in somehow. Whether it is a natural lure or not, everything has to eat sometime. It's opportunistic and its nocturnal. Owls are an indicator of its presence and it likes to toy with the remains of its victims. It likes to put them on display for others to come look for their fellow man. This is a vicious predator and nothing more. Anything else is in my head. It might own the woods here, but it doesn't own me. I have to stay focused. I have to keep these woods out of my head. I have to think about the hunt and nothing more. It knows I'm here. It thinks. It comprehends. It looks for weakness and vulnerability.

Animals can sense people. Not just the presence of people, but what's in a person's heart. They know what a person's motives are with or without seeing the person's demeanor. This thing has a keen sense on both things. It likes to toy with a potential prey. It likes the worthy hunt and not the easy takedown. Just like what I prefer. It prefers a challenge in a hunt. James was right all along. Is it smart enough to sense a bait? Does it comprehend enough to know where I am? Would it mistake me for another local hunter like it did last time? Whether it thinks it's me or some other hunter passing through, it might come if it had reason to believe it was a quick meal or a notable opponent. I would do the same thing out on any other hunt, too.

I will give it signs to follow. Enough to know someone is here. He may think it's someone else. But if those owls communicate with it somehow while it is dormant in the daylight hours, then it'll already know it's me out here and it will make its presence known. It will scurry and sneak around to scare me until I have a chance to see it coming, like last time. It will try to scare me into running or having to stand my ground again with no choice but to fight back. Deer seem to be close by like the last time I saw it too. Was it hunting some poor doe to rip apart before it found the other hunter and then me? That has to be it. That's what makes it opportunistic. Always go for the bigger fish. Next to this creature, this sea of pines offers the next bigger fish of hunters, maybe bear, coyotes, then deer, then whatever else is beneath them. The food chain is a beautiful thing out here.

I leave James' old camp sight and make my way out to my old hunting area. Wherever I take down a deer, doe, or otherwise, is where a new encampment needs to be set up. Set up the stronghold maybe, hang a dead deer for carving up and slaughter. That will at least draw it in a make it curious to know if it is me out here hunting again or not. White tails are more active just before nightfall and throughout the night. That doesn't give me a lot of time to work with. The sleet turns to frozen rain again as my feet crunch through the snow that has stayed on the ground. It takes a few hours of fast walking and near jogging to get back to my hunting site from memory. I stop to pull out the hand warmers to place them on the interior of my camel back to melt my frozen water supply. I use the scent blocker and mud to cover my own scent and the smell of gun oil on the Henry. I leave my ruck buried under brush and more snow before getting any closer. I'm faster without all that weight on my back.

I move between the trees to get closer to my area. I stay unnoticed by even the rabbits that jump from their burrows to eat and drink some of the moisture that has settled on the weeds. Each step is slow and methodical. I move my feet from heel to toe, not to snap any branches or twigs too loudly or crunch sand mixed with frozen snow. The remains of the salt brick deer feeder I left are in sight, but nothing else is around it. I get closer to it to realize that salt has been licked away clean down to the stake in the smaller tree that held it up. I remember the rut marks all over the trees in this area. There is even a small watering hole nearby that the deer used to drink fresh spring water that always flows out of it. As long as the spring water flows it may not have frozen up by now. I stay low to the ground and hunched over to observe droppings that aren't covered in snow.

They're still here in this small clearing. They'll keep coming back to an area that has what they want. Salt feeders and pine needles freshly fallen from the snow that are rich in nutrients, more than enough spots to rut and mate some poor doe that gets killed in the process. Once daylight goes away again, they'll come back still thinking this is the perfect spot to do what they do best. I pull out the knife from my boot and clean it off with my clothes and jacket. I pull out another bottle from my cargo pocket and pour some deer scent all over the area surrounding a new salt brick. Moving what's left of the old mineral salt brick feeder, and add it to the new and take it to an open area that several have laid down in. I slice the knife through my hand to cover it with a noticeable amount of blood. I grunt quietly in a quick pain as I squeeze my blood through a clinched fist onto the blade. I slam the handle of the knife upright in the salt brick to stick into the air. I place more deer scent and my blood all over the sides of the blade and stick more salt to it covering all the metal with salt, except for both edges.

If a white tail can remember a location, then this creature can do the same thing. It'll know I've been here from the slightest changes from the last time it attacked me here. Deer won't get spooked by a specific location or remember that gunshots happened here. But this creature may be smart enough to know a location regarding gunfire that happened near it last time. I move back to my ruck to grab my ghillie blanket, and water to bring back to the clearing. By the time I get back to a vantage point of the clearing the salt brick is set up on, a cluster of deer has trickled into the area. If they come this soon with daylight hours still remaining, then they are that comfortable with the location and unaware of me.

I set up my camouflage in a hurry. An entire family of them enters the area with noses down to the ground, sniffing. Full grown does and younger ones that have tiny black nubs sprouting for future horn racks. They find the brick within an hour after getting their fill of pine needles, and a six pointer joins the herd of maybe nine or ten in total. I watch as they lick the remnants of the brick first, but the six-point buck is the first one to lick the salt from the knife. He gives a slight twitch away after a small and sudden sharp pain to his tongue but goes right back to licking the salt covered blade. He loses interest so others can do the same thing. They all do the same thing, with more than one licking the blade at the same time.

The buck comes back in again, but his tongue is hanging out and dripping blood as he approaches the blade for another taste. They all seem quiet and content as they take turns. A two-hundred-pound animal has to lose at least two or three pints of blood before dropping, and it is never quick to bleed them out with such a minor wound. But they just keep licking the knife and the salt brick more and more. Soon enough, the knife no longer has salt on it, but they only covered it in their own blood that is filled with the same taste of their desired minerals of salt that they need to stay fit through the winter. The taste keeps them coming back each time as they keep licking each other's blood off the knife. It's hours into the evening like this. They take a lick of the salt brick, then take a lick of the blade covered in salty blood, and then keep slashing their tongues open more and more to create a mortally ending wound that they cannot feel, see, or hear.

The darkness comes and my water freezes again. The sleet filled flurry has turned to a quiet snowfall, but all remain calm during the twisted and deranged end of life that I have created while watching from my vantage point. A familiar death that I have created again for many things in the past. Only this time, there are no screams of pain. No concerns of the one deer moving slower than the other in a dizzy trance from loss of blood. More of the herd have joined the feast with each other. A dining in their own blood that they keep coming back to repeatedly. One of the smaller doe finally drops to lie on the ground, panting, with her bleeding tongue sticking out her mouth in a limp manner. She has no worries or concerns beyond what nature demands of tasting more of the same thing that the others keep eating too.

Something that tastes so good and full of salty minerals that the body needs for them to live but will kill all of them. Are we so different in our own human ways? These animals will go peacefully though. Simply fall asleep, not to wake up in the cold anymore. Whereas we make the end for others as violent as we can think of. To generate suffering as harshly as possible to others. That is our difference here, but we are the same in always coming back to the things that kill us. We know what kills us. We watch others go to their deaths without a second thought. Do we convince ourselves that death is nonexistent for ourselves and others in some delusion? The deer do not have to convince themselves that death isn't near because they never knew of it beyond their own natural instinct of safety.

It is a comparison that is easily comprehended and commonly misunderstood. Our own nature. I could get up and scare the other deer off before more continue to take that deadly taste of the blade, but I sit and wait for the doe to lay her head down. I will sit and wait for the deer to stop coming in to end their own life. If I only knew when the same could come for me, I would want to go in the same way. I would watch others I know drift away quietly and content. Without struggle or worry and simply fall asleep with them at the end of it all. But we don't do that to ourselves. That is only a dream left to be desired when waking back up in the reality that pains us all.

Younger deer start to drift off and wobble. Panting in slight concern but more in confusion why the taste of salt doesn't leave their mouth. None of them think to look at the doe that has already gone to sleep near them. To them, it just makes them want to do the same in the illusion of safety she gives them. I watch this for hours as they all slowly drop and go away into the night. The larger bucks that joined in are the last to drop. I try to tell myself that there was no good time to stop it all from happening, or I have convinced myself out of necessity that they were dead already with the first taste. They pant in the snow while lying on the ground. Some raise their heads up to see the rest of the group laying comfortably too. Their tongues stay out while still bleeding and dripping out their own blood. Their chests eventually stop raising and lowering. Their bodies are still warm for a while and snow melts as it touches their coats. Some of the ones already on the ground begin to pant heavily as the buck grunts and snorts, realizing what he has allowed his family to do to themselves.

But it's too late for him and the others. He has just burdened himself with being the last one to fall asleep after knowing what has happened to his herd. Knowing what he has allowed to happen to his family. I hope animals will never have to know a level of guilt like us people. I watch a dozen of them drain and drink their own blood with plenty of opportunity to stop any more than I needed from dying. Yet I stood by and only watched. I feel nothing for them or me now. The snow falls on them and no longer melts away, for their warmth in life has completely left them. Their purpose as bait can now be served, as I am no different from the monster I have returned here to hunt. Its bait to lure me in is my fellow man, whereas my bait for it is my humanity.

Twelve or more dead deer will do just fine for now…

Chapter 19: The Call to Arms

My day begins heading back to the station after a sleepless night in Maggie's room. My first stop in the patrol SUV is Jeppiess Pawn. They're decent folks and have had this location set up in town since I was a kid. Had a lot of business with them in the past but they're not one for keeping their doors open much these days. They helped me out a few years back getting my Smith and Wesson model 69 when they first came out. I know they stay there more and more these days because they can't afford the electric bill in their home and the store. I give them a break a lot when they bring in stolen goods on pawn. Try finding a city cop that doesn't bring them up on charges for that. They're just working folk like anybody else around here that just need a hand now and then.

I pull in front to park on the roadside, but the open sign isn't lit yet and I realize the time is still before the curfew that I had put in place. Even if they tried to open up, they wouldn't get many visitors in the snow like this, anyway. I knock on the door and see his wife's silhouette approach through the tinted glass and peek her head outside with the sliding bar gates still in place.

"Hello Miss. Is your husband in. I know you guys aren't opened up, but I'm bit pressed for time."

"Oh, yes… Um… Just a sec. He's getting cleaned up, but I'll go get the keys and let you in, Sheriff. We didn't plan on opening today with the blizzard and all. One sec."

"Not a problem Miss Jeppiess. I'll wait here."

She closes the main door and moves to the back. I can't see or hear much through the front door, but I hear his voice and some scrambling around. He could still be in pj's for all I know. Poor guys, just trying to hold on to what they got left in this town.

Even their daughter left the area after her kid was on the same bus as Maggie was.

Mr. Jeppiess comes to open the door and the sliding bar gate.

"Oh, uh... Hey there Sheriff. We weren't gonna open today. We know about the curfew and stuff, but come on in."

I walk in to look around and his wife is moving things around in the back and starting the fresh coffee that leaves the scent throughout the store daily.

"Sorry I ain't dressed decent yet, Sheriff. What can I do for ya?" he asks.

He seems stunned I am here. I haven't come by the shop in a while. But there hasn't been word of them taking in stolen goods on pawn in a while either. Most of the store is still dark and I can see my breath in the main lobby area. His wife comes out and closes a curtain that they used to keep the heat in their living area through the wintry nights.

I cup my hands near my mouth to warm them up. "You guys staying warm in here when you spend the night?" I ask. They both appear cold enough that anyone not knowing them would assume they've just seen a ghost. This is not like them and something is off here.

"Uh... Yeah... Yes, Sheriff. We... Uh... We rarely heat up the entire store at night. Just the back rooms and the kitchenette area. So, what brings you in today, Sheriff? We ain't had no visitors in a few days or anything. I would've given ya a holler if I brought in something suspicious on pawn. Just like you said when that happened last time."

His wife sits near the register in front of the gun racks that still have their own bar gates over them and a dust cloth to keep them cleaned up for customers to view. Some of their goods have sold off since the last time I was here. A lot of camping and outdoor gear is missing. Though all the fine jewelry and watches are still in the display case. He keeps a dust cover on it to keep customers or their kids from scratching up the glass too much. But the dust cover for the gun display case is on the opposite side today. She avoids eye contact as she gives the appearance of reading an outdoorsman magazine. Not her typical reading beyond Better Homes and Garden that I remember seeing in her hands.

"No worries. I wish I could stop by more often than I do. They keep me busy there at the station. Anyway, I had some 44 magnums ordered up a few weeks ago and sent here for pick up. Got the notification they arrived here but I haven't had the chance to swing by and pick them up yet."

"Oh yeah… I remember those. They came in and I put them right in the system. I called the station to let them know they were in, but the message may not have got to ya."

"No, I got the message. You're totally fine. Like I said. Just been busy."

"Right then. Let me grab them under the case here."

He bends over out of sight and I unclip the safety of my holster. He raises up and sits two boxes of Hornady 44 Magnum on the counter.

"These came in a few weeks ago, like I said. Hornady Leverolutions with over 220 grains of stopping power."

I open the box and examine the rounds. The red tip makes them faster and hit harder, but they're for hunting out of rifles, if you can find a rifle that can accept them that it is.

"Are you sure the little model 69 Smith can handle something that powerful?" he asks.

"Well, hopefully I don't have to find out the hard way." as I put the round back in and close the box up. "Do I owe you anything for the rounds?"

"No sir. They handled all that on the online retailer they shipped from and your Law Enforcement carrier permit is still on file here. You're good to go, Sheriff."

"All right then. Thanks for holding them. You guys stay warm through the blizzard out there. You guys need anything, just give the station a call."

I grab the two boxes and move to the front door and hear a sigh of relief from his wife at the register. I turn back around to give them a last glance and hope for a simple gesture of "*come again*" or "*thanks, Sheriff*", but they say nothing until I look back at them when I stop at the door.

"Oh… Uh… Thank ya Sheriff. Don't be a stranger and be safe out there."

He is usually chattier, but I got the entire town on edge these days. I nod my head back at the both of them and head back out to the SUV. The wife quickly moves right back to the front door and closes the sliding bar gates before I even pull away.

Drake sits patiently in the passenger seat on the other side of my AR holstered in the center console rifle holder. It is meant for holding shotguns in the center, but if you shorten the collapsible stock of the AR, it sits in firmly. Drake only gets to ride up front with me before the day starts on our way to the station and when we are on our way home. I put his law dog vest on him before we left the house. Had some special patches made for him to stick on it. One that says Sheriff's Department, and another that says do not pet without permission, though he doesn't always go by that one either when kids approach him. We make our way to the station, and the group is already there inside. Me and Drake both hop out to go inside. Rachel sits by the front desk waiting to be greeted by Drake, as they always do.

"What do we have now, Rachel? Talk to me…" as I move to my back office and she and Drake follow.

"I stopped by Ricky Clauson's house before I picked up Sherral this morning to see if his wife could have something for Drake to sniff him out when we get out there, but she wasn't home. Talked to the neighbor, and they said they had gotten in an argument before he went out hunting and she took off to the city. She hasn't been back since then."

"So, she called him in missing, took off, and doesn't even know he is still out there missing? Wife of the year right there…"

"Pretty much. The neighbors said that they get into it and argue all the time and she runs off to the city for a while. They didn't even know we still considered him missing. But the garage door was still open, and I found one of his old factory uniforms. It's covered in dust and warehouse oils, but I hope Drake can use it to sniff him out."

"That will have to do for now." as I open the office door and find Greeves looking at the map and making dry erase marks on the board. Davis sits comfortably on the couch sipping on coffee and Sherral makes her way out of the bathroom from outside the office.

"Hey there, Greeves, how are you doing today?" I ask. His face is freshly shaved and broke out from razor burn around his lower neck.

"I'm good, Sheriff. Just marking up the map if that's ok?"

"No, that's good. Are these all the locations of attacks so far?"

"Right. All that's missing is Clauson's body."

"Ok, that's good work. We don't have an exact location yet." as I grab the marker from his hand and mark up the board in the same manner. "All we got a lead on so far is within a five to six miles inwards of the old refueling station on the coastline." I mark the fueling point on the board. "The other location is the school bus attack from the last time, right here. Then, we have the location of the remains where we found the cold one from yesterday, here. Lastly is the bus driver, also from the school bus attack. Now his body was found here in this general area a few days after we found the bus. Davis, if you don't mind getting up off your fat ass and looking at this."

He gets up and joins everybody behind me to look at the marks all over the map.

"Did the coroner identify the cold one from yesterday yet?" I ask Sherral.

"No, nothing back from him, yet."

"Anything from the State PD on help for a search party to recover a body?"

"No, Sheriff. Sorry, but we got nothing back from Game and Wildlife either."

"Dammit… Does anyone in any of the surrounding counties do any work anymore?"

"Not during a blizzard apparently, Sheriff.", says Davis sarcastically.

"Well thank you, Davis. I didn't notice it was still snowing outside, smart ass."

"So, what's the plan here, Sheriff? Are we going after Ricky's body?" asks Greeves.

"That's right. Now when these hunters go in, they go in deep. Some are too drunk to realize how deep they go in. But I know of a few areas that stay prominent with the deer hunters that they go to a lot within the areas discussed. Once we are that far in, let's hope Drake can pick up the trail from there. It may take to about midday to get to the area with heading out this early. So, that leaves us only a few hours to search the area and to work a crime scene. We are looking for any clearings that are best used by hunters to get a vantage point and take a shot. There's more of those the closer you get to the shoreline." I continue on after another mark on the map.

"A key point here at these spots are these various watering holes and spring that deer will make their way to for drinking fresh water. That's the first place we head to. There's been tons of weather, rain, sleet, the last week and it's still snowing out there, but blood trails take several days to clear out before a scent can't be picked up anymore by most service dogs. If it's there, Drake can find it."

"What about the guy that got out yesterday?" asks Rachel. Even though she knows what I told her last night, it's her signal for me to inform these guys the same thing.

"Right. There's a high probability that he's pushing out there too. I want vests on and full gear for all of us. Shotguns and multiple service pistol magazines loaded up on your person. I want everyone that makes their way out there with me and Drake to have at least two flares on their person. We are not taking any chances out there. If we spot him, we move from body recovery to pursuit of him. Depending on how much time we have, or even if he is really out there, we have him point out the location of the body as he says, and this search gets a lot easier for us. He is armed and we already know he is potentially dangerous, but for the most part we believe he is heading out there to hunt this thing down too."

The office phone rings at the front desk and Sherral moves to pick it up as I continue on with these guys.

"What is this thing, Sheriff? You try tellin me it's a bear again and I'm walking away." says Greeves with a concerned tone. I look directly at him as I put the cap back on the marker and motion for everybody to bring it in close. Even Drake comes in close to listen in.

"Check it out, guys. There's only four of us left, and Drake here. You're right, Greeves. It's not a bear. Truth be told, I don't know what the hell this thing is. I'm trying not to make this personal, but you all know it already is personal for me. One way or another, blizzard or no blizzard. I'm heading out there. I don't care about the remains, but that's our job. To investigate and put these matters to rest. All a dead body tells us at the end of the day is that someone was killed by something. That *something* is what concerns me the most right now..."

Sherral interrupts yelling across the station, "Sheriff, it's for you."

"Is it an emergency call?"

"No, it's some doctor's office."

"Take a message and tell them I'll be calling back within a few minutes."

I continue on with all of their full attention. "We are short staffed, up against some serious weather elements, and back up support is, well, you guys already heard that part. Most of you know what the last body looked like by now and I won't lie to you anymore. I can't order any of you to come out there with me anymore with this station on the verge of its doors closing down for lack of manpower. If any of you want to walk away from this one and stay to enforce the town curfew here with Sherral, then speak now and nobody will judge you otherwise. Don't answer me yet. I'm not looking for somebody to be a hero if it comes to it. People are dying out there, and we gotta go soon. You guys think about it for a sec amongst yourselves while I make this call back."

I walk away from the group and make my way to the front desk to make the call back to whatever doctor's office tried to call in.

"Hackensack Medical Center, how may I direct your call..."

"Yes, someone from Dr. Hernan's office may have just tried to call within the last few minutes."

"Please hold while I transfer your call..."

Rachel comes over to tap me on the shoulder while I'm on hold. I turn around to see all of them shaking their heads in agreement with what needs to be done. She gives me the thumbs up too, but I keep looking at her as the phone gets picked up. She tries to motion as to who it is that is calling, but I'm not getting my hopes up until I know who it is for sure.

"Mr. Williams?... Jason Williams, is that you?"

"Yeah it's me. Is this Dr. Hernan's office?"

"Yes, it's his P.A. We've been trying to get ahold of you on your cell and home phone."

I look down at my phone to see several missed calls. I must have left it on silent last night. "Ok, well, what's going on?"

"We have one, Jason. We have a donor organ for you."

I nearly drop the phone in shock and Rachel keeps staring at me, trying to figure out why a weight has been visibly been lifted off my shoulders right in front of her.

"Jason... Are you still there?"

"Um... Yeah... Yes, I'm here. Jesus, this is just some great news, finally."

Rachel puts two and two together after she looks at the number on the collar ID for the medical center. She covers her mouth to prevent shouting in the same level of relief that I have. I shake my head yes for her.

"The donor came in last night. We couldn't get it transported fast enough in the winter storm to some of the surrounding areas to get it to people that were above

you on the list. A few others already rejected it for high risk factors. You're next in line Jason! You're it!"

"High risk? What do you mean high risk?"

"We can discuss all that when you come in."

"How long can this thing stay stable?"

"With the perfusion method we have available to us here, the donor kidney can last up to 48 hours out of the human body, but we can't wait that long. We need you here within the next 12 hours for pre-op measures and blood testing before we can move forward. There are some tests we can do here while you're on your way from the samples we have already on file, but the sooner you get here the better. They need you now."

"Ok, what if I can't make it within that 48-hour window?"

"In all reality, if you can't make it within a 36-hour window, the donor organ may go to waste. Mr. Williams, I can't stress enough how critical time is of the essence. You have been told what to do if this call comes months ago now. There's nobody else on this list willing to take the risk factors on this donor organ in the area and we can't risk transporting it to others on the list that are outside the immediate area because of the weather."

"Ok. Count me there in the next 36 hours, then. Run whatever tests you can while I'm on my way. I'll keep my phone close.

"OK. Get here ASAP. If we don't hear from you within 36-hours, then you give up your spot on the list for this donor organ and we gotta start calling other potential recipients before we lose the donor organ. But there isn't anybody else we would get it to in time at that point. You're really it, Jason. Just get here. I'll let them know you're gonna try to push through the winter storm."

"Ok, I gotta go. I'll keep you posted."

"Ok, don't stop if you can. Just get here."

I turn to look at Rachel, but I don't have to say anything. She can tell by the look on my face. She always could tell what was going on with the look on my face, even when I was being a hard ass on the job in uniform.

"Was that the call?" she asks.

"Yeah. That's it. I got just over a day to get there… They got one."

"Holy shit, that's awesome, Jason!" as she jumps and hugs me, all teary eyed. I nearly drop to the floor with her arms wrapped around me.

"You're going in now, right?" she asks. It takes just a split second to think about what to say. They need me there at the hospital the sooner the better, but I know I have the time to find this dead body out there. I have to stay on the creature's trail and any evidence is still evidence, dead or alive.

"No, they want me in later tonight. As soon as we find the body, I'll break away in the SUV and head down into the city. From there you need to take charge and investigate the scene. You know the drill. You have watched me do this a dozen times. No matter what, body or no body, I head out on my own after the search is over. Can I count on you for taking in Drake for me?" I ask her.

"Um…" Davis and Greeves grabbing our attention and acting like they clear their throats. "So, are you two gonna get a damn room finally or are we gonna go for a walk in the woods or what?" asks Davis. Me and Rachel forgot we were standing in the middle of the station with an audience. I can always count on Davis to be the buzz kill at the party.

"Davis, have I fired you recently?" I ask as he slumps back down on the couch again.

"Not since that whole public intoxication bit with the fireworks display on the county fairgrounds last year."

"Yeah, I remember that one. But at least your eyebrows grew back… So, we are all in?" I ask.

"Yes Sir, Sheriff." says Greeves.

"Got nothin better to do in a storm like this." says Davis.

Rachel lets go of my hand I didn't even realize she was still holding. I move back to the front desk after Sherral makes her way back.

"Sherral, we're heading out soon to search for the second missing individual."

I reach into my back pocket and pull out my wallet to get the business card out for the rehab center. I hand it over to her and she looks at it, confused at first. Then she looks back up at me after knowing what

212

the entire town already knew after last night. I lean in to talk to her, so the others don't hear me while they are gearing up for the cold.

"After we leave, I want you to call in and get an update on her. I want to know she's making it through her withdrawal symptoms well. She's about 48 hours into not having that crap in her system. So, last night and today will be the worst for her. They won't let anyone talk to her during that portion, but I still want to know she is ok. You tell them to tell her, when they feel she is coherent enough to understand, that my name came up on the donor recipient list. That everything's gonna be fine now. Things are gonna get better now. She just needs to focus on getting clean and staying clean now. Ok?"

"Oh, Sheriff. That's such good news. I can call before you guys leave."

"Just hold off. Nobody here needs to hear that conversation. Send me a message on my phone or over the radio. A verbal thumbs up and nothing more. These guys need to focus out there on what needs to get done, then we can all come home."

"Ok, Sheriff." as she shakes her head. "What do you want me to do here while you guys are out?"

"Any 911 calls come in have them transferred to the state PD or the surrounding sheriff's office. Whichever they are closest to. I see little happening with most people in a blizzard like this beyond sliding off into a ditch. But, you never know. Keep reaching out to the game warden and animal control to see if they are willing to change their mind and get out there with us and do their damn job for once."

"Oh. The coroner over at the hospital morgue just got back to me on the other line. He put in a request for further info of the crime scene."

"What does he want?" I ask.

"He wants to know if the male's heart was in the body's vicinity. If not, then the radius needs to go larger for an additional search."

"I take it they haven't identified him yet?"

She shakes her head *no* while looking down.

"As soon as I find a set of arms and a lot of missing skin out there, I'll gladly track down a missing heart. Until then his focus needs to be based on identifying the individual. Leave the searching to me. Be sure he keeps his mouth shut until we at least know who it is."

"Ok, I'll be right here if you need me, Sheriff. Please, you guys just be careful out there."

I turn around to see the group gearing up for the cold and vests on top of it. The inmate transport keeps more than enough water for us, and they checked all radios for the same frequency. Davis grabs the shotguns, and each person has additional 45 ACP magazines for service pistols. Drake keeps sniffing up the old shop uniform that Rachel grabbed from his residence as I put a GPS tracker on him if he gets too far ahead of us when we get out there.

"Ok, Davis... I want you in my patrol SUV with the four-wheel drive on the entire time ahead of us. Move my AR and the gear in the passenger seat into the passenger seat of the Inmate transport van."

"Alright then, Sheriff. It'll be like muddin' in the winter, right?"

"You're an idiot Davis. Don't make me fire you again. Greeves, be sure the crime scene gear is stocked, bagged, and loaded up in the back of the van."

"It's already there, boss." he says.

"Ok then. You'll be driving the van behind Davis. Davis, I'm gonna need you to take it slow. If that SUV is struggling through the snow, then you know the van will have a hard time too. It will be just a matter of you making the tracks that we need to follow in the van right behind you. I want constant radio communications on anything that any of us may see out there the closer we get. I want the 24-hour flares set up on the roadside where we dismount from the vehicles to push into the wood line. From there, it's just a matter of following Drake in, but we scatter out in a wave to look for anything that can give us an indicator of foot traffic. We are limited on time, daylight, and the weather is against us nonstop right now. If anyone feels any symptoms of hypothermia, then we abort efforts and return to the station. If anyone gets lost out there, abort and return to the vehicles, simple as that. What questions do you guys have?"

"How will we know where we need to stop while we are traveling on the road?" Greeves asks.

"I'll give the one-to-two-mile warno and we find a safe area to unload from there. The only other thing that might stop us is if Drake picks up a scent before then, but that is unlikely while he is in the back with Rachel. Other questions? Spit it out now guys, we gotta roll soon."

"Wait… Why am I in the back of the van with the dog?" Rachel asks.

"Because Drake likes you better than Greeves or Davis and I call the shots 'round here last I checked." as I smile back at her.

She gives me the typical *eat shit and die* look that any woman is good at, but I act like I don't catch it and move to my office to grab my gear and vest. "You guys go load up and I'll be right out." I hear the guys rushing out the door, banging desks as they move, and Rachel calls for Drake to follow her to the van. I move to my locker and grab more ammo for the AR and a few speed loaders for my model 69. I take off my shirt and put medical tape all over my torso to protect the catheter from breaking again under the vest. A butterfly knife, some additional flares to throw in my cargo pockets. A black camel back full of water is already on my desk. I slam the locked office door behind me as I head out and I hear the phone ringing before Sherral picks it up.

"Hello, Sheriff's Department… Ok… Ok… Just one moment please.", as she covers the mic on the phone with her hand. "It's the State PD. What do you want me to say?"

"Are they on their way to assist?" I ask.

"No, they just said they needed to speak with you. They said it's urgent." she whispers.

I roll my eyes in disbelief. "This is urgent too. If they need me that bad they can come out and find me, then assist in a search effort for once. Anything else and they can leave a damn message after the beep." I reach around her and tap the hang-up button on the phone with a single finger and Sherral looks at me, stunned, while she still has the phone held up to her ear.

"What do ya know. It beeped… We're headed out, time now. You know what to do, Sherral."

Chapter 20: The Hunter

The younger ones are easier to throw on top of my shoulders to move to a suitable clearing. I drop the lifeless bodies on the ground one at a time, lined up next to each other and see the eyes are still wide open in their confusion and dizziness. The heavier doe and bucks need to be dragged by the legs or antlers. Before I get back to each one to drag it to the campsite, a cluster of coyotes makes themselves known surrounding me in the woods. They draw in closer and closer, but they spook off to run back into the woods when I grab the last buck. I leave my knife sticking upwards on the last of the salt brick, just in case they get too curious for their own good.

All of them leave a blood trail from their mouth and slashed up tongues to follow. That will bring in more attention from the woods. As long as I see coyotes floating around me, I'll know that there isn't anything out here much more aggressive than them for now. I lay them all out to create a large C shape with the rounded center facing inward and westward from the shoreline winds. That will send the smell scattering into the woods even more. I find a few good tree branches and hang them all facing down with cord. A few twitches and jerks out of the younger ones when blood flow rushes back to their heads. But all of them are more than dead once I slice the jugulars down the line. Enough blood fills the ground below them to generate a steam in the snow. Another thing me and this creature have in common. We like to hang what's left of our victims. I think I have it beat this time though. I move to my ruck and look for my field dressing knife.

I dig around the pelvis areas with a field dressing knife for a short while to tie off the anus areas off all of them, one at a time. I don't want them to spray hormones or piss in place before I drop their innards to the ground. That would only bring in more deer. I don't want that. I want something deadlier than me to come in looking for a free meal when I scatter these insides around me. I step away once they drain what's left of the blood out of their gushing throats. I leave a large cut all the way down through the torso to the rib cage. The larger bucks start opening up through the deep cut to show their stomachs and intestine. I move to the high ground and set up a vantage point. The ground stays soft enough to dig deep into the marshiness of the sandy soil. I dig with a small e-tool style shovel I picked up at the pawn shop. I stop often to see the coyotes bounce back and forth near the blood trail left in the snow. The frigid air freezes the blood stains to the ground. There must be at least five or six of them sneaking around.

I hear a sudden whimpering from one of them and drop the shovel to sling my Henry rifle back over my shoulder. I point it in their general direction down the blood trail where all the deer were dragged through. A lone coyote trots down the trail with its mouth open and red tongue hanging low. Its blood drops out its mouth fast. It must have taken a taste of my other knife too fast without knowing the blade was there. It stumbles around in the visible clearing, looking for the rest of its pack for help. They roam around the lone and injured coyote to approach. It turns to catch a side glimpse of its large pregnant belly. She must be the head mother of the pack, but she is clearly injured. They approach her faster each time and take licks of her open mouth. I kneel on my belly and move in closer to them.

I've lost count of how many times someone has asked me if I ever killed anyone, but they never ask if you've watched someone or something slowly die by your own hand or another's. This will be the second time in a short time period for that now. The pregnant female coyote sits on her back legs now, too dazed to understand what goes on

218

or why the rest of her pack no longer takes licks of her mouth. Now they move closer to her each time to take bites of her while growling. She tries to turn and snap back at each of them as the others move in closer to her. She attempts to get up and walk around to a nearby tree to keep the rest of the pack away from her. She is too weak and dizzy to move quick. She looks down at the ground and sniffs her own blood before looking around at the rest of the pack that growls at her.

All of their teeth are visible as she attempts to keep moving away from them until she drops to the ground with her belly sticking up from the side. Her chest rises and falls, showing she is out of breath with her bloody tongue still drooping. A larger male goes into her front side. Coyotes will always take their prey from the front. The male takes a serious gnaw at her neck first and she whimpers loud enough to echo. The rest join in, cautiously at first, bouncing back and forth in concern, until that first taste. She struggles and continues to whimper and bark at them when her neck is free from one's jaws. They didn't chomp at her neck hard enough the first few times. The blood is only coming from surface cuts and bites, but not deep enough into her major arteries yet. I watch as these ugly and smelly varmints kill off their own chance of this year's litter of pups from the only female that appears of breeding worth in their pack.

Her legs twitch with the last few attempts to snap her jaws back at one of the other coyotes. Her chest and lungs raise slower and slower now, while a few others rip out her tail. Smaller one's bite on her back legs and paws. The larger male, though, he keeps going at her mouth and throat. Survival of the fittest. The choice of living or dying is left up to so many others. Help from our fellow species is only an option, especially if helping a weaker one live becomes a burden to the rest. That makes you just as weak as the injured one out here. They'll come for you too if you try to help. They'll eat you alive for helping others weaker than you. I try to tell myself they are only doing what nature intended them to do. Put her out of her misery, but she's still breathing and fully aware of how she will end by her own kind. Only the healthy survive, but they slow the continued production of their own species in the process.

A larger footprint lurks from behind. A heavy and slower movement. I know that larger rustling sound that nature always provides. I turn around to see a black bear moving around near my gear and sniffing. I low crawl to a nearby tree, as it isn't paying any attention to me. It moves down into the low ground near all the hanging deer and the pack of coyotes that still bite at their own female, with a few taking curious licks of the hanging deer. I keep the tree between me and the bear as it wobbles by me unnoticed. My rifle is raised if it turns and notices me. Jesus Christ... It's so close to me I could reach out around the tree and touch it. The marshy ground shudders underneath me as it walks. It must be a solid 400 pounder trudging by me on the other side of the tree I propped myself next to.

Its breath lingers in the cold in front of it as it moves closer to the coyotes and away from the tree. It stops before reaching the low ground and stands up on its back legs to send a menacing roar through the woods. The coyotes look up but refuse to leave their free meals to a larger prey. They scurry around as the black bear fake charges down at them. They'll stand by for a continued effort, but they know they can't take on something of its size with the few they have in their pack. The bear fake charges again but stops close enough to scare them into the woods away from the female coyote that is still struggling to breathe with its snout in a melted pool of snow and blood. The coyote pack stays near the bear in the wood line but won't approach it any closer.

The bear sniffs around the dying female coyote before placing a heavy claw down on its pregnant belly. The female coyote yelps in shock and raises her head in a last glimpse of pain and suffering, but the bear clamps those massive jaws around its neck to twist and snap it. It sniffs around at her fresh bite marks and blood but loses interest from the horrid smell a dead coyote gives off. The bear turns to the hanging deer that the coyotes are struggling to get to without jumping off their hind legs. Once they notice the bear is approaching them again, they attempt to snap at its legs and thighs, just to be slapped around a few good times. The larger male coyote won't risk another hit like that from a larger animal. He scurries off into the wood line for good this time, and the others follow behind to leave the bear to its new buffet.

The bear moves around near the deer and rips them apart to make my effort easier to bring in larger prey with all the blood and meat scattered around below. Now a new bait is set. The largest natural animal these woods offer is here and chowing down. I move to continue digging with my e-tool while the bear stays occupied with its free meal. It takes a while to dig in, but the bear eats enough the entire time I dig to drop down near the snow-covered blood trail to take a rest for its filled belly. He sees me from below but has no interest in me. My entrenchment goes deep and about three feet around is more than enough.

I always told her I wanted to be cremated when I die, but maybe placing a body upright in a fox hole wouldn't be too bad either. I have already spent more than enough time in one of these. I remember staying warm many of the winter nights in the desert in one. A smaller hole like this is easier to keep warm in verses a tree stand out in the open. Why not just stay in one of these after I'm gone too? Makes sense to me now that I think about it. I move to throw my ruck down in the hole with all my gear, except for the tent and last ghillie blanket.

I use the field dress knife to tear apart the tent in larger pieces. I gather up larger tree limbs and place them on top of the fox hole and leave an opening large enough to see everything at the low ground. I find a few limbs strong enough to hold the weight of at least my body weight on top of the fox hole. I don't know if it will be strong enough to hold up much more than that, but hopefully I won't have to find out otherwise. The layers of tent nylon material go on next to keep the moisture off of me and keep the body heat in the hole. Next layer on top is the ghillie cloth to cover up the bright colors of the tent material. Then more shrubbery from nearby and the dirt that came out from digging the hole. I move the rifle in first to set it down slowly to the ground and crawl back in through the opening.

My hands are frozen for being out here this long without cover. Not too many hand warmers left, but they need to be used to keep my water supply from freezing. I'll just hold my hands in my armpits and groin area. I move back into my ruck to look for more ammo and install my rifle stock ammo holder. I look through the rifle opening of the fox hole and see the bear is gone already. Only the hanging bodies of a dozen deer and a smelly pregnant coyote that I have some credit for killing as well. I check the magazine tube of the Henry and see that it is down to its last round from firing off into the tree line hours ago now. Or maybe that has been as far back as yesterday now? I really can't remember right now. I load up the stock ammo pouch and the magazine tube with the heavy grain hand loads. I hear a slight rainfall trickling its way down onto the canvas of the tent material. Some of the dirt and sand will turn to mud to help solidify my cover before the nightfall.

No coyotes, no owls fluttering their wings, it's just the winds through the pines to make them moan into the hours of the day. I am just left with the sound of frozen rain droplets made of teeth sprinkling down as the cold comes in while only leaving enough visibility to see my breath that disappears into the coming darkness. The overcast keeps dimming the skies so much I can't tell if it is supposed to be daylight hours or not. How long I have been out here already? The rain and moisture may cover and dissolve the scent, but the wind stays in my favor long enough to scatter the smell throughout the area. My Henry stays at the ready pointed outside the foxhole towards the hanging deer.

Too tired to move, but too tense to sleep. Hours pass. The pattering of raindrops turns to snowfall, and the freezing air sets in fast enough to shiver into my bones. My eyes adjust to the darkness, enough to see each silhouette of the pines all around me. It's out there and it's watching, waiting. Only watching because it knows it does not have enough cover of surrounding ambient noises now to hide its movements this time. Only the cover of night, but that isn't enough for it to attempt to end me again. It's a better hunter than that, but not a better hunter than me. I pull the lever of my Henry in and out to chamber a round, release the safety as slowly as possible, just in case it is desperate enough to come in to the open. Just once is all I need. Give me one excellent shot to see if you bleed like me. I reach down into my ruck again to pull out my monocular to look around.

The deer just sway around from recent smaller varmints taking a bite, but nothing worth shooting at. The snow bleaches out the night vision, but something is moving fast beyond the clearings. If it is a single creature, then it is a predator. I look for movement from other animals to give me an idea if it is more than one animal roaming around out there. Until I think I hear owls hooting and fluttering from above. They are on a nearby tree behind me and can't get a good visual on them. I'll take the shot on this creature as soon as it gets curious enough for a free meal. Movement again from beyond the wood line. Go ahead. Just stick your head out once to see all the death lying around the clearing waiting for you to enjoy. I know you like to rip them apart.

The movement I see from the tree line slows down, but I see a certain sliver of shrubbery still shaking with the fading night vision of the monocular. It moves again, but it is too fast to catch a glimpse when jumping over the area where the blood trail was left from dragging the bodies down in there. I catch a set of horns moving by in a brief glimpse. It's here.

I lower the night vision and move to the rifle. I hear a tree being scratched on in the area. It scratches the pines to sharpen its claws like any animal would. The last time I had a good glimpse of it, we were higher in the tree line. It's good to know that it is real enough to move around on the ground level too. I just need visibility for a single second. I move the hammer back as I slow my breathing and cover my mouth with my gator neck. Any movement at all will have a 45-caliber slug headed its way with the slightest squeeze of the trigger.

I raise my stock to the cheek bone.

The limbs are still moving near the shrubbery.

Rain and sleet throw off my sight picture, but it beats a scope fogging up.

Slow that breathing down low.

Just give me a visual of this mother fucker.

My finger tenses on the trigger and I see its eyes light up.

All remains quiet for the exception of my heartbeat.

You're dead now and you don't even know it.

I take the shot and it sends a shock wave of recoiling pain into my injured shoulder again. Enough that makes my eyes water and jaw line clinch with a growl. The blast sound echoes loud enough through the ringing of my ears again to drop several snow piles to the ground from the trees above. I push through the sharpness of my arm and sling the lever action in and out before I crawl my way out of the fox hole. I look up first to see that there are no owls above me. I move to the lower ground and still hear the grunts and snorts of the creature. It's still breathing but injured. Too injured to come at me now. The human teeth and rain come down harder and harder the closer I get to the struggled breaths. Each human molar and tooth scratch my jacket sleeves as they bounce off my arms and hands. I keep my weapon at the ready in case it has the strength to fight back before I end it.

I move fast but don't run to it. My eyes still have to adjust to the darkness after the muzzle blast lit up the entire area. I keep the Henry on my right arm and move tree shrubbery out of the way with my left arm.

"Oh my God... No..."

The white stag lays in front of me gasping for air. It doesn't show concern, it only looks at me in contempt for what I have done. The side of its chest has a bullet entry wound larger than my hand as I kneel closer to it in my desperation. It does not raise its head in bewilderment. It does not show fear of my presence. It only looks back at me as it takes its last few struggled breaths. I move to feel its neck, and it only blinks at my touch. I've killed again, but this was not a needed take down. Even though I came back to these woods to hunt this one down over a week ago now, I started to believe it is one that could not be gotten like James said. But I was wrong in thinking that. I was wrong in hoping that the last little bit of good in anything I know could not be destroyed by my own hand.

"Did you come to warn me? I thought you couldn't die..."

His 9-point rack is massive, and the white coat is as soft as a newborn's hair. I only wish I had the power to give life back to something. The only power we may possess is the means to take a life, nothing more. I drop my rifle down below its lifeless legs that don't even

224

flinch. He just looks at me as I cry next to him in his last moments. I don't remember the last time I cried that wasn't in anger, but I can only be furious at myself for not knowing how to comfort him.

"I'm so sorry…"

A deer will have their eyes left open when they die. He slowly closes his eyes in front of me before the final raise of his chest. A last breath exhales, and he is gone. He leaves right in front of me without a sense of peace or understanding why. He is simply gone, the same as I am lost. I pick him up by his hind legs and drag him back to the others that have been hanging. I grab my rifle back up off the ground to keep it at the ready with my non-firing hand. The bear had his way with most of them, as select organs and rib bones lay scattered everywhere. I look up to see it is no longer deer hanging in front of me. It is only the faces of the dead that hang there lifeless and staring back at me.

"Koja tu?" the boy says.

He hangs there with them again. He repeats himself, over and over, just reaching out to me for help. His palms open and covered with his coughing blood. Another body struggles and grabs the rope. Legs remain tense but start to shake more and more. They are dying in front of me. Their deaths are being repeated in front of me, but only backwards. One has his skull blown off. One is burned alive. One is missing lower limbs that a blast has ripped off. One has enough bullet exit and entry wounds to be more like a human sponge dispensing his own bile and blood. I walk down the line of hanging bodies and recognize all of them. Every one of them already tagged and ready to be bagged.

How long will they hang there struggling? Will they come down and be back to life enough to bring me a similar death most of them did not deserve? They are all such familiar faces frozen in fear before their demise, except for one. I walk down the line of hanging and struggling bodies that reach for me as I pass. Their toe tags flap around beneath them before being drenched in their own blood and piss. I walk to the end and see a person I have never seen before. A naked woman hanging from the rope. But she does not reach for me. Her hands remain tied in front of her.

"I don't know you." I say, as she only stares back at me. I move closer to her.

Her tits dangle down like swollen utters of a mother cow waiting to be drained by her young. Her stomach has multiple stretch marks and appears more like a deflated balloon. The smell is horrible as blood drips from her hairy and unkept cooch. A small piece of intestine hangs from it. At first frightening glance it's as if the rope just hangs down behind her to the ground, but I know it is part of her insides hanging from her inner groin. She only stares back as I move closer to hear what she is trying to whisper to me in a gargled struggle.

"My child... My boy comes for your soul."

I back away, still not remembering her. Her legs begin to thrash around like the others. She grabs at the rope around her neck, struggling more and more than just a few feet in front of me. She screams. Her screams are unbearable. Her screams of pain grow louder as I back away in horror, and they all yell at the same time. Yelling at me. Yelling why has this happened to them. I have no answer for them. The woman in front of me thrashes around her legs, harder than the rest of those hanging further down the line. A splash of her insides land on the ground a few feet in front of me. They are not intestines like a few of the others have still hanging from their torso. That is a fetus sac wrapped by an umbilical cord and covered in bloody fecal matter from her bowels.

I walk to the backside of hanging bodies and try to tell myself they are not real. These are deer I have left to hang, not people. I pull out my knife and reach up to cut them down, one by one. Their squirming bodies drop to the ground like struggling worms, looking for a means to go back into the ground beneath them. They all continue to reach for me as I grab their legs and pile the bodies up, one by one. The mother first. Then the boy. Then all the others. They all touch me as I grab them to drag them to the pile.

I throw the pregnant coyote on top of the bodies. Her dead smell lingers on my jacket. They are dead and cold enough not to melt the snow that falls on them, but they still reach for me, hoping I can save them, but it is too late for all of them now. The pile of carcasses is up to my chest when I drag the white stag next to the pile to throw on top last. Small hands keep reaching for me and touching my boots and pants from the bottom of the pile. It takes all my efforts and nearly breaking my back to lift the white stag and lay it on top of all of them as they moan and cry. I know my end will be worse than the pile I stare at. The crying and the screaming never stop and fill my sleepless nights.

I walk away with my rifle and make my way back to the salt brick. It still sits upright on the last few pieces of the frozen salt brick. Another coyote lay near it but has also gotten too curious for its own good, like the mother coyote from earlier. I look at my knife after ripping it from the frozen ground the salt brick sticks to. The blood also remains frozen as I re-holster it to my belt. I grab the dead coyote and begin dragging it back to the pile. The winds pick up in the short walk back to the pile. The trees loose branches and the winds cast on my face that makes my nose numb. I can see my brows are accumulating ice. I cannot see the blood trail from the other deer anymore. All I can see is the clearing from the vantage point.

The snow is white enough to light up the entire area. I see the body pile and look around for other animals that may have come in for a taste in my brief absence while dragging back another dead coyote. And then I see it sitting high above in the trees. His glowing red eyes in the white out give its demonic presence away. I drop the dead coyote where I stand and move behind the first largest tree I can see. I don't know if it saw me. I don't hear any movement or that same roar it gave last time, but it is taking the bait. I get a better glimpse for the first time. It's a creature like I have never seen before. A beast of biblical origins that only nightmares are made of. Nightmares that still frighten humankind, even though they are thought to no longer exist in the realms of reality.

Its powerful wingspan shakes the needles and snow out of the pine trees with each flying pass as it hovers over the rotting carcasses of multiple deer and coyote. It scurries through the trees and clamps down on the bark of the pines to crawl upside down again. Like the last time we met. It moves in a roach like manner crawling to the forest floor down through the tree it landed on. It ravages the decaying and frozen bodies of the deer I laid out, as if it were still hunting a living creature that had no chance of survival. Its mighty claws and teeth rip away at the lifeless doe's neck and legs like an entire pack of wolves that has found a free meal. Though it is only one terrifying, monstrous thing that chills me to the bone more than the frigid air has for the last several days now, it has taken the bait that landed it right into the sights of my Henry. I only have taken one shot with five remaining rounds left.

It's only about fifty yards out from me, and I can hear it growling as it eats. It turns to see the dead coyote I just dropped, but it doesn't see me for being too low to the cold and freezing ground. It moves up closer to the dead coyote. Those eyes are so red. It stands and walks on its rear clawed feet. Its arms and upper claws are massive inside that eight-foot frame. A thin but muscular build underneath a furred body. A mangy body that belongs on a sick or strayed dog that just escaped the pound. It drools constantly. Blood and saliva roll out from between those wolf-like fangs. Its horns are smaller than most bucks with only a few staggering points on it. Its back is hunched over in a painful walk while its wings are closed in on its backside. Each step closer, it leaves a short-tempered growl of a bear.

It keeps coming in closer while my rifle is at the ready. When it gets close enough, it moves down to all four again like a panther. The closer it gets to the coyote, the slower it moves. Its torn and leathery wings raise and lower with a flutter on its back like a vulture that just landed on a power line looking down at roadkill. The wings have a massive span twice the size of its height. It keeps moving closer, and I can smell its breath from the other side of the tree. Its tail seems to have a mind of its own as it sways behind it. The breath is that of salty and metallic fresh blood being gulped down in devastating bites. It gets close enough to investigate the dead coyote I just dragged back and move my sight picture of the iron sight to its head. I don't know if it's the numbness of the cold or absolute fear that makes my finger move so slowly to the trigger. I feel the moisture of the snow dripping through my torn jacket. My neck is freezing more than ever before, but I have to stay still.

I have to keep my breath slow.

It sniffs around the coyote before it takes a bite.

It doesn't see me less than a few yards away now.

The barrel is stationary right on its head.

A good shot will send a round straight through its spine as it's down on all fours.

I move my finger to the trigger from outside the trigger housing.

Squeeze don't pull.

Just breathe and take the fucking shot.

The round goes off before I register how hard I am squeezing the trigger. The creature flinches and screams as the round goes right through the supporting bone for its wing. It raises back up on its feet to look right back at me. I stand up in a hurry to jerk the lever action back and forth to take another shot at its torso. The recoil bashes the rifle into my shoulder. The creature is stunned, but I sling the lever back and forth. It starts to leap toward me as I take another shot aimed at its head, but the round hits its neck. It has tremendous speed coming at me, with claws reaching out for me. I sling the lever to load another round and take a shot at its leg to see it stumble, but it keeps coming and screaming that high-pitched roar. I walk backward as I chamber another round. I drop on my back to keep it from getting a good grip on me again, as it lunges up before I can take another shot. I raise the rifle quick and its stomach lands on the end of the barrel. The weight of it on my barrel is pressed down on my entire upper body and it feels heavy enough to bury me without digging. It reaches out and claws at my face, and I yell out in pain. I turn my head before it thrashes around its other claw that catches my cheek and earlobe as it continues to swing its arms around at me. The barrel length of the rifle keeps me just out of its reach while it keeps swinging those claws at me in a furious rage.

I look back at it and pull the trigger again. The round blasts through its midsection and sends the flaming shock-wave through its backside through the other wing. I position its stunned body with the rifle to fall over next to me. I scoot away on my ass in a hurry to reload. It is stunned from that last shot and its bullet holes pour blood. I reach for the spare rounds on the stock holster of the rifle before it gets up again. I keep loading the side gate of the Henry as it looks at its crippled wing laying lifeless next to it, then it stares back at me. It stands upright and opens up its upper claws to show their fierce length and sharpness. It sends a roar at me that knocks my hat off my head. The bullet holes in its torso are closing up right in front of me as it hesitates to come at me again for another attempt. I don't get all the rounds loaded, but I fling the lever action to chamber a fresh round and take another shot at its chest.

It just stares at me, then moves to keep walking toward me. Another shot at its head goes through one eye, but it keeps coming. Its claws stay close to its side, but the fingers are outstretched. Another shot at the leg and it jumps over me onto a tree behind me. I keep the rifle pointed up at it as it crawls up the tree. It moves back up the tree in a hurry. Its rear claws grip right into the frozen bark and I can hear every time it makes a new grip on the tree while moving upwards. Blood pours down my face into my eye. Everything goes red, but I keep the rifle pointed upwards as it disappears into the top layers of the pines and darkness. Only the snow that comes down from the black sky is all I can see beyond my blood. I stay frozen and at the ready, waiting for it to come back down for me. All that it does is give a blood chilling roar from the canopy of pines as it moves away now.

I look to my stock ammo holster on the rifle and load up more rounds of the hand loads. These things done it some damage and nearly knocked my arm outta socket again. I move the lever action back and forth again to make sure I chamber around this time. I get up and start cleaning my face from fresh snow on the ground, but I look up with the rifle at the ready every split second. I go over to where I took a shot at it from laying on my back. It splattered blood everywhere. Its blood is on the ground near the coyote and all over the surrounding trees.

I pick up the rifle with my exposed hand and look at the blood this thing poured out with all the shots I took at it here at the ground level. It's injured. It had to crawl back up the tree and not fly back up the tree. It's hurt and bleeding all over the place. This isn't a normal creature. This is worse. This is a devil that came right outta Hell. Ok, then Leeds. You got one up on me once, now I got one on you. You're not as smart as you thought you were, and now *I know you bleed.*

If you can bleed like me, then I know you can burn.

Will you burn like me too?

Chapter 21: The Hunted

I unholster my revolver before I get in and throw it on top of my bag. Greeves waits for the signal from me to roll out and brings up Davis on the radio to tell him the same thing. The snow and frozen rain plow down on the roof of the van as we move through town at a snail's pace, then Davis picks up some speed when we get on the state routes that the plow trucks have already rolled through at some point late in the night. Davis seems to be keeping it steady in the four-wheel drive of my patrol SUV in front of us. Greeves is too nervous to take a risk of sliding off a road. Had to pull his Crown Vic out of a ditch last winter now that I think of it. He keeps looking over at me.

"You ok kid?" I ask him.

"Yeah... I think so, Sheriff. Looks like the roads were frozen underneath all the fresh snow."

"You'll be alright. Just keep it steady and follow in Davis' tracks. His ass end gets squirrelly in front of us then just back off a lil more."

I open my bag and pull out the newer 44 magnum rounds I just got from the pawnshop in town before I got to the station. I unload the revolver of the standard target rounds and load it up with the grizzly killers. If it wasn't heavy enough of a weapon before, it is now. I unclip the two speed loaders from my belt and do the same thing after I re-holster on my drop-thigh rig. I don't know how some of these guys keep their Glocks holstered on their hip beside all of that gear. Davis' belly would get in his way for a quick draw situation. Luckily he hasn't had to do that since he's been with the department.

I look in the back to see Rachel and Drake shaking hands on the other side of the inmate lock cage. She taught him how to do that a while back. They know how to high five each other too. He tries to jump up on the bench next to her to lick her face, but resorts to just keep his head and front paws on her lap. She doesn't see me watching her with Drake from the corner of my eyes. She holds his paws and pets his forehead as his ears adjust to relax downward. He enjoys being held by her, always did. She looks up at me and I turn away to look forward to the road. At least she isn't still giving me the fuck off look at my backside for sitting in the back with the dog.

"Did anybody load up the shotgun?" I ask.

They both shake their head no. I reach into my bag and pull out the box of rounds to fill the magazine tube with buckshot rounds. I don't chamber a round, not until out of the vehicle for the shotgun. The center console dual mount for long guns keeps the weapons pointed at the roof of the vehicle, just in case someone is stupid enough to keep a round chambered and touch the trigger. It would only put a hole in the van's roof and not somebody's head for a quick grab when jumping out the vehicle and your sidearm isn't enough for the task. I switch over the shotgun to move my AR closer to my side in the console mount and pull back the slide to ensure the chamber is clear. I pull an empty magazine from the AR and move to the next box of ammo to load it up when Sherral calls in on my cell.

"Hey there Sheriff. State PD and AC PD are still trying to contact you, but I told them what's going on with you guys out there to locate a potential crime scene."

"Like I said, if they're not coming out to assist, then they are wasting my time. Did you get anything back from the rehab center? How is she doing?"

"No call back on that one yet, either. If the staties or the AC PD come out, where do I need to send them?" she asks.

"Radio into Davis in the vehicle ahead and let him know we'll be stopping near where he found the white pickup the other night. That's our best rally point for them, unless we see something sooner. Once we push out into the wood line, Rachel will stay in the rear with both vehicles to maintain radio contact between us and you. These hand mics have a low range, and we are gonna lose cell reception once we get so far in. We radio in our findings to Rachel, then she maintains contact with you back at the station. Simple as that."

"I ain't stayin' by the damn vehicles. Oh... Hell no!" says Rachel from behind the cage.

"Excuse me?"

"You heard me. I'm going out there too." she says.

"I need you here by the road with the radios if the state comes out to assist, dammit."

"Then leave the fat one in SUV here with them. You're not stopping me this time."

I turn to look at her as she is still petting Drake on the forehead while he looks up at me, too. I still have Sherral on the phone, blabbering something as I glare at Rachel.

"Take that back Sherral. We're *all* pushing out there when we stop. I'll maintain communications with you via radio as long as I can, but you'll at least have the location of our stopping point in the vehicles if anyone else in this fucking state does some work today."

"Ok Sheriff. I'll be right here."

"Roger that. Be in touch soon." and then I hang up the phone before turning to look at Rachel.

"Happy now?" I ask Rachel sarcastically.

She flips the bird at me before I turn around, shaking my head. I keep loading the AR rounds into the magazines. One tracer and one hollow point round over and over. Four magazines total loaded up to 30 rounds each. I release the slide to not chamber a round and check the safety. Three mags go into the vest holsters and one goes into the AR. I flap the ejection port over to be closed, and I do a functions check on the surefire light and optic for battery life. She's ready as she'll ever be. We push through the snow for several miles and then Davis slows down ahead. I pull him up on the radio.

"Davis, Sheriff here. What's going on up there? Are we getting close to the location where you brought in the white pick up?" I ask.

"Roger that. We're less than a mile out. But there's something in the road less than thirty meters out. Looks like a dead animal or something. A few birds hanging around it."

"Ok then. We're gonna push forward a little behind you and then come to a halt. I want you to drive around it and pull ahead so you can stop ahead of it. When you're close enough for a visual on whatever it is, radio in what you see. Then I'll move on foot to get a closer look if needed. Take it slow folks. Ain't no tow coming out here to the rescue."

"Roger that."

Greeves pulls up behind Davis and turns the strobes on after Davis moves forward.

"Greeves, pull into the right and back up diagonally to block the road and keep the lights on."

He does as I ask, and the tires slide around to catch grip on the frozen road surface. We all watch as Davis attempts to move around whatever he is seeing. The couple of birds near the dead animal start to fly away as Davis approaches them in the SUV.

"Sheriff, those are owls up there..." says Greeves as his hands shake on the steering wheel.

"I know. Just sit tight right here."

Rachel gets up from her seat in the back and approaches the inmate cage of the van. I unlock it so she can have a better view out the windshield, too. Davis struggles in the SUV for a sec to stay away from whatever is once the road. Once he has a good grip on the road surface in the SUV, he rolls down his window to look down on the road. He comes to a stop with his head out the window and radio in hand. I grab the radio to wait on his response.

"Jesus Christ!... Sheriff?!... Sheriff, it's a damn arm. It's somebody's fucking arm I'm looking at on the road here."

"Don't stop Davis. I want you to pull forward ahead, like I told you. We gotta close this section of the road in both directions."

"It's got blood all over it!"

"Pull forward, dammit! Keep that vehicle moving. You got the whole right side off the road already. Move forward like you are told and stop ahead to block the road a little ways up."

"Jesus... Uh... Ok. I'm moving." he says and puts his head back in the vehicle to roll up the window.

Once he stops, I turn to Rachel and Greeves, who are shivering and sweating bullets at the same time.

"So much for heading out to fetch another dead guy. At least a full body anyway... Ok guys. This is what we came out here for and we knew we would see something like this soon enough. I'm going out to the road on foot. Once I give the thumbs up, radio to Davis. I need you guys to get out on foot and keep your heads on a swivel on the road surface. Maintain 360 as best as you guys can, but stay near the vehicle you came in until I say otherwise. Rachel?"

She just looks out the front windshield gazed in fear. I raise my voice to snap her out of it.

"Rachel?!"

"Yeah... What?" she says, still in shock.

"Keep Drake in the vehicle. If this is what I think it is, then the other arm is not far, but we may need him to sniff it out. We can't have him do that until we know for sure, though. Ok?"

She just keeps staring out the windshield at the same bright red spot on the road a few meters ahead. It's been put there within the last few minutes. The snow hasn't even had the chance to cover the blood yet.

"Rachel?... Rachel, focus dammit?!"

"Ok..." she says and then I turn back to talk to Greeves.

"Wait for my signal."

"Ok..." he says, but he focuses on the same thing Rachel sees.

I step out of the van and hear him radioing into Davis. The road looks more like a hallway corridor surrounded by pines. The snow lightly falls as my feet crunch the ice underneath it. I look all around for any sign of life, but the only sound is that of the engines still running in the SUV in front and the van behind me. I unholster my revolver and keep it at the ready once the arm is in full view. That's way too much blood to be from the body I saw yesterday. This is the blood of something beyond just one arm that's been ripped away from a body at least 24 hours ago. The fingers are purple and blue while curled up in a freeze. I look back and give Greeves the thumbs up to step out of the vehicles. Davis gets out and yells from the distance.

"What the hell did that, Sheriff?!" he says.

I ignore him and shake my head as I get closer. The snow falls harder, and Davis is almost out of sight from white out. The snowfall picked up in the few minutes I have been staring at the sad remains of a human limb. The wind sends a cold chill down my spine underneath the layers of winter gear and vest. A demonic whisper come through the woods into my ears that startles Davis, too.

"She's here with us..."

"What the fuck was that?!" yells Davis.

"Come feast with us..."

Ol' Leeds brought us here.

"Davis, get back in the SUV, right now dammit!!! Now!!!"

I turn to look at Greeves and tell him the same thing, but he just keeps shaking his head, as if he is confused or doesn't hear me. I can hear Drake barking viciously from the back of the van.

"Get back in the van now, Greeves!!" I yell from the road.

I keep yelling at him to get back in as I run to the van and holster my revolver. Another blood-soaked arm is thrown from the wood line onto the windshield of the van and Rachel screams her lungs off. Greeves looks at the hood of the van, frozen in shock. The woods send a blast of frightening roars. Roars so loud it hurts to hear them without covering your ears. I keep yelling at Greeves, but he can't hear me over the terrifying howls from behind the trees. The wind, the snow, Rachel's screams, the devastating roars of the creature all together deafen me. The powerful winds pick up to send a line of pine trees falling on the white road. I look to see a tree coming right at me. I hesitate long enough to see where it is going to land and dodge it.

A tree falls over on top of the van and hits Davis on the back of the head. The siren goes off in a struggled and mumbling effect, but Rachel stops screaming. The van roof and windshield are caved in, and Drake is still barking. I can only see Greeves' feet next to the tire, covered in limbs, when another tree falls in my direction. I miss the bulk of the tree, but a large enough branch catches my leg to pin me down before I get out of the way and yell out in pain from my lower leg. I look back up at the van to see Drake trying to bite and claw his way through the busted windshield. No movement from Greeves or screaming from Rachel. I look back to see Davis hobbling towards me, and other pines fall on the road in the distance ahead of the SUV.

"Sheriff!!... Holy shit... Are you ok?"

"Get back to the SUV now and radio in. Two officers down... Right now, Davis! Go!" as I attempt to pull my leg out from under the branch. My leg isn't hurt yet, but all the weight of the branch and my thrashing around will sprain my ankle if I move too forcefully.

Davis attempts to run back to the SUV but freezes in a panic when we hear another gut-wrenching roar. He pulls out his service pistol and yells back as he fires off several rounds into the woods. The creature remains unfazed as he unloads an entire magazine at it. It rushes from the wood line with claws stretched out at him. Its wings stay low and streamlined to be faster on the ground level. The tail is as straight as a speeding arrow. Those teeth open wide when grabbing him and pinning him down on the ground with its weight. Davis flails around in horror as it drags him to the other side of the road. Those eyes. I remember those eyes. The glow of burning bright red through the whiteout of the snow as it lunges back and then in to clamp on Davis' face as he still screams. He keeps hitting it with the bud of his pistol until it twists his head off his shoulders mid-yell. His arms go limp and it sets a rear claw on his belly as it glares through the snow and back at me now.

It steps over him and walks towards me. A slow walk. A tormenting walk that makes a victim know what's coming. It opens and closes its tattered and holey wings until the bright snow shines through it and then wraps them around itself. All I see coming my way is a slender

238

silhouette, raised horns, and red eyes as its breath releases into the cold with a foggy growl. I unholster my revolver and struggle to aim it through the branches of the fallen pine on top of my leg still.

BANG!!!

The echo of the grizzly killer rounds sends my ears into an instant ring. It keeps walking toward me, unfazed, with the bullet hole in its chest closing up.

BANG!!

"She'll burn with you..."

BANG!!

The revolver breaks through the sound waves and recoils in my hand like a rocket launcher that belongs mounted on the hood of a military HUMMVEE. A shoulder hit that creates a slight shudder in its pace, but it's still not stopping.

BANG!!

It takes a hit on the thigh like it was fucking nothing. It keeps coming and walking towards me, stuck under this fucking tree. A near eight-foot stance upright. Its lower claws tap into the icy road as a dragon would to keep a grip. Smaller claws made up of two fingers hold the top pieces of its leathered wings in place.

It crouches down lower on all fours again, creeping like a cat that comes to play. I take aim at its head as it climbs over the fallen limbs. It grunts and growls as its monstrous upper claws tear away at limbs and branches to get to me. One shot left before reloading. I reach for my secondary speed loader on the lower part of my vest that I can't get to under the branches that hold me down. I keep aim as it forces through the brush. I need it in as close as possible for a headshot.

Closer... Ignore the leg pain...

Keep that aim... Steady with two hands...

It slowly moves in at me within reach of my revolver. Its long face and mouth full of jaggedly sharp teeth that will scare your soul straight to the hell it came from. Those burning red eyes pierce down into my tormented heart. It reaches out an arm with outstretched claws with a growl.

A barking comes from my side and startles both me and the demon. Drake jumps up from nowhere and latches on to its outstretched arm that makes it scream in pain. It thrashes and claws away at him until thrown down on the ground, but he gets back up again. They stand off and stare at each other as they each pace in a circle. Drake lunges at its neck for a kill tug after the creature opens its wings and claws with another hellish roar. The creature struggles with Drakes clamping force around its neck for a few seconds. He throws Drake to the ground and then he goes for the horned tail of the creature. They are both pushing each other back towards the SUV and away from me. I take aim and make my last shot below the gas cap of my patrol SUV.

BANG!!

The shot doesn't faze either of the two vicious fighters as Drake keeps coming at him and clamping down on one of its lower legs now. The gas tank is leaking down to the ground, but the thick snow doesn't let it travel far in a puddle. I reach for the flare I left in the lower cargo pocket of my free leg. I pop the cap and its flash blinds my eyes even after looking away. The flare spits out a glow from my hand, a foot tall.

"DRAKE, Heel!!!" as loud as I can. My ears are ringing so much I can't hear myself yelling.

Drake holds his ground with the creature but hesitates when I make the command.

"FIND!! SEARCH!! Just go!! Get out of there dammit!"

As Drake glances at me briefly, the creature grabs Drake up by his torso. Drake yelps in pain as the creature returns the favor with a furious bite into his midsection.

"No God Dammit!... No!!"

The creature holds Drake up in the air like a new trophy kill as it spits out a bone from his torso. It raises his flinching body high into the air and opens its mouth to drink his blood that drip down to him. The creature gazes back at me with a roar, with my dog held over its head. Drake jerks and flinches around until it throws him into the wood line while he still whimpers. The creature stares off into the direction it just threw my friend away, like unwanted leftovers. I toss the flare towards the SUV behind the creature while it still looks away. The flare ignites the puddle of fuel that has pooled up into the snow. A streak of flame moves faster than my eyes can register and burst into the back end of the SUV in an explosion that sends more fuel all over the creature.

It's startled, but the flaming debris catches the creature's massive wings and sets it on fire. It screams in pain again and again. Then stops to stare back at me with the flames that cover its body sizzling away at the mangy fur that chars away. It rolls around in the snow to get rid of the flames on its head and torso, but moves back into the wood line, out of sight again. I can't see it, but it still screams and still burns. The roars and growls fade away into the wood line.

I catch a breath of relief and hold it to force my leg out from under a branch. I hear a popping sound that sprains my ankle. I get up to limp towards the burning SUV to yell into the woods.

"Drake! Drake, where are you?!"

The patrol SUV has its entire ass end engulfed in flames. I won't step any closer as I look for Drake. The front end could catch fire and ignite just like the gas tank did.

"Jason!!" yells Rachel from the transport van. I turn and look to see her struggling from the back underneath the collapsed safety cage. Drake pushed the front windshield outward in several chunks of glass before he came at the creature.

"Hold on. It's gone, but I don't know for how long. Are you hurt?!!"

"My shoulder and arm's lodged under the cage and seat, but I don't think its broken."

I hear whimpering from the wood line beyond the SUV.

"Drake!! Drake, is that you? Where are you?!"

"Jason! Help me. Get me outta here. Please! Where are you going?!" yells Rachel.

I look to see Drake at the lower part of the ditch line of the side of the road, but he isn't moving beyond his chest struggling up and down. I run over to him with the pain shooting down my foot and slide down on the frozen ground to be next to him.

"Drake? Drake, buddy… You're hurt. You're hurt again. We gotta get you to a vet. They'll fix you up again. Ok? They'll fix you up just like last time…"

I lift him up off the ground and his entire stomach area bleeds all over my vest and mag pouches. His eyes are blinking. He is conscious and alert, but nothing more than being limp in my arms. A piece of his insides falls back down onto my boot when I get him off the ground. I walk with him in my arms and hold in the pain from my ankle. Limping through the snow is hard enough. Now I add in the weight of my best friend hurting and bleeding out in my arms.

"Stay with me, buddy. Just stay with me and we'll get you to a vet. I swear it. Just stay a bit longer." I reach the van and hear Rachel still struggling inside. I reach out with a hand, while still holding Drake to open the sliding van door, and it falls off the sliders to hit the ground.

"Jesus. It got Drake? Jason… I… I tried to keep him in the van, but he busted through the windshield after the tree fell. Is he gonna be ok?" she asks.

Her arm is clamped down under the inmate transport cage behind the driver's seat. I sit Drake down at the edge where the van door was supposed to be. I reach over to the CSI bag and grab the crowbar. I hear Drake still struggling to breathe and whimpering as I step over him to get to Rachel. I pry up the cage and use my bodyweight to push the driver's chair out of the way and it releases her arm that is mangled in two different places.

"Oh my God, Jason! My arm is all to hell!" as she cries out and screams in pain.

I grab a body bag tarp used to hide a crime scene from onlookers in crowded areas. They rip easily and I tear it in two to cover her arm and secure it to her chest.

"I know. Just don't look at it right now. I need you to sit up straight and take a deep breath. Tell me, do feel pain in your chest? You gotta talk to me, Rachel. Try to sit up straight."

"This side of my chest hurts to breathe."

"Ok, your collar bone might be broken or fractured. Keep it still and lower your breathing. Sit up straight against the seat there or on the floorboard next to Drake. Has Greeves made any movement since the tree went down?"

She looks at Drake and back to her arm in a panic.

"Rachel... Look at me... Just look at me. Has Greeves said anything since the tree fell?"

"I... Uh... I don't know. I couldn't hear anything in here. I just saw that driver's side roof cave in when the tree fell. He was standing on the same side."

"Ok then. Stay here with Drake. Get down next to him and keep talking to him. Just talk to him. He knows your voice."

She does as I ask, and I hop back out of the van, forgetting my ankle is twisted when I land on the road. I limp around the front of the van in a hurry to see his legs are still twitching, and I feel a glimmer of relief again. But it was no use. His entire head is crushed in from his face to his chest area between the van and a massive branch of the pine. I try to look for a pulse or a reflex with his hands, but there is no response from either. His leg just lays there on the road twitching. I try to shake his body in some blind hope to pry him out. And maybe he would be alive and alert. A fresh piece of brain matter drops on his pool of blood underneath him in the snow.

"Fucking, Christ! He was just a kid. He was just a fucking kid!?"

I limp back around the front of the van to get back to Rachel and Drake. She still lays next to him crying.

"Jason? He's slipping away. What do we do?"

"You're not a fucking vet! No, he isn't. He's fine. We're gonna make it all better, Drake. I promise... Rachel, hand me the other half of that sheeting. I gotta stop the bleeding somehow."

I try to lift him up and get the sheet wrapped around his torso, but it was all gone. It has bitten all of his insides out. There is no stomach area, only a hollow bit mark that has torn everything out. It broke a piece of his rib off that punctured both lungs. I wrap it around him anyway and he whimpers again as I lift him up and put him back down on the floorboard again.

"Drake... Drake! Stay with me, buddy. You're gonna be fine. You're gonna be all right. We've been here before, buddy. Remember? Remember how they tried to get you in the desert. They didn't get you then. They ain't gonna get you now! I promise!"

I hold his head in some mad sense of hope that he can make it, but he only looks back up at my face to see me in tears. I start tying off the sheeting to stop the bleeding. It's everywhere. My friend is bleeding out in my hands in the back of a van. My last good friend is going away.

"Drake... Drake, buddy don't go. Please just stay with me. Don't go."

I hold my head next to his forehead, wishing I could trade places.

"Drake, just stay... Please... I'm so sorry. You won't have to do this ever again. Drake?"

I raise up and he looks at me one last time with those two different colored eyes before they close. I keep talking to him, asking him to come back, and Rachel sits back in tears and covers her face with her good hand. I know he's gone when I hear his last whimpering exhale. I drop to my knees on the outside of the van, crying tears that freeze to my face from the cold. A furious burst of anger and hate fills my hands and I pound the side door of the van, denting it inward multiple times. I am so angered and covered in tears that I don't hear myself screaming. I can't feel anything when I keep punching the door. When I am out of breath from yelling and my bloodied knuckles have busted through my gloves, I drop down on my ass next to the van. But the tears don't stop.

"Jason?" says Rachel from inside the van. "Jason... I am so sorry."

I get up and limp back over Greeves body on the other side of the van. His leg finally stopped twitching. I reach for his service pistol and both magazines on his belt and move back to Rachel. I drop the magazines on the floorboard next to Drake's now lifeless body. Rachel keeps trying to get my attention and saying something, but I ignore her. I don't even know what she is saying to me right now. I muscle the sliding door upright from the ground. I try to fit it back on the sliding door mounts and it latches in place. The sliding mechanism is bent from the tree fall distorting the metal tracks, but it closes enough to lock after a few tests back and forth.

"Jason. What are we gonna do?"

"You're gonna radio in, to Sherral back at the station. The state PD and the Fire Department have to come out now. They gotta put that patrol SUV out. The snow may stop it from spreading more of a fire, but it could catch the pines from higher up and spread from there. Let her know we need EMT services and there are four deputies down. Three are more than likely DOA." I reach through the remains of the crushed cage door and grab the dash mic to hand it to Rachel. "Do it now."

"Oh my God. Greeves is dead?" she asks.

I reach into her leg pocket and transfer her flares into my lower cargo pocket. I check Greeves pistol to discover he never even had a round in the chamber. I slide the hammer back, check the safety, and then hand it to her.

"Get your Glock out and have it at the ready."

I move to the passenger side door and reach for the shotgun to hand it to her, too.

"This is your last resort. If anything comes opening this door that ain't got a gun and a badge, you start blasting those pistols with your good hand until they are empty."

"Jason. No. Don't do this..." she says.

"Don't try to reload. Just move to the next loaded pistol. If that doesn't stop it, then give it a single blast to the head with that shotgun. You won't be able to re-pump and chamber a round with your arm busted up, but at that point you just need to get out, run your ass off, and find cover. Keep all those spare magazines in your pocket so you can reload when you find cover. Just don't stop moving or shooting at that point."

"Three men DOA? What do you mean?" she asks.

"Keep this door closed and try to stay warm until they show up. If you gotta start shooting, it will only startle it for a second or two. That's all the time you need to keep moving."

I go back to the front passenger and grab my AR and slide it back to chamber a round. I look through the bag and reload my revolver with the same heavy Hornady loads again. I check to make sure the speed loaders are still up.

"Hand me all the flares outta that bag next to you and a spare flashlight."

She does as I ask, but her good hand is shaking from the cold. I look back in the CSI bag for a space blanket and open it up to wrap around her.

"Please don't go out there, Jason. I'm sorry. I'm so sorry about Drake. I'm sorry for everything."

"Don't talk like that right now."

"I'm sorry I didn't believe you. I should've believed you. Just don't go back out there. Just stay here. Please Jason!?" as she keeps trying to touch my face while she begs and cries. She grabs my arm as I get the blanket wrapped around her.

"You'll be fine. Trust me. Just stay here and call it in. Do as I say now."

"Please don't go. I'm sorry I left you all those years ago. I'm sorry I couldn't give you a baby like you wanted." as she looks to see me crying through eyes that are filled with anger.

"Don't do this. Not right now, Rachel. It wasn't your fault. None of this was your fault." as I hold my forehead on hers to keep her calm. I wipe her tears off her cheeks as she keeps sobbing.

"I'm sorry I was so mad at you for so long when I came back. I wanted to be Maggie's mom. I wanted to be a mother, but I couldn't. I wanted to be a mother for your kid, our kids. I can go back to the fertility clinic and try again. I'll take whatever meds they want me to this time. That's the only reason I left, but I came back still wanting to be with you. Just stay here with me till they get here. Please?! We can go away. We can leave all this behind..."

246

"I can't do that, and you know it. That thing is still out there."

"They got an organ for you, it's just waiting. We can go. We can start over again, Jason."

I step back into the van and grab her hand to put the pistol in it. I hold the back of her head and kiss her cold and chapped lips before looking her directly back in the eyes that are still tearing up. It's freezing inside the van, but I haven't felt her sense of unforgotten warmth in so long and I let her hold my face to kiss me back.

"Don't go… Why are you doing this?" she cries.

"Because my Maggie's still out there and I'm gonna go find her."

"Please, Jason. I love you… Please don't go. I'm so sorry."

"I'm so glad you came back in my life."

I hold my hands on her face to touch her lips once more. I let her hair go, but she tries to reach out for my arms again with her good hand and drops the pistol. I rush out the van and close the sliding door to hear her screaming my name behind me.

"Jason!!... Jason!!"

I pull out my hand cuffs and put them on the handle of the sliding door and the front passenger door to lock her in place. Her screams turn to moans the further away I walk. I come up on Davis' headless body and reach for his service pistol out of his hand and the holster clipped to his belt. I attach it to the top piece of my vest above the magazine pouches and holster his pistol after unloading the empty magazine for a fresh one full of rounds.

I look back to see Rachels hands pressing against the bashed-up windshield, still crying and screaming for me not to leave her. I lean back down at his body again to grab the flares from his cargo pocket and add them to mine. The SUV is smoldering hot as I walk by it. The wood line is filled with smoke and white snowfall. Ol' Leeds has left me a trail to follow covered in blood and chunks of burnt hair. I leave the road and I look back to see the smoke covers my view of the carnage it has caused. The hurt and pain this monster has left in my path to pick up the pieces for months now. I'm done with this. I'm done with waiting on the next move from you. I'm coming to you this time…

Chapter 22: Run and Gun

We all burn, and we burn everything before ourselves. This creature takes injury. It bleeds, though it seems to recover fast. It's nocturnal by choice. I may have crippled it enough to keep it from flight. That's its only vantage. I have to keep it at the ground level. Then it becomes a fair fight. If it bleeds, then it will burn. I make my way back to James' campsite and leave the pile of bodies behind. The daybreak comes in through the overcast of snow clouds. I run most of the way with a ruck sack rubbing my backsides raw as it bounces up and down. I stop every hundred meters to watch and listen. To listen if anything is following me in the distance. I make it back to the shoreline and I hear gunfire from the distance. Several gunshots. The first set of nine or ten come from a smaller caliber or pistol of some sort. A long pause and then five staggered shots from a larger caliber.

They must be several miles out at least and closer to the main county roads. I make my way over to James' hut and ignore the gunfire. It is too far away to decipher what is going on. His hut is crumbled to the ground and I have to move large sheets of wood and brush out of the way to get to it. I pause every few minutes to look around and blow breath on my bare hands to keep them warm. I get to the bottom of the rubble. The smaller five Gallen barrels say fuel oil and others say 15% ethanol on corroded barrel stickers. I don't know dick about boats or boat fuel. All that matters to me is that they all have an explosive hazmat sticker on the side of all of them. I gather up six barrels from the pile of rubble. I move over to the shoreline and see the remnants of an abandoned pier that are barely holding on to the posts that keep it in place. The high tide and low tides of the beach front have left a goldmine of boating fuel for the taking.

I move down to the shorefront and start checking them. Some barrels have corroded open and are empty. Some are still sealed, but there is more than enough to get the job done and burn this creature out into the open. I move the loaded barrels back up near James' hut. I grab a random hand pump stuck in the sand and cycle freezing cold ocean water through it to clean it out. It still has the needed threads in place to mount it on the sealed cans. I move them back up off the shoreline to add them to the rest of the pile repeatedly to accumulate almost a hundred gallons. I don't need to take all of them back to the hunting sight, just enough to lure it back to the mass pile of more barrels waiting to ignite. Strategic placement throughout the woods will bring it out into the open as long as it stays at the ground level. It can still climb trees and jump from one to the next. It may not risk staying on a tree that is engulfed in flames.

I set up my snare with the last of the cord just out of reach of the ground and near the fuel sources I can't take with me as I trek back into the woods. An enormous pile of wood and rubble waiting to tip off into the shoreline's ledge holds the snare in place. I build a sled with some more of the scrap wood from James' shed. I load my pockets with more ammo out of my ruck and make sure I have enough melted snow turned into water to fill my camel back. I have to stay light and as fast as possible. The moment trees go up in flames, this entire forest will do the same thing. Then it gets lured out into an open area away from flames but near a fuel source. I drag the sled into the wood line, and I pause to see the owls watching at me from the trees again.

"You lil shits are gonna burn with that thing!"

I keep dragging it through the trees and the brush underneath them as they stare. The sled is heavy, but the ground is frozen. The bark is dried and cold, but enough fuel will catch anything on fire. I stop underneath the tree they stay perched on and move to the sled to attach the rusted hand pump to one barrel.

"You tell that son-of-a-bitch I'm gonna burn that mother fucker out!"

I pump fuel all over the tree at eye level, above the frozen ground and snow, all around the bark of the pine. I do the same to the tree next to it and they still look down at me.

"It will burn before I do if it doesn't come out here and face me. I know where it came from. I'm here to send it home! You tell 'em that!"

I pull the sled away a reasonable distance and then walk back to the tree the owls are perched on while trying to scare me. I pull out the flint and steel from my pocket and start sparking it.

"I know what I am, and it doesn't scare me anymore…"

I set the tree on fire and the flame sits where the fuel was splattered first. The flame travels where it dripped down, but the bark catches flame by the time it gets to the ground. I back up knowing that the two trees are burning and not just the fuel splashed on them to get them started. I move back to the sled and look back at the owls that still sit there on an upper limb. The smoke has engulfed them out of sight, but the pine needles catch flames faster. They try to fly off and struggle, but they falter fast. One by one, they fall over to the ground for lack of oxygen and too much smoke. None of them get away. Some pass out and fall to the ground. Others fall on the limbs of the tree that are already ablaze. They squeal and flap around, trying to escape what comes for them. Their yellow eyes turn to glare at me without blinking. A nearby tree's needles and pinecones catch sparks from the heat.

I move the sled full of fuel away further into the woods. A strategic layout of burning trees first. The more fuel on other trees to ignite and draw it out into the open. It will have a trail of openings to follow to stay away from the flames. So long as it still can't fly off from that one shot it took in the wings. I zigzag back and forth for hours from one tree to the next in the woods. I create a funnel all the way back to the hunting site and the winds pick up, coming from the east heading west, away from the ocean. It sends the smoke from the first two trees in my direction, but I am way too far away to know if other trees nearby have also caught flames too. The smoke is black and grey, so I know something is burning hot near the shoreline. I move the sled faster, the lighter it gets from spraying boat fuel on any tree I walk past now. The gap is nearly closed off and I reek of ethanol.

I see the pile of deer and coyote bodies that other wildlife has picked at more and more. A faint glow of orange follows me in the darkness. I look back toward the freezing Atlantic Ocean that I haven't seen for hours, and the smoke fills the skies. I look to my west and above the tree line to see a faint snow make itself known. I grab the last few barrels by hand and carry them to the area where the salt brick was and douse more trees and brush. The blood trail from last night is already covered in the snow that falls harder. As long as I place the fuel at eye level on the tree, the moisture from the snow won't wash it off the bark and it will set fire. As soon as it comes in, I will light the area behind it to close it in. From there, it becomes a matter of leading it to get back to James' campsite to lure it on top of the rest of the fuel. Then I'll send this fucker back to hell.

I empty one of the last two fuel cans on top of the pile of bodies. The white deer lay lifeless on top of all of them, but nothing has touched it, looking for a free taste like the others below it. The body pile is far enough away from the other fuel-soaked trees for now. I lit it up and all the dead deer and coyotes turn to my nightmares again. People I've killed, to people I have witnessed being killed. They all keep reaching for me a moaning in pain along with the screaming. The screaming never stops. The ringing of gunfire never stops. They can move but they just reach out for help and cry.

"You did this. You had this coming. We all got it coming…"

I watch as they change from people I know to wildlife again, back and forth in my own twisted mind. I turn away as they still scream under the flames. My foxhole is still left in place, and I make my way to it. The snow and the winds pick up, but the orange glow to the east gets brighter. I take a good look around the area before I work my way away from the burning pile of bodies. It's nighttime, and the air smells of a pine scent that you leave hanging in your rear-view mirror, only to add in the smell of flaming coals made from bark. I get to the fox hole and readjust the top of the tent material and ghillie blanket, but I hear something. Something is breathing near me. Is that bear still nearby? I look around to see a wave of wildlife running away from the direction of the shoreline. Dozens of them moving through the dark smoke and snow. More deer and a bear with her cubs that walk beside her. Squirrels and rabbits scurry around on the lower part of the trees, but they all travel in the same direction. Away from the flames.

I pause for a while as all the animals pass by me without a second glance. More coyotes and a cluster of foxes run away, and the orange glow gets brighter. That or it was already that bright, and the sky has just gotten that much darker. The winds pick up, bringing more smoke into the area. There is so much smoke it becomes hard to decipher what is snow and what is smoke. I see a few more animals trotting away into the distance, and I go to lift the cover of my foxhole that is covered in a light layer of frozen snow.

A blood curdling roar comes out from the foxhole and the creature reaches out at me. Its red eyes are the only thing I can see in the grave's blackness I was about to curl up into. I slam the heavy brush pile covered in frozen snow on top of its head. It thrashes through it with ease and climbs out of the hole. I have the rifle pointed at it, but I wait for it to stop thrusting around its arms before I shoot. It expands its battered and holey wings and yells again while outstretching its claws. It closes its wings around itself and stands upright, grunting and growling with every movement. Its red eyes just glare back at me, but I keep the sights right at its shoulders and wings now. It takes a step closer, but I hold the rifle up to its head and it stops.

"So, you know what this is now?"

I take a step towards it and it takes a step back.

"What the hell do you want?"

"Come feast with us."

I keep my eyes on the creature and keep the rifle steady on its head. This is how it thrives. Within your fears and nothing more. It speaks through the winds of the woods, right into your heart and soul. It hesitates and opens its wings while lowering its head. Its mouth full of teeth slowly open.

"Your heart of darkness is mine!!!!"

It lunges at me again, but I shift aim just in time to point the rifle over to the side of the creature and fire at the last fuel can that creates a blast to send me and the creature into the air to hit the low ground near the pile of bodies already covered in flames. It screams as we are both pushed through the air and its backside is on fire. It rolls around in the snow to keep its wings from burning even more.

I scramble around and look for the rifle while my jacket is on fire and grab up the rifle to chamber another round. We walk in circles around the pile of burning bodies and I keep the rifle aimed at it while sliding another round into the side loading gate of the rifle. My jacket has caught fire too much from the splashed fuel all over me. I struggle and try to get it off while keeping the rifle aimed, but I throw it toward one of the last trees I doused in fuel. The tree goes up in flames from the heat that the body pile has created to dry it off. It stops circling the flaming body pile between us as I do the same. We face off through the blaze and its eyes glow through the fire. It jumps into the air over the fire and roars its chilling sounds through the woods.

Time to run and gun...

I shoot while it is midair, and it throws it off balance and I run through the opening of trees that don't have fuel on them. It gets up to lean back down on all fours and chases after me with lighting speed from its streamlined body. The trail of smoke from its burned-up wings follows behind it and mists into the smoke already in the air. I break off a tree limb as I run and fire back at it blindly without looking. The rifle recoils into the air, but I still maintain my grip with numb and frozen hands. All I hear are more growls and roars from behind as I sprint. I stop to look back to see it gripping one pine to the next several feet up and not staying on the ground level. It pauses briefly and then climbs the pine tree until it lands on a few meters away. It is trying to reach the high ground in the smokey mist to stay out of sight so I can't shoot at it. It will try to jump down on me from higher up.

I pull the flint and steel out of my pocket after I sling the Henry over my back. I rip a cargo pocket off of one side of my trousers and wrap in around the end of the branch I broke off. I look for the nearest tree that I already doused in boat fuel and stick it into the puddle that dripped down into the snow. I hit the flint and light it up and bring my rifle back up to the front at the ready.

I turn around with the torch and it jumps down from a random limb right in front of me to scream and claw my stomach. I yell out in pain but hit it with the edge of the torch in the face. I crouch over, holding my stomach, but keep moving back to the shoreline. I ignore the pain and take another shot from behind while running at its torso to. I sling the rifle backwards to pull the lever to chamber another round. I light up every tree I can see as I run. It's just a matter of lowering the torch to the bottom of any tree that looks familiar or smells like fuel. I stop to pause before lighting another tree and to look back, just long enough to get a visual on the creature. I can hear it moving from above again. It won't risk landing near me again. It's gonna try to land on top of me this time.

I look up to see it crawling face down to the bottom of the tree at me in a fury. I light the tree and the flames shoot upwards right at its face and I keep moving. I catch a glimpse of it jumping from one tree to the next from the corner of my eye and then back down to the ground level. I turn, knowing it is on the ground level, and I take a solid shot at its face to stun it again. It freezes in place to scream in pain and hatred for me. I use its hesitation to keep loading the side gate of the Henry and keep running. I drop the torch by another fuel-soaked tree to see it light up in a flash of heat. I run long enough to be out of breath and hold in place to just listen as I try to lower my breathing. I grab another branch to prepare for a new torch, but not until I know where Leeds is at now.

I lift my collar to cover my breathing and sink lower down the tree I stand next to. I hear grunting and growling from above, but no visual yet. Trees are scraped and clawed as it moves around above me.

Only a little further and I'll be able to use the lighting from the fires closer to the shoreline to my advantage. It glows now, like the sun setting behind the woods, but darkness has been here for what seems like days now. Movement from above stops and I move my Henry back to the low-ready to keep running.

I dodge trees and brush left and right. I don't remember ever running faster, even when taking enemy fire from down-range. Its massive claw blindsides me from the back side of a tree during my epic sprint. It stuns me to the ground, but the rifle stays slung behind me between my back and the ground to not be able to grab it. My nose bleeds in an instant and sends a sharp pain between my eyes. It grabs my leg and almost breaks my ankle with its ridiculously powerful grip and drags me faster than my own sprint. My rifle dangles behind me as I am dragged through the frozen forest floor and brush on the ground. I try to beat its claws as it drags me along with the torch that I didn't have the chance to light yet. I abandoned the torch, and it rolls away on the ground behind us as it keeps dragging me along. I reach for my rifle and take a shot at its spine. It lets go after a scream and I run back to the torch I dropped. I pull out my flint and steel as it stands there, trying to re-cooperate from another direct hit. Then it drops down on all fours to run at me. I get the torch lit up, and it stops dead in its tracks, ready to lunge, but the lit torch makes it pause.

"I told you I knew where you come from and I'm here to take you home." as I lower the torch to the nearest tree.

I can't remember if I poured fuel on this one or not, but it isn't calling my bluff. It sits still on all fours but motions back and forth, ready to pounce me like a rabid grizzly bear. I touch the torch to the tree, and nothing happens. I rub it up and down the bark to try to light it. Still nothing.

"Shit…"

It roars before it takes another fast lunge as I throw the torch to another tree. Any tree surrounding us has to have fuel on it. I duck behind the tree I just tried to set on fire, and it leaps by me as I shoot and shout back at it. I blast a round through its wings and pull the lever back again. It climbs another tree that the torch lit up into a blaze. The trail of fire follows it up the tree as it climbs. It looks down and gives that same demonic and ear-piercing scream before it jumps to another tree, out of sight again. I change my direction in running to the other side of the funnel I have set up. Only a few of the trees with fuel on them on the other side of the funnel have lit up on fire, but the smoke is getting heavier the closer I get to the shoreline. I can't hear any movement from the trees. I don't even have time to catch my breath before I pull out the flint and steel again. I hit the flint right next to the tree and set it on fire with flames that shoot up to the branches. I do it over and over as fast as I can with the other line of trees.

The winds pick up and knock over one of the first trees I set on fire earlier. The roots of pines are never in the ground deep enough to keep it steady under stress. I look around to see more trees, some engulfed in flames and some catching, but they are all swaying in the wind while uprooting themselves from the frozen marshy ground that cannot hold them. They begin to topple over like a child's game of dominos. The creature hangs on to a tree as it swings over to break its fall. This entire forest is about to go up in flames around us both. It jumps off the branch of a flaming pine before it hits the ground and attempts to look around the area for me. I hunker down behind an unlit tree to watch what it does. Its fur is burnt away, and its wings are scalding hot with steam rolling off the back side. Pieces of charred flesh fall off its torso, but it still attempts to heal somehow.

The chase is more important to this thing. The thrill of the hunt and a kill from a being that it terrifies its prey into submission before ripping it apart. As soon as it turns its back, I jump up to a full-scale sprint again towards the shoreline. It screams before it continues its efforts to chase me again.

Run and gun…

Run and gun all night if I have to. Just to get it right where I want it.

Chapter 23: The Lake of Fire

I limp through the woods for miles. Everything hurts and my ankle is throbbing. I can feel that it is swelling to the point of filling up my boot. Feverish, cold, and exhausted, but I have to keep going. I cough uncontrollably into my hands. I look at my gloves through my mag light and see my palms covered in blood. It takes forever to get to any area that I am familiar with. The small watering hole area that hunters used to bait in deer is already frozen. Hard enough to step on and keep moving forward.

I keep the surefire light of the AR on, along with the mag light I attached to the shoulder strap of my camel back. It lights the way for a few meters into the darkness, but I have to stop often to give my ankle a break and catch my breath. My eyes are tearing up. Not from pain, but from more toxins rolling through my bloodstream for lack of dialysis treatment. The snow is coming down but not enough to give a white out condition yet. These woods are so quiet out here. I wish I had made it out here more often on my own terms to enjoy it more. The stories that surround these woods are, mostly, just stories. But it has proven to me otherwise earlier today when I saw my best friend ripped apart. I knew it was real. I just didn't want to admit it. Now more are dead.

I'll be out here as long as it takes to find this thing and fill it with enough lead to send it to the grave. I keep trudging through the snow. Some areas are still soft and marshy underneath all the white, but some are frozen solid. The trees creek and moan with a slow breezing wind that makes my eyes tear up even more with the freezing air. I pass by a tall pine tree with its roots, trying to uplift from the ground like a multitude of bodies attempting to come up from the grave. I move to stay out of its way in case it falls. It would be hard to see where it may land when the wind topples it over. I come across an open clearing in the woods. A type of vantage points a hunter would use for the kill.

I try to pick up the pace, but tire too quickly. I trip in a deep spot to fall on my side and keep the rifle away from the dirt. I fall into a small freshly covered hole that has been dug into. My mag light falls off my shoulder mount outside the hole and I reach for it to see what I have fallen into. The light reflects off of an orange his vis-vest a hunter would wear, but it is torn to pieces. A boney skeletal hand reaches out for me from underneath the dirt and grabs my vest. I shudder back in panic and kick myself backwards, away from it. A gurgle and choking sound come from under the dirt and snow.

"What the fuck!!" I scream in horror.

It twists my arm when grabbing at me. As I try to back away, it uses its grip on my leg to pull itself out from under the snow while I back far enough away. I try to shake off its grip and I point the AR at it to see it in the light. It falls over outside of the hole while still reaching for me with a single boney arm. One eye is missing, but the other is hanging down to the check bone. This can't be real. It raises its head to look at me. The scalp is torn and ripped off to see bone and brain matter budging from underneath. It uses its single arm to drag itself out of the hole more. It slowly crawls towards me as I freeze in place and keep pointing the AR at it. It's a body. A dead body that has been out here for days. It raises its head to look at me through the surefire light and the AR I keep aimed at it.

"It wants us to burn." in a cracked a struggling voice.

It grabs ahold of my leg again, but not to try to hurt me. But to reach for help. It releases another struggled breath and then goes limp in front of me while still outstretching its skeletal arm. Its entire lower body is buried under the snow or missing. I reach to turn my radio volume back on and Rachel it still calling for me. I get back on my feet and keep the AR light pointed at the body.

"*Jason... Jason? Are you there? Please God, just radio back in Jason...*"

"Yeah, it's me. Sheriff Jason Williams here. Over..."

"*Oh, thank God. Jason, where are you?!*"

"I'm about five or six miles in, and I found another body. I'm pretty sure it's Clauson, over."

"*Jason, we don't care about that right now. They need your location to come to you.*"

"Negative..."

"*There are state PD and Game and Wildlife all over this. I'm in the EMT ambulance talking to you. They are gathering an entire hunting party to get out there to you. They want you to sit tight wherever you are.*"

"Negative. I'm pushing forward to the shoreline to get to the old marina fueling point area. I'll be placing a flare marker here at this body's location. Over..."

"*Jason?!... Please just hold in your current position...*"

Static and mumble comes over the radio as I ready the next flare.

"*This is New Jersey State Police Captain Smith. Do you read?... Over.*"

"This is Sheriff Williams... Nice of you, assholes, to come out and assist."

"*We're here now, and you have two dead deputies and one injured. We need you to halt your investigation, mark the body, and make your way back to the county route. If you do not comply, you will be arrested for tampering with a police investigation and indicted under federal charges. This isn't your investigation anymore, Jason. Bring it on back in before more people get hurt. How copy? Over..*"

"Eat a dick Smith! I'm out here and I'm going in further. You can come in and arrest me or help me out. Either way. I'm out here to finish this, so stay the fuck outta my way. How do you copy that one? Now, this is Sheriff Jason Williams, over and out, shithead."

I reach up to my shoulder and turn the radio down low, but not off. I need to hear what they are communicating and their locations, but I don't want to keep the radio on loud enough to give away my position. I pop the cap on the flare and a massive set of teeth growls at me at eye level. A monstrous silhouette raises its arms to charge me.

"God Dammit!!!"

I dodge its roar and move to the side of the nearest tree in a hurry and I ready the AR and shine the light on it.

It's a bear. A black bear and her cubs following behind her and they walk past the tree I stand next to. I keep the AR raised at them, but they pay no attention. I look around with the flare and the AR light attached to the barrel. There are more animals moving in my direction. A cluster of coyotes, rabbits bouncing around in the snow like ping pong balls, and then the cluster of deer follows behind. They are all moving in the same direction. They all pass by me with only a few glances of concern. I cough more blood into my hands as they walk by, and still no alarm in my presence. I have never seen so many animals at once, much less moving in the same direction to the west of the shoreline a few miles out.

I jab the flare into the ground to mark the body location as the last few deer and beavers scurry by me in a hurry. I look back up to a higher ground and see a single doe standing there looking down at me. As I struggle on my feet to move closer, it does the same thing. I keep my AR raised at the ready in case I stumble on another bear, but I only see the doe closing in on me as I walk in the opposite direction of the herd of wildlife leaving in the distance. It stops walking towards me, but lets me get closer to it, despite an automatic rifle being pointed at it. Can it see me behind the light? Why doesn't it follow the rest of the animals moving in the same direction? I get closer to it and it remains stationary. I can't believe my eyes when I turn the radio off to silence all the frantic chatter.

"Wow... Look at you..."

It's a white albino doe. Fully matured and fearless of me walking closer to it. I keep coughing up more mucus, but I don't care right now. This is the most gorgeous thing I have seen in a long time after being surrounded by all this death. Hard to catch my breath and I feel lightheaded. I can't believe what I'm seeing in front of me. The moment

I don't feel cold from the snowfall and sleet is when I should worry. But nothing worries me right now in seeing such a sight so close. I lower my rifle as I get less than a few feet away. It lowers its head in a bit of concern from me being so close, but still not running away from me.

"I wish I knew you a long time ago."

Never a good idea to pet wildlife. If you get your scent on them, they may be pushed out of their group. It looks at me and raises its ears as I reach out to it. Random gunfire fills the woods from out of nowhere. It doesn't startle it. It just looks back in the same direction as the gunfire. It's heavy gun fire, but staggered. A large caliber of some sort. Not the gunfire of a semi-automatic rifle, either. Could be a shot gun with a pumping action between each fire being shot, but it's too hard to tell. The white doe turns and looks back at me before turning around to the gunfire and start walking towards it. It gets a few meters away before turning back to look at me. More shots go off and it keeps looking back and forth at me and then back at the direction of the gun fire.

I walk towards it, and it moves ahead a little further up the higher ground before looking back at me again in a frozen stance.

"What? Am I supposed to follow you?"

With no idea where it leads me, I follow anyway. It stops at a high ground in the forest but keeps looking back at me until I catch up. I walk up beside it to hear more gunfire. More concerning is the orange glow that comes from the shoreline. Several pine trees are on fire and one falls down in a blaze as I stand next to the white doe and watch in dread. I drop to a knee beside it.

"What the hell is going on out here."

The white doe keeps looking back at me, but I remain out of arm's reach, away from it.

"Ok… Ok… No more of this. It ends now."

I reach up to my hand mic and turn the radio back up to hear more chatter. The gunfire is changing directions somewhere in the woods. It's moving away from me, closer to the shoreline. The tree line that is on fire appears to be a giant V shape all the way to the old marina dock. But burning pines are falling over more and more as I watch.

Whoever did this didn't account for how out of control this could get. As much as I don't want to lead anymore people out here, got no choice. I turn to speak into the mic as the white doe runs off in the same direction with the other wildlife. I watch it fade away into darkness and snowfall before I talk into the radio.

"Rachel, Sheriff here. Do you read? Anybody? It Sheriff Williams here, over?"

"*Roger, State PD still. Sergeant Harris here. They are making their way to you still. Are you remaining stationary or returning? Over…*"

"Negative… Still moving to the shoreline. We got a bigger problem. Did the fire department come out to put out the patrol SUV that was on fire?"

"*Sheriff, they have instructed me to tell you to return to the nearest county road and wait for…*"

I block the last of the transmission by holding the mic call button in place. Blah… blah… blah… And I still hear the shots going off closer to the fire.

"Dammit Harris, did they put out the SUV fire or not? Is the fire department sill there? Over."

"*Roger Sherriff. That fire is still lit but has been left monitored in a controlled burn status.*"

"Harris, listen to me. We have another massive fire going on out here. This fire is out of control and covering a few square miles already. Do you have air support available in the fire department?"

"*Roger, they have a Heli tanker down in AC, but it could take a few hours to get filled up.*"

"We're next to the Atlantic, dummy. I don't think it's gonna run out of water soon."

"*Roger that. It's the middle of winter and everything is frozen. Sheriff, it is snowing over here at the wreck site where your van was at. How is it a damn wildfire over there?*"

"Can you get them to get it in the air or not?"

"*Roger that, but there gonna want a solid location before they go through all that trouble. This isn't in my scope of things.*"

"Well, get in your fuckin scope because it is coming your way if the wind keeps pushing it. Tell them to get it in the air and head due east from your location. Believe me, they won't miss this one. Over and out." as I reach up to turn the mic off again while I can still hear gunfire in the distance.

He's here. That bastard got to it before I did, just like he said he would.

That's one determined prick. Either determined or crazy one...

Chapter 24: And Hell Followed Him

I can't tell if my eyes are tearing up from the cold or from a broken nose from the last hit. Anytime I stop to listen all around me, my body shivers from the freezing air despite all the flaming trees that surround me. The more blood I lose, the colder it will get, no matter how close I get to the flames. I kneel low near the tree I hide behind and lift my shirt to see the fresh claws marks that have only gone through the meat, but no organs are hit. I touch the inside of the gashes to make sure and my icy fingers make me cringe in absolute anguish, but I can't scream. Not now.

I turn around and look behind the tree and it walks upright, scanning the area for me. I get back on my feet but stay behind the tree with the Henry pointed at its already charred and burned up body. Its wings are mere bones, with little skin hanging on. There are more than enough trees around it in a furious blaze to get a good visual and I can see it is trying to heal itself somehow. It slows its step and looks around again before dropping on all fours to curl up into the ball. It screams in the fetal position, and I watch its wings recuperate in front of me. Hell no. Don't give it the chance. I take another shot through its wings and the bullet goes through and shatters the lower bark of another burning tree behind it. It jumps back into a full run at me with arms stretched forward. I sprint again with it catching up from behind. A burning tree is starting to topple in my path, and I speed underneath it just in time. It lands in front of it to block its pursuit.

I turn around to see its eyes through the flaming tree that has fallen between us and I take another shot at its torso. It dodges and jumps to another standing tree to keep chasing me. It jumps from one tree to the next as I keep firing at it. Another round hits its leg, and it drops to the ground, then I turn around to keep running to the shoreline. I lost my jacket when it jumped me from the foxhole. It was full of most of the ammo I had for the Henry. I reach to feel my pant pocket as I run, and there's nothing in them beyond the flint and steel. All that remains for rounds is what I left on the rifle stock ammo holster. I pause in place, hoping I crippled it from that last leg shot, and I load the rifle from the side gate again while looking around for it. I look around into the dozens of burning trees that surround me. The funnel of flames is closing in, and I know I am close to the shoreline with the last of the boat fuel.

I turn around to work my way back to the shoreline and the creature stops me dead in my tracks to lift me up by my throat while roaring into my face before I get the chance to keep running. It taunts me now as my feet dangle off the ground, despite having more than enough strength to cave my head in. I struggle to grab my Henry, but I have to keep some grip on its claws, so it doesn't break my neck off. The number of teeth it opens up, available to sink into my midsection, but I grab my fillet knife still holstered in the back of my belt to jab it in the throat with my free hand. I keep jabbing it in the neck until it tosses me to the side like a rag doll and gurgles in its own blood.

The monster crouches down into a fetal position again to heal itself, but I refuse to wait around for it to keep running after me. I give it another shot to its backside. It lunges from its crouched position and climbs the nearest unscorched tree to get the high ground vantage again. It goes from one tree to the next, whether it is in flames or not, just to get ahead of me. I take another shot while running, only to see tree bark and fire sparks splattering off into the distance, away from it. I hurdle over the crispy dead owls and hear the creature slam back down to the ground level behind me. It runs behind while screaming at me, but I slow down to a jog once I see the snare. Closer and closer it runs and then moves down to all fours again, ready for the kill. I turn around to see it still coming at me at full speed and ready the rifle, but it doesn't slow down this time.

It tangles a single leg up on the snare but keeps running at me. The hook is set, and I move to the other side of the barrels before it jumps over them. I knock over the weight of last rubble of scraps and wood from James' hut into the nearby ledge into the shoreline. It tightens the snare cord that it still doesn't see on its foot. It lands only a few feet in front of me and reaches with that terrifying claw. It gets jerked into midair to dangle and thrust around, using its wing and claws to try to escape. It is more anxious with reaching for me now than it is to release from the cord while hanging upside down. I drop, not only to avoid its reach so close to the top of my head, but to try to breathe while I grab another tree branch to cover in the last of my cloth. The flint and steel have trouble striking a flame on the cloth from my sweat and moisture of the snow but lights up.

I slowly back away, closer to the shoreline as it still struggles and screams, while hanging over the last fuel barrels. I follow the fuel trail from the beach front I left before I made my way back into the wood line with the sled. It opens its mangled and leathery wings to fly before looking down to see what it is almost directly below it. I just hold the flaming torch in one hand and my rifle in the other to see this creature roar in frustration. The trees all around it light up the night sky with a heat that blazes so much the snow does not have the chance to touch the ground before melting. The tree with the snare has flames traveling up it, but not high enough to burn the cord yet. I lower the torch to the fuel trail on the ground to watch it close in on the barrels below the monster.

I unload the last of my ammunition in the Henry to stun the creature so the flames can do what I intend for them to do. The trail flames ignite at the lower barrels and the rest send a wave of an explosion upwards to engulf it in flames. Its body chars to black in front of me. Its red eyes still glow brighter than the flames that surrounds it. The demon screams and roars in pain, fright, and anger. It thrashes around harder to reach up and slash the cord. Only to drop its scorched and dying body down into the barrels and scrap wood that has heated up like lava beneath it. It struggles and moves slower. A claw raises up beside a wing made of bones and scorned skin that is melting from the heat. More screams and roars struggle to mere growls and grunts before those blazing red eyes fade away into the fire in front of me.

I walk backwards to keep eye contact, but the flames have consumed the entire area where James' campsite used to be. The trees are falling more rapidly out in the wood line the longer I wait to make sure it is dead and burning in Hell. The tree that held the creature's snare topples over on top of it and the burning barrels. The winds have attempted to push the flames away from the shoreline. The beach is the safest place to be right now. I look for an area that isn't engulfed in flames to make my way over the ledge to get to the beach. I look back at the burning pile of fuel barrels one last time and see something I can't believe.

The flames separate and a white light appears out of the fire. A white light that walks on two feet. It does not have wings, but more like a massive cloth of white that trails in the wind and flames, remaining unharmed from the fire. If devils are real, then angels must be real too. The chaos and the fire and all the scorching heat that surrounds me, yet I stare at an angel closing in that walks right up to me. Lost and confused as to who I am and where she is.

"Am I dead?" I ask. "Did I get burned up?"

I look to my left and right to see more like her. Multiple shining lights brighter than the flames of the Hell in my own darkness. The world felt as if it completely closed down all around us. There were no concerns, and no more worries, and all became peaceful. I must be dreaming. I must be dead. I hope I am dead this time. I don't remember this moment, but I never want to leave this moment. I hope I can stay here and not have to leave this time. My legs collapse underneath and send me to the ground in exhaustion mixed with pain. Her soft hands touch my face while I try to understand what she is saying through the ringing of my ears from the gun fire. The child just looks at me in concerned tears but isn't afraid of me. They all slowly approach in linens of white and brightly shining light. Walking through the flames unharmed from the blaze. I lean in to hear her speaking in my ear.

"I wanna go home..." she says to me.

"Me too..."

"Are you my Daddy?"

"No... I... I don't know you..."

"You look like my Dad."

"Where did you guys come from? How many of you are there?"

A sudden and familiar roar comes from under the flames of the blazing pile of fuel barrels. The metal cans move, the fallen pine rumbles around to see it come back from the land of the dead that it refuses to remain in. Its body is entirely engulfed in flames. There is no flesh or muscles. Only blackened bones, those sharp claws, the rows of teeth, and its glowing red eyes. Not a red glow of evil, but the glow of a hatred hotter than the flames coming through its eyes. It struggles to move and continues screaming at us. It looks right at me and sinks my heart into my stomach in an absolute fear.

"Run! Run dammit!!!"

I tell all the kids, and they scream in terror as they rush behind me. I raise my rifle and sling the lever in and out. I pull the trigger as it still attempts to stumble out of the flames. A click from the hammer fall and nothing happens. I am totally empty. It walks and limps closer with flames all over it that seem more crazed than the fuel barrels and trees burning combined behind it. I keep the Henry pointed at it for no reason other than hoping for a miracle to fill the chamber with a fresh round. The girl cowers at my leg in fear. I pick her up to run in the same direction as the other children to the shoreline. I turn around, just to see a brighter light blinding me. The light is attached to a rifle barrel pointed at me from less than a few meters away.

Rounds go off just beside me and above me. I drop to the ground with the girl and my rifle still in hand. Tracer rounds that seem to go everywhere from an automatic weapon. She screams while holding me tight. Three-round bursts over and over. An entire magazine full of rounds. The rounds hit the creature over and over and send it back into the burning flames it spawned from before my very eyes. The automatic weapon is reloaded in less than a second, and the person keeps firing again and again. As if their finger is just stuck on the trigger.

Pow, Pow, Pow.

Pow, Pow, Pow.

Pow, Pow, Pow.

It doesn't stop. The gun shots never seem to stop!

They won't fucking stop!

The ringing in my ears, they don't ever fuckin stop!

Pow, Pow, Pow.

Pow, Pow, Pow.

Gun shots fired!

Pow, Pow, Pow.

The creature falls over backwards into the flames with arms and bony wings stretched out. Its skull and multiple rib bones fractured from dozens of bullet holes. Teeth seem to be shattered into the back of its skull. The children have scattered closer to the beach. I get up with the girl and rifle still in hand to see another cluster of tracer rounds still being fired at the now lifeless creature. It gives out that same scream louder than my own terrors and the screams of the children. Through the flames it continues to reach for me and the girl. Its arm goes limp again as several bones turn onto fiery red and orange coals. The rounds stop firing, but he reloads again to point at me. He steps into the light of the surrounding flames to point an AR styled rifle at me.

"Put the kid down now, God Dammit!!!"

He keeps his sights on me, but he is stumbling. His walk is weak, and his eyes are yellow as he moves closer while out of breath. I drop her while she is in tears and she moves out of the way, but I keep the weapon in hand. Only cops talk like that. Once the kid is outta the way, then there is no collateral damage for taking the shot. The girl moves to the side and ducks down. I can see his breath being forced out as he tries to keep his bearing.

"Put the weapon down, now!!!" he says

I keep the weapon in hand and start walking towards him.

"Stop where you are!!! Put the weapon down, now!!! God Dammit. I'll shoot you where you fucking stand. Put the fucking weapon down, NOW!!!"

A familiar hovering sound comes from the distance and a light shines on both of us. A helicopter from above with a search lamp that shines down. It hovers close by and looks around at the several children that scurry around to the beach. A smaller attachment dangles by rope several feet below the chopper from a cable as it dips it into the ocean to be filled up with gallons of water. It pauses to shine the spotlight back on me and the Sheriff. A loudspeaker comes on from the chopper.

"This is the Atlantic City Fire Department! Move closer to the shoreline now and stay away from the fire! I repeat, move away from the fire! We are giving out your position now! Get to the shoreline and help will arrive soon!"

The Sheriff looks away from me and at the chopper. The wind from the helicopter blades fuels the surrounding flames. I raise my rifle while he is distracted. I don't need a miracle now. I just want him to shoot as I walk closer.

"Did you do this?!!?! Did you fucking do this?!?!? I told you to put the gun down and drop to your knees or I will end you right here, God Dammit!!" he tries to yell over the passing helicopter as it moves out.

Just shoot. Just end it. I step closer...

"You have to the count of three to drop the weapon and get down on the ground, right fucking now?!" he screams as he coughs all over his weapon while keeping the barrel fixed on me.

"ONE!!!"

I keep the Henry in hand as I take another step forward.

"TWO!!!"

Just do it. Just fucking do it as I close my eyes.

"Daddy?!"

She runs up to him as his weapon is still pointed at me.

"Maggie?!" he says as he tries to turn and look at the girl while keeping me in his sights.

270

He drops to a knee and looks at her and holds her while he still pointed the AR in my direction. He uses his off hand to look at her. It's as if he thinks his eyes are playing trick on him. He pushes her behind him but keeps his non-firing hand on her as he raises back up on his two feet. He sees I have lowered my weapon, and he lowers his AR. The chopper we just saw, or maybe a different one, comes by to shine lights all over the area. It dips its cable rig and bladder back into the ocean the same as the other. The chopper lights up the area and the Sheriff looks to see more children cowering by driftwood and brush closer to the beach. She holds his leg tight and screams something to get his attention, but he still appears hesitant to raise his AR back at me. I see her shaking her head no for whatever they are trying to say to each other over the sound of the helicopter, but he keeps his eyes on me. It's her. It's his daughter. It's all the kids he was looking for.

"Are they all here?!" he asks as the chopper flies away again.

I don't know how to answer that. I just shake my head yes, but I never counted how many came out of the woods. He picks her up and backs away. He keeps the weapon raised at me. He turns away with her wrapped around him to make his way down to the beach. He turns back to look at me in a moment of hesitation. Wondering if he should leave me. Wondering if I can be trusted long enough to turn his back on me.

"Who are you?!" he asks as the chopper leaves out of earshot again.

I look back at him when all goes quiet, except for the flames that rage behind me.

"Four percent."

I can think of nothing else to say to him.

He lowers his AR to point down at the ground. He pauses for one last time to look at me and nod his head in agreement. He motions a hand signal telling me to move out. He turns and continues down the ledge with the girl in hand and other children come out from their hiding areas on the beach. They follow him on the sand. All of them dressed in white linens that flap with the slightest breeze. He motions for them to follow him and points the flashlight at himself to make his presence known. He tells them he is with the Sheriff's department. The one girl is still wrapped around him closely with all her grip. He pops a flare, and I can see all the children. Nine, no, ten kids total follow him as they walk away from the fires.

"Manana" says a voice from behind me.

I turn around to see another child walking towards me. A small middle eastern boy also dressed in white linens but wearing their customary hat. He stops in front of me as I grow in shock from seeing something that can't be real. I kneel back down to see if he is really there.

"Dera Manana" he says again.

It's their Pashto language, but it's the same boy I remember, or at least I think it is. I don't know anymore, but he just looks at me.

"I can't understand you, kid. I'm sorry." as I shake my head and point to my mouth. I point over to the Sheriff as the other children still follow him on the beach. Strobe lights are closing in from a convoy of emergency vehicles traveling on the sandy beach in the night to get to the Sheriff's location. The boy looks at all of them with the flare the Sheriff holds up as his only signal, and then the boy looks back at me.

"You have to go with them now. You have to go with the policeman." I tell him as I point at the Sheriff walking closer to the emergency vehicles, closing the distance. He looks at the strobes of the approaching vehicles and back at me. Then he wraps his arms around me to give me an unexpected hug.

"Dera Manana" he says again before letting go.

He runs barefoot down the ledge with a less drastic slope on it and meets up with the Sheriff. He runs fast. I remember they all could run fast. The chopper comes back to refill from the ocean and shines the lights down on all of them to give their position to the EMT vehicles. I see them all. The sheriff, the girl he holds tight still, and eleven more children following right behind him. Was it a ghost that just hugged me? Am I still seeing things? I never thought you could touch a ghost, but I think I just did. I guess ghosts aren't as scary as we are led to believe. I never thought I could actually talk to one.

272

Chapter 25: The Ferryman

She doesn't look a single day older than the last time I saw her going to school that fateful day. I hold her the entire way to Atlantic City in the back of the ambulance. Medics and EMTs try to get me to let her go as she keeps her arms wrapped around me, but I only reach for my weapon the more that they try. They can do everything they need to do while she stays in my arms and my arms only. I say nothing when they try. They only receive a look from me that tells them that standard procedure does not apply right now. They loaded multiple kids up in ambulances and patrol vehicles. Several surrounding counties had to come in with their emergency service vehicles to keep all these kids together. My cell phone keeps going off in my pocket once we get back into service range and the radio chatter becomes too much to care to keep up with.

We convoy through the snow with a plow truck in front of us. We drive what seems like for hours into the night and the dawn finally arrives before we get to the emergency entrance. Everything seems to be a blur now and I feel faint. I know I need to get plugged in soon. A nurse approaches my ambulance, with Maggie still holding on to me. A few other kids are on a gurney, but other nurses go to them first before one looks to me.

"Sheriff Williams? Are you Sheriff Williams?"

I shake my head yes and she helps me up off the bench seat in the back of the ambulance. She has a wheelchair waiting for me. I sit down in the wheelchair and try not to bang-up Maggie's knees on the arm rests as the chair moves.

"One of your deputies and your assistant back at your station made us aware of your condition. Do you feel lightheaded or cold?"

I shake my head yes again.

"Ok, just hold on to her and we'll get you both checked out in the dialysis ward."

I hand over my AR and Davis' pistol off my chest rig to a State PD patrolman, and he nods in agreement to what needs to be done with them. He reaches down to try to unholster my revolver, but I stop him from pulling it out while the wheelchair moves into the hospital. They place Maggie on a bed right next to me as they shred through my layers and take my vest off to get to my catheter. Maggie watches nurses surround me as they do all the checks, and she screams when another doctor touches her and attempts to move her bed to the side, out of arm's reach. I grab the rail before he has a chance. My left hand stays outstretched to keep holding her hand, but the doctor gives me a foul look. I wave the nurses away from me to get the doctor's attention before he has time to separate us. I put my hand on my revolver but keep I it holstered.

"She just wants to hold my hand and be next to me. Is that gonna be a problem, Doc?"

He backs off and gives the same gesture with his hands. I turn to Maggie and they are covering her up in more blankets to get her warm again. They move to check her vitals, but she still seems scared.

"They're just gonna help you. Nothing's gonna hurt you now, ok. I'm not going anywhere."

She shakes her head and releases my hand, so she can drink from the water cup they bring her. She sets it to the side and returns to holding my hand again. As soon as the nurses step aside, I move the beds closer together when they aren't looking. They bring in the IV tubes and dialysis machine. The tubes seem to be everywhere to my other side, but I pay them no attention as we just keep looking at each other. She looks the same as I remember. Like what she looked like when she just woke up from a nightmare in her room. I want to stay awake right now, but my eyes tell me otherwise. I can feel myself fading in and out as the poison leaves my body from a medical tube. She just stares back at me. The doctor dims the lights and orders the nurses out.

"He's plugged in, and her vitals are good. We gotta look at these other kids and start working with the police to contact the parents…"

They all step out of the room and other officers stay outside my room. Nurses, doctors, and more police and EMT personnel rush through the hallways back and forth. A nurse comes in and out to check the machine and Maggie, too.

"Is my Daddy sleeping?" she asks the nurse.

"No… No, I'm still right here." I say, or mumble more or less.

"Daddy has had a long day, so he might be tired for a bit. But he'll be fine." says the nurse.

She steps back out after giving Maggie more water and an entire tray of food. She eats like she has missed every meal for the last year. I doze in and out until the machine makes that God awful noise. I could sleep for days at this point, but it isn't the kind of tired you get when you're sick anymore. It's just a tired from a lack of sleep. That I can deal with better than the sick kind of tired. When I think I wake up, I see Maggie dressed in sweats and wearing hospital slippers. Her hair has been washed and her white skin has returned to her natural glow I remember.

I sit up moments later after another dark spell and drink the first glass of water that I see to ease my dry lips. I look around the room to see Rachel sitting in the corner. She gets up to brighten up the lights, and she calls out to the nurse in the hallway. One comes in before I have time to stand upright.

"No. Not now. You've got to stay seated, Mr. Williams."

"I gotta go talk to the other police to get the parents here for all these other kids."

Rachel and the nurse try to keep me sitting down on the bed and I look down at the machine that has run multiple cycles.

"They are already on it, Jason. A few sets of parents have already showed up." says Rachel as she tries to keep me seated.

I look up at her, still in uniform, but they wrapped her arm up in a sling. I hear phones and shouting from across the hallways that are filled with flashing lights and more police trying to push the reporters out. The nurse comes in to close the door to keep the noise out. She moves to work on the machine and moves the tubes out of the way. I thought Maggie was here, but she isn't on the bed now.

"Where's Maggie? Where is she?"

"Just calm down, she's with one of the other nurses. She wanted to see some of the other kids that came in for a sec." says the nurse.

"I don't care where she is. I just want her in here now, dammit."

"Ok, Sheriff. I'll call in on the nurse and have her bring her back in."

She steps out but keeps the door closed from behind. Rachel jumps from her corner and hugs me from behind. She just sits on her knees on the bed and keeps holding me from behind.

"What the hell happened? How long have I been out?" I ask her.

"The State PD, AC Fire department, even game and wildlife showed up a few hours after you left me in the van. They all came. They had so many questions, but I just stopped answering them at one point. I'm so glad you guys are safe."

"Did all the kids make it back?" I ask.

"Yeah Jason. You did it. You brought them all back. The doctors and nurses said they are all healthy. The fire department said they spotted you guys from the helicopter in the forest fire. They said you guys were lucky to get out alive, knowing how bad the fire was out there."

"I gotta get a hold of Dr. Hernan's office over at Hackensack. How far away are we from his office? Does anyone know where my cell phone is?"

She breaks her hug and comes around to the front of me, dragging a chair to sit on with her good hand. She sits down in front of me already in tears, but it isn't good tears. These are bad tears rolling down her cheeks. I lift a finger to hold up her head and whip them away.

"Talk to me, Rachel. What's going on?"

She hesitates to get her bearing but sits up and holds my hand in my lap while still in the chair.

"The kidney didn't make it, Jason. They tried to get ahold of you while you were out there. They thought they would have a chance when they heard you were coming in on the ambulance this morning. They tried to ready it for transport here, and they were gonna move through with the surgery, but they just couldn't keep it stable any longer... I'm so sorry, Jason."

"They said I had 36 hours to get there. Has it been that long?"

"They wouldn't give me a lot of details. You can't give up now, though. We just gotta stay closer to the hospital for now until another good one comes in. Just pray and that call will come again. Just sleep outside the hospital in a patrol car if you have to. Just stay close to here from now on."

My heart sinks, but it isn't a total loss. I got my girl back. Rachel cries more and lays her head on my lap. I don't know if I need to comfort her or if she is trying to comfort me.

"How's Maggie doing?" I ask and she raises up and tries to wipe away her nose.

"I haven't gotten to see her yet. I came as soon as they said your treatment was almost done, but they had already taken her out. They said she was healthy somehow. No signs of shock or anything. She still looks like she was the same age even. It's like some sort of miracle happened out there after all this time."

"Yeah, I know. I held her the entire trip here in the ambulance, just to make sure I wasn't seeing things. I haven't gotten to talk to her about any of it yet. But it looks like I'm about to get my chance."

I look down the other hallway to see Maggie, with a nurse holding her hand, walking beside her. Rachel turns to look and see what I'm seeing. She gasps in amazement and cups her hand over her mouth. She looks back at me and then back at Maggie. Rachel just smiles in disbelief as the nurse brings her in.

"Look, it's Rachel…" she says to the nurse. She raises her head up at the nurse, as if to ask for permission to let her hand go. She lets go anyway, to come up and hug Rachel.

"Oh my God. It's Maggie…"

They just hold each other. I know Maggie just sees Rachel as a good friend. But Rachel always wanted to be more than just a friend to Maggie. I reach for my cell that was sitting on the meal stand beside the bed. I just didn't see it.

"Who are you calling?" asks Rachel, and I look down at Maggie.

"Well, I'm gonna get a hold of Mommy to see if she can talk to you."

"Where is Mommy?" She asks, while sitting on Rachel's lap.

"Well… Uh… She got sick and had to go to a different hospital to see another doctor. But you don't have to worry, because she should be almost all better by now."

"I already saw Mommy." she says while fidgeting with Rachel's cast and sling.

"What do you mean?" I ask as Rachel and I look at each other in confusion. I pick Maggie up off her lap and sit her next to me.

"Maggie, baby girl, Mommy's at a different hospital. What are you talking about?"

"I saw her get on the boat. The boat that took her away on a river. A skinny white man wouldn't let us get on with Mommy, because we didn't have any coins."

"Skinny white man? What are you talking about, baby girl? Help Daddy understand."

"Everything was like a dream. But it was a good dream. A new little boy we didn't know played with all of us after we got off the bus at school. Some of the other kids were scared of him, but he still played with all of us at the playground. Then we all went to a river and a skinny white man came up to us in a boat. He asked if we wanted to go for a ride.

The only people he let get on the boat was Mommy and the new boy that played with us at the playground. She hugged me before she left

278

and said to tell Daddy she's sorry she wasn't strong enough. She was sad and said she missed me so, so much. Then she took the little boy's hand and got on the boat with him. We watched the boat float away before a black man came for us at the river to take us back to school. He was a doctor too."

"A black man? You mean you like a doctor here at the hospital that helped you? Or maybe helped Daddy out when I was sleeping?" I ask as she lays down on the hospital bed beside me.

"No, he was a black doctor in the woods. He was a funny man that made us laugh a lot. He took us all to the beach first, though. Then I saw the man that looked like you. Did Mommy get on the boat to go to the beach too? Are we gonna see her at the beach?" she asks.

"Maybe it was just a dream, baby girl. I don't know what you saw. Mommy's at a different hospital. She's totally fine. I just saw her the other..."

A knock on the observation window and I see two men in suits holding up a State PD detective's shield. Rachel gets up to go talk to them, but I motion her to stay in the room with Maggie. She sits back down in front of her as I get up and walk out the door, looking back to make sure the door was closed behind me. I stare them down and shake my head at them.

"New Jersey's finest State Police. Glad to see you, assholes finally made it to the party. Oh, but don't worry. All the hard work is done."

"We're glad you found them, Sheriff. We're glad you found all of them. You're a damn hero Sheriff." one of them says nervously.

"Ain't no fucking heroes here, boys. What the hell do you people want from me? I got my daughter in there that has been missing for months now that I had to go find on my own, no thanks to you guys. Do you see her in there? Healthy, happy, alive, and well." as I point inside the room.

"We know Sheriff. We tried to get ahold of you, but your lady back at the station said you were tracking down a lead out there. There's something we needed to talk with you about. There's been an incident."

"There's been lots of *incidents* these last few days. What makes this one so important?"

"This one is about your wife…" he says.

"What are you talking about? Spit it out." as I look them dead in the eye, as serious as can be.

"There's been an incident at the rehab center you had her admitted to. I'm sorry, Sheriff, but…"

"But what?" I ask.

The other one raises his head to look up at me. "She's gone, Sheriff. We're sorry to inform you at a time like this, but she's gone."

I look down and shake my head no. Hoping none of this is true. Wishing I didn't hear those words as my stomach churns. My heart can't sink anymore. I turn to put my hand on the observation window to keep my balance before collapsing. Rachel sits inside with Maggie, clueless, as she looks back at me through the window. She gives me another look of confusion before Maggie gets her attention again. But they are both smiling as they chat. I look back down, trying to hold back tears.

"She was in a secure facility. I paid them thousands to help her during her relapse. How the hell did this happen?"

"I don't think this needs to be discussed right now, Sheriff."

"How the hell did it happen! Just give me a straight answer!"

"Ok… During the worst of her withdrawal symptoms, she managed to break one of her straps holding her torso, but it got wrapped around her neck. We're still looking over the remains, but it is all diverting to a botched suicide attempt on her part. But it's not the first time something like this has happened at that facility. We have shut the entire operation down pending further investigation from similar incidents."

"Sorry? You're fucking sorry? You're damn right you're fucking sorry. I am launching investigation on your entire precinct and anyone else that had knowledge of a County Sheriff's office in need of assistance but refused to respond. Every last one of you! I'll take this all the way to the top beyond the State PD if I have to."

"Sheriff, you gotta calm down. I know this is hard…"

280

"You don't know shit, mother fucker!... I lost two men out there! Two men dead and it all could have been avoided!"

I walk up closer to them and stare them right in the face. They know they fucked up.

"My wife is dead, and I got two men dead now too... I gotta go tell that little girl in there that Mommy died strapped to a bed choking and pissing herself. I gotta go tell the family of my two deputies that they died a fucking hero, but I know they were scared shitless when they were fucking killed by something out there... You gonna go lie to my two deputies' parents and tell them they're heroes too? You gonna lie to me, detective? You gonna lie to me and tell me you didn't know about a fellow officer needing help out there? Will you lie to me? Do it just once, I fucking dare you. Just lie to me once..."

Neither of them can look me in the eye. They just stare down in shame, knowing they have nothing to argue with. Knowing that there is no valid reasoning for leaving a comrade behind, fallen or not. One reaches into his coat pocket for the typical contact card to pull it out and hand it to me.

"We're all happy you found them. All of those kids have you to thank for being with us today. I know more parents are on the way. Try to enjoy this time with your daughter, because you have her back now, Sheriff. Call us before you leave town to head home with your girl."

I turn away to look back at the room. The other detective put a hand on my shoulder.

"We really are sorry to have to tell you this, Sheriff."

"Get your damn hand off me, asshole, before I yank your fancy tie off and watch you choke to death on it too. Then we'll see how much you fucking like it."

They both stand there in shock for a moment, not knowing how to take a threat of violence from another officer.

"You're still standing there. That was your cue to leave, shit heads."

One detective taps the other on the shoulder to motion them both to turn and walk away. I think to myself, what I have done. What has Maggie seen out there all this time? My wife can't be dead. This can't be happening. I want to go back to sleep now, but I wipe my tears away before Maggie and Rachel can see they are there. My best friends gone. More deputies are dead. I just gotta breathe. I just need to think, but the more I think within these first few seconds, the more I think the worst as to what has happened during all this. I don't want to know, but I have to know. This can't be real. I pull my cell phone out of my pocket and wave back at the girls through the glass. I have to call to confirm my fears.

"Hackensack Medical Offices, how may direct your call?"

"Dr. Hernan's office please."

"Sure thing. I think he may be out of the office right now. Can I ask who's calling."

"Then just get his PA. Tell them it's Jason Williams calling in and they'll answer."

"Ok, please hold."

A brief pause before she answers and out of breath.

"Jason… Oh my God. Jason are you ok. We've been trying to reach you. We heard everything going on out there."

"What happened to the donor?"

"Jason, we tried to transport it to you. These things happen. It was… It was just too long. We held it for too long. I am so sorry, Jason. This has never happened before when we get a donor organ in during a winter storm like this. The organ just wasn't stable enough to be held up anymore during transport."

"Shut up and listen to the question please… What happened to the organ donor? Not the organ, the organ donor?"

"Jason… Mr. Williams, we can't disclose any information regarding the donor for confidentiality reasons."

"The organ donor is dead. I don't think they are gonna give a shit now."

"I… I know this is heart breaking, but…"

"Don't give me that crap. You know damn well I can come in there with a warrant and an ROI from the courts within 24 hours and make you give me the information I want while you're put in cuffs… I just want to know the cause of death of the donor. No names or personal details. Cause of death and nothing more…"

She types something in on a computer and shuffles through some papers for a bit, but she fell for it.

"*Jason… Are you still there?*"

"I'm waiting…"

"*Asphyxiation… The cause of death was asphyxiation…*"

I almost drop the phone hearing what I just heard. The PA continues to babble something, but I hear nothing. I look at them through the glass observation window still, but I haven't really seen them until now. Rachel is high fiving Maggie, and they fist bump each other while laughing about something together. She taught my best friend the same thing what seems like forever ago. They hold each other and smile and giggle over something they catch on the TV in the room's corner. They both wave again and look at me through the glass as they sit on the bed. I just smile back at them. It hurts to smile, because I don't do it enough.

"*Jason… Jason, are you still there? Listen to me, there is still time. You are young and healthy enough to still only be a mild risk for another donor operation transplant. They are gonna keep somebody in your current condition high on the list for the lack of risk factors involved.*"

"Take me off your damn list. I don't want it anymore."

"*What? Jason? We need you to come in. I know this seems so daunting right now for you, but you can't just give up like this. There are going to be more donors eventually, and you don't realize how close we were to making this happen…*"

I hang up the phone and turn it off as I slip it into my pocket. I don't care to talk anymore. I think I will just watch my two girls for a bit longer from right here. The last two loves of my life stay so close to me, but somehow so far at the same time. My Jay bird has flown away now. My wife has left me by my own hand. But at least I'm not alone. At least I found a Mother for her, before it was too late.

Even if my wife is gone, that seems to be a decent enough trade for now. Not a fair trade, but good enough.

And I still get to be Dad just for a little while longer.

Chapter 26: The Marlin

Exhaustion is an understatement as I watch the blue sky of the dawn appear over the Atlantic. The area is filled with smoke to darken the sun that attempts to pierce its way through, but I know that blue sky is coming. I find my rucksack with the last of my ammo for the Henry. I keep it loaded as I watch the flames turn what I left of the beast to mere ashes. I dig around in my ruck to find a half empty flask of Captain and turn it upright in celebration, alone. It's a good thing I snagged the last bottle I had in the truck before I came back out here. The fire department choppers continue to hover around, almost three or four of them at one point, and they dip their bladders into the ocean and spray the flames down.

I climb up to the ocean lookout over James' camping area. There is nothing left of his home and still no sign of him. I squat under a tree to stay out of sight, but still keep a full view of the ocean and the smoldering fire. The water is more than freezing, but when I get to see it beyond the smoking darkness of the forest, it is as blue as the sky that sits above it. My legs are wobbly, and it isn't the booze making that happen. Not yet anyway. I'm lucky the scratches all across my gut have already scabbed up. I could just sit here and drink myself into a nice deep sleep for days now, but then what. Where am I supposed to go from here? What am I supposed to do? No one will believe any of what has happened the last few days.

A slight breeze picks up when I get settled in, propping my back against the tree with my bottle in hand. The morning is cool and clear and freezes my nostrils, but the cold filling my lungs allows for a full breath for the first-time in days. I don't know how long I sat here before all the choppers hover out of earshot. A crackle of leaves and twigs startles me from behind further into the wood line. A slight grunting noise from something raises my heart level more. I jump up in a hurry to move back into the open, closer to the drop off area that leads to the sandy beach. I raise my rifle and it takes all my efforts to keep it aimed in my near drunkenness. There is no way that thing lived being burned up like that. I watched it turn to nothing but ash.

"James?... James, is that you?" I ask.

My eyes are playing tricks on me again. My ears are still ringing from the gunfire as I try to convince myself that what I am seeing isn't real. The wood line that is covered in looming smoke is cleared from the breeze. I lower my rifle and stand upright as it approaches closer to me.

"I thought you were gone."

The white stag stands there looking right at me after reappearing from the grave I thought I put it in. I walk closer to it. The thing I came out here to kill and then killed by mistake stands tall right in front of me. My heart is still racing out of my chest. He's magnificent to look at and his head raise is massive with that nine-point rack. He is almost completely invisible with the remaining snow in the background with that bleached white coat. I drop to a knee in awe and fatigue again, but it still slowly approaches.

"You really are the one that's not supposed to go down." as I prop my weight on my rifle with the stock on the ground.

It moves closer within arm's reach now and it is so amazing to see this close. I lay my rifle on the ground to touch him. To see if my humanity is still real and not buried in some distant battlefield in an unknown land. I reach my shaky hand out and it flinches around for a bit until it lowers its head into my palm. My heart sinks into my chest and I can't keep my eyes from watering when I feel down its neck so close to me. I lower my head as it sniffs me for a bit, and then it places its forehead to mine.

"I'm so sorry..."

It walks in closer while my head is still lowered, and I cry. Its chest comes in close to my head now, like a father in nature that holds their child closer to their heart. I can hear it beating through the ringing of my ears. It backs away to stand there perfectly still as I stroke its neck. The winds pick up and the last few of the pines that didn't burn sway around. Ashes and smoke flutter past us as we both look at each other in amazement.

"What are you?" I ask, as it still stares back at me.

The whispers of the woods and trees grow louder until I can hear what is being said to me. The white stag keeps looking at me without movement until I can recognize what the winds of the forest is trying to tell me.

"The one you feed..."

It repeats itself until I acknowledge what is being said, somehow. I shake my head yes.

"Ok... Ok, then. I know what I need to do now. I knew all along, but I just... I just lost my way is all. It's just so hard to go back, but I know I gotta try." as I wipe my own tears. The deer turns around to walk away back into the woods. It trots off and vanishes as mystically as it appeared.

I pick up my rifle and my bottle, just to tilt it down and pour the rest of it out all over the ground. There's one for the fallen. I gather up my ruck and place it on my shoulders, despite the agonizing pain all over my body. It takes most of the morning to make my way back to my truck and uncover it from underneath the snow and brush that I hid it under on the side of the road. She starts right up like a champ and chugs through the unplowed road of deep snow from the last few days. I drive past a cluster of firetrucks and police vehicles. A sheriff's van is busted in from a tree falling on it, but I don't see anybody that appears to be injured. A state police trooper directs me past them as they attempt to cut up multiple down trees off the road. I drive by them without getting a second glance in my direction.

An hour's drive puts me back into the empty town and I pull up right beside the pawn shop. Getting out of the truck is a task after a hike like that in the woods. Not to mention my multiple cuts, bruises, and burns that ravage my body. The store appears closed, but I knock anyway. The lady approaches the door to open the theft gates back up and looks at me in shock.

"He's here! Honey, he's here!" she says to her husband in the back room.

I stand there wobbling around, ready to fall over with any stiff breeze. She unlocks the doors in a hurry and still calls for her husband in the back of the shop.

"Oh my God. Are you ok?" she asks with extreme concern while looking me up and down.

"I'm here for my Marlin."

"Please, come in. Are you hurt? Where's your jacket? I thought you had a good jacket last time we saw you. You must be freezing out there." as she holds the door open.

I take one step in and fall over on their floor to hit my face instantly. The shop owner runs to help me back up and then takes a good look at my face to see the claw marks all over it. It takes both of them to lift me upright and sit me on a nearby chair. The old man just stares at me in disbelief and his wife comes back over with water and a small medical kit. I guzzle down the water and spit half of it out on their floor from choking on it. I sit back in the chair to see him still staring at me as his wife tries to clean my face.

"You look like you've seen a ghost…" I ask him.

"No. I thought you would never be back here, honestly." he says back to me in near shock.

"Yeah, me too."

He moves outta sight to go to some of his clothing racks and gathers an outfit. His wife keeps lifting the glass of water to my lips to drink and I take it in slower this time.

"You're a really nice lady." as I look back at his wife and she smiles.

He comes back over with a full set of clothes

"You get your bearing back and go get yourself cleaned up in the back. Come on, were gonna help you out. Can't have you fallen over like that. You ain't too big, but we're too old to keep lifting you up like that again."

They lift me off the chair to take me through the back of the shop area. A small TV and a few recliners sit next to a kitchenet. Their bathroom is small, but he turns on the warm water for the shower. They both get me in, still fully dressed, and I just stand there for a bit.

"Don't worry about them old clothes. We got you some new ones for ya. Use whatever soaps you need to clean up. Do you need a doctor or something? Some of those cuts need stitches." she says.

"I think I'll be ok. I just wanna stand here for a bit."

They step out discussing something, but I don't care to listen in. Any slight movement sends pain all over as I strip naked to shower. Blood and dirt from my clothes wash away down the drain. I get cleaned up in a hurry, hoping I don't outstay my welcome. I slide open the shower curtain to see a pair of fresh clothes on the toilet. They must have taken my boots off at some point and cleaned them up. My belt with a few pieces of gear sits next to it. I have no clue how long I have been standing in the shower. I step through their living area after getting dressed and see them sitting at the small lounge table near the entrance of the shop area.

"Do you feel better?" asks his wife.

"I do. Thank you."

"Come over here and get a decent meal in ya." says the shop owner.

I sit at their small table and gobble down a plate of eggs and microwaved meat of some form. Bacon or patty sausage, whatever it is, it's fake meat, but anything is edible at the moment. I look up to see them both gazing at me in awe.

"I'm sorry. I guess I forgot the last time I had a meal of any form. I just came in here and kinda fell on your floor like a drunken idiot."

"It's ok. As soon as she saw your face, I knew it was you." he says.

"What do you mean?"

"It's all over the radio right now. They say the Sheriff found all the kids alive from all those months ago now. Been almost a year ago this winter, actually. The fire department claimed that another person was with him, but he disappeared back into the woods somewhere before the state could come in a talk to him. Is that you they were talking about?" he asks.

"The state PD never came that far in. They're cleaning up a mess on the side of the road right now. A bunch of trees went down on a Sheriff's van or something."

"So, it was you?" his wife says with an excited tone and smiles.

"I just want this to stay quiet, guys. I just came back for my Marlin, but I really do appreciate your kindness."

"Keep it quiet? You're a damn hero in this lil town now. Do you know how long them kids have been gone? Some parents left the area months ago after they called off the search." he says.

"I'm sorry, mister. Ain't no heroes out there. Only survivors are all there is now."

"Well, you're a hero to folks 'round here anyway, whether you like it or not." as his wife chimes in and proclaims to us.

I stand up from their table to straighten out my clothes. His wife jumps up from her seat and moves to another clothing rack. She comes back with a jacket in hand and holds it open. She signals for me to put it on.

"Here. This will help keep ya warm. It ain't as good as that last one we saw ya wearing, but you gotta stay warm out there before you get sick." she says.

"Oh crap. One sec and I'll be right back." I step back outside, and the cold sends a chill to my chest after the warm shower I just had. I reach into the cab of my truck and grab the Henry rifle to take it back inside. The old man already has my Marlin sitting on his glass display case and I sit the Henry right next to it.

"The Henry is a damn good rifle. It's tempting to keep it too, but the Marlin's more important to me."

The shop owner picks it up to clean it off after a quick function check.

"You sure put some serious rounds through this one, young man."

"You have no idea, mister. How much do I owe you guys for the clothes and all your troubles from when I stumbled in here?"

"You don't owe us anything. We all owe you at this point." she says before the old man can answer.

"Ok then, how much to trade back for my Marlin?"

The shop owner just slides the Marlin closer to my side and shakes his head no.

"You don't owe us anything. We owe you everything." he says.

I don't even have any money to give them, even if they said they needed more than what I gave them last time. I look back over at his wife.

"Miss, do you still have that letter you were gonna send out for me?"

"Oh yes. We hadn't sent it out yet, being the weekend and all. We were gonna push it out Monday for ya." she says.

"May I have it back, please?"

"Of course." And she hurries into the back room again.

"Why are you guys being so nice to me?" I ask the shop owner as he continues to look over the Henry.

"Our grandson was out there with all those other kids. We got the call last night from his mother that they found him. She's already there now. We were getting ready to head over to the hospital in the city to see him and then you knocked on the door."

His wife comes out from the back room again and hands the letter back to me. It was stamped and ready to go, just like they said they would do. The shop owner reaches out to shake my hand.

"We can't thank you enough for going out there and finding our lil grand boy. This town thought they lost all of them kids. Where you gonna head to next?" he asks as he grips my hand. I look behind him on the display counter under the rifle case and see a picture of his family together. The shop owner's daughter looks like her mother. A handsome young man holds her with a baby boy in her hands.

"Can I convince you to come over to the city with us? Pretty sure the Sheriff and the news crews wanna know how you guys found them out there after all this time." he says.

"Sorry, but no. I don't think you want someone like me in front of a news camera right now. I think I gotta head home now, Mister."

His wife comes around the display case to hug me and lower my neck to kiss me on the forehead. She straightens out the jacket and collar to place her hands on my chest.

"You just be careful driving out there, will ya? Where's home at for ya?" she asks.

"Not sure yet, Miss. Gotta go find it." as I slip the letter back into my new jacket's inner pocket.

I walk out the door with the Marlin in hand and I turn to look back at them before I leave.

"You good folks take care of your grand boy. They need you more than you know."

They smile and give their thanks again while waving me goodbye as I walk out the front door. I stop at a street side trash can outside of another empty shop near my truck. I pull the letter out of the jacket pocket and rip it up to throw the pieces into the garbage before I jump back in the truck to head out of town for the last time. I look up to see another fire department chopper heading over to the Pine Barrens area for another pass. They may be putting out the last of the fires.

I'm only half a day's drive away from there, but I'll have to speed my way there to get there by morning. I blast north through New York City during the night. Little to no traffic makes the trip seem faster, but overall quieter to get into Portland, Maine. The closer I get, the more anxious I get, but I know I have to stop and get a few hours of sleep while in route. My anxiousness turns to nervousness when I try to sleep at a rest stop just to close my eyes. My nervousness turns to being downright terrified. I have faced the enemies of our nation, over and over again. I have watched men fall in ways that are undeserved on so many levels. I have battled a demon that could only exist in some nightmare. Never have my hands shook more than being so close to her. The dawn returns to more blue skies and I give up on sleeping in the rest area in my truck. I move inside to clean up in the mirror before heading out again.

All of my doubts for reappearing here come to mind, making me reconsider turning around and going in any other direction. What if I am different? What if she doesn't recognize me anymore? What if their lives have moved on and things got better without me? This is a weight we carry that weighs more than any amount of gear or bullets we can carry. That terrible idea that we become ones that are no longer missed. Only forgotten about in an effort nobody cares to remember after so many years of being a part of it. What if they really cast us aside as nothing when the wars are over? Do any of us have a home to return to where we are wanted when the battle ends?

My hands shake uncontrollably as I turn into a residential area full of cookie cutter homes. It's early in the morning, but some are awake already to come out and shovel their driveways covered in a few inches of snow. I pull up to her house. *Her* house used to be *our* house before I left for Georgia as my last duty station. What if she tells me to go away and wants nothing to do with me? What if I get the cops called on me again? I hit my chest several times to get myself to calm down and get my bearing back before getting out of the truck. I take a deep breath before I close the truck door and I already see her on the porch outside the front door.

I walk up the walkway just looking at her, but nothing can be muttered out of my mouth for reasons I can't explain. There is no smile on her face and there is no warm welcome for me outside of my own home that I left behind so many times.

"Hey" she says with a forced smile to give the appearance of being glad to see me.

"Hello."

"I was wondering when you would show up."

"I had to take care of some things first... Did you get the checks I sent?"

"Yeah."

We stare at each other in silence. I look her up and down. She always looked more beautiful to me first thing in the morning like this. I never knew how to say the words to her, though. Her hair has gotten longer. I want to touch her to be sure I'm not seeing things again. To make sure there is still a heartbeat after hurting her so many times, but I only stand outside the house we used to call *our* home, speechless and too afraid to say anything. I stay away from the porch to keep my face and recent scars hidden behind my hat.

"I take it you're staying close now that you're discharged?" she asks.

"Yeah. I got a place close to here. Some apartment complex nearby. Haven't even seen it yet, but it's a start. I guess."

"You could have stayed here for a bit if you needed to."

"I didn't think you wanted me around for a while."

"Why would you think that?" she asks.

"I don't know, really. I... I missed you."

She just stares back at me, emotionless. I wish she would say something back to give me a sign if I can stay or if I need to go away. Even if it's on the sidewalk. No matter what she is thinking, I have to tell her at this point. I have come too far to back down now.

"Listen. I have something I need to say. I don't care if you hate me or not at this point, but I gotta say it. I'm not here to apologize. I wouldn't know how to make amends even if I wanted to. There's just something that needs to be said now. You're right. You were right all along. I am changed. I am different now. Everything is different now and I don't know how to go back. Maybe I'm broken and I don't want to go back to the way we were before. I just don't know how if I could.

There're parts of me that are missing now because I changed over there. These are changes that happened to me that will never fit your criteria of being accepting again. I don't think I'll ever meet anybody's criteria anymore."

"What are you talking about?" she asks.

"I don't know what I'm trying to say. I just... I... I feel dead in some places. Broken somehow. I have for a long time now. But those places someone like me has to go to, on the inside too, we choose to go so nobody else has to."

"Yeah... I know." she says while sitting down on the porch steps.

"It's there to stay, whatever is broken in me. It will always be there. Maybe it will get worse or maybe I can use it for something better or, maybe, something good. I just don't know anymore. I do know that I'm here and still going. Still moving forward anyway I can and still fighting for something."

"You know... It's gonna be hard for you and me to go back to what we were. I don't know if it can be like that again." she says while gathering her thoughts while trying to speak at the same time.

"Yeah. I know that. But I didn't come here to beg you. I just wanted to try for him. I just want to be here for him, now. And I will fight for it if I have to. It might be the only thing I have left to fight for now... Am I gonna have to fight for it?" I ask.

She stays quiet for a few moments while thinking about how to answer me.

"No... You don't have to do that anymore." she says finally.

"Ok."

"But you should tell him that yourself." she says.

"He's here now?" I ask nervously.

She gets back up off the porch step and moves to open the door to call for him inside. I stand there with my heart pounding through my chest.

"Hey there! Come outside here! There's a surprise waiting for you!" she says.

My hands shake as my knees get weak enough to drop to the cold ground. The sound of small feet run through the home I left behind so many times before. He comes out the door around her and stops with a smile from ear to ear. My heart freezes in place as I stare at my younger self from over twenty years ago. It's like looking at a mirror full of memories.

"Dad! You're home!" as he runs down the porch skipping stairs several at a time. He nearly knocks me over as he wraps around me. He pushes me back to look at me while cupping his hands over his eyes, and I do the same as he moves in closer until our hands touch.

"Remember Dad? The dark isn't that scary. Remember?"

"Of course, I remember, little man. I never forgot."

We lower our hands to look at each other.

"Mom said you were still fighting. Do you have to go back again? Did the bad guys scratch up your face?"

"No. I think it's over for a while now. I'm here to stay this time, I hope. The bad guys didn't get me."

I bring him back in close again to hold him just a little longer.

"Dad's home now and I'm gonna try to stay as long as I can."

There will always be a new fight ahead of us. But none of it matters if we forget why we fight. What we fight for, or even who we fight against. I gaze at a miracle that can turn back time for a second chance to do it right. It hurts to smile as I keep my arms around him for as long as he will let me. But it feels good to feel again. To see that my boy hasn't forgotten me.

It feels good to do this one thing right.

I have to do this one thing right for both of us.

I hope I can do this right.

I will gladly follow you wherever you go to make it right.

I will go down fighting for you again and again if I have to.

So long as I still get to be Dad just for a little while longer.

I won't have it any other way…

And let it be, that the tale ends of his warriors having laid down their swords to escape thy own hearts of torment that begats eternal damnation. For the given love of those in purity and innocence shall only be recognized by that of a true faith so that it may always be a guide for him back to thy father's house. Never again he having to fulfill the unwanted burden to journey through the nine gates that always remain wide for the broken and weary, but instead to remain in the narrow light that the son giveth. Let it be that he hath fought the good fight for his brethren and remember them not as they were but as they lived for thee. Go now and rest, ye truthful warrior.

Rest and rage in war no more.

About the Author

Corey Phillips was born and raised in Newport, TN, and graduated from Cosby High School in 2007. After 7 ½ years of active-duty service in the U.S. Army, with two combat tours to Afghanistan, he moved on to study screenwriting at Grand Canyon University, Phoenix, AZ. He then transferred and studied creative writing to graduate with a Bachelors of the Arts from Southern New Hampshire University, NH, in 2021. LEEDS serves as Corey's debut novel.

Made in the USA
Columbia, SC
04 May 2022

59873450R00183